D0032034

BEST NEW ROMANTIC FANTASY

———

BEST NEW ROMANTIC FANTASY

Edited by
Paula Guran

BEST NEW ROMANTIC FANTASY

Copyright © 2007 by Wildside Press

Cover art copyright © 2007 by Timothy Lantz
www.stygiandarkness.com

Cover design © 2007 by Stephen H. Segal

ISBN-10: 0-8095-5784-3
ISBN-13: 978-0-8095-5784-4

Library of Congress Control Number: 2007925915

Publisher's Note:
No portion of this book may be reproduced by any means,
mechanical, electronic, or otherwise, without first obtaining the
permission of the copyright holder with the exception of reviewers
who may quote brief passages in published or broadcast reviews.

Juno Books
Rockville, MD
www.juno-books.com
info@juno-books.com

To Ellen Datlow.
always "the best"

———

Contents

TITLES & THINGS
An Introduction

Paula Guran

WELCOME TO THE SECOND IN OUR . . . uh. . . series . . .
The first volume in this series of annual anthologies was titled *Best New Paranormal Romance*. It was published in November 2006 and featured short fiction from 2005. The volume you now hold in your hands is *Best New Romantic Fantasy* (covering fiction from 2006). It is being released about six months or so after the first book rather than a year later (as one might expect for an annual series).

The two are, despite differing titles, still the first two of a series of anthologies from Juno Books. Juno Books didn't exist a year ago, so we could not have published the first book then. Our intention, from this point forth, is to appear in the spring—so we are now getting "on schedule."

The title change? The first anthology's lengthy introduction by the editor (me) explained why we used the term "paranormal romance" to begin with and why we think a new genre is emerging which, for lack of (literally) a better term, is known to many as "paranormal romance." (You can read that essay and other adventures in paranormality on our Web site www.juno-books.com. Just look for the "essays" link on the blog.)

The introduction was really rather impressive, if I do say so myself, and reviewers said nice things about it. But the fiction in the anthology was, as such things should be, *much* more impressive and we hope you pick up a copy and read it.

We think the stories here are just as outstanding, but don't get your hopes up about this introduction. This introduction won't be nearly as lengthy, informative, or controversial. You can skip right over it and get on with the great fiction this anthology compiles and not miss much, if anything, at all.

THE SECRET MEANING OF "PARANORMAL ROMANCE"

I STILL CONTEND that to the world at large, the term "paranormal romance" means a broad range of fantastic fiction that is not necessarily "romance" as defined by those who think the word must apply *only* to uplifting stories with happy endings. Some romance readers evidently assume the whole world knows their definition and agrees that "romance" must possess the sanctified H(appy) E(ver) A(fter) ending. Some of these folks even feel using "their" word in the title of a book is somehow deceptive and part of a conspiracy to foist faux romance onto the hallowed shelves of bookstore romance sections, thereby wreaking havoc on the normal order of the world. (That was, of course, never the case.)

Inaccurate or not, like it or not, "paranormal romance" is commonly used for "paranormal romantic non-romance" as well as "paranormal romance romance." But it's not the *only* term in use.

In the last year or two, the phrase "urban fantasy" has started to be used as a label for one type of paranormal romance. Urban fantasy has been used for quite some time in the field of fantastic literature where its definition varies, but usually includes something along the lines of (as John Clute puts it in *The Encyclopedia of Fantasy*) "texts where fantasy and the mundane world intersect and interweave throughout a tale . . ." set in a city.

So, some paranormals can be called urban fantasy by the already established meaning, but not all. It doesn't even work well as a label for the specific type of fantasy usually meant. Charlaine Harris's Sookie Stackhouse started out in the very non-metropolitan Bon Temps, Louisiana. Is it "small town fantasy"? Juno Books author Maria Lima's *Matters of the Blood* is an "urban fantasy" set in and around a very small town in Texas. Is it "rural fantasy"? Then there's the paranormal suburb of Mysteria, Colorado that Mary Janice Davidson, Susan Grant,

P.C. Cast, and Gena Showalter each wrote a novella about for a Berkeley Sensation anthology in 2006. Suburban fantasy! I'm sure there are novels set in areas consisting of one or more adjacent municipalities situated around an urban core with a population of at least ten thousand. Census agglomeration fantasy! Stories set in the south of France: Provençal fantasy . . . set in long inlets from the sea with high steeply sloped walled sides: fjord fantasy . . . .

If you were paying attention (and I hope you weren't by the time I got to fjords) you might have noticed I slipped the plural of "paranormal" in as a noun. "Paranormal fiction" is also bandied about. Neither is any more accurate than the other terms, but they are being used by those as desperate as I to call this very popular cross-genre fiction *something*.

Not that any of the above truly describes the fiction in this anthology.

THE SECRET MEANING OF THE TITLE OF THIS BOOK

NO, WE DIDN'T CHANGE THE TITLE because some radical romance readers burned our blog in virtual effigy. (They didn't.) Nor did we change it because fantasy readers were ashamed to be seen in public with a "romance" book. (I did hear one person mention she'd be embarrassed reading the first volume in public because "romance" was on the cover.) But we did feel we wanted a term that would be descriptive but still convey "this kind of fiction" without getting further tangled up in definitions.

So, what label best describes the stories? Juno Books publishes fantasy and these stories are fantasy. (Those attempting to define fantasy can get contentious, too, but they would probably accept these stories as literature of the fantastic.) Easy. Does this preclude science-fictional stories? No, not really, but it so happens that this year there is no SF. "Romantic" is not "romance" and it applies . . . and keep the "best new" part . . . . It'll do. Besides, the acronym is now *BNRF* and we can pronounce it "ben-riff," which is an improvement over *BNPR* ("ben-per"), don't you think?

The new title gives me a little more freedom in my editorial choices, too. *Best New Romantic Fantasy's* stories do not necessarily deal with the establishment or continuance of a relationship. Nevertheless, I think readers will see each of them, despite their variety, as romantic stories.

The settings for these stories also present a delightful diversity. You'll find love (or at least echoes of it) on the streets of modern New York City . . . on an ancient Mediterranean shore . . . in the library of an early 19th century alternate England . . . on the rocky shoals of a lighthouse island in the past and (simultaneously) a coffee shop of the present . . . in West Virginia on a day that might be tomorrow . . . in a powerful place beyond space and time . . . in a version of medieval Japan . . . beside the timeless sea . . . in a world of a world of magic and carnivals . . . in a suburban "anyhome" . . . in an enchanted forest of the American Northwest . . . in twentieth century Taiwan . . . in an exotic land of deserts and palaces . . . in twentieth century Key West, Florida . . . and in Paris during the upheavals of 1868-1870.

Although this year's stories may seem darker than last year's selections, this was neither intentional nor (I don't think) a matter of taste. There seemed to be fewer lighthearted stories to choose from (and, trust me, the search was made). Perhaps this is merely the mood of the times just as, in 2005, there seemed to be an unusually high number of stories dealing with soldiers published.

But let's not waste any more time with introductions. Read for yourself and draw your own conclusions. As always, I'd love to hear your ideas and thoughts, so visit www.juno-books.com and let me know what you think.

Paula Guran
April 2007

AN AUTUMN BUTTERFLY

Esther Friesner

THE SUBWAY WAS ALWAYS THE FIRST PLACE she noticed the change of seasons in New York. Spring offered causeless smiles from strangers and room to breathe as heavy coats were doffed like old cocoons, a brief, glad freedom soon snatched away by summer's suffocating heat. When autumn came, the smells of food and drink carelessly dropped and gone to rot, of sweat trapped against packed bodies on plastic seats, all ceded to the crisp, cold tang of endless stone tunnels and star-bright bursts of ozone from the tracks. Winter showed itself in the faces of huddled, bundled passengers, hugging themselves for warmth. Straphangers shed icy onionskins of snow from their shoulders. Luckier riders who could claim seats dealt with heating units that crisped the backs of their calves but left the rest of the body to freeze. All the dancing times were done. Even the beggars moved more slowly from car to car. Children of ice, a single tap from a living human fingertip could shatter them down to their bones.

She didn't like to think about winter. When autumn came, she tried to put the thought of its inevitable arrival as far from her mind for as long as possible. From the day she'd left college for business school, winter always depressed her. The long walks through Philadelphia streets sodden with dirty snow were not cheerful memories. Even the gemmed reds and greens of Christmas in the stores, the small, conciliatory sparkles of white and blue Chanukah decorations, could not distract her into a smile. Grim as any Grail knight, she trudged from class to home to class until she had done what was expected of her and she could pack up her M.B.A. and fly away forever. They claimed that in New York no one cared about who you were or where you'd come from or whether or not you had a place to go, just as long as you did your job. She wanted that. She gulped down deep, welcome draughts of anonymity as if they were drugged wine.

It was autumn when she saw the butterfly, and it was nothing she had ever wanted.

Autumn elsewhere meant harvest home, apples red and ripe, corn golden in the ear, barns fat with promises of winter fireside feasts, rich plenty in the teeth of icy barrenness. Autumn in New York meant the last of September's false summer, the forced cheerfulness of Back-to-School sales, the first whiff of chestnuts roasting on streetcart braziers. Most of the tourists left, except for the momentary flood-tide at Thanksgiving, and the hansom drivers near Central Park brought out blankets for their horses. The city drew a long, half-regretful breath, like an old woman who rejoices to see her grandchildren come to visit but settles gratefully back into the sweet, familiar peace of her own little house when they go.

She was just coming in to work when she saw it. At first she thought it was the crumpled wrapper of a candy bar, bright orange scribed with black. It huddled in a little niche beside the great glass doors that led into her office building, a small inlet of stone choked with the crushed cigarette butts of refugee smokers. The smell of burnt tobacco seeped into the pores of the fluted concrete archway, clung in an oily film to the gilt-brass handles of the doors. Afterwards, she never could say what made her glance its way once, let alone twice. It was only rubbish amid other rubbish, no rarity.

But she did look twice. In fairy tales a third look would be called for, but the city was too shored up with rock and iron to have any need for fairy tales. A second look sufficed, a look that traced the fragile curve of one drooping wing. It moved. She thought it might be some trick of the captive winds that swirled through city streets, birthing dust devils in the entryways of skyscrapers, casting sand into lovers' eyes. Then she saw that none of the rubbish crowding the creature moved, and knew that the small, shy stirring of the wing meant life.

Something drew her, nothing spawned by sense. She came nearer, stooped down. Eyes like shining poppyseeds glowed beneath the quivering filaments of antennae thinner than breath. Without thinking, she stretched out one hand and the butterfly made no move to flee as she used the other to scoop it gently into the wooly palm of her navy blue glove.

Impossible, she told herself as she walked inside the building and waited for the elevator and soared up through steel-boned shafts to her proper place in the world. It's small, it's barely still alive, I'm wearing gloves, and yet . . . what is that tiny pulsing in my hand? Surely not a heartbeat? No. Impossible. Insane.

Her co-workers noticed her find at once. How could they do otherwise? It was more than just the city-worn body of a butterfly in her hand; it was a spell of binding power. It rippled outward from the wafer-winged insect to envelop her in its enchantment. While she held the thing, she couldn't walk the same way she'd done before. Her old, quick, clipped stride would jar away the last delicate splinter of life to which the creature clung, the life now in her care. So now she moved more slowly, with the dreamy, alien grace of a Minoan priestess gliding forever across a ruined palace wall. By the time she reached her desk, she'd acquired acolytes.

Someone brought a coarse brown cardboard drink-holder from the coffee shop on the first floor. Someone else brought tissues to line it, a third person begged them both to wait and bustled up a fine white box lined with cotton wool, the kind that was meant to carry jewels. Holding her breath, she slid the butterfly from her trembling hand onto its cloud-soft bed. The people who had come to gawk now ringed her, their eyes filled with black and orange wings, pilgrims of faith waiting for a sign. When the butterfly's eyelash legs curled in and out and in again, when the bright wings dipped and rose, they were finally free to smile.

Questions from her co-workers flurried around her head, hints and plans and offers of help assaulted her. Already one man had taken charge, calling up the Bronx Zoo for information on the care and feeding of rescued butterflies. Another sneered this effort away and went instead to ring up the Museum of Natural History. A third began to tell, in great and unrequested detail, about his perfect family vacation to a place in Georgia where butterflies of a thousand warring beauties lived inside a building like a giant circus tent. None of it sounded real.

"Rotten bananas," he was saying. "That's what they feed them there. That's what we'd better get for this little guy: Rotten bananas."

Well. That sounded real enough. He promised that he'd go down to one of those little fruit peddlers on the street and hunt up a nice piece of browned and sickly-sweet banana as soon as lunchtime rolled around.

She thanked him. She thanked them all. She didn't tell a single one of them that she was certain that the butterfly would be dead by lunchtime. She molded it a tiny water dish made of foil wrap taken from the coffee room and left it under the warming glow of her desk light. She tried not to look at it all morning.

Just before lunch, she had to go to the bathroom. When she came back, she found the creature's box splashed with the petals of a rose. Someone had bought a flower and given it to the butterfly. It had wrapped its legs around the stem and was resting its head on the blossom. She brought her eyes to the edge of the creature's shining cell and thought she saw its curlicue of a tongue plunged deep into the heart of the flower. She watched it until someone came by her desk to remind her that there was a meeting scheduled for lunchtime.

After the meeting, the butterfly was gone; not dead, but vanished. She stood beside her desk, staring down at the place where the little white box had been, and the silvery wink of the water dish, and the rose. All had been whisked away. Questions flew up to swarm the inside of her skull: What had happened? Where was it? Had someone taken it? Why? It was far too early for the cleaning staff to come through, and even they never touched things left out on the desktops. Might it have been knocked off by some careless passer-by? She dropped to hands and knees, peering under the desk. Viewed so closely, the pale gray-green carpet reminded her of something she'd once seen growing in a Petri dish. She was still searching under desks and chairs when the man who'd promised her the rotten banana came back. He was sorry, none of the street vendors had anything but fruit at the very moment of ripe perfection. Successful city trade demanded nothing less. When she told him that it didn't matter, that the butterfly was gone, he gave her a short, cutting look and walked away.

Things changed then; the morning's warmth dwindled off and died. Whispers blew little breaths of late autumn chill through the office.

How could someone manage to lose a butterfly? A few people stopped by to extend unwanted sympathy, as if this were the only loss her life had known. Mostly they kept their distance, unwilling to believe her when she claimed she didn't know how it had happened to vanish, where it had gone. One man emphatically declared that things in offices do not simply fly away, and no one seemed to see anything in his words worth even the ghost of laughter. Their smiles were tight, their nods supposedly offered acceptance of her assertions, but she knew dismissal when she saw it. She worked through the remaining hours of the day striving to feel nothing, feeling instead the encroaching cold.

She left at five, which had never been her way. Why hurry home when home held nothing to hold her? She didn't need a man to complete her, or another woman, or even a dream, but completeness was not the same thing as connection. That, she did need. The longer she worked, the longer she belonged to some part of the human world. She knew that her manager adored her for this quiet devotion to her job, mistaking it for a sign that she valued his approval. To her, he was no more than a ghost among ghosts, only some of whom knew they were dead.

This evening, though, she found herself unable to wrap herself in a cloak of shouts and shadows, to block out all things that made the city less than a sweep of noise, a swash of faces, a blur of rainbow light. For the first time, she found herself riding down from the office in an elevator filled with persons, not people. To her left, the fat, balding man with the moustache coughed into his hand. She counted the bristly black hairs on his knuckles at a glance, saw the pale place at the base of one finger where a wedding ring no longer shone. The woman to her right already had the fleecy collar of her brown suede coat turned up against the cold night awaiting her outside, but she smelled of the same rose that had fed the butterfly and her smile was sleepy with anticipated love. A young man fidgeted just at the corner of her sight, one gloved hand clenching and unclenching around the handle of his attaché case, leather creaking and squeaking against leather, skin embracing skin. Each small thing touching her fellow passengers snapped at her notice, drew her eye, forced conjectures as to who they really were, where they'd come from, what they hoped to find in the world outside. Images fell easily one into the next, a cataract of thoughts and questions that she was powerless to flee. When the doors finally opened on the ground floor, she almost flew out of the car, desperate to breathe air that was not thick with stories.

She strode away from the building, eyes straight ahead. She did not dare to spare a glance at the place where she'd found the butterfly that morning. She was afraid that despite the darkness and the hour and the cold impossibility of it all she would see it waiting there for her, its black and orange wings aglow like embers among ashes. By the time she reached the subway stairs, she was running.

The platform was packed. The trains that rumbled past on the other side of the station were full, their windows jammed with faces. Her own train quickly filled and she rode it home with her eyes fixed sometimes on the floor between countless pairs of shoes, or on the overhead advertisements, or on the air just a hand-span above the heads of the other passengers. Riders boarded in wedges and debarked in waves, a dozen and more at each station. It would be the same at her stop, with a crowd for her to ride up out of the underground, and streams of people in the streets to wash her all the way home.

But when she reached her stop and the doors slid open, she was the only one who wriggled through the press and stepped out of the car. She walked three steps, then stopped. Only then she recognized her isolation, how she stood alone on the platform with no one striding past her, no one heading for the turnstiles. The far side of the station where the uptown trains ran was deserted too, not a single soul there waiting to ride back to the city. She heard the fading rumble of her train as it rushed farther away down the tunnel. The echoes fled after, leaving behind only herself and the silence.

She shrugged it off—this was a city, stranger things happened here. These small coincidences of solitude that had somehow come together in this way were nothing to unnerve her. She had lived with worse. She would go home.

The first turnstile she tried was frozen. So was the next and the next, all the way down the line. The revolving gateway too was locked; she could feel the chill of the iron bars biting into the palm of her hand even through her glove. She called for help, but there was no one near the token booth, or in it. The empty glass box shone with the pale green of aquarium lights. When she saw this latest desertion, she was already so numbed to mystery that she felt more annoyance than fear or surprise.

She thought she would try to climb up and over the turnstile, but her heels were too high, and the station floor too cold for stocking feet, and when she set down her briefcase and tried to reach through the gateway she encountered a torn place in the curtain that screened her waking mind from dreams. She watched with widening eyes and shuddering breath as her hand disappeared to the elbow, sinking from sight into solid air. When she gasped for dear life and pulled it back, it was covered with butterflies.

They were all the colors of a spring sky at sunrise, pink and blue, yellow and rose, pale greens and bright, blazing oranges streaked with the black of bare winter trees. They clambered over the thick wool sleeve of her winter coat, leaving trails of golden pollen that sparkled against the old, always-so-serviceable iron gray. She felt them in her hair, tiny legs stumbling every now and then against her cheek, gentle as a willfully forgotten caress. She began to shake. She began to cry.

They settled over her eyes, tongues uncurled to sip her tears. She shouted out her fear, blinded to everything but their swarming colors. No sooner would she sweep a host of them away from her eyes than fresh waves of wings tangled themselves against her lashes. Was this payment for the kindess she had shown the long-gone morning's castoff creature? She could have walked on by, left it there with all the other scraps and sheddings of city life. Was this bright terror her reward?

Her voice escaped her in a shriek as she begged the cold and empty air of the abandoned station to save her. The harsh sound startled the butterflies and they rose up from her in a radiant cloud, bodies blending into the shape of a clothesline-tethered sheet that traced the soft billows of one May morning's breeze before sailing away down the empty tunnel. She swallowed hard to keep the lurching pulse in her throat from bursting out of her mouth in the shape of some fresh monster, and stared after their massed farewell flight. For a moment she found herself thinking of a manta ray's measured underwater progress, its fleshy wings fantastically transformed into a cloak of flowers. She watched the butterflies fly away until they were lost in darkness.

Their departure stole the uncanny silence. She began to hear the old, familiar sounds returning, the background noises proper to this place. The uptown tunnel breathed out the hollow, heralding roar of a train's imminent arrival. The turnstiles hummed to life behind her, stiff metal arms groaning and clanking as people came back to share the platform with her, one by one by one. Their battered faces were equally empty of nightmare and miracle. She could smell stale cigarettes and the frosty spectre of oncoming winter clinging to their clothes.

As she edged her way past them, picking up her briefcase where she'd dropped it, making for the turnstile and her life, she wondered whether these people could read her recent brush with madness just by looking at her. She stole a dozen furtive sideways glances as she moved past them, but saw nothing in their faces, not even the effort of indifference. She told herself that she should be relieved, but her chest ached, and her throat closed around a hunger she was too ignorant to name.

When she stretched out her hand to lay it on the turnstile bar, she saw the butterfly. It was suddenly there, perched across the softly gloved bumps of her knuckles, orange and black and jewel-eyed. The scrawled pattern on its wings was indistinguishable from the petaled livery of all its countless kin, and yet she risked dreaming that it was the same one she'd discovered a thousand years ago that morning, half crushed amid the city's scourings. Against every fact and finely reasoned lesson of reality, it had come back.

It would take her half a breath to swat it to a smear against the turnstile's gateposts. It would take less than that to shake her hand free of it and go her way. She did not, would not do one or the other. She knew it was no choice for a sensible person to make.

She remembered sensible choices. She remembered hard words, and a closed door, and her mother's voice telling her how much better off she was for having left a man who'd never amount to anything worthy of her.

She remembered cold nights, and colder sheets, and the false warmth she'd wrapped around herself. Her ears ached with countless tellings and re-tellings of how hopeless it was, how badly his wild dreams accorded with her expectations for a life of security, order, substance.

She remembered then that not a single one of all those expectations had ever been hers, not truly. They had been handed her from her childhood, gifts bestowed with the same smiles that said Thank heavens we'll never have to worry about you; you're such a good, sensible girl. That was her parents' highest form of praise.

She remembered his hand, and a rose.

The butterfly's tongue curled out and pierced the thick cloth of her gloves, piercing deep into her blood. She felt it, sharp and sweet, and all the brittle arguments of intellect melted and flowed away. She let them go, knowing and accepting that she was now irrevocably lost to sanity. She was not afraid.

Someone at her back barked for her to move it or lose it. Bodies jostled all around. She pushed her way through the subway gate half waking, eyes fixed upon the strong, deliberate opening and closing of the wings against her glove. The butterfly rode her hand with the calm assurance of a hawk on the falconer's wrist. She brought it up out of the subway to give it to a night bright with streetlamps, striped with neon, scattered with stars.

As soon as they stood on the sidewalk, she felt the small legs tighten to her hand. The wings began to move, slowly at first, then faster, to a gradually accelerating beat. It merged with the breathless tempo of her heart and blurred onward into speeds beyond imagining as the creature took flight into the face of heaven, taking her with it.

It rose into the night, lifting itself away from hard streets and harder eyes, soaring for the open reaches of the sky. It would not let her go, its grip upon her strong, and she gasped, helpless as the sidewalk spun away below. She dangled awkwardly as the tiny body towed her along, until the two of them cleared the rooftops. She felt the air of the high places slide beneath her, cradling her with a lover's tender care. She realized that somehow she had let her briefcase drop away, this time for good, and didn't regret it at all. The city slipped by in her wake, ribbons of silver rock and golden light. She turned her eyes to the snowfield of stars and laughed into the wind.

Echoes of old voices streamed past her, trying to turn her flight aside with dire warnings. Couldn't she see that this was madness? Wasn't she afraid of flying so far from the solidness of earth? What if she were never to return? Didn't she know how much she risked? Hadn't she learned this lesson before, at a cost still paid? Didn't she care what others would think of her? Where was her common sense, where, where had it gone? She closed her ears to keep out all the fretful chitterings and opened her eyes even wider to the light. It was brighter now, a clean, blazing white that rimmed the butterfly's wings with blue. She gazed into the heart of the onrushing star until it shattered her sight into a million swirling flakes of dazzlement.

Earth scraped abruptly against the soles of her shoes. The tip of one high heel caught itself against a lip of pavement. Her sight returned as she fell forward against a flight of brownstone steps already dusted with snow.

"Are you all right?" A hand was strong at her elbow, helping her to stand. She held back recognition, drawing it deep inside her like a drowning man's last breath, refusing to admit she knew the voice that asked: "Did you hurt yoursel—? Oh."

She was amazed to see how easily he remembered her. She'd expected the years to have changed them both beyond memory's power to redeem. Only now, holding his face with her eyes, with her soul, she realized how little time had passed. For a while they both stood there, drinking silence.

Then he said, "I heard you were living in New York." She acknowledged that this was true. She explained nothing, and his smile shyly told her there was nothing that she needed to explain. She found his lips as casually and as naturally as she'd lost the old city.

"Well," he said at last, and cleared his throat, and added, "Are you hungry? Want some tea?"

She followed him up the steps to a door she'd slammed behind her in another life than this. By the time they reached it, their misted breaths were a single silvery cloud against the old-fashioned panels of glass etched with Easter lilies. Her last practical thought was to wonder how many times he'd had to replace them, on account of vandals. So many things of beauty smashed so easily to dust. She reached for the doorknob without thinking any more at all.

"Ah! What's that on your hand?" His own fingertips ventured to touch the trembling wings. The butterfly turned and rested its two foremost limbs on the ball of his thumb, pollen staining his fingertip gold. "They're usually all gone by this time of year, you know."

"I know." The doorknob turned, the pale glass lilies sparkled, and the autumn butterfly flew before them through the door.

Esther Friesner *is the Nebula Award-winning author of thirty-one novels and over one hundred fifty short stories, in addition to being the editor of seven popular anthologies. YA novel* Nobody's Princess *was published in April 2007. Other recent publications include* Tempting Fate *from Dutton/Penguin and short story collection* Death and the Librarian and Other Stories, *from Thorndyke Press.* Nobody's Prize, *the sequel to* Nobody's Princess, *will appear from Random House in spring 2008. She received a B.A. degree in both Spanish and Drama from Vassar College, an M.A. and Ph.D. in Spanish from Yale University, where she taught for a number of years. She is married, the mother of two, and lives in Connecticut.*

A LIGHT IN TROY

Sarah Monette

S HE WENT DOWN TO THE BEACH IN THE EARLY MORNINGS, to walk among the cruel black rocks and stare out at the waves. Every morning she teased herself with wondering if this would be the day she left her grief behind her on the rocky beach and walked out into the sea to rejoin her husband, her sisters, her child. And every morning she turned away and climbed the steep and narrow stairs back to the fortress. She did not know if she was hero or coward, but she did not walk out into the cold gray waves to die.

She turned away, the tenth morning or the hundredth, and saw the child: a naked, filthy, spider-like creature, more animal than child. It recoiled from her, snarling like a dog. She took a step back in instinctive terror; it saw its chance and fled, a desperate headlong scrabble more on four legs than on two. As it lunged past her, she had a clear, fleeting glimpse of its genitals: a boy. He might have been the same age as her dead son would have been; it was hard to tell.

Shaken, she climbed the stairs slowly, pausing often to look back. But there was no sign of the child.

Since she was literate, she had been put to work in the fortress's library. It was undemanding work, and she did not hate it; it gave her something to do to fill the weary hours of daylight. When she had been brought to the fortress, she had expected to be ill-treated—a prisoner, a slave—but in truth she was mostly ignored. The fortress's masters had younger, prettier girls to take to bed; the women, cool and distant and beautiful as she had once been herself, were not interested in a ragged woman with haunted half-crazed eyes. The librarian, a middle-aged man already gone blind over his codices and scrolls, valued her for her

24

voice. But he was the only person she had to talk to, and she blurted as she came into the library, "I saw a child."

"Beg pardon?"

"On the beach this morning. I saw a child."

"Oh," said the librarian. "I thought we'd killed them all."

"Them?" she said, rather faintly.

"You didn't imagine your people were the first to be conquered, did you? Or that we could have built this fortress, which has been here for thousands of years?"

She hadn't ever thought about it. "You really are like locusts," she said and then winced. Merely because he did not treat her like a slave, did not mean she wasn't one.

But the librarian just smiled, a slight, bitter quirk of the lips. "Your people named us well. We conquered this country, oh, six or seven years ago. I could still see. The defenders of this fortress resisted us long after the rest of the country had surrendered. They killed a great many soldiers, and angered the generals. You are lucky your people did not do the same."

"Yes," she said with bitterness of her own. "Lucky." Lucky to have her husband butchered like a hog. Lucky to have her only child killed before her eyes. Lucky to be mocked, degraded, raped.

"Lucky to be alive," the librarian said, as if he could hear her thoughts. "Except for this child you say you saw, not one inhabitant of this fortress survived. And they did not die quickly." He turned away from her, as if he did not want her to be able to see his face.

She said with quick horror, "You won't tell anyone? It's only a child. A . . . more like a wild animal. Not a threat. Please."

He said, still turned toward the window as if he could look out at the sea, "I am not the man I was then. And no one else will care. We are not a people who have much interest in the past, even our own."

"And yet you are a librarian."

"The world is different in darkness," he said and then, harshly, briskly, asked her to get out the catalogue and start work.

SOME DAYS LATER, whether three or thirty, she asked shyly, "Does the library have any information on wild children?"

25

"We can look," said the librarian. "There should at least be an entry or two in the encyclopedias."

There were, and she read avidly—aloud, because the librarian asked her to—about children raised by wolves, children raised by bears. And when she was done, he said, "Did you find what you were looking for?"

"No. Not really. I think he lives with the dog pack in the caves under the fortress, so it makes sense that he growls like a dog and runs like a dog. But it doesn't tell me anything about . . ."

"How to save him?"

"How to love him."

She hadn't meant to say it. The librarian listened too well.

"Do you think he wishes for your love?"

"No. But he keeps coming back. And . . . and I must love someone."

"Must you?"

"What else do I have?"

"I don't know," he said, and they did not speak again that day.

SHE DID NOT ATTEMPT TO TOUCH THE CHILD. He never came within ten feet of her anyway, the distance between them as impassible as the cold gray sea.

But he was always there, when she came down the stairs in the morning, and when she started coming down in the evenings as well, he came pattering out from wherever he spent his time to crouch on a rock and watch her, head cocked to one side, pale eyes bright, interested. Sometimes, one or two of the dogs he lived with would come as well: long-legged, heavy-chested dogs that she imagined had been hunting dogs before the fortress fell to the locusts. Her husband had had dogs like that.

The encyclopedias had told her that he would not know how to speak, and in any event she did not know what language the people of this country had spoken before their world ended, as hers had, in fire and death. The child was an apt mimic, though, and much quicker-minded than she had expected. They worked out a crude sign-language before many weeks had passed, simple things like *food,* for she brought him what she could, and *no,* which he used when he thought she might venture too close, and *I have to go now*—and it was ridiculous of her to imagine that he seemed saddened when she made that sign, and even more ridiculous of her to be pleased.

She worried that her visits might draw the fortress's attention to him—for whatever the librarian said, she was not convinced the locusts would not kill the child simply because they could—but she asked him regularly if other people came down to the beach, and he always answered, *no.* She wasn't sure if he understood what she was asking, and the question was really more of an apotropaic ritual; it gave her comfort, even though she suspected it was meaningless.

Until the day when he answered, *yes.*

The shock made her head swim, and she sat down, hard and not gracefully, on a lump of protruding rock. She had no way of asking him who had come, or what they had done, and in a hard, clear flash of bitterness, she thought how stupid of her it was to pretend this child could in any way replace her dead son.

But he was all she had, and he was watching her closely. His face never showed any emotion, except when he snarled with fear or anger, so she did not know what he felt—if anything at all. She asked, *All right?*

Yes, the child signed, but he was still watching her as if he wanted her to show him what he ought to do.

She signed, *All right,* more emphatically than she felt it, but he seemed to be satisfied, for he turned away and began playing a game of catch-me with the two dogs who had accompanied him that morning.

She sat and watched, trying to convince herself that this was not an auspice of doom, that other people in the fortress could come down to the beach without any purpose more sinister than taking a walk.

Except that they didn't. The locusts were not a sea-faring people except in the necessity of finding new countries to conquer. They were not interested in the water and the wind and the harsh smell of salt. In all the time she had been in the fortress, she had never found any evidence that anyone except herself used the stairs to the beach. She was trying hard not to remember the day her husband had said, casually, *A messenger came from the lighthouse today. Says there's strangers landing on the long beach.* Little things. Little things led up to disaster. She was afraid, and she climbed the stairs back to the fortress like a woman moving through a nightmare.

Her louring anxiety distracted her so much that she asked the librarian, forgetting that he was the last person in the fortress likely to know, "Who else goes down to the beach?"

The silence was just long enough for her to curse herself as an idiot before he said, "That was . . . I."

"You?"

"Yes."

"Why? What on earth possessed you?"

His head was turned toward the window again. He said, "You spend so much time there."

At first she did not even understand what he was saying, could make no sense of it. She said, hastily, to fill the gap, "You're lucky you didn't break your neck."

"I won't do it again, if you don't want."

She couldn't help laughing. "You forget which of us is the slave and which the master."

"What makes you think I can forget that? Any more than I can forget that I will never see your face?"

"I . . . I don't . . ."

"I am sorry," he said, his voice weary although his posture was as poker-straight as ever. "I won't bother you about it again. I didn't mean to tell you."

She said, astonished, "I don't mind," and then they both, in unspoken, embarrassed agreement, plunged hastily into the minutiae of their work.

But that evening, as she sat on her rock beside the sea, she heard slow, careful footsteps descending the stairs behind her.

Come! said the child from his rock eight feet away.

Friend, she said, a word they'd had some trouble with, but she thought he understood, even if she suspected that what he meant by it was *pack-member.* And called out, "There's room on my rock for two."

Friend, the child repeated, his hands moving slowly.

No hurt, she said, and wondered if she meant that the librarian would not hurt the child, or that the child should not hurt the librarian.

Yes, he said, and then eagerly, *Rock!*

"What are you doing, this evening?" the librarian's voice said behind her.

"Teaching him to skip stones." She flung another one, strong snap of the wrist. Five skips and it sank. The child bounced in a way she thought meant happiness; he threw a stone, but he hadn't gotten the wrist movement right, and it simply dropped into the water. *Again!* he said, imperious as the child of kings.

She threw another stone. Four skips. The librarian sat down beside her, carefully, slowly.

She said, "What is the sea like, in darkness?"

"Much more vast than I remember it being, when I had my sight. It would do the generals good to be blind."

"Blindness won't teach them anything—they have never wanted to see in the first place."

"You think that's what makes the difference?"

"We learn by wanting," she said. "We learn by grieving."

Shyly, the librarian's hand found hers.

The child threw a stone.

It skipped seven times before it sank.

Sarah Monette *grew up in Oak Ridge, Tennessee, one of the three secret cities of the Manhattan Project. Having completed her Ph.D. in English literature, she now lives and writes in a 101-year-old house in the Upper Midwest. Her novels are published by Ace Books. Her short fiction has appeared in many places, including* Strange Horizons, Alchemy, *and* Lady Churchill's Rosebud Wristlet. *Visit her online at www.sarahmonette.com*

THE MOMENT OF JOY BEFORE

Claudia O'Keefe

FELICE COULD NEVER REMEMBER WHO THE MAN WAS five minutes after he left. She could tell you neither his name nor describe his face. Was he tall or short? Fat or thin? Muscular or soft? What type of clothes did he wear? What were his politics? Or could he not care less what they did in Washington these days?

They talked. That much she knew. Each time he visited her crappy little log cabin outside Cherry Lick, she came away with the impression that they had talked for hours. He also preferred to visit her outside. He was adamant about it, always refusing her invitation to come indoors, one of the few memories it seemed she could keep. In the late spring, they sat on limestone boulders that ruined the pasture behind the cabin as a potential gardening space, misaligned grey rocks that erupted through the March violets and wild onions like impacted wisdom teeth. When summers came, she hauled out her pair of five-dollar camp chairs and they anchored them side by side in swells of waving grass, while trying to ignore the flies and stench of cow dung that wafted over her landlord's property. They stood sheltered under the bare, wet-black branches of her sugar maple in the fall, her boot toe trying unsuccessfully to push aside layer upon layer of sodden leaves to find bare ground where she could scratch a note to herself about him, just one word. Even in winter he made her stand out on her ice-slimed back porch while they conversed. He kept her shivering and captive for entire afternoons, so that when she found herself inside at last, with no recollection of coming in to warm her hands over her stove's only working coil, her fingers were white and bloodless from the tips down to the palms.

Each time she witnessed his arrival on the sloping gravel drive, she told herself that *this time* she would remember. She would save his name somewhere in her head, some place safe he couldn't pilfer. She'd paint the shape of his hands on the insides of her eyelids, sketch his eyes on her palm with one of her daughter's felt markers, like a student trying to crib a test.

Twice she found her clues, within minutes of his departure, but they were useless, as if she'd scribbled them while asleep and dreaming in that language which makes no sense upon waking. Her depiction of his eyes was equally baffling and disturbing. She'd drawn a pair of whirlpools, violent, watery tornadoes flying across her life and heart lines.

Felice had only two other vague pieces of information about the man. One, he was kind sometimes. Two, a vein of cruelty ran through him darker and thicker than in the richest Appalachian coal mine.

"ARE YOU IN TROUBLE, MOM?" her daughter Risa asked one afternoon when Felice picked her up after school.

"What?" Felice said. Looking at her daughter in the rear view mirror, she was unable to conceal her startled reaction. Risa sat next to her friend, Sheila, in the back seat, whom they were giving a ride home.

Light filtered out of the dull September sky like sun through old sheet plastic. It cast yellow reflections at the port wine stain on Risa's otherwise delicate left cheek, turning the birthmark orange. A little more than three months remained until Risa's thirteenth birthday. Though shades of grey emotion often eluded her daughter, as was to be expected with someone her age, she was highly intuitive about moods both black and deliriously bright coloring the world around her. She picked up on them immediately and never hesitated to question that world openly, even in front of strangers.

"No, honey." Felice laughed. "I'm fine."

She had no intention of telling Risa she sat behind the wheel in total dread because she'd run over a wooly-bear caterpillar on the drive here. Not just one caterpillar, but hundreds. Thousands of them. All crossing Hwy 382 going in the same direction, from west to east. For some reason it had made her think of her odd visitor and want to scream mindlessly.

Now, pulling out of the school parking lot and turning north again, she realized she'd have to drive over the bizarre phenomenon all over again.

Laboring up the road, the car crested the hill that marked the edge of the town where Risa went to junior high and the beginning of their fifty-minute drive back to Cherry Lick. Felice's foot hesitated on the gas pedal when confronted by the stain along the asphalt below, spreading clear to the first bend in the highway, black and inky red and creamy pus all mixed together.

The stain moved.

Risa frowned. "What is that?"

"Woolies," Felice said. Unable to avoid them, her tires crushed the first wave of worms, fat as a little girl's pinky, but covered in fur as dense and appealing as a teddy bear's.

"Oh, God, yuck!" Sheila said, her face and hands pressed up against the window on her side of the car.

Sheila had refused to wear her seat belt and now Felice worried about the girl, who was her responsibility, somehow opening the door and falling out. She heard Risa unbuckle herself. Her daughter grabbed the front passenger's side seat and pulled her upper body over it to better see through the windshield.

"Sit back," Felice warned them both. "Both of you buckle your seat belts. That's the last time I'm going to ask, Sheila."

Both girls ignored her. Her fingers clutched the wheel so hard her knuckles ached.

"Go around them," Risa pleaded.

"How?"

Woolies, living and dead, covered the road from one side to the other.

A pickup truck skidded around the first curve, sliding on the remains of previously smashed caterpillars, while its tires threw up a spray of the newly crushed behind them, splattering their car's passenger window. Sheila jumped back reflexively, giggling in delighted fright.

"Stop, mom."

Felice, wishing she could, did not apply the brake.

"Stop killing them, Mom!" Risa was frantic, her lips twisted and blotchy from biting down on them as she watched.

"I'm sorry, Risa."

This was their only route home, over miles and miles of the gentle creatures, whom Risa liked to pick up and cuddle in her hand each time she found one.

"I'm sorry."

An hour and a half later, drained and still upset, Felice dropped down on her daughter's bed and hugged the girl tightly. Risa resisted at first, but then finally relaxed in her mother's arms.

"Did you see that they were all black?" Risa asked.

"Yes."

"Do you know what that means?"

Wooly-bear caterpillars normally had black at both ends and a reddish brown striped midsection. Folklore dictated that the narrower the brown stripe, the harsher the winter. Not one of the woolies whose lives she'd just extinguished had even had a brown stripe.

Her fingers pushed Risa's tousled hair out of her face, gently untangling the knots in it without feeling herself doing so. Her eyes grew unfocused. For a split second it felt as if her body was elsewhere.

Felice rocked in a bitter spring breeze, arms around her knees, drawn up on one of the boulders in the back pasture. She saw a man's hands. Strong, long-fingered, cleanly kept. Hands which blurred just a little as they moved, deft and never to be questioned. Hands of warning.

"Winter's finally coming," Felice said. "It comes from west to east, taking as many as the woolies gone. It's coming for everyone we love."

"Yes," the girl agreed softly, not even questioning the ridiculous thing her mother had just said.

FELICE AND RISA SHARED their dingy nineteenth century cabin with Felice's mother, Karena. Both Felice and Karena had fallen on hard times financially during the late 1990s, so it was agreed that they would join together as a semi-extended family. They'd moved to the Virginia-West Virginia border from the Tucson area four years earlier, pushed out by the real estate boom which took everything beyond Section 8 housing out of their reach. Very few places in the U.S. remained unaffected by double digit gains in housing prices at that time. Cherry Lick was one of them.

Karena hated the place. She hated that the nearest city with a bookstore was almost three hours away. She couldn't stand the winters, which she claimed lasted fourteen months of the year. In cold weather she complained loudly and often about the missing chinking between the cabin's heavy log walls, fallen out years ago and never replaced by their landlord, a sweet, old hippie whose pot habit left him in a permanent fugue state. She told Felice she missed her turquoise skies and tacky billboards with long-legged cowboys in neon cowboy hats selling "authentic Indian souvenirs" made in Pakistan.

Of all the things that drove her mother nuts, however, Felice knew she resented the Fundies here the most. Born and raised a firm believer in religious exploration versus religious dogma, Karena felt herself drowning in a population who interpreted the bible literally and supported what she saw as Washington's desire to conquer the Middle East in the name of Christ.

"Is this the twelfth century?" she'd ask. "Are we living through the Crusades?"

Felice couldn't say what made her decide on Cherry Lick. It wasn't their sort of town. Outsiders were always outsiders here, each of the families who surrounded their rented home having been on this land since before the two Virginias were separate states. She had to admit that the fervent pursuit of a Christian life dominated her neighbors' lives, socializing, work, schools, and politics. Sex, though it happened as readily here as any place else, was given a crust of sin too difficult to discard. She could go months without hearing someone make a joke that didn't begin or end with the words, "time to come to Jesus."

Curiously, she couldn't remember what her own religious leanings were, be they one of the many flavors of Christianity, anti-Christian, or outside that debate entirely. She felt fairly confident that she wasn't into Judaism, Hinduism, or the Muslim tradition, simply because she hadn't been raised as such. She knew she had once had very definite opinions about the order of the universe, but somewhere along the line a hole had appeared in her mind and into it those opinions plunged, never to be resurrected. Instead of trying to remember what her beliefs were, she fought to remember when and where she'd lost them. She thought it may have occurred slightly before she had packed her family into the car, hooked up a U-Haul trailer, and fled Arizona.

Fled *him*.

Not that it had done any good. He'd found her immediately, been waiting the day they moved in.

Rather than dwell on the downsides of her current home, Felice preferred the positives. Spring was glorious here, mostly because it followed winter. She didn't mind using a flashlight to navigate the living room, which sucked all the light out of the house even on the sunniest of days. Nor did the hundreds of thousands of spiders thriving in the cabin's crumbling timbers frighten her. She could flick them away when they crawled over her in the night. Cherry Lick's social isolation didn't bother Felice. She knew she had sought it out. She definitely didn't belong here, but then she'd never really belonged anywhere, even in her home town of Los Piños. Rather than feeling straitjacketed by this area's religious proclivities, she felt comforted living amongst people who let someone else tell them what was what when it came to spiritual matters. Rules were good. Rules meant emotional safety.

Unfortunately as life continued into October, with its harvest festivals and corn mazes, Day-Glo green plastic pumpkins giving way at the megacenter to an avalanche of resin Christmas trinkets before Halloween, while Risa underwent daily tweenie emergencies, discovering Sheila doing the dirty behind the FFA pig barn with the twelve-year-old hunk over which she herself mooned, and Karena hid in her bedroom with a 2.5 liter bottle of Carlo Rossi Mountain Red, watching late night reruns of *Hardball*, *Meet the Press*, and *The Capital Gang*, Felice paced. She walked. She dreaded. She knew. She slogged through lakes of cow pies out back day after day, knowing her family had only a little while to go now. Just days until life changed and couldn't change back.

In the early morning hours of November 11th, Felice lay in a hypnagogic state, at the far threshold of sleep, the night's dreaming done. Or so she thought. Though she'd recently taken to sleeping with the three-way light bulb in her bedside lamp turned to its highest wattage, she could feel the dark outside, its mastery over her part of the world still unchallenged. Cobwebby frost lay over the pasture outside, paralyzing every growing thing, from the bent and rotted stems of summer's thistles to the copperheads that shut their eyes and felt themselves harden into knots, stored beneath the icy ground like so much frozen chicken.

She dreamt the type of dream that feels like real life, and in it her three-way bulb glowed darkroom red. Her sheets, damp with sweat, pooled around her, a slurry of blood pouring over bare legs. Above her dresser, the tiny, frameless mirror she'd found at a yard sale blinked crimson, reflecting an ambulance's revolving lights as they shone in through the window.

"What is it? What's happened?" she sat up and demanded.

Her mother stood at the foot of her bed. She was transparent. She looked happy and young, dressed in a suede mini-skirt and fringed leather vest from the early seventies, her hair an amber beehive of hairspray and Peter Max curlicues.

Oh, my God, Felice thought. *She's dead.* Her ghost was here to say good-bye.

"Mom?"

"I loved Arizona," Karena said. "I loved where I grew up. T-bird convertibles and sunburn. The red rocks of Sedona. Why did we have to leave?"

Felice didn't know what to say to this.

"Something awful has happened," Karena announced, then disappeared.

Felice opened her eyes, now truly awake. Her pulse coursed through the blood vessels in her ears, sounding like floodwaters trashing through a cave. Her lungs expanded painfully as she gasped in surprise.

Her mother wasn't dead. She sat watching Felice from the little chair by the window, looking every one of her sixty-six years. Her shoulders drooped, her cheeks were flush with an unhealthy excitement, her eyes completely resigned.

"God, you scared me," Felice said. She told herself to calm down, breathe more slowly. She figured it must be close to three or four in the morning.

"What's wrong, Mom? Can't you sleep?"

"I think . . ." Karena was uncertain. "You should come see CNN."

THE PLAGUE HAD BEGUN.

World Health Organization experts figured the virus entered the U.S. in Seattle, on a jet from Indonesia carrying 435 of the first 500 to die. Only a small percentage of the passengers lived in the Puget Sound area or terminated their travel there. Of the 362 travelers who switched planes at Sea-Tac, the majority continued on to Chicago, Denver, and Tampa, but a single couple, whose final destination was Dayton, Ohio, proved potent enough as carriers of the disease to fell the passenger lists of three additional flights, each full to capacity. Seventy-two percent of those infected died within a week.

Dubbed the Tsunami Flu because it appeared to originate on a small, remote island flattened by the 2004 disaster, the pandemic confounded epidemiologists who decided early-on that they were dealing with a brand new cousin to A(H5N1), better known as the avian flu. Once it was proved beyond doubt that the world was not dealing with bird flu, theories multiplied, among them that the waves decimating the island nation had set in motion a series of events which took years to unfold. Some said the Tsunami Flu had been around for nearly a century, but isolated until the waters made the tiny speck of rock in the South Pacific where it lay dormant unlivable, thus forcing survivors to migrate to larger population centers and carry the virus with them. Others contended that a certain animal species, perhaps wild pigs, weakened by the disaster and the destruction of their natural habitat, were transported on floating wreckage to unsuitable ecosystems where a previously low-grade strain of flu was encouraged to mutate into something fatal, then spread to humans.

Felice didn't care. She cared only that the virus came on fast and hard, the mortality rate highest among those younger than eight and over sixty years of age. It incubated and was infectious for far longer than the average flu, but severe symptoms didn't appear until the last stages of the disease, when fatal pneumonia flared up and killed patients within hours. Officials had kept news of the virus under wraps for nine days, badly underestimating how quickly and completely it was able to mushroom.

When CNN first broke the story, the media had no idea what was going on, only that hundreds of people had succumbed overnight to a mystery ailment that appeared without warning in several major metropolitan areas. People collapsed in dressing rooms at the mall, while hailing taxis, repairing downed power lines, or cruising up to the take-out window for a triple-decker combo.

Karena hugged her parka around her shoulders as she and Felice sat on the edge of Karena's bed, three feet from the TV. Outside, the temperature dropped into the teens. They didn't have enough blankets in the house. Felice noticed her mother shivering under the parka, but didn't feel the cold herself. Hypnotized by LIVE shots of ambulances backed up at emergency rooms, she watched frustrated EMTs waiting to unload their cargo, like limos mobbing the Kodak Theatre on Oscar night.

Footage of a frenzied mother attempting to carry her comatose teenage daughter into a trauma ward unaided, replayed over and over in a continuous loop. Felice and her mother glanced up nervously at the ceiling. Risa slept in the room above.

"We're safe here," Felice said, more to convince herself than her mother.

"You think?" Karena asked sarcastically. "I don't believe that for a second."

"Mom, there's a reason this place is the butt of every late night comedian's jokes. Cherry Lick didn't even have electricity until the sixties. We're lucky our telephone isn't on a party line. Risa told me her friends' kindergarten memories are of picking up the phone and listening in on their neighbors' conversations. We're forgotten back here, isolated."

"We have an interstate and a Wal-Mart. That's all this thing needs."

"The store!" Felice jumped to her feet, reached for her boots. "I should take what we have left in the bank and buy some extra food."

"And get yourself killed by terrified mobs?" Karena reached out and gripped Felice's wrist, fingernails biting into it.

"There aren't going to be any terrified mobs," Felice said. "Not yet. If anyone's awake right now they're either watching wrestling reruns or the Weather Channel. No one is calling this a plague yet. I doubt the locals are bright enough to look at people dying five states away and think they could be next."

Her mother let go of Felice's arm and sighed deeply. "You know what's right. Go ahead if you think you have to."

"Would you rather starve two weeks from now?"

Karena's features hardened with suppressed anger and familiar fear, the fear that something would happen to Felice, leaving her alone. "You don't talk with the old farts at the post office like I do. If they aren't trying to drag you to a tent revival, they're retelling their family stories about 1918."

"World War I?"

"The Spanish Flu." Karena saw her daughter's blank look and snorted in frustration. "Killed fifty million worldwide, more than the bubonic plague? How many people in the city know about the pandemic of 1918? Hardly any. So little happens of consequence around here that what memories people do have become concentrated. Thousands died in these mountains. They remember it like it was yesterday."

"Which is why I should go now. While I still can."

"Fine. Go."

"Mom? Grandma?" Arms hugged to her chest from the chill, Risa stood in the doorway. Her slippers scuffed the old pine floor with each step as she headed toward the bed. "What are you fighting about?"

"I'm sorry we woke you, sweetie," Felice said.

"We're not arguing, sweet pea," Karena assured her.

"We have some breaking information," said a voice from the television set. All three turned to listen. The tawny-haired man was CNN's top anchor. Disheveled after twelve hours on camera without a break, he looked little better than the unfortunates being hauled out of Denver's ambulances. "This just in. The CDC has confirmed the itinerary of Val and Judy Piets, the couple whose domestic flight from Seattle to their home in Dayton, Ohio included connecting flights in Chicago and two other cities. CNN is being told that their two other stops were at Louisville, Kentucky and Charleston, West Virginia. No word yet on whether the couple disembarked for any length of time at either of those airports. As soon as we have that information . . ."

Felice sat down on the bed again, pulled Risa into her lap and crushed her protectively to her.

"We may already have it," Karena said.

Felice's stomach soured. 'I don't think so. Not yet. I've got to go get us what we're going to need."

She sent Risa back up to bed. She rose. She dressed.

She never left the driveway.

He stood waiting for her by the car.

AN HOUR AFTER SUNRISE the phone rang. Fighting a mental fog that left her uncertain what she'd been doing moments before, Felice drifted into the kitchen to catch the call before the answering machine picked up. Risa sat calmly with one of their white-washed flea market chairs faced away from the center of the room, staring through the multi-paned glass door to the back porch and watching something disappear into the woods. Her morning bowl of mini-wheats rested and wobbled on her legs, milk dripping unnoticed onto her pajamas.

Felice grabbed the receiver, while at the same time trying to see what mesmerized her daughter. Herds of deer were an every day occurrence, flocks of wild turkeys less common. Rarely, they glimpsed the flame-red tail of a fox shooting by, or the monstrous, glorious form of a pileated woodpecker.

A black smudge, taller than it was wide, blighted the pasture, shrinking in size by the second as it traveled farther away. It bobbed up and down slightly like a person traveling over uneven ground, but Felice couldn't make out a head, arms, or legs. It was a shadow, walking like a human. Her breath sped up frantically as she prayed for the forest to hurry and swallow up the dark, smutty thing.

"Hello?" Felice said into the phone.

"Is this Risa's mom?" asked an unfamiliar voice.

Risa turned to look at Felice. Tears ran unhindered down her daughter's cheeks, the sides of her nose, around her mouth. Wetted by them, her birthmark darkened, the color grew more vivid, as if varnished.

"Mom?"

Not vacillating for a second, Felice dropped the phone. "Just a minute," she said absently to the caller, but the receiver had already banged to the floor.

"Risa, what is it? Did you see it? What was that? Did it scare you?"

Risa, clinging to her mother, refused to speak.

Frowning, Felice gently pried herself free and picked up the phone again.

"Sorry," she apologized. "Who is this?"

"This Risa's mom?"

"Yes."

"I'm Darla Heiney. Sheila Heiney's mom."

"Yes, of course."

"I'm guessin' you know by now about the plague." The woman was terse, matter of fact.

"They haven't labeled it—"

Darla Heiney rolled right over that. "We aren't waiting for them to close the schools. We're sending our children to safety."

"We? Sending them where?"

"The parents here, Cherry Lick. Jerry, the bus driver's calling in sick and taking a load up to the old school house on Muddy Stump Mountain while they're still healthy. Peg'll look after them."

"Peg, who?"

"Old school nurse, she and her boys has a camp next to the school house."

"How do we know *they* aren't infected?"

Darla's dull laugh sounded like lard choking a garbage disposal. "You don't know much about us, do you? Peg ain't been off that mountain in years. Clyde and Hubert only come down to ride the Rattler at the state fair and that was back in August. They don't got it."

Felice's heart convulsed at the thought of sending Risa away with these hicks. Could strangers be trusted to keep her warm enough? Would they feed her anything remotely edible? What happened if

Risa became ill? Felice wished she didn't have to go out into the world to make a living. She could simply keep her daughter home until the danger passed.

Darla interrupted the silence between them as if guessing her thoughts.

"Hon," she said, "I don't really care what you decide. It's Sheila made me call. She's worried about her friend."

Risa's tears had evaporated, whatever she'd seen through the back door thrust aside once she intuited adults were talking about her.

"Mom—" she began.

Felice didn't hear the rest. Memories only hours old and already fading wormed their way back to the surface.

Her car keys dangling from slack fingers, the emergency run into town now a non-issue. Not a whisper of light fell from the night sky, the new moon not yet exited her womb, clouds obscuring every star. Yet she saw him clearly, the back of his head as he walked away from her. Hair black as clotted blood, each glassy strand sharp enough to cut naked flesh.

"Felice," his voice crawled inside her ear on ticklish insect feet.

She shuddered.

"I want her," he said.

"Jerry will stop at the end of your drive an hour later than usual," Darla said, bringing her back to the present. "He'll wait two minutes."

"Yes," Felice said. "We'll be there."

WISPY, GOOSE-DOWN SNOW SWIRLED about mother and daughter as they stood just the other side of the icy cattle guard separating their drive from the road. They were located on a blind corner, the opening to their drive hidden by fir trees and wild hedge rows of leafless greenbrier.

Anxious that the bus driver might not see them and opt not to stop, Felice felt a soothing touch and looked down to find Risa's hand on her arm.

"Jerry can see me from here."

"Okay," Felice said.

Pick-up after pick-up truck passed by, drivers nodding to them sadly. How many similar scenes had they witnessed along this road?

"God bless you," an elderly farmer called to them as he cruised by, window rolled down despite the frigid temperature.

Felice stroked her daughter's hair. "You know I love you—"

"—a whole big bunch," Risa finished the habitual phrase for her. "I love you, too, Mom."

"I'll come get you soon. I promise. We'll get your favorite quadruple fudge brownie at the mall in Roanoke. We'll get two of them, smash them together and make it octodruple fudge!"

Risa smiled, but didn't laugh. Even as a baby, Risa had been gifted with a beautiful laugh, never a giggle, but melodious, uninhibited laughter that made the air shiver and clear. Felice remembered the last time she'd heard it. When they still lived in Los Piños. Unlike a toddler's fierce attachment to her favorite blankey or a five-year-old's innocent belief in Santa Claus, something in Felice told her those joyous sounds should not have been allowed to lapse. Her daughter's beautiful laughter had been a language in itself. Her bilingual nature should not have been suppressed, even when the adults around her forced her to use only the tongue with which they felt comfortable.

Felice would give her life to hear her daughter laugh like that right now.

Jerry roared up the hill and around the sharp bend, his bus already overloaded with children. They sat dangerously high in seats piled with luggage. Backpacks and crates of food and an avalanche of sleeping bags filled the aisle. Spotting Risa and Felice, he hit the brakes, sending children tumbling off their perches to the floor.

"Sorry 'bout that," Jerry said, when he opened the door. His hand trembled on the wheel. He wore a sterile paper face mask.

Perceiving Felice's alarm, he pulled down the mask in order to speak more clearly. "Don't worry. I ain't got it. It's made some of the parents feel more easy sending their kids off with me is all."

Felice nodded. She kissed Risa's forehead and held her close. Jerry would have to pry her away if he expected Risa to get on the bus.

"Ma'am," he said.

Felice gazed up at him.

"Lots of kids to pick up. Lots more worried sick parents. We've got a long way to go."

Felice nodded again and released her child, righted the heavy, adult-sized camping pack on Risa's shoulders and gave her a gentle nudge toward the bus.

"Mom, guess what!" Risa pivoted suddenly on the step, her eyes strangely bright and out of character for this somber good-bye. "He spoke to me."

"What? Who spoke to you, honey?" Felice asked urgently. "What's his name?"

Risa started to answer, but Jerry pushed the lever to close the bus's hinged doors, putting glass and metal between them, and Felice couldn't read lips. The bus rumbled away in an explosion of grinding gears, diesel smoke and burning oil, leaving Felice standing precariously on the cattle guard, the life drained out of her the farther Risa rode from their drive. She felt fragile, old, less of a person. She wanted to scream, knew she could because no one lived close enough to hear her. Instead, she turned and headed back down the drive, quiet, eyes growing hot with held-back tears, not knowing what came next.

Sixteen hundred dead that evening. Twenty-three hundred by the next morning. Thirty-four thousand within two days. Two hundred and seventy-eight thousand by the following week. Neither of the Tsunami Piets, as the media began calling the married, ill-fated disease carriers from Ohio, had disembarked in Charleston. As Karena predicted, a Wal-Mart trucker stopping at the Covington store in Virginia brought it to those living on the border. Though nothing happened for more than twelve days, on the thirteenth day, the first cases of the flu cropped up along the Alleghenies, reaching into every hollow within an hour of the Interstate. Nor was the trucker the only source of transmission, just the first of hundreds infected to bring death to the Mid-Atlantic.

Rather than being safer, the Appalachian hills turned out to be one of the places with the highest per capita ratio of fatalities. Though those in high population centers had a greater chance of contracting the disease, after more than a million deaths in the U.S. it was thought the better, more readily available medical care in the cities gave victims an edge. Emergency production of medicines and an eventual vaccine would lead to a tapering off of deaths in the cities, the talking heads on MSNBC forecast. In the nation's poorest, most rural areas, however, that same help would be slow arriving and more difficult to distribute. Events were cancelled and most public buildings closed. Felice's boss called her and told her not to come in; the office would be shut down until further notice.

Days, then weeks went by without a single opportunity for Felice to speak with Risa. No phones, not even party lines, were installed atop Muddy Stump Mountain. Cell phone coverage was non-existent more than a few miles from the Interstate. Who communicated with the old school house and how? Felice wanted to know. Her sole link to her child was the surly Darla Heiney, hardly a font of information.

"They's not hacking or coughing or wheezing or anything like that," Darla told her over the phone.

"But have you heard anything about Risa?" Felice asked. "Has your daughter said anything to you about her? Is Risa scared? Is she homesick? Is she eating?'

"Hon, I just don't know," Darla said. God, how Felice had come to hate Darla's 'hon's'. "They's not talking to us at all right now with the Tsunami spreading so much."

"Can you send a message? Can you get a message to her?"

"No!" Darla bawled into the phone, drawing out the word in that peculiar mountain way that mimicked a heifer giving birth at the bottom of a sink hole. "I done told you that before."

"But I don't even know where Muddy Stump Mountain is. No one will tell me and there aren't any maps of this area for sale. I've never lived any place where you couldn't buy a damn map!"

"You're not thinking of trying to get up there, are you?" Darla asked, "'cause the way things are right now, Clyde and Hubert will shoot you on sight if you get anywhere close, no questions asked."

"Are you telling me I can't go get my child if I want to?" Felice said.

"That's exactly what I'm tellin' you."

"You can't stop me."

"Maybe not me, but Hubert's twenty-gauge Mossberg sure can," Darla said. "Felice, you're just going to have to put your trust in the Lord 'til this thing's over. Be strong in knowing that Jesus is looking out for her as we speak."

Apparently the savior wasn't looking out for Darla Heiney. She died the next morning.

CUT OFF FROM EVEN THIS FEEBLE SOURCE OF NEWS about Risa, Felice moved into full-panic mode. She called the school again, hoping someone might have been left behind to field questions after it closed its doors. Now not even the answering machine in the front office picked up. She found the bus driver listed in the phone book with his address and raced to his house next to a rarely visited Civil War battlefield. His front door stood open, the place deserted. A litter of starving, flea-bloodied puppies abandoned by the family whined and tripped her up as she made her search of the home for clues to Risa's whereabouts. Nothing. Nor had a crumb had been left in the house for the dogs. After filling an old enamel roaster with fresh water for the animals, the best she could do, she moved on, pounding on door after neighbor's door. No one answered. Cars sat in many of the drives, but she detected no movement in any of the houses. If the residents were home, they remained in hiding. She drove to the junior high. It proved a useless trip. A thick chain and industrial-sized lock put the place off-limits. Officials hadn't even left information at the gate.

Her Chevette wound for hours along one-lane country roads, passing yard after yard of brown ice and toys forgotten in mid-play, but she saw no children. Her concern wasn't that she'd miss spotting the mountain school house amongst the leafless trees and hills so convoluted and covered in mud they were like dirty blankets piled in a laundry basket. What drove her to near madness was the unhelpful, unconcerned behavior of the people she did find to question. Judging by their accents they'd lived here for years, if not their entire lives, yet none confessed to having heard of the old school. They listened to her frantic, gradually more strident story and shrugged.

Her gas gauge rode below "E" for over twenty miles before she found a service station. Though only a little after three in the afternoon, dusk overpowered the winter-short day and blackened every hollow. Pulling up to the pump, she sighed in relief to see a light on inside the cozy general store adjacent to the station. If she could just buy a cup of coffee and fill her gas tank, she'd continue her search until last light. Digging into her purse for her wallet, she looked up, reached for the door handle, and found a shotgun barrel aimed at the spot between her eyes.

"Don't, ma'am," said the station owner through the rolled-up car window.

"I just want some gas and a cup of coffee," she said.

"No coffee. No food," he said. "We got gas, but we's got new rules for the duration."

"Alright."

"I'm going back into the store. I'm going to trust in the Lord that you is an honest person and will pay me for what gas you take. Leave the money inside that there tire over there."

He pointed at an old tire laying in the dirt next to the pump, filled with soil and the desiccated remains of last year's hollyhocks. His gaze never left her as he backed into the store as if she were the one with gun about to pull the trigger.

"Wait!" she called after him. "Do you know where—"

He shut his door quietly, yet firmly.

Felice followed instructions, filled her tank, paid, and drove home.

She didn't sleep that night, couldn't stop twisting and turning various scenarios over and over again in her mind, each involving Risa sick or in trouble and calling out for mommy, who wouldn't answer, wouldn't come to her aid.

"How could you just let her go like that!" Karena said to Felice's back, as her daughter paced anxiously in the cave-like living room at dawn.

Felice turned to see Karena enter from the kitchen. With the morning sun at her back, her hair half-wild from sleep, and resentment she'd suppressed for days carving a look of fury into her features, her mother resembled a ship's figurehead cutting through the gloom. Felice felt that anger plowing toward her and cringed with guilt.

"How could you let them take her without knowing where they were going?" she asked.

"They did tell me where they were going. Muddy . . ."

Fear made it hard to focus. *What am I going to do? How do I get her back? I don't have anyone to help me. I'm alone.*

"Muddy Hump—"

"Muddy Stump Mountain," her mother said. "For God's sake, you don't even remember the name of the place, let alone know how to get there. What kind of a mother are you?"

"A terrified one. Okay? I admit it," Felice shouted. "I'm absolutely terrified we're never going to see Risa again. It was Jerry, the bus driver. It was the school bus that came to pick them up. Shouldn't you be able to trust a God damned school bus? How was I supposed to know these frickin' people were totally disorganized? It was all happening so fast, the deaths, the thousands of deaths, the train wreck spread of this thing, the inevitability that it would come looking for us here. I figured everyone else was just as terrified as me. Jerry would rush our children off to safety and then be in touch with us immediately to let us know they were safe and what was happening to them. I don't understand the people in this place. I've tried to figure them out, what goes through their heads, but I don't get it. It's like they care about the sanctity of life, about others, about their children, but they don't care. They're like Darla Heiney, shrugging it off their backs and then dropping dead."

Felice felt as if she was physically coming apart. A thousand horrible emotions flooded through her, tumbling her about inside herself, dragging her under like an invisible riptide.

"I was afraid for her when I sent her off," she said. "That's why I did it. I was afraid *he'd* get her."

"He? Who are you talking about?"

"The man, the person who's always visiting us."

"What man? Felice . . ." Her mother reached out to her. "Do you have a fever?"

Felice pushed her mother's hand aside before she could lay it against her forehead.

"Don't touch me."

"Why, are you sick?"

"Yes."

Did she imagine it, or did her mother hesitate, retreat a step in self-preservation? A moment later, Felice glimpsed her mother's instant shame over a purely human reaction. Saw and forgave.

"Sick with worry," Felice said.

"I'm sorry," Karena said, softening her attitude. "I know you were just trying to protect Risa. I'm worried, too."

"Mom, I don't know what to do."

"We go look for her, is what."

"What do you think I did all of yesterday?"

"But you didn't have my connections."

Felice frowned. Had her mother been out where she could catch the flu? "What connections?"

"There's this old geezer at the post office. He hovers inside the door almost all day long. Now that they've discontinued counter service and the postmaster is no longer there, he doesn't have anyone to talk to. His mind is half-gone, but there's enough left that he recognizes me every day and keeps hitting on me. I'll ask him where they've taken Risa."

"But if he's as far gone as you say—"

"He's still got fingers," Karena said. "He can point."

Hope, a small sliver of it, pushed through Felice's monologue of inner dread.

"I don't want you getting too close to him. Even yesterday, I did my best to stand a few feet away from people." She thought of the gas station owner. "Not that they would let me come near."

"Don't worry about me. Our biggest problem is what to do once we find the school house."

"What do you mean?" Felice asked.

"They're armed, aren't they?"

Felice thought for a minute, pacing again. "I wish I had a bull horn."

"Signs," her mother said.

"Big signs!" Felice agreed. "We won't drive up directly to the school house. We'll get just close enough for them to read our signs."

"Doesn't Risa have some white poster board in her room?"

Felice hugged her mother. "I'll get busy making them. You drive down to the post office and talk to this guy."

Karena grabbed the car keys.

"Remember, don't get too close," Felice said.

She went to work, thankful her mother forgot to question her about the visitor. She regretted having blurted out what she did. It was as if by telling another person about him, it made him more than figment, gave him a life she dared not let him have.

Half an hour later, she capped the ultra-fat permanent marker, finished with the signs asking for her daughter's release, and suddenly realized her mother hadn't returned. Their post office was less than a mile away. It shouldn't have taken Karena this long to ask someone a simple question. Felice went to the front window and glanced uneasily up the drive. She gasped.

The top of their driveway was gone. Her mind tried to understand what she saw in its place, but refused. It recoiled at the total absence of reality it perceived, the hole in the world it saw just two hundred yards away. Whatever was there was literally beyond her comprehension. Unable to identify it, her brain filled in the gap with something more reasonable, the way human vision colors in the natural blind spot every person possesses by copying and pasting what surrounded it.

A black stain. A floating miasma which erased ground and gravel and cattle guard.

Everything in Felice tensed, came to a stop, her heart, her breath, her thoughts. The sight paralyzed her completely.

Intelligent, the thing reacted the moment Felice came to the window, as if it could see her, roiling swiftly down the drive toward the house.

"Stop."

Felice knew she had spoken, though she didn't feel her lips move, couldn't hear her heart beating or see her chest rise and fall.

The phenomenon slowed its progress and halted in place, consuming the empty parking spot in front of the house and the volunteer sumac shading it.

Her thoughts unlocked themselves long enough for hysteria to set in. What was that thing? What did it want? Had it hurt her mother? She knew in her soul that Karena needed her right now. Something horrid had or was about to happen. She had no car. Her mother had taken it, which meant she'd have to rush the mile to the post office on foot.

Past that.

"Go away," she said.

It didn't move.

"Please just go away."

It came closer, past the four-story fir tree where owls hooted at night, past sleeping forsythia bushes, over the ring of stones marking the bed where peonies and poison ivy flourished in late spring, around the front porch, halting only when it was in arm's reach of the window where Felice stood.

The wrongness of it swallowed everything. Incredulity struck Felice blind seconds before the stain formed fingers to touch the window glass inches from her face.

When her world finally came back to her, she discovered herself racing down the final quarter-mile to the main road. How had she gotten here? Had It put her here? Had she managed to get around it, through it?

Her throat burned, her body unaccustomed to exertion in the raw air, as she sprinted through a church parking lot and arrived at the post office. Parked in front, the Chevette's engine was still running, but no Karena. Instead, an elderly man dressed in a puffy silver jacket that belonged on someone sixty years his junior attempted to flag down a rusted-out minivan speeding by on the highway. It wouldn't stop and the man, drained by the effort, crumpled to the asphalt parking lot like a discarded ball of aluminum foil. As he fell, his arms wrapped around something at his feet.

"Mom!" Felice cried.

"This your ma?" asked the man, who had only three teeth and smelled of moldy carpeting.

She nodded. He released his protective hold on Karena and crawled aside.

"She fell down," he said.

"Felice?" Karena wheezed and clutched her chest. Her body shuddered. Her skin was tinged a cross between vein blue and shocky white. She labored to sit up and failed. "I can't breathe."

NINE-ONE-ONE PUT HER ON HOLD with an estimated wait time of thirty-one minutes. Cherry Lick's local volunteer fire and rescue didn't answer their direct line. Karena tried but was already too weak to stand, let alone walk as her daughter assisted her to the car's passenger seat. Sweet, very sweet, though he knew the risks, the old man did his best to help, but mostly got in the way.

"You should stand back," Felice told him. "I don't want you to get it."

"My son is dead," he began, shaking his head. "I'm tired of winter."

Felice nodded her understanding and laid her hand lightly on his shoulder. It sagged beneath her palm. Though uncomfortable saying it because his sense of the divine was not her own, she wanted to give this man something to ease his pain. She smiled at him.

"God is standing right beside you," she said. "I see him. His hand is on your other shoulder. He will be there when he brings your son to welcome you home."

The old man's lips trembled. "Thank you," he said.

She climbed in behind the wheel, backed up and tore out of the parking lot as fast as the ancient hatchback would take mother and daughter toward the nearest hospital.

A National Guard roadblock barred her way half a mile from White Sulphur Springs.

"I'm sorry, ma'am," the female soldier with bleach-fried hair and an M-16 rifle told her, after instructing her to roll down her window no more than a crack. Most of her face hid behind a mask that Felice guessed must have dated to the first Gulf War. "I can't let you pass. White Sulphur Springs, Lewisburg, and Ronceverte are under quarantine."

"Quarantine!" Felice cried. "The flu is everywhere."

"I know, ma'am."

"But I have to get my mother to the hospital."

"The hospital's full."

"The clinics?"

"Those resources have been deployed elsewhere."

Felice made a choking sound. "Deployed? Where? How do you deploy a building? This is an emergency! My mother needs immediate care."

"I understand, ma'am, but I can't let you pass."

Felice gazed beyond the military Hummers and barricades, attempting to see what went on farther down the road at the edge of White Sulphur.

"Don't even think about it," the soldier said.

"Think about what?" Felice asked innocently, but knew her thoughts were transparent.

"We have all the roads, all of them. You can't get into town."

"My mother is . . ." she didn't want to say, dying, not when Karena could hear her and give up before they could find help. "My mother is extremely ill," Felice begged.

For the first time since their encounter, the soldier bent down and looked into the car at Karena slumped in the passenger's seat, laboring to breathe. "I can see that, ma'am," she said finally. "Here." Latex clad fingers pushed a slip of paper through the crack between window glass and door frame. It fluttered into Felice's lap. The phone number for a rural aide worker.

"They usually have Tamiflu and some of the other drugs. That's all I can do," the woman said. "Now, please, if you'll turn around over there."

Felice turned and drove all of fifty feet to a pay phone. She dialed. The line picked up.

"Give me your address," said a sour-sounding man on the other end of the line.

Felice hesitated, not knowing if she'd heard right.

"You're calling from the pay phone next to the Hardee's, aren't you?"

"Yes."

"What's your address?"

"Can I come to you?"

"No."

"My mother, it was so sudden. She wasn't showing any signs, but I'm scared. I think it's really bad."

"She's not alone," the man said.

His cold, impersonal tone caught Felice by surprise. "No, you're not hearing me," she said.

"No, you're not hearing me. Give me your address and go home. My wife will be there when she can."

A cold drizzle slicked the highway as Felice rushed toward Cherry Lick. It turned to hard rain once the barricade was out of sight and the wind picked up. Passing Risa's school with its construction paper Thanksgiving turkeys still in the windows and the forlorn look of someplace that would never reopen, hail peppered the windshield. Icy rain came next, slashing at the trees, streaking by the side window like globs of frozen spit. Her tires shimmied on the curves. The road changed course and they charged into gale force winds where the spit became wet snow. The roads were eerie, untraveled by anyone except for a car heading the opposite way with an urgency Felice recognized.

Karena complained every moment of the way home, growing less lucid by the mile. Felice worried the freezing temperatures in the car exacerbated her rapidly deteriorating condition. Their heater was broken, but she cranked it on high anyway in hopes it would miraculously revive. Her mother coughed uncontrollably. Now that professional medical care proved to be out of reach, Felice cursed herself for making the decision to drive rather than go straight home and continue to call for help from there. Alarm settled in her chest and permanently altered the tempo of her heart. She couldn't get home quick enough, couldn't turn the wheel and slide and fish-tail through this white crap mounting up on the roads fast enough.

Get Mom to warmth, she thought over and over again, concerned the aide worker would arrive at their cabin, find no one there and pass them by. *What's in the medicine cabinet? There's got to be something in there I can give her.*

Turning onto their road it occurred to her that she hadn't seen their home since the stain had come. What would she find when she rounded that final bend? Would the top of the drive still be a black hole? Would there be a drop-off into nothingness where she normally parked the car? Would *It* be waiting for them? What had she been thinking to give the aide worker's husband this address? She could have lied and taken Karena to any number of empty houses she'd visited yesterday, the bus driver's place, for instance.

Five-inch drifts as coarse and sloppy as ice rink shavings covered the drive. No holes, no dark, boiling fog. Just snow and—she lifted her foot off the gas momentarily when she spotted them—tracks. Not knowing what to expect, she veered down their steep drive, obliterating the signs of human visitation leading to their porch.

A slight figure in a quilted pink coat she didn't recognize huddled against the door, taking shelter under the overhang. Hearing the car rattle over the cattle guard, the obviously miserable refugee looked up.

"Risa?" Felice whispered. She forgot to be careful in the snow and slammed on the brakes, barely able to keep the car from sliding sideways into the pasture.

"What?" Karena blinked. "Did you say, Risa? Is she back?"

"Yes, Mom. Risa's back."

Yesterday she would have endured any torture, any loss to get her daughter back, see her running toward the car, made clumsy by the snow. Would have stomped on the parking brake, thrown open the door and gathered Risa in her arms in delirious reunion, swearing to never let her daughter go again.

Today, she honked the horn, beat on it several times until Risa got the message and stopped twenty feet from the car. Its headlights spotlighted her confused face through the heavy flakes falling between them, her nose and birthmark reddened by the cold, hands made blotchy by it. She was soaking wet from her sneakers up to her knees from hiking through drifts. The thin, unfamiliar coat could not have kept her warm on her journey.

Felice opened her window.

"Stay away!" she shouted. "Grandma's not feeling well."

"But, Mom—"

"No, Risa, stay back!"

"I couldn't find the spare key under the snow."

"Risa, listen to me. I'm going to turn off the engine and throw my keys to you."

Felice didn't know if she was already contagious, didn't know if objects could pass this disease to others, but didn't want to take the chance.

"I want you to take off one of your socks and put it over your hand."

"What?" Risa, expecting her mother to comfort her, not bark orders at her, began to cry in exhaustion and fear.

"It'll be okay, sweetie. Just do what I tell you."

"But, Mom—"

"No, listen to me!" she said. "Open the house, leave the keys in the lock, and go to the kitchen. I want you to make yourself some hot chocolate in the microwave and take it up the back stairs to your room. Change out of your wet clothes and get under every blanket you have. Do not come downstairs, no matter what you hear. As soon as I have grandma settled in her room, I'll be up to see you."

Risa, ignoring everything she'd just said, started toward the car again. Felice laid on the horn and, eventually, her daughter grasped the seriousness of the situation.

"I love you, Risa," Felice said. "I don't know how you got here, but I'm so glad." She lobbed the keys into the snow. "Now, go!"

"YOU'RE LUCKY," said Trina, the home aide worker, a fortyish woman with a New Jersey accent, sterile gloves, and a face mask tied so tightly around her head it creased her cheeks. "You're the last house I'll be able to visit tonight. If I don't start now, I don't think I'll make it home."

"Yes," Felice said, "come in, please."

Felice gave the woman points for achieving the near impossible, finding their half-hidden drive in white-out conditions and having the guts to navigate down the driveway.

"Oh." Trina grunted thoughtlessly when she saw Karena. The look she gave Felice offered no hope whatsoever. "She has it."

After all she'd been through already, and the undignified struggle dragging her mom through the snow, scraping and bruising them both because she wasn't strong enough to carry her, tearing the medicine chest apart and throwing every last useless thing on the floor in her frantic search for something that could make Karena feel better, sitting by her bed and holding her hand and reassuring her again and again and again that medical help was on its way, would be here any second—

to have this stranger come in and dismiss her chances so casually made Felice want to rip the woman's throat out.

"Please." Felice gestured for them to step into the next room. She spoke in a low voice. "You're going to tell me there's no chance for her and I don't want her to hear that."

"I can give you some OTC flu medications, Sudafed, Benadryl—"

"What?" Felice was stunned. "I thought you were going to bring us real help. The woman at the barricade said you carry Tamiflu."

"I'm not a doctor," Trina said. "I'm not even a nurse. The rules don't allow aide workers here to dispense prescription mediations."

"Rules! What do the rules matter now?"

"I'm sorry."

Trina dug into the bulging carry-all hanging from her shoulder and retrieved a package of non-prescription flu tablets.

Felice begged for the second time that day. "Please," she said, forgetting to whisper, her voice steadily rising. "My mother is the only family my daughter and I have. We're all each other has. Please, you must have something else in that bag. My mother should be in a hospital right now."

Trina set the package of flu tablets on a table and stared at Felice for several seconds, undecided. Finally, she reached into the bag again and brought out a small, black book.

"A Bible?" Felice said.

"Our savior is the hope you're seeking right now," Trina said.

From the other room, Karena burst into the conversation. "Does everyone here have to be a turd for Jesus?"

Felice's eyes widened and she felt herself blush.

"What?" Trina asked, as she ventured into Karena's room again.

Karena, hysterical at the onset of chronic pneumonia, fought the confines of her blankets. Every word she spoke came out like the moan of wind sucking rain through a bed sheet. "I said, does everyone here have to be a turd for Jesus?"

"Turd?" Felice forced her voice to be light. She didn't want her mom to drive this woman away before she could convince her to help. "You haven't been hanging out with Risa's friends, have you?"

Her mother wouldn't be jollied out of her anger. "Felice, what on earth made you decide to bring us here? The moment we moved into this house, I knew it would be the last one I'd ever live in. I knew I'd die in Cherry Lick. I love you, Felice, but I'll always resent you for this. I just don't get it. Why here? This isn't your home. Christ, these people live, eat, breath Him. They're so obsessed with the Bible they fart and belch in scripture."

Clearly offended, but retaining her professionalism, the aide worker backed out of the bedroom. Sitting on the edge of her mother's bed, Felice looked over her shoulder at Trina. The woman appeared ready to bolt for home, but Felice put every thing she could into communicating their need using her eyes alone. She had the feeling that behind her mask, the aide worker's lips pursed in a stern frown.

At last Trina nodded and the corners of her eyes softened in a smile, one Felice felt certain was pity.

"God bless your family," she said. A moment later, the front door clicked shut.

Felice rose to turn the lock and saw it, a small, brown paper sack next to the package of OTC flu remedy. She opened it and peered inside at two sample packs of prescription medicine, the type doctors often gave to their patients as free trials.

She dosed Karena immediately, then sat in the chair next to her mother's bed, with the phone to her ear, on hold with 911 for another hour before she gave up. Upstairs, Risa would be lying frightened in her bed. Karena's anger had eased after she received her medicine. Felice knew she should go up and reassure her daughter, yet when she started to leave, she noticed her mother's gaze searching timidly about the room.

"Mom?"

Karena didn't answer, showed no signs that she heard Felice. Her eyes grew weepy and red around the rims. Gone was the confident, outspoken woman.

"Mom? What is it? What can I get for you?"

Felice didn't really need to ask. She could see it in Karena's eyes. Only one look had that type of desperation. Her mom wanted her own mother, long dead.

"I want to go home," Karena stated.

"I know," Felice said, softly stroking her mother's damp brow.

"Back to Los Piños."

"Home," Felice nodded and said.

"I miss it so much."

"Get well!" Felice said, her own eyes hot, ready to spill over. "Get well and I promise you I'll get us home. I will."

"Mom?" Risa called to her from her bedroom.

"I'll be up there in a minute," Felice told her. "Did you do what I said? Are you warm?"

"Yes, Mom, but there's something I have to—"

Felice couldn't handle things a moment longer. She needed escape. "In a minute, sweetie."

She rushed out the back door, not even stopping to put on a coat.

Snow blew under the porch eaves. It frosted the old slatted swing, which gyrated wildly in the wind, suspended by twin lengths of chain. Felice paced up and down the narrow portion of decking free of drifts. Flakes landed in her eyes and melted in her tears. She'd never felt guilt this heavy. What possessed her to bring her family here? Her mother was among the seventy-two percent. She would die tonight without seeing home ever again. More than anything, she wished she could make this hideous form of death easier for her.

Though she'd told Risa she'd be only a minute, she paced until her energy ran out and her feet stumbled. Uncaring that the wind and snow plastered her back, she brushed off the porch swing's painted slats and collapsed into it. Her weight calmed its fierce movements and she stared out into the back pasture. Snow made the wind visible. Its currents and whirlpools, tossing and thrashing, a stormy sea not normally seen, hypnotized her. Her emotionally exhausted mind groped for understanding, the reason for all of this, the reason for everything. What was the black stain and why did it come here? Why couldn't she remember her mysterious visitor the moment he left? Who was he?

"Felice," he'd said. *"I want her."*

Finally, the cold and wet penetrated her overexcited, overheated body. Dusk encroached, turning the storm midnight blue. She realized she had to go in. Half-blinded by the snow, she almost missed the tiny spot of red under the barren sugar maple.

Curious, she shielded her eyes and descended the steps, then punched through the drifts toward the shelter of the tree, where the snow was only a couple of inches deep.

At first she thought they were plastic, blown here across the miles from the cemetery in town, where wreaths of fake flowers adorned nearly every grave. Then she crouched down and touched the poppy-like petals. Each blossom had a black spot at the center in the shape of a three-pointed star. She dug snow away from the slender olive-green stems and discovered that they were firmly rooted in the earth. Her mind wouldn't accept what she'd found.

How? she asked herself. "How?" she said aloud.

The small cluster of desert wildflowers didn't belong here. Native to Western Arizona, they did not grow in winter, Felice knew, nor east of New Mexico. In fact, there was only one place she'd ever seen this particular strain.

Blast after blast of wind flattened the blossoms to the ground, but not a petal was lost. In wonder, Felice picked them, protected them in her arms, ran up the steps, through the back door, and into her mother's bedroom.

Two startled heads popped up, when she rushed into the room.

"Risa!" Felice said.

Chair pulled up to the bed, her daughter sat with her upper body lying across her grandmother's bedcovers, gently hugging her. She jerked upright at Felice's entrance.

Alarm Felice imagined would assault her system only during the last moments of her own life, crushed the breath from her lungs. Adrenaline lit her nerve endings painfully on fire.

"Oh, Risa!"

"Mom, you don't have to worry."

"Risa, leave."

"No, Mom."

Felice approached the bed, still clutching her haphazard bouquet of wildflowers.

"Please, for me, honey. It may not be too late."

Karena's glassy eyes fixed instantly on the flowers in her daughter's hands and lit up in pure joy.

"Mariposa lilies," she said. A feeble hand reached for the gift her daughter brought her. "Is it spring already?"

Felice cupped her mother's hands around the bunch of lilies and assisted her in lifting them toward her face. Her mother attempted to gather their warm, dusty perfume into her nose. Though Felice knew she couldn't possibly smell anything in her condition, Karena pretended the fragrance was magnificent. She sighed and her fingers petted the blossom's large, soft petals as she smiled up at her daughter.

"Thank you for keeping your promise, Felice. Thank you for taking me home."

"Los Piños," Felice whispered to her and touched her hand.

"Los Piños."

Her mother sighed again, closing her eyes.

"WHY, RISA?" Felice asked when the two stood in living room together, allowing Karena some fitful sleep. "You're exposed now."

"Mom, I've already got it."

"No!" Felice denied it. "You're not sick."

"I've been trying to tell you, but you won't listen."

"How did you even get here?"

"Mom, listen to me!" Risa almost shouted.

Felice steered her daughter into the kitchen so she wouldn't agitate Karena.

"They all have it up on Muddy Stump."

"What? How? They weren't supposed to let anyone near the school house. They wouldn't let me near it. Wouldn't even tell me where it was. I drove around for hours looking for you."

"Sheila snuck out to see her brother," Risa said.

Felice thought about her last conversation with Sheila's mom, Darly Heiney, the news the following morning.

"Sheila's mom is dead," Felice said.

"So is Sheila. So are half the kids at the school. Sheila gave it to all of us. When that old lady and her two sons who were guarding us died, a bunch of us got in their trucks and got out of there."

"Drove?"

"Don't be so shocked, mom. The girl who drove me home was about to go for her learner's permit when Sue hit."

"Sue?"

"Duh. Short for Tsunami."

"Risa, this thing doesn't infect everyone automatically. You shouldn't have gone into your grandmother's room. You shouldn't be near me without protection. Go get one of those painter's masks from the tool box in the furnace closet and put it on."

Risa shrugged. "But, Mom—"

"Do it!"

Felice waited until Risa headed toward the storage room at the back of the house, then returned to her mother's room. She halted one step inside the door.

He stood at Karena's side.

His lips were beautiful.

His hands, exquisitely carved in flesh and bone and skin flawless as alabaster, spoke of a will no one on Earth could resist. His cruel posture dismissed everything and everyone because whatever anyone wanted truly didn't matter. His hair might have been sharp as prison wire and the icy hue of a meteor shower in mid-winter, but his lips couldn't hide what he thought sometimes.

Sorrow, genuine and final.

"I'm sorry," they whispered.

Why is he in my house? Felice wondered dully. *He's always refused to come indoors.*

"You said you wanted her," she said. "Why did you want my mother?"

This isn't memory. This is now. I'm seeing him now.

"I can see you changing, Felice," he said. "You aren't quite forgetting, but you aren't remembering. Time is short."

She tried to force herself to look into his eyes, but she couldn't move her gaze above those terrifying, seductive lips.

"Whatever you have left to do to prepare, you must hurry."

If she looked into his eyes she would know everything and everything would be lost. She had to forget again.

During the precious seconds she wasted thinking this, he placed his hand over Karena's heart. One moment her mother was there, living in agony. The next, an empty husk grew still and sunk deeper into the mattress. Felice saw nothing, no light, no mist, no ghostly apparition. She sobbed at the lack of what her expectations told her she should experience when her mother left her. She'd had no time. She hadn't had the chance to prepare.

Though he didn't actually touch her as he passed her, his aura, the black stain, brushed her cheek and she glimpsed a thousand happy memories, a thousand ugly ones, her entire life compressed into a single sensation, one sound, a mixture of rushing water and sun shining on dreaming eyelids, and the half-life of the human body decaying one cell at a time, day by day.

Ten minutes, twenty minutes, an hour later, she still hadn't forgotten his visit.

She closed her mother's door quietly, as if any noise, however slight, might disturb her.

Outside, the worst happened, snow changed to heavy sleet. Icy pellets, identical in size to coarse sand, poured from sky to roof as if from a dump truck loaded with twenty tons of the stuff. They scoured the shingles, hissed down the drain pipes and overflowed the gutters, cascaded from eaves and overhangs into great piles. Atop the eight-inch drifts already on the ground, even an additional two inches of sleet would make shoveling by hand difficult, if not impossible. Whenever this had happened in the past it always froze rock-hard afterwards, trapping them for days.

No one else would be coming tonight, nor tomorrow. No one to comfort or assist them, no one to take Karena away. Felice knew she had to protect her daughter from the smell now seeping through the house. Even if she could have managed the dead weight, Felice couldn't bear to put Karena out into the storm. Opening the bedroom window, then closing the door on her mother was the only option she had.

Risa waited nervously in the hall, wearing her mask.

"Grandma?" she asked.

Felice smiled a smile that wasn't one. "She's peaceful now."

"She's dead?"

"Yes."

Felice wasn't certain what reaction she should expect from Risa—tears, anger, accusations, disbelief. Instead, her daughter bobbed her head numbly in acceptance, turned and climbed the stairs to her room.

"Risa?"

"I'm okay."

Felice knew for a fact that she wasn't, Risa's fatalistic attitude upsetting her more than the blame for which she had braced.

It's okay. I'm going to die. You're going to die. We're all going to die, her daughter's eyes said.

She had to do something. She had to turn this around immediately.

She scrubbed herself raw in a hot shower, put on fresh clothes, then found a second mask in the furnace closet. Food for Risa came next. Scrounging in the refrigerator, she considered making her daughter's favorite soup, French onion, but ultimately decided on a warming, yet non-descript vegetable instead. If Risa ate French onion now, she would hate it forever, always reminded of her grandmother's death when it crossed her lips. She baked biscuits to go with the soup, slathered them in butter and jam and placed everything on a tray.

Risa's room was terrifyingly neat. She'd picked up everything off of her floor and thrown away the trash, changed her bed linens, arranged stuffed animals, slipped papers and odds and ends into drawers, stacked and sorted books into two piles, those belonging to the public library and her school. Most frightening of all was the clothes basket on the floor next to her dresser. Not only had she swept every piece of dirty clothing into the basket, she'd lined it with a thirty-gallon trash bag.

Felice's throat tightened. That a twelve-year-old would think of this, prepare like this, undid her.

"Are you okay, Mom?" Risa asked from the bed where she sat stiffly upright.

"Sure," she said. She placed the tray across her daughter's lap. "I brought you some soup."

"I don't want to eat."

"I think you should. Scoot over. I'll sit next to you and we'll watch some TV."

Risa gave her control of the remote. She flipped through the channels, finding more than half had gone off the air. With the exception of a few news networks, snowy static replaced any channel or program requiring live or recently recorded content. Eventually she found a cheesy romance flick on a station which appeared to be computer automated rather than manned by living persons, and made no mention of the plague.

"I'm scared for you, Mom," Risa surprised her by saying forty minutes into the movie. "I don't want you to be all alone."

"Honey, you're not going to die. You're not even showing symptoms. Even if you got it, I know you'd survive."

"How do you know? Grandma died so quick."

"Grandma was older. This flu strikes older people the hardest. Older people and the very young. Now, I know you're not eligible for social security, are you?"

Risa giggled.

"And you're not a little girl any more. You're almost thirteen."

"Tomorrow," Risa said with evident pride.

Oh, God. Her birthday's tomorrow. The special birthday.

"That's right. Tomorrow. And I have something special planned."

She had no such thing. With all that had happened, she'd forgotten. It seemed ghoulish to even think of celebrating, but kids had a different reality from adults.

Risa choked softly and suddenly rubbed her neck.

"What is it? Did you swallow something the wrong way?"

"My throat hurts," Risa said.

SHE VOMITED THE SOUP AND BISCUITS within the hour. By midnight she had a fever. Karena hadn't lived long enough to use much of the prescription meds, so Felice, hoping it might help if she was aggressive from the start, gave Risa a double dose. She got on the phone with 911 again, which this time didn't even answer, let alone put her on hold. Children's grape-flavored expectorant initially quieted the cough Risa developed around two-thirty in the morning, but less than thirty minutes later it was back, and Felice heard it working its way down into her bronchial tubes and finally her lungs.

I will not lose her. I won't, Felice promised herself over and over through the night, while she phoned Trina, the health department, ambulance companies, the pharmacy at the megacenter, every doctor in their meager rural phone book, seeking help or even advice. Yes, it was the middle of the night, but given the times, she expected at least one phone to be answered by a live person.

At dawn, the sun rose shrouded behind weather dark as a funeral veil. Fifteen hours and still the sleet continued, entombing them in a foot-and-a-half of solid ice. Piles topping twice that height lay in front of the windows and doors. Almost no light reached the ground. Instinctively, Felice glanced toward the drive, but couldn't see it through the gloom, anticipating, steeling herself for the fight she knew lay ahead. She had no hope.

Karena had struggled to breathe, Risa didn't. Karena's soul, her person had wrestled with the confines of a body that sought to smother her, wanting out, wanting freedom. Risa's did not. Her figure lay limp beneath the covers, hair slick with perspiration, lips blue from lack of oxygen. She choked on every breath, no longer having the energy to cough. The only movement came when she clawed ineffectually at her chest. A bloody, wadded tissue fell from her fingers.

"Happy Birthday, sleepy head," Felice said.

Risa's eyelids, pained slits, worked to open all the way.

"Hi."

Felice carried a zippered plastic bag, printed with mod pink and orange flowers.

Risa saw the pouch.

"What's that?"

"A present for someone who's all grown up."

Make-up was all Risa had talked about this last year, when she would be allowed to wear it. Since the age of ten, she'd requested foundation to cover her birthmark, plus the mascara and lip gloss she swore—with a straight face—that the other girls wore.

Felice unzipped the pouch, removed astringent towelettes, a bottle of moisturizer, and another of foundation. All were hers, but they'd work well enough to make her daughter happy now, when time was so precious.

"Shall I give you a makeover?"

"Yes, please."

Felice hated putting anything on those pale, yet perfect cheeks. Her daughter's cryptic beauty needed no enhancement. Like most girls her age, however, she equated artifice with sophistication and the drive for sophistication was every thirteen-year-old's secret aspiration.

Covertly wiping away blood and spittle from the corners of her daughter's mouth, Felice dotted beige liquid on forehead, chin, nose, and—

"Not the birthmark, mommy."

"Are you sure?"

At that moment a bead of sweat rolled into Felice's right eye from her browline. Something that felt like a lead butterfly contorted, then drowned in her lungs. Dizziness rocked her from side to side. She couldn't suppress a hacking cough that labored to clear her throat of mucus that quivered and unexpectedly blocked her airway.

"I'm sure," Risa said. "He has to know I love it."

"He?"

If Risa answered, Felice didn't hear it. She put a hand to her temple, instinctively trying to squelch the throbbing that began there.

No. Please not yet. I have to help my baby.

She fumbled through the rest of the makeover, worried that the weakness infecting her so suddenly would result in a heavy handed job too close to make-up on a corpse.

When she held the mirror up to her child's face, however, something glorious happened. Her daughter's color came back, her eyes brightened, and she laughed, that unaffected music which was uniquely Risa. For just a moment, Felice glimpsed the joyful adult her daughter was meant to be.

"It's been so long since I heard you laugh like that," Felice said.

"Thanks, Mom. I'm gorgeous."

"Yes, you are," she said and passed out.

He was bent over her daughter when Felice woke. The ends of his long, black hair tickled Risa's throat. His fingers lovingly caressed the side of her chin, still baby soft.

"No," Felice cried. "You can't have her. She's mine. She belongs in this world."

"In my world, now," he said. "She's thirteen. That was our agreement."

He lowered those exquisite lips to Risa's cheek, the one with the mark laid on her since birth. Odd, why had she never noticed it before? Her birthmark took the shape of a partial kiss. The instant lips met cheek, the kiss completed itself, then disappeared into Risa's face.

She opened her eyes.

"Daddy!" she whispered.

"I'm here, little dove."

"I'm afraid. I can't breathe anymore."

"I know," he said. "Time to come home with me."

"No, please," Felice said. "I love her so much. I need her."

For the first time she found the strength of will to look up into his eyes.

At once she knew everything, and everything was lost.

"Wake up, Felice. It's time to stop dreaming your human dreams."

"You took her," Felice accused, unable to fight the weight of eyelids that no longer responded.

"I didn't make you choose the place where sickness would be the worst."

"You're Death," she said.

"And you are The Moment of Joy Before," he told her. "It's time to stop pretending. To see with your real eyes again, so thousands need not suffer each day you forget."

But hadn't she suffered, too?

"I've missed you, my love. I need you. Our daughter needs you."

No. No one needed her. She was all alone now in the cabin in Cherry Lick.

"Wake!" he ordered.

Felice got up. She sat up through her cooling skin, through her face and those dead eyelids, shrugging off hideously rigid muscle and disgusting, congealing flesh.

He laid the fingers of one hand against her face and moved her so she was forced to meet his eyes.

They were kind. They hungered. She knew the man who lived within them.

"I am Eternity. I am Love. I am your Last Dream," he said, "Come to me."

On the other side of the door, the sun broke free of its black veil, just in time to set. Sleet became snow once again. Slanted, late day light transmuted snowflakes from ice white to gold, sunlight given mass that soothed her fevered cheeks.

She took his hand.

Claudia O'Keefe's *work has appeared in* The Magazine of Fantasy and Science Fiction, Salon.com, Writers on the Range, New Mexico Magazine, *and* American Libraries. *In 2004, she competed with 2,500 other writers from 96 countries to win the Shell Economist Prize for her essay, "The Traveling Bra Salesman's Lesson." Her short fiction was chosen for inclusion in* Best New Paranormal Romance *and* Horror: The Year's Best 2007. *Among her five books are the novel* Black Snow Days, *and the family-themed anthologies,* Mother, Forever Sisters, *and* Father, *which include original fiction from Whitney Otto, Winston Groom, Jonathan Kellerman, Marilyn French, and Joyce Carol Oates, among others.*

JANE. A STORY OF MANNERS, MAGIC, AND ROMANCE

Sarah Prineas

Miss Jane Bigg-Wither reached her twenty-first year and, as a single woman must do upon attaining such an advanced age, resigned herself to spinsterhood.

That is to say, she embraced it with all her heart.

Jane was not ugly; she was not without family connections; she was in possession of a comfortable inheritance. Really, she had hardly any reason to remain unmarried.

Yet instead of marrying, Jane lived as quietly as possible under the circumstances in the country with her uncle, who was fascinated with all things to do with the magical element though he had no practical ability himself.

"My dear Jane," said Sir Percival over toast and tea one afternoon, "I've just received the most wonderful news." He held up a letter as proof.

Jane looked up from her book. "What is it, Uncle Percy?"

"Well, it's the Thameside College of Magic and Technology. It seems they want to name a new building after me! Isn't that lovely?"

"Oh, indeed." Jane sighed, closed her book, and prepared to listen.

Sir Percival beamed. "You know I gave them a little money last year. A trifle, really, nothing much."

"I remember it well, sir," Jane replied, smiling briefly at the thought of calling fifteen thousand pounds a 'trifle.'

"And by way of saying thank you, they want to name the new building after me. The Sir Percival Bigg-Wither Laboratories. It sounds rather good, does it not?" He glanced down at the letter. "The Dean of the college wishes me to attend a dedication ceremony in a fortnight. Would you like to come along, Jane?"

"Oh, not again," Jane muttered.

"I beg your pardon, my dear?"

Jane sighed. How could she say no? But visiting the Thameside College of Magic and Technology meant encountering . . .

. . . Warlocks. Ugh. Jane shuddered.

The previous year Sir Percival had invited several newly qualified warlocks to Wither Castle, and every one of the young men had proposed to Jane. They had followed her around the estate; they had challenged each other to duels over who would escort her in to dinner; they had taken every opportunity to accidentally-on-purpose brush up against her or take her hand. Poor Sir Percival had been devastated when Jane had turned down every proposal, for he would have delighted to call a warlock his nephew-in-law. But Jane was adamant: absolutely no warlocks.

And so she remained a spinster.

"You will come, won't you my dear?" her uncle asked.

Jane composed herself. "Yes, of course I will, Uncle Percy."

Sir Percival gave a satisfied nod. "Very good." He cocked his head and gave her a sly wink. "I believe the Viscount Sanditon will be in attendance."

"That's what I'm afraid of," Jane murmured. Of all her persistent suitors, Sanditon was the worst.

"I beg your pardon?"

"I am quite sure he will be, Uncle Percy."

Sir Percival patted her hand. "Then it's all settled. Thameside College a fortnight from today. Lovely!"

As Jane had expected, the dedication ceremony consisted of one tedious speech followed by another, which were in turn followed by a tedious celebratory tea held in the Dean's gardens overlooking the river. Jane kept an eye on her Uncle Percy; as the center of attention, his round face grew pink with happiness and sherry. Jane, of course, was besieged by admirers, warlocks-in-training and several professors of magic. At the earliest opportunity she pleaded indisposition and escaped with a cup of tea to a quiet, shaded pergola.

She was not alone for long.

A lean figure wearing a fashionable high-collared black cape, an embroidered waistcoat, and a quizzing glass hanging from a ribbon around his neck approached: Sanditon. He was rich, handsome, dashing, titled, everything a spinster might desire.

Jane raised the teacup before her face and shrank into the shadows, but it was too late; she had been spotted. "Oh damn," she murmured.

As the viscount spied her, he gave an elegant bow. "My dear Miss Bigg-Wither!"

In response to his unctuous smile, Jane lifted the corners of her mouth and showed her teeth.

"Alas," he said, seating himself with a flourish on the bench beside her and seizing her hand, "that the fairest flower should hide herself away to bloom unseen."

Jane remained silent; she could hardly agree or disagree with such a statement and she refused to waste a simper on this particular suitor. Instead she sipped her tea.

"I have been speaking with your uncle," Sanditon said.

Jane looked up, alarmed. "Upon what subject, sir?"

Sanditon stroked her hand. When he spoke, Jane thought she could see tiny blue sparks—the lingering presence of the magical element— winking from his teeth. "We spoke, Miss Bigg-Wither, about Wither Castle. I overheard Sir Percival mention to the Dean that his estate is somewhat . . . troubled."

Troubled wasn't the half of it, Jane thought. Despite Uncle Percy's inability to practice magic, the Bigg-Wither estate was strangely fraught with elemental storms and the odd occurrences that accompanied them. The castle's west tower had been rebuilt repeatedly after being transformed by elemental bolts into ice and, on one memorable occasion, butter. The knot garden was infested with homunculi. The ha-ha had migrated from one field to another, and sheep continually stumbled into it, the stupid creatures, breaking their legs. The maze was dangerous; nobody knew, any longer, what lurked at its center and the gardeners refused outright to enter it.

"In order to explain all the odd phenomena," Sanditon was saying, "Sir Percy and the Dean of the College have requested that I, as their most capable recent graduate, pay you a visit to investigate." He gave Jane's hand a lingering kiss. "As a warlock, I was delighted to agree; as a man I am even more delighted. I shall join you at Wither Castle in five days' time."

"Oh," said Jane. "How nice." He'd made a mistake. Now that she knew when he was coming, she could make arrangements to go on a shopping trip to London or on a visit to friends. One way or another, she'd not be at Wither Castle when Sanditon arrived.

LATER, AFTER JANE HAD MANAGED to scrape Sanditon off, she entered the Dean's house in search of her uncle. She'd had enough tea and had fended off several more unwanted advances by young warlocks. It was time to return home.

As she padded down one long, carpeted hallway, she heard raised voices coming from a room at the end. Jane continued, more quietly, and peered through the crack in the door into the Dean's study. The Dean himself was seated behind a wide, polished desk. Standing on the patterned carpet, his back to Jane, was another man. The first thing Jane noticed about him was his height, which was exceptional; the second thing was his anger, for it was evident in the set of his shoulders and the clenched fists at his sides.

"Absolutely not," the man was saying.

The Dean leaned back in his chair and laced fat fingers over the waistcoat stretched across his belly. "You haven't any choice, Day. To begin with, someone must go along to keep an eye on Sanditon and his . . . er . . . you know. His condition. And I shouldn't have to remind you that you still owe the tuition from your last semester, and you shan't be granted a diploma until it is paid."

"I realize that," Day replied. He sounded as if he were speaking through gritted teeth. "So now I've got to drop everything to trot out to some nobleman's estate to find out why his damned sheep are behaving strangely?"

The Dean nodded. "Better that, Day, than reading the Political Register and fraternizing with Cobbett and his lot."

"On the contrary," the man replied. "The efforts of the Luddites are far more important than the Bigg-Wither shrubbery. Elemental magic must never be used to run machines that take work away from honest craftsmen. We will stop it any way we can."

"Machine breaking, you mean," the Dean said, shaking his head. "Diploma or not, Day, you're the finest warlock the college has ever produced, and you're wasting your talent on radical activities that will only land you in prison."

The tall man shrugged. His coat, Jane noticed, was rather shabby, and his dark hair needed cutting. This, she felt sure, was no fine gentleman. His next words confirmed her suspicion. "Then I'll go to prison," he said. "But at least—" Suddenly he broke off and straightened, head cocked as if listening to something. Jane was certain she hadn't made a noise, but somehow he'd sensed her presence. Slowly, he turned to face the door.

As his eyes met hers, Jane caught her breath, feeling as if his angry gaze were penetrating the door and the silken folds of her tea gown and her skin to the very core of her self. To a place where no one had ever been before. What did he see there, she wondered, and why did it make him look so fierce? She broke the gaze, looking down to compose herself. After taking a deep, calming breath, she smoothed her dress and opened the door wider.

As she entered the room, the tall man's frown grew deeper. "You've been eavesdropping!"

"You have a very loud voice," Jane replied and, retreating into the forms of politeness, held out her hand. "I am Jane Bigg-Wither. I believe you have been invited with Viscount Sanditon to investigate the odd things that have been happening at my uncle's estate."

The man named Day continued to stare, stepping closer, as if drawn against his will, to take her hand. "You're Jane Bigg-Wither."

"As I said, that is my name."

His eyes narrowed. "I've heard about you."

Jane cursed inwardly and gave him a tight smile. From Sanditon, she had no doubt. What on earth had the Viscount told this man? "How very interesting."

He nodded. Still gripping her hand, he moved closer, peering down at her. His eyes were gray, she noted, and his nose was rather long. "What they say is true," he said. "How do you do it?"

"Do what, sir?"

He opened his mouth to speak, then gave himself a little shake and released her hand. "My name is Aubrey Day."

"I am pleased to make your acquaintance, Mr. Day," Jane said. "You will be arriving at Wither Castle in five days?"

"I don't seem to have any choice."

Jane smiled, and he blinked. "Good." She nodded at the Dean, who bobbed a hasty bow in return, and left the room.

In the hallway, Jane leaned against a wall, knees weak. Mr. Aubrey Day was a warlock like all the others, but she'd never encountered anyone like him, anyone who made her feel so . . . exposed. And he was odd in a way that all the others were not, from his radical politics, to his anger, to his unusual height. Perhaps she would be at Wither Castle after all, in five days' time.

IF MISS JANE BIGG-WITHER TOOK EXTRA CARE with her dress and coiffure on the fifth day hence, one might argue that she did so at the behest of her uncle, who wanted her to appear at her loveliest for the visiting warlocks.

Those two gentlemen arrived in Viscount Sanditon's private carriage followed by another carriage packed full of baggage and the nobleman's valet, hairdresser, and bootblack. The carriages rattled over the cobblestoned courtyard and to a halt before the castle, which loomed in all its moated, turreted majesty before them. Jane and her uncle came out of the keep's great double doors to meet their visitors. The afternoon was cold and blustery and Jane's skirts blew against her legs and tendrils of her hair loosed themselves from their pins. The air felt prickly, the way it did before the advent of elemental storms.

"My dear Viscount!" Sir Percival cried, beaming and clapping a hand to his old-fashioned wig, which threatened to fly away in the wind. "And Mr. Day. Welcome, indeed!"

"See to the baggage, Day," Sanditon ordered. Tossing a fold of his cape over his shoulder, he bowed, then advanced upon Jane and took her hand. "You are a most gracious host, Sir Percival, and your niece! As always, a delight. Miss Bigg-Wither, I greet you." He bent to kiss her hand. Jane let it lie limp in his grasp.

Aubrey Day, who wore a woolen muffler around his neck and the same shabby coat he'd worn before, turned from where he had been unloading a crate from the second carriage and greeted her uncle with a brief bow. To Jane he gave a nod and a look of suspicion. Then he turned back to the baggage.

Sir Percival was intrigued. "Mr. Day! What is that you've got there?" He pattered down the steps and out into the courtyard. "Did you bring . . . Equipment? And, perhaps . . . Instruments?"

Aubrey Day nudged one wooden crate with his foot. "This is a portable Tuppence device."

Leaving Sanditon at the front door to instruct his servants, Jane followed her uncle, noticing that Aubrey Day edged away from her to stand behind another pile of crates.

"Portable! Really! And this one?" Sir Percy asked, pointing to a cloth covered dome.

"Good afternoon, Mr. Day," Jane said.

Ignoring her outstretched hand, Aubrey Day muttered a greeting and turned to her uncle. "This, sir," he said, "is a bellweather."

"Indeed!" Sir Percival stooped toward the dome. "For predicting the onset of elemental magic storms? Is it a bird? Might I have a look?" Before Aubrey Day could answer, Jane's uncle had swept the cover from what proved to be a domed cage. The animal within, a small, brown mouse, lifted its nose at the disturbance, twitched its tail, and settled again into a furry ball. "It stirred!" Sir Percival said, squatting down to peer into the cage.

Aubrey Day crouched beside him, frowning. "Yes, it did. As far as I know, no elemental storms are forecast for this area. It's very odd."

As he stood up, Sir Percival laid a sly finger alongside his nose. "Ah ha, Mr. Day!"

Aubrey Day got to his feet. Without seeming to realize it, he had moved to stand close beside Jane. "Ah ha, Sir Percival?"

Jane answered. "He means, Mr. Day, that elemental storms do not behave as predicted around Wither Castle. We have many, many rather unexpected manifestations of magic, in fact. That is part of the problem."

Aubrey Day frowned down at her. "Part of the problem," he repeated. He gave himself a shake, as he had in the Dean's office, and stepped away from her.

At that moment, Sanditon minced down the steps from the front door of the castle. As he stepped toward them, he sucked a few minuscule sparks of magical element from his fingertips, which he wiped with great fastidiousness on a handkerchief. "Be sure the device is handled carefully, Day." He seized Jane's arm. "And, my dear Miss Bigg-Wither, we must immediately get you in out of this nasty wind."

LATER, AFTER THE VISITORS HAD SEEN TO THEIR BAGGAGE and their rooms, they gathered in the drawing room for conversation, to be followed by tea. Jane tried to ignore Sanditon, who had squeezed in beside her on the sofa and kept pressing his thigh against hers even while nibbling sparks from his fingertips. Her uncle sat opposite her in a comfortable armchair, and Aubrey Day stood with an elbow on the mantel, glaring at the fire.

After an exchange of pleasantries, Jane's uncle introduced his favorite subject. "My dear Viscount, now that you're unpacked, have you had the opportunity to consult your aetherometer?"

Sanditon gave an elegant shrug. "You must ask Day, Sir Percival. I leave all of the more instructive tasks to him, as he has not yet taken his degree. It is good practice for him, you see."

Aubrey Day continued to frown at the fire. "You were right, Sir Percival. The glass is falling. The bellweather is agitated enough that I think a storm will arrive by tonight."

Uncle Percy beamed. "Then we will certainly see some magical transformations."

"Indeed," said Sanditon, reaching beneath the tea table to place a hand on Jane's knee. "The storm will offer a perfect opportunity for me to conduct a few experiments." He caught Jane's eye and gave her a glinting smile. "I like experiments, Miss Bigg-Wither, don't you?"

Jane responded by reaching down to push his hand off her knee.

Sanditon continued, unfazed. "Now that you have an expert on hand, Sir Percival, I will have the odd occurrences explained in a trice, I assure you."

"I do hope so," said Uncle Percy. He went on to describe the major and minor transformations wreaked upon his estate by elemental storms during the past ten years. "We have," he concluded, "had some very odd chicks hatching from the eggs laid on the home farm. The pullets are not fit for eating, of course."

After this comment, a brief silence fell. Aubrey Day stirred at his post by the hearth. "What about you, Miss Bigg-Wither? Have you an interest in elemental magic?"

Jane blinked, surprised at being brought so suddenly into the conversation. "Yes I do, Mr. Day," she replied. "I have long wished to commence a course of study, in fact, in order to educate myself."

Aubrey Day nodded. "You should begin with Sally Tuppence's work."

"I have long wished to read Miss Tuppence's treatises," Jane said. "I think it would be interesting to replicate some of her experiments. Uncle Percy, did she not attend Thameside College?"

"Well, yes, my dear Miss Bigg-Wither," Sanditon interrupted. He gave Jane a benevolent smile and returned his hand to her knee. "But a lady such as you are ought not pursue such studies. Those sorts of things are not appropriate for study by the gentler sex."

At the hearth, Aubrey Day straightened. "How can you say, that, Sanditon? Tuppence was a genius, the greatest scientist we've ever known. Without her work, we'd know almost nothing about the operations of the magical element."

Sanditon gave a dismissive sniff. "Day, we all know that Mistress Tuppence was a very great scientist. But she carried out her research fifty years ago, and then the world was a very different place. Our age is more refined, more polite. We would never think of training up ladies to be scientists. In any case, Day, you are not a suitable advisor to a young lady of Miss Bigg-Wither's class."

Scowling down at the carpet, his hands thrust into his pockets, Day replied, "I don't see why Miss Bigg-Wither shouldn't study magic if she wants to."

Jane opened her mouth to state her enthusiastic agreement, when she was interrupted by her uncle. "Viscount Sanditon is quite right, Jane. Magic is not for ladies. And now, my dear, you may ring for tea."

Jane bit her lip to hold back her comment. Her uncle's gentle commands were to be obeyed. With a sigh, she rose from the sofa and crossed to the bellpull, where she rang for the maid. Aubrey Day returned to his morose contemplation of the flames.

When the tea tray was brought in, Jane reseated herself by the tea table and poured out, offering sugar and lemon and cucumber sandwiches. "Sugar, Mr. Day?" Jane asked with a sigh, holding up his teacup. "Lemon?"

"No." He looked up, hesitating before crossing the room to her. As she held out his tea, their hands met and his jerked back; the cup and saucer fell to the floor between them, making a mess of delicate shards and tea on the patterned carpet.

"Oh, damn," Jane cursed quietly. Aubrey Day looked up, his expression shifting from dismay to amused surprise.

"I beg your pardon, my dear?" her uncle asked from his armchair.

Jane picked up a napkin and bent to dab at the tea, which had stained the hem of her skirt. "I said 'Oh bother,' Uncle Percy. I've broken the cup."

"You could never be so clumsy, Miss Bigg-Wither," Sanditon interjected with his glinting smile. "It was clearly Day's fault."

"No matter, my dear," Sir Percival said. "Ring for the abigail; she will clean it up."

"My lord Viscount, would you be so kind?" Jane asked.

Sanditon agreed, rising from the sofa to cross to the bellpull. As he stood, Aubrey Day knelt down beside Jane and began picking up broken pieces of china. His bent head was very close to hers. The frayed collar of his coat, Jane noted, was turned up at the back, untidy. She restrained the urge to reach out to smooth the collar, instead leaning closer to whisper, "I wish to speak privately with you, sir."

Aubrey Day placed a handful of shards onto the tea tray. "Why?"

"Hmm. You might give me a reading list." She straightened and put down the napkin.

Aubrey Day remained on his knees beside her. "Really."

"Yes," Jane whispered.

"Really?" he repeated, leaning toward her.

"Well, no, sir." What excuse might she give? "As my uncle indicated, something very strange is going on here."

"I am aware of that."

Having rung for the maid and explained the accident, Sanditon was returning to his place on the sofa.

Jane let out an exasperated breath. "Quickly, sir. Might we meet later?"

"All right."

Jane gave a relieved nod. "Good. The library, then, in one hour."

As EVENING FELL, the storm predicted by the bellweather and the aetherometer advanced. Though she was not a witch or warlock, Jane felt a tingling excitement in the air as she entered the library. The room took up two stories in the castle's south turret and consisted of tiers of shelves built into the curving walls, each shelf jammed with books on every subject. The shelves were interrupted, here and there, by tall windows, which had replaced the original arrowslits, and by a set of French doors, which opened up onto a veranda, which in turn looked over the infested knot garden and the maze. Through the windows, Jane saw an elemental storm crouched over the distant hills, ready to pounce. Now and then a blue flash of magical element flickered on the underbelly of the gray-green clouds.

Moments after Jane had arrived, Aubrey Day joined her, closing the door behind him. "I wasn't sure you would be here," he said, crossing the room to stand before her, frowning.

"Frankly, sir," Jane replied, "I thought the same thing of you." He was standing rather close and in the dim light he appeared very tall and dark.

He is a radical and a warlock, Jane reminded herself. She took a step back.

"Oh, no," he said, following. "I came. I didn't want to, but I did."

"You didn't want to, sir?"

"No." With a visible wrench, he turned away from her and, as if seeking protection, went to stand behind a reading table. "I can't figure it out. You are the niece of an idle nobleman. I should hate you on principle."

Jane thought about protesting, but it was true: Uncle Percy was, indeed, idle. So was she, for that matter, though she had long ago tired of idleness.

Day continued. "Even so, I can't stay away from you."

Jane nodded. "You're just like all the rest."

He looked up, and suddenly his face seemed alert and not quite as angry. "Just like all the rest? What do you mean?"

"Warlocks." She shuddered.

"What do you mean, warlocks?"

"Whenever I meet a warlock, he . . ." Jane paused, embarrassed, then told herself to be practical. "He attempts to take liberties with my person."

Aubrey Day raised his eyebrows. "You mean you were not encouraging Sanditon? He is not your lover?"

"Certainly not! He simply will not leave me alone."

"That is very interesting." Day looked around the room. "Go and stand over there, Jane, by the window. And I will stand here, by the door."

Jane went to stand by the window. The room darkened as, outside, the storm clouds advanced over the setting sun. "We ought to light a candle," she said.

"Just a minute. Stay over there."

He really should address her as "Miss Bigg-Wither." Most ladies would not put up with such behavior. "You are not very polite," she noted.

"No," he agreed absently. He frowned down at the carpet for a long, silent minute, then looked up at her. "There's definitely something. I can still feel it, but it's not too bad. I'm coming closer now. Stay where you are." He took a few steps toward her, keeping the table between them, avoiding her eyes. "All right." He swallowed. "Don't be alarmed, Jane. I'm coming right up to you." He did so.

Jane closed her eyes. But she felt his presence, very near. When she opened her eyes, he was standing before her, arms folded as if restraining himself, again staring at the floor. "What is the matter, Mr. Day?"

"It's stronger here." He drew a shaky breath. "I'd better go back to the door." He retreated, leaning against the door, clinging to the knob as if to anchor himself. "There's only one explanation for it." He fell silent, gnawing his lip.

"What explanation, sir?"

He did not answer.

"Tell me at once, or I shall come closer!" she threatened.

He looked up, alarmed. "No! Don't do that." He looked around the room. "Sit down in that chair next to you. I'll sit down here, and we'll be safe."

She sat down next to the window. "Now tell me."

"All right." Without seeming to realize what he was doing, he stood up and began pacing across his side of the room. "We know of three types of magical creatures. The first are the Reservoirs, which draw the element within themselves and store it. Extremely rare. Maybe one in a generation, and none in England since last century. Then Bellweathers, like the mouse I brought." As he lectured, his pacing continued, but with each pass he was drawn closer to her side of the room. "Bellweathers are somewhat common." He halted and stood before her chair looking down at her, his eyes alight. "But you, Jane, are something else altogether."

Jane slowly rose to face him. The room had grown very dark. From the windows came, at frequent intervals, flashes of elemental lightning. Thunder growled, even through the thick stone walls of the turret. Jane saw elemental sparks twinkling from the ends of Aubrey Day's hair, and then she saw nothing but darkness, for he had bent down to seize and kiss her.

Jane expected to feel repelled, for in her experience warlocks were repellent. For some reason, she did not. Instead, she returned the kiss, with interest.

At that moment the elemental storm broke with a crashing roar over the castle and the library door flew open to reveal a lean, shadowy figure: Sanditon.

Jane and Aubrey Day drew apart, but it was too late—they'd been seen.

The Viscount advanced, his mouth asnarl and his black cape aswirl. "I might have known! Sneaking away, Day, to assault this innocent young maiden!"

Beside her, Jane thought she heard Aubrey Day mutter a comment on who was assaulting whom.

Sanditon circled the table and advanced. "Fear not, Miss Bigg-Wither!" He paused and gave what sounded to Jane like a high-pitched cackle. "I will avenge you! This blackguard will not live to rue the day he stole you away from me!" The storm punctuated his challenge with a ferocious strike of elemental magic.

There goes the west turret again, Jane thought.

Aubrey Day took her hand and they backed away from the advancing Viscount. "What is the matter with him?" Jane whispered.

"He's addicted to the element," Day replied. "It makes him . . . Well, you can see for yourself."

As they watched, the magical element saturated Sanditon's body. He stood before them, lighting the room, cobalt sparks sizzling from his skin and the ends of his hair, surrounding him like a scintillant aura. "I challenge, you, Day, to a duel!" he shouted.

Aubrey Day glanced at the window. The storm crashed and rolled outside, the sky flickering with elemental bolts. "All right." He shrugged. "Name your weapon."

Jane gave an exasperated shake of her head. "Oh, this is stupid. You can't fight him, Aubrey."

Ignoring Jane's comment, Sanditon sneered. "Of course you wouldn't know this, Day, as you are not a gentleman, but it is for you to name the weapon."

"Fine," Aubrey Day said. "Magic."

For a moment, Jane thought she saw Sanditon hesitate.

But then he gave one of his shrieking laughs. Without waiting for Jane to get out of the way, he shouted out a spell, which emerged from his mouth as a roiling ball of element. After floating in the air for a second, as if orienting itself, the spell flew through the air toward them, shedding sparks as it came.

Calmly, Aubrey Day stepped out of the way, pulling Jane with him.

The ball of element splattered into the French doors, which dissolved into a whirl of sawdust and sand.

Invited in, the storm blasted through the open area. Thunder shook the turret, and bolts of elemental lightning ricocheted across the room, striking the shelves; each book hit by the element transformed into a bewildered white dove that floundered in the buffeting gusts. Sanditon was forced to his knees, the cape wrapped around his face.

Over the howl of the wind, Aubrey shouted, "Too dangerous in here, Jane! Go outside!"

"But the storm!" she shouted back.

He grasped Jane by the shoulders and bent to speak into her ear. "It won't hurt you, Jane—it can't. The element—" He paused to glance over his shoulder at Sanditon, who was struggling to his feet. "—It loves you." With that, he pushed her toward the veranda and turned to face Sanditon.

Jane stumbled outside. The storm had pounced upon the castle and was shaking it as a cat does a mouse. Playful, she thought, but with rather serious effects for the mouse. Elemental bolts sizzled through the air. Peering through the darkness, Jane saw the knot garden writhing with the gyrations of thousands of tiny, green-skinned, dancing homunculi. Beyond, a dark shadow loomed up out of the maze. Across the lawn, with the sound of cracking branches, an ancient oak toppled beneath the onslaught of wind and magic.

Yet not a single stray bolt threatened her. Even the wind seemed to caress, rather than buffet. Aubrey Day was right. The magical element loved her. She was not a witch or warlock, so she could not use the element to transform the world. But if she called to it, might it come to her?

Jane stepped to the edge of the veranda and opened her arms, hardly expecting any response. At once, the storm whirled into a vortex above her, snapping with elemental lightning and blue-black clouds. Her skin tingled, and sparks effervesced from her fingertips. A great bubble of joy expanded in her chest. She threw back her head and rose up on her tiptoes, felt her skirts swirling about her legs and the pins explode from her hair, which writhed about her head like enchanted snakes.

As the focus of such exaltation, Jane cried out with happiness. She let the joy fill her for another moment, then composed herself. *Very well,* she told the storm, catching her breath. *I've very much enjoyed your visit, but I'm afraid you must leave now.*

From inside the library came a flash of sapphirine light and a crash of thunder as the element being used by the dueling warlocks rushed to obey Jane's request. After swirling about her for another minute, the storm reluctantly drew off. Jane felt the element tingling against the surface of her skin, then fizzing slowly away. As the magical storm departed, the clouds opened up and an ordinary rain pelted down.

From the hole in the turret where the French doors had stood, Jane saw a tiny lizard-like creature emerge. Peering through the curtain of rain, she saw it skitter across the veranda, down the steps, and into the maze. The bushes there twitched, as if a large shape had shifted, and were still.

Next, a few battered-looking white doves fluttered from the opening, and then Aubrey Day appeared. He looked a bit ragged but, to Jane, otherwise unharmed. She breathed a sigh of relief.

He approached her, cautious. "Are you all right, Jane?"

Jane smiled. She felt far beyond all right; she felt transformed. Even her uncle would not be able to determine her fate from now on. She would refuse to be idle; she would study magic, if she liked. Perhaps she'd even attend Thameside College and become a scientist, like Sally Tuppence. "I am quite all right, thank you."

Aubrey Day glanced at the storm, which was trundling off over the distant hills. "Good," he said. Then he turned his full attention on her. "Jane, I will leave you alone now, if that is what you want."

"No, sir," Jane said. "I think—" She paused. The lingering elemental magic seemed to be sparking in her bones, making her want to rise up on her toes and do . . . something . . . to the man before her. She restrained herself. "In the library, earlier, sir. We were interrupted."

Aubrey Day swiped the ragged fringe of hair from his eyes. "Right. Interrupted."

Jane couldn't stop herself from smiling, thinking of the kiss they had begun. "You were about to tell me what kind of magical creature I am," she prompted.

"Ah. Right. You are a Lure, Jane."

"A Lure?"

"The Lure attracts the element to itself, which is why you have so many storms here. You lure them, Jane. Warlocks and witches, too, nearly always have a very low level of the element present in our bodies. Not enough to effect a spell . . ."

"But enough that you respond to the Lure," Jane noted.

"Yes. So it's mechanical."

"What is?"

"My attraction to you."

"What a relief that must be," Jane said, "You can go away and never think about me again."

"Yes," Aubrey Day agreed.

Jane frowned. He'd answered just a bit too quickly. Well then, it was up to her. "I suggest an experiment."

He raised his eyebrows but did not speak.

"You must kiss me, sir, and I will kiss you, and we will determine whether the attraction is, as you say, mechanical or whether it is, as I suspect, not."

Without hesitation, Aubrey Day bent down and kissed her. She, at the same time, kissed him. After a few minutes he stopped. He looked at her, and caught his breath. "Not," he said.

"Not, sir?"

"No, Jane. Not."

Sarah Prineas *lives near the Iowa River in Iowa City, Iowa, where she works at the University of Iowa. She really, really loves Iowa. Her short fiction has appeared in lots of online and print venues; a bibliography can be found on her Web site, www.sarah-prineas.com. Sarah's first novel, Magic Thief, the beginning of a YA fantasy trilogy, will be published in 2009 by HarperCollins and by many other publishers around the world.*

JOURNEY INTO THE KINGDOM

M. Rickert

THE FIRST PAINTING WAS of an egg, the pale ovoid produced with faint strokes of pink, blue, and violet to create the illusion of white. After that there were two apples, a pear, an avocado, and finally, an empty plate on a white tablecloth before a window covered with gauzy curtains, a single fly nestled in a fold at the top right corner. The series was titled "Journey into the Kingdom."

On a small table beneath the avocado there was a black binder, an unevenly cut rectangle of white paper with the words "Artist's Statement" in neat, square, hand-written letters taped to the front. Balancing the porcelain cup and saucer with one hand, Alex picked up the binder and took it with him to a small table against the wall toward the back of the coffee shop, where he opened it, thinking it might be interesting to read something besides the newspaper for once, though he almost abandoned the idea when he saw that the page before him was handwritten in the same neat letters as on the cover. But the title intrigued him.

AN IMITATION LIFE

THOUGH I ALWAYS enjoyed my crayons and watercolors, I was not a particularly artistic child. I produced the usual assortment of stick figures and houses with dripping yellow suns. I was an avid collector of seashells and sea glass and much preferred to be outdoors, throwing stones at seagulls (please, no haranguing from animal rights activists, I have long since outgrown this) or playing with my imaginary friends to sitting quietly in the salt rooms of the keeper's house, making pictures at the big wooden kitchen table while my mother, in her black dress, kneaded bread and sang the old French songs between her duties as lighthouse keeper, watcher over the waves, beacon for the lost, governess of the dead.

The first ghost to come to my mother was my own father who had set out the day previous in the small boat heading to the mainland for supplies such as string and rice, and also bags of soil, which, in years past, we emptied into crevices between the rocks and planted with seeds, a makeshift garden and a "brave attempt," as my father called it, referring to the barren stone we lived on.

We did not expect him for several days so my mother was surprised when he returned in a storm, dripping wet icicles from his mustache and behaving strangely, repeating over and over again, "It is lost, my dear Maggie, the garden is at the bottom of the sea."

My mother fixed him hot tea but he refused it, she begged him to take off the wet clothes and retire with her, to their feather bed piled with quilts, but he said, "Tend the light, don't waste your time with me." So my mother, a worried expression on her face, left our little keeper's house and walked against the gale to the lighthouse, not realizing that she left me with a ghost, melting before the fire into a great puddle, which was all that was left of him upon her return. She searched frantically while I kept pointing at the puddle and insisting it was he. Eventually she tied on her cape and went out into the storm, calling his name. I thought that, surely, I would become orphaned that night.

But my mother lived, though she took to her bed and left me to tend the lamp and receive the news of the discovery of my father's wrecked boat, found on the rocky shoals, still clutching in his frozen hand a bag of soil, which was given to me, and which I brought to my mother though she would not take the offering.

For one so young, my chores were immense. I tended the lamp, and kept our own hearth fire going too. I made broth and tea for my mother, which she only gradually took, and I planted that small bag of soil by the door to our little house, savoring the rich scent, wondering if those who lived with it all the time appreciated its perfume or not.

I did not really expect anything to grow, though I hoped that the seagulls might drop some seeds or the ocean deposit some small thing. I was surprised when, only weeks later, I discovered the tiniest shoots of green, which I told my mother about. She was not impressed. By that point, she would spend part of the day sitting up in bed, mending my father's socks and moaning, "Agatha, whatever are we going to do?" I did not wish to worry her, so I told her lies about women from the mainland coming to help, men taking turns with the light. "But they are so quiet. I never hear anyone."

"No one wants to disturb you," I said. "They whisper and walk on tiptoe."

It was only when I opened the keeper's door so many uncounted weeks later, and saw, spread before me, embedded throughout the rock (even in crevices where I had planted no soil) tiny pink, purple, and white flowers, their stems shuddering in the salty wind, that I insisted my mother get out of bed.

She was resistant at first. But I begged and cajoled, promised her it would be worth her effort. "The fairies have planted flowers for us," I said, this being the only explanation or description I could think of for the infinitesimal blossoms everywhere.

Reluctantly, she followed me through the small living room and kitchen, observing that "the ladies have done a fairly good job of keeping the place neat." She hesitated before the open door. The bright sun and salty scent of the sea, as well as the loud sound of waves washing all around us, seemed to astound her, but then she squinted, glanced at me, and stepped through the door to observe the miracle of the fairies' flowers.

Never had the rock seen such color, never had it known such bloom! My mother walked out, barefoot, and said, "Forget-me-nots, these are forget-me-nots. But where . . . ?"

I told her that I didn't understand it myself, how I had planted the small bag of soil found clutched in my father's hand but had not really expected it to come to much, and certainly not to all of this, waving my arm over the expanse, the flowers having grown in soil-less crevices and cracks, covering our entire little island of stone.

My mother turned to me and said, "These are not from the fairies, they are from him." Then she started crying, a reaction I had not expected and tried to talk her out of, but she said, "No, Agatha, leave me alone."

She stood out there for quite a while, weeping as she walked amongst the flowers. Later, after she came inside and said, "Where are all the helpers today?" I shrugged and avoided more questions by going outside myself, where I discovered scarlet spots amongst the bloom. My mother had been bedridden for so long, her feet had gone soft again. For days she left tiny teardrop shapes of blood in her step, which I surreptitiously wiped up, not wanting to draw any attention to the fact, for fear it would dismay her. She picked several of the forget-me-not blossoms and pressed them between the heavy pages of her book of myths and folklore. Not long after that, a terrible storm blew in, rocking our little house, challenging our resolve, and taking with it all the flowers. Once again our rock was barren. I worried what effect this would have on my mother but she merely sighed, shrugged, and said, "They were beautiful, weren't they, Agatha?"

So passed my childhood: a great deal of solitude, the occasional life-threatening adventure, the drudgery of work, and all around me the great wide sea with its myriad secrets and reasons, the lost we saved, those we didn't. And the ghosts, brought to us by my father, though we never understood clearly his purpose, as they only stood before the fire, dripping and melting like something made of wax, bemoaning what was lost (a fine boat, a lady love, a dream of the sea, a pocketful of jewels, a wife and children, a carving on bone, a song, its lyrics forgotten). We tried to provide what comfort we could, listening, nodding, there was little else we could do, they refused tea or blankets, they seemed only to want to stand by the fire, mourning their death, as my father stood sentry beside them, melting into salty puddles that we mopped up with clean rags, wrung out into the ocean, saying what we fashioned as prayer, or reciting lines of Irish poetry.

Though I know now that this is not a usual childhood, it was usual for me, and it did not veer from this course until my mother's hair had gone quite gray and I was a young woman, when my father brought us a different sort of ghost entirely, a handsome young man, his eyes the same blue-green as summer. His hair was of indeterminate color, wet curls that hung to his shoulders. Dressed simply, like any dead sailor, he carried about him an air of being educated more by art than by water, a suspicion soon confirmed for me when he refused an offering of tea by saying, "No, I will not, cannot drink your liquid offered without first asking for a kiss, ah a kiss is all the liquid I desire, come succor me with your lips."

Naturally, I blushed and, just as naturally, when my mother went to check on the lamp, and my father had melted into a mustached puddle, I kissed him. Though I should have been warned by the icy chill, as certainly I should have been warned by the fact of my own father, a mere puddle at the hearth, it was my first kiss and it did not feel deadly to me at all, not dangerous, not spectral, most certainly not spectral, though I did experience a certain pleasant floating sensation in its wake.

My mother was surprised, upon her return, to find the lad still standing, as vigorous as any living man, beside my father's puddle. We were both surprised that he remained throughout the night, regaling us with stories of the wild sea populated by whales, mermaids, and sharks; mesmerizing us with descriptions of the "bottom of the world" as he called it, embedded with strange purple rocks, pink shells spewing pearls, and the seaweed tendrils of sea witches' hair. We were both surprised that, when the black of night turned to the gray hue of morning, he bowed to each of us (turned fully toward me, so that I could receive his wink), promised he would return, and then left, walking out the door like any regular fellow. So convincing was he that my mother and I opened the door to see where he had gone, scanning the rock and the inky sea before we accepted that, as odd as it seemed, as vigorous his demeanor, he was a ghost most certainly.

"Or something of that nature," said my mother. "Strange that he didn't melt like the others." She squinted at me and I turned away from her before she could see my blush. "We shouldn't have let him keep us up all night," she said. "We aren't dead. We need our sleep."

Sleep? Sleep? I could not sleep, feeling as I did his cool lips on mine, the power of his kiss, as though he breathed out of me some dark aspect that had weighed inside me. I told my mother that she could sleep. I would take care of everything. She protested, but using the past as reassurance (she had long since discovered that I had run the place while she convalesced after my father's death), finally agreed.

I was happy to have her tucked safely in bed. I was happy to know that her curious eyes were closed. I did all the tasks necessary to keep the place in good order. Not even then, in all my girlish giddiness, did I forget the lamp. I am embarrassed to admit, however, it was well past four o'clock before I remembered my father's puddle, which by that time had been much dissipated. I wiped up the small amount of water and wrung him out over the sea, saying only as prayer, "Father, forgive me. Oh, bring him back to me." (Meaning, alas for me, a foolish girl, the boy who kissed me and not my own dear father.)

And that night, he did come back, knocking on the door like any living man, carrying in his wet hands a bouquet of pink coral which he presented to me, and a small white stone, shaped like a star, which he gave to my mother.

"Is there no one else with you?" she asked.

"I'm sorry, there is not," he said.

My mother began to busy herself in the kitchen, leaving the two of us alone. I could hear her in there, moving things about, opening cupboards, sweeping the already swept floor. It was my own carelessness that had caused my father's absence, I was sure of that; had I sponged him up sooner, had I prayed for him more sincerely, and not just for the satisfaction of my own desire, he would be here this night. I felt terrible about this, but then I looked into his eyes, those beautiful sea-colored eyes, and I could not help it, my body thrilled at his look. Is this love? I thought. Will he kiss me twice? When it seemed as if, without even wasting time with words, he was about to do so, leaning toward me with parted lips from which exhaled the scent of salt water, my mother stepped into the room, clearing her throat, holding the broom before her, as if thinking she might use it as a weapon.

"We don't really know anything about you," she said.

To BEGIN WITH, my name is Ezekiel. My mother was fond of saints and the Bible and such. She died shortly after giving birth to me, her first and only child. I was raised by my father, on the island of Murano. Perhaps you have heard of it? Murano glass? We are famous for it throughout the world. My father, himself, was a talented glassmaker. Anything imagined, he could shape into glass. Glass birds, tiny glass bees, glass seashells, even glass tears (an art he perfected while I was an infant), and what my father knew, he taught to me.

Naturally, I eventually surpassed him in skill. Forgive me, but there is no humble way to say it. At any rate, my father had taught me and encouraged my talent all my life. I did not see when his enthusiasm began to sour. I was excited and pleased at what I could produce. I thought he would feel the same for me as I had felt for him, when, as a child, I sat on the footstool in his studio and applauded each glass wing, each hard teardrop.

Alas, it was not to be. My father grew jealous of me. My own father! At night he snuck into our studio and broke my birds, my little glass cakes. In the morning he pretended dismay and instructed me further on keeping air bubbles out of my work. He did not guess that I knew the dismal truth.

I determined to leave him, to sail away to some other place to make my home. My father begged me to stay, "Whatever will you do? How will you make your way in this world?"

I told him my true intention, not being clever enough to lie. "This is not the only place in the world with fire and sand," I said. "I intend to make glass."

He promised me it would be a death sentence. At the time I took this to be only his confused, fatherly concern. I did not perceive it as a threat.

It is true that the secret to glassmaking was meant to remain on Murano. It is true that the entire populace believed this trade, and only this trade, kept them fed and clothed. Finally, it is true that they passed the law (many years before my father confronted me with it) that anyone who dared attempt to take the secret of glassmaking off the island would suffer the penalty of death. All of this is true.

But what's also true is that I was a prisoner in my own home, tortured by my own father, who pretended to be a humble, kind glassmaker, but who, night after night, broke my creations and then, each morning, denied my accusations, his sweet old face mustached and whiskered, all the expression of dismay and sorrow.

This is madness, I reasoned. How else could I survive? One of us had to leave or die. I chose the gentler course.

We had, in our possession, only a small boat, used for trips that never veered far from shore. Gathering mussels, visiting neighbors, occasionally my father liked to sit in it and smoke a pipe while watching the sun set. He'd light a lantern and come home, smelling of the sea, boil us a pot of soup, a melancholic, completely innocent air about him, only later to sneak about his breaking work.

This small boat is what I took for my voyage across the sea. I also took some fishing supplies, a rope, dried cod he'd stored for winter, a blanket, and several jugs of red wine, given to us by the baker, whose daughter, I do believe, fancied me. For you, who have lived so long on this anchored rock, my folly must be apparent. Was it folly? It was. But what else was I to do? Day after day make my perfect art only to have my father, night after night, destroy it? He would destroy me!

I left in the dark, when the ocean is like ink and the sky is black glass with thousands of air bubbles. Air bubbles, indeed. I breathed my freedom in the salty sea air. I chose stars to follow. Foolishly, I had no clear sense of my passage and had only planned my escape.

Of course, knowing what I do now about the ocean, it is a wonder I survived the first night, much less seven. It was on the eighth morning that I saw the distant sail, and, hopelessly drunk and sunburned, as well as lost, began the desperate task of rowing toward it, another folly as I'm sure you'd agree, understanding how distant the horizon is. Luckily for me, or so I thought, the ship headed in my direction and after a few more days it was close enough that I began to believe in my life again.

Alas, this ship was owned by a rich friend of my father's, a woman who had commissioned him to create a glass castle with a glass garden and glass fountain, tiny glass swans, a glass king and queen, a baby glass princess, and glass trees with golden glass apples, all for the amusement of her granddaughter (who, it must be said, had fingers like sausages and broke half of the figurines before her next birthday). This silly woman was only too happy to let my father use her ship, she was only too pleased to pay the ship's crew, all with the air of helping my father, when, in truth, it simply amused her to be involved in such drama. She said she did it for Murano, but in truth, she did it for the story.

It wasn't until I had been rescued, and hoisted on board, that my father revealed himself to me. He spread his arms wide, all great show for the crew, hugged me and even wept, but convincing as was his act, I knew he intended to destroy me.

These are terrible choices no son should have to make, but that night, as my father slept and the ship rocked its weary way back to Murano where I would likely be hung or possibly sentenced to live with my own enemy, my father, I slit the old man's throat. Though he opened his eyes, I do not believe he saw me, but was already entering the distant kingdom.

You ladies look quite aghast. I cannot blame you. Perhaps I should have chosen my own death instead, but I was a young man, and I wanted to live. Even after everything I had gone through, I wanted life.

Alas, it was not to be. I knew there would be trouble and accusation if my father were found with his throat slit, but none at all if he just disappeared in the night, as so often happens on large ships. Many a traveler has simply fallen overboard, never to be heard from again, and my father had already displayed a lack of seafaring savvy to rival my own.

I wrapped him up in the now-bloody blanket but although he was a small man, the effect was still that of a body, so I realized I would have to bend and fold him into a rucksack. You wince, but do not worry, he was certainly dead by this time.

I will not bore you with the details of my passage, hiding and sneaking with my dismal load. Suffice it to say that it took a while for me to at last be standing shipside, and I thought then that all danger had passed.

Remember, I was already quite weakened by my days adrift, and the matter of taking care of this business with my father had only fatigued me further. Certain that I was finally at the end of my task, I grew careless. He was much heavier than he had ever appeared to be. It took all my strength to hoist the rucksack, and (to get the sad, pitiable truth over with as quickly as possible) when I heaved that rucksack, the cord became entangled on my wrist, and yes, dear ladies, I went over with it, to the bottom of the world. There I remained until your own dear father, your husband, found me and brought me to this place, where, for the first time in my life, I feel safe, and, though I am dead, blessed.

LATER, AFTER my mother had tended the lamp while Ezekiel and I shared the kisses that left me breathless, she asked him to leave, saying that I needed my sleep. I protested, of course, but she insisted. I walked my ghost to the door, just as I think any girl would do in a similar situation, and there, for the first time, he kissed me in full view of my mother, not so passionate as those kisses that had preceded it, but effective nonetheless.

But after he was gone, even as I still blushed, my mother spoke in a grim voice, "Don't encourage him, Agatha."

"Why?" I asked, my body trembling with the impact of his affection and my mother's scorn, as though the two emotions met in me and quaked there. "What don't you like about him?"

"He's dead," she said, "there's that for a start."

"What about Daddy? He's dead too, and you've been loving him all this time."

My mother shook her head. "Agatha, it isn't the same thing. Think about what this boy told you tonight. He murdered his own father."

"I can't believe you'd use that against him. You heard what he said. He was just defending himself."

"But Agatha, it isn't what's said that is always the most telling. Don't you know that? Have I really raised you to be so gullible?"

"I am not gullible. I'm in love."

"I forbid it."

Certainly no three words, spoken by a parent, can do more to solidify love than these. It was no use arguing. What would be the point? She, this woman who had loved no one but a puddle for so long, could never understand what was going through my heart. Without more argument, I went to bed, though I slept fitfully, feeling torn from my life in every way, while my mother stayed up reading, I later surmised, from her book of myths. In the morning I found her sitting at the kitchen table, the great volume before her. She looked up at me with dark circled eyes, then, without salutation, began reading, her voice, ominous.

"There are many kinds of ghosts. There are the ghosts that move things, slam doors and drawers, throw silverware about the house. There are the ghosts (usually of small children) that play in dark corners with spools of thread and frighten family pets. There are the weeping and wailing ghosts. There are the ghosts who know that they are dead, and those who do not. There are tree ghosts, those who spend their afterlife in a particular tree (a clue for such a resident might be bite marks on fallen fruit). There are ghosts trapped forever at the hour of their death (I saw one like this once, in an old movie theater bathroom, hanging from the ceiling). There are melting ghosts (we know about these, don't we?), usually victims of drowning. And there are breath-stealing ghosts. These, sometimes mistaken for the grosser vampire, sustain a sort of half-life by stealing breath from the living. They can be any age, but are usually teenagers and young adults, often at that selfish stage when they died. These ghosts greedily go about sucking the breath out of the living. This can be done by swallowing the lingered breath from unwashed cups, or, most effectively of all, through a kiss. Though these ghosts can often be quite seductively charming, they are some of the most dangerous. Each life has only a certain amount of breath within it and these ghosts are said to steal an infinite amount with each swallow. The effect is such that the ghost, while it never lives again, begins to do a fairly good imitation of life, while its victims (those whose breath it steals) edge ever closer to their own death."

My mother looked up at me triumphantly and I stormed out of the house, only to be confronted with the sea all around me, as desolate as my heart.

That night, when he came, knocking on the door, she did not answer it and forbade me to do so.

"It doesn't matter," I taunted, "he's a ghost. He doesn't need doors."

"No, you're wrong," she said, "he's taken so much of your breath that he's not entirely spectral. He can't move through walls any longer. He needs you, but he doesn't care about you at all, don't you get that, Agatha?"

"Agatha? Are you home? Agatha? Why don't you come? Agatha?"

I couldn't bear it. I began to weep.

"I know this is hard," my mother said, "but it must be done. Listen, his voice is already growing faint. We just have to get through this night."

"What about the lamp?" I said.

"What?"

But she knew what I meant. Her expression betrayed her. "Don't you need to check on the lamp?"

"Agatha? Have I done something wrong?"

My mother stared at the door, and then turned to me, the dark circles under her eyes giving her the look of a beaten woman. "The lamp is fine."

I spun on my heels and went into my small room, slammed the door behind me. My mother, a smart woman, was not used to thinking like a warden. She had forgotten about my window. By the time I hoisted myself down from it, Ezekiel was standing on the rocky shore, surveying the dark ocean before him. He had already lost some of his life-like luster, particularly below his knees where I could almost see through him. "Ezekiel," I said. He turned and I gasped at the change in his visage, the cavernous look of his eyes, the skeletal stretch at his jaw. Seeing my shocked expression, he nodded and spread his arms open, as if to say, yes, this is what has become of me. I ran into those open arms and embraced him, though he creaked like something made of old wood. He bent down, pressing his cold lips against mine until they were no longer cold but burning like a fire.

We spent that night together and I did not mind the shattering wind with its salt bite on my skin, and I did not care when the lamp went out and the sea roiled beneath a black sky, and I did not worry about the dead weeping on the rocky shore, or the lightness I felt as though I were floating beside my lover, and when morning came, revealing the dead all around us, I followed him into the water, I followed him to the bottom of the sea, where he turned to me and said, "What have you done? Are you stupid? Don't you realize? You're no good to me dead!"

So, sadly, like many a daughter, I learned that my mother had been right after all, and when I returned to her, dripping with saltwater and seaweed, tiny fish corpses dropping from my hair, she embraced me. Seeing my state, weeping, she kissed me on the lips, our mouths open. I drank from her, sweet breath, until I was filled and she collapsed to the floor, my mother in her black dress, like a crushed funeral flower.

I had no time for mourning. The lamp had been out for hours. Ships had crashed and men had died. Outside the sun sparkled on the sea. People would be coming soon to find out what had happened.

I took our small boat and rowed away from there. Many hours later, I docked in a seaside town and hitchhiked to another, until eventually I was as far from my home as I could be and still be near my ocean.

I had a difficult time of it for a while. People are generally suspicious of someone with no past and little future. I lived on the street and had to beg for jobs cleaning toilets and scrubbing floors, only through time and reputation working up to my current situation, finally getting my own little apartment, small and dark, so different from when I was the lighthouse keeper's daughter and the ocean was my yard.

One day, after having passed it for months without a thought, I went into the art supply store, and bought a canvas, paint, and two paintbrushes. I paid for it with my tip money, counting it out for the clerk whose expression suggested I was placing turds in her palm instead of pennies. I went home and hammered a nail into the wall, hung the canvas on it, and began to paint. Like many a creative person I seem to have found some solace for the unfortunate happenings of my young life (and death) in art.

I live simply and virginally, never taking breath through a kiss. This is the vow I made, and I have kept it. Yes, some days I am weakened, and tempted to restore my vigor with such an easy solution, but instead I hold the empty cups to my face, I breathe in, I breathe everything, the breath of old men, breath of young, sweet breath, sour breath, breath of lipstick, breath of smoke. It is not, really, a way to live, but this is not, really, a life.

FOR SEVERAL SECONDS after Alex finished reading the remarkable account, his gaze remained transfixed on the page. Finally, he looked up, blinked in the dim coffee shop light, and closed the black binder.

Several baristas stood behind the counter busily jostling around each other with porcelain cups, teapots, bags of beans. One of them, a short girl with red and green hair that spiked around her like some otherworld halo, stood by the sink, stacking dirty plates and cups. When she saw him watching, she smiled. It wasn't a true smile, not that it was mocking, but rather, the girl with the Christmas hair smiled like someone who had either forgotten happiness entirely, or never known it at all. In response, Alex nodded at her, and to his surprise, she came over, carrying a dirty rag and a spray bottle.

"Did you read all of it?" she said as she squirted the table beside him and began to wipe it with the dingy towel.

Alex winced at the unpleasant odor of the cleaning fluid, nodded, and then, seeing that the girl wasn't really paying any attention, said, "Yes." He glanced at the wall where the paintings were hung.

"So what'd you think?"

The girl stood there, grinning that sad grin, right next to him now with her noxious bottle and dirty rag, one hip jutted out in a way he found oddly sexual. He opened his mouth to speak, gestured toward the paintings, and then at the book before him. "I, I have to meet her," he said, tapping the book, "this is remarkable."

"But what do you think about the paintings?"

Once more he glanced at the wall where they hung. He shook his head, "No," he said, "it's this," tapping the book again.

She smiled, a true smile, cocked her head, and put out her hand, "Agatha," she said.

Alex felt like his head was spinning. He shook the girl's hand. It was unexpectedly tiny, like that of a child's, and he gripped it too tightly at first. Glancing at the counter, she pulled out a chair and sat down in front of him.

"I can only talk for a little while. Marnie is the manager today and she's on the rag or something all the time, but she's downstairs right now, checking in an order."

"You," he brushed the binder with the tip of his fingers, as if caressing something holy, "you wrote this?"

She nodded, bowed her head slightly, shrugged, and suddenly earnest, leaned across the table, elbowing his empty cup as she did. "Nobody bothers to read it. I've seen a few people pick it up but you're the first one to read the whole thing."

Alex leaned back, frowning.

She rolled her eyes, which, he noticed, were a lovely shade of lavender, lined darkly in black.

"See, I was trying to do something different. This is the whole point," she jabbed at the book, and he felt immediately protective of it, "I was trying to put a story in a place where people don't usually expect one. Don't you think we've gotten awful complacent in our society about story? Like it all the time has to go a certain way and even be only in certain places. That's what this is all about. The paintings are a foil. But you get that, don't you? Do you know," she leaned so close to him, he could smell her breath, which he thought was strangely sweet, "someone actually offered to buy the fly painting?" Her mouth dropped open, she shook her head and rolled those lovely lavender eyes. "I mean, what the fuck? Doesn't he know it sucks?"

Alex wasn't sure what to do. She seemed to be leaning near to his cup. Leaning over it, Alex realized. He opened his mouth, not having any idea what to say.

Just then another barista, the one who wore scarves all the time and had an imperious air about her, as though she didn't really belong there but was doing research or something, walked past. Agatha glanced at her. "I gotta go." She stood up. "You finished with this?" she asked, touching his cup.

Though he hadn't yet had his free refill, Alex nodded.

"It was nice talking to you," she said. "Just goes to show, doesn't it?"

Alex had no idea what she was talking about. He nodded half-heartedly, hoping comprehension would follow, but when it didn't, he raised his eyebrows at her instead.

She laughed. "I mean you don't look anything like the kind of person who would understand my stuff."

"Well, you don't look much like Agatha," he said.

"But I am Agatha," she murmured as she turned away from him, picking up an empty cup and saucer from a nearby table.

Alex watched her walk to the tiny sink at the end of the counter. She set the cups and saucers down. She rinsed the saucers and placed them in the gray bucket they used for carrying dirty dishes to the back. She reached for a cup, and then looked at him.

He quickly looked down at the black binder, picked it up, pushed his chair in, and headed toward the front of the shop. He stopped to look at the paintings. They were fine, boring, but fine little paintings that had no connection to what he'd read. He didn't linger over them for long. He was almost to the door when she was beside him, saying, "I'll take that." He couldn't even fake innocence. He shrugged and handed her the binder.

"I'm flattered, really," she said. But she didn't try to continue the conversation. She set the book down on the table beneath the painting of the avocado. He watched her pick up an empty cup and bring it toward her face, breathing in the lingered breath that remained. She looked up suddenly, caught him watching, frowned, and turned away.

Alex understood. She wasn't what he'd been expecting either. But when love arrives it doesn't always appear as expected. He couldn't just ignore it. He couldn't pretend it hadn't happened. He walked out of the coffee shop into the afternoon sunshine.

OF COURSE, THERE WERE PROBLEMS, her not being alive for one. But Alex was not a man of prejudice.

He was patient besides. He stood in the art supply store for hours, pretending particular interest in the anatomical hinged figurines of sexless men and women in the front window, before she walked past, her hair glowing like a forest fire.

"Agatha," he called.

She turned, frowned, and continued walking. He had to take little running steps to catch up. "Hi," he said. He saw that she was biting her lower lip. "You just getting off work?"

She stopped walking right in front of the bank, which was closed by then, and squinted up at him.

"Alex," he said. "I was talking to you today at the coffee shop."

"I know who you are."

Her tone was angry. He couldn't understand it. Had he insulted her somehow?

"I don't have Alzheimer's. I remember you."

He nodded. This was harder than he had expected.

"What do you want?" she said.

Her tone was really downright hostile. He shrugged. "I just thought we could, you know, talk."

She shook her head. "Listen, I'm happy that you liked my story."

"I did," he said, nodding, "it was great."

"But what would we talk about? You and me?"

Alex shifted beneath her lavender gaze. He licked his lips. She wasn't even looking at him, but glancing around him and across the street. "I don't care if it does mean I'll die sooner," he said. "I want to give you a kiss."

Her mouth dropped open.

"Is something wrong?"

She turned and ran. She wore one red sneaker and one green. They matched her hair.

As Alex walked back to his car, parked in front of the coffee shop, he tried to talk himself into not feeling so bad about the way things went. He hadn't always been like this. He used to be able to talk to people. Even women. Okay, he had never been suave, he knew that, but he'd been a regular guy. Certainly no one had ever run away from him before. But after Tessie died, people changed. Of course, this made sense, initially. He was in mourning, even if he didn't cry (something the doctor told him not to worry about because one day, probably when he least expected it, the tears would fall). He was obviously in pain. People were very nice. They talked to him in hushed tones. Touched him, gently. Even men tapped him with their fingertips. All this gentle touching had been augmented by vigorous hugs. People either touched him as if he would break, or hugged him as if he had already broken and only the vigor of the embrace kept him intact.

For the longest time there had been all this activity around him. People called, sent chatty e-mails, even handwritten letters, cards with flowers on them and prayers. People brought over casseroles, and bread, Jell-O with fruit in it. (Nobody brought chocolate chip cookies, which he might have actually eaten.)

To Alex's surprise, once Tessie had died, it felt as though a great weight had been lifted from him, but instead of appreciating the feeling, the freedom of being lightened of the burden of his wife's dying body, he felt in danger of floating away or disappearing. Could it be possible, he wondered, that Tessie's body, even when she was mostly bones and barely breath, was all that kept him real? Was it possible that he would have to live like this, held to life by some strange force but never a part of it again? These questions led Alex to the brief period where he'd experimented with becoming a Hare Krishna, shaved his head, dressed in orange robes, and took up dancing in the park. Alex wasn't sure but he thought that was when people started treating him as if he were strange, and even after he grew his hair out and started wearing regular clothes again, people continued to treat him strangely.

And, Alex had to admit, as he inserted his key into the lock of his car, he'd forgotten how to behave. How to be normal, he guessed.

You just don't go read something somebody wrote and decide you love her, he scolded himself as he eased into traffic. You don't just go falling in love with breath-stealing ghosts. People don't do that.

Alex did not go to the coffee shop the next day, or the day after that, but it was the only coffee shop in town, and had the best coffee in the state. They roasted the beans right there. Freshness like that can't be faked.

It was awkward for him to see her behind the counter, over by the dirty cups, of course. But when she looked up at him, he attempted a kind smile, then looked away.

He wasn't there to bother her. He ordered French Roast in a cup to go, even though he hated to drink out of paper, paid for it, dropped the change into the tip jar, and left without any further interaction with her.

He walked to the park, where he sat on a bench and watched a woman with two small boys feed white bread to the ducks. This was illegal because the ducks would eat all the bread offered to them, they had no sense of appetite, or being full, and they would eat until their stomachs exploded. Or something like that. Alex couldn't exactly remember. He was pretty sure it killed them. But Alex couldn't decide what to do. Should he go tell that lady and those two little boys that they were killing the ducks? How would that make them feel, especially as they were now triumphantly shaking out the empty bag, the ducks crowded around them, one of the boys squealing with delight? Maybe he should just tell her, quietly. But she looked so happy. Maybe she'd been having a hard time of it. He saw those mothers on Oprah, saying what a hard job it was, and maybe she'd had that kind of morning, even screaming at the kids, and then she got this idea, to take them to the park and feed the ducks and now she felt good about what she'd done and maybe she was thinking that she wasn't such a bad mom after all, and if Alex told her she was killing the ducks, would it stop the ducks from dying or just stop her from feeling happiness? Alex sighed. He couldn't decide what to do. The ducks were happy, the lady was happy, and one of the boys was happy. The other one looked sort of terrified. She picked him up and they walked away together, she, carrying the boy who waved the empty bag like a balloon, the other one skipping after them, a few ducks hobbling behind.

For three days Alex ordered his coffee to go and drank it in the park. On the fourth day, Agatha wasn't anywhere that he could see and he surmised that it was her day off so he sat at his favorite table in the back. But on the fifth day, even though he didn't see her again, and it made sense that she'd have two days off in a row, he ordered his coffee to go and took it to the park. He'd grown to like sitting on the bench watching strolling park visitors, the running children, the dangerously fat ducks.

He had no idea she would be there and he felt himself blush when he saw her coming down the path that passed right in front of him. He stared deeply into his cup and fought the compulsion to run. He couldn't help it, though. Just as the toes of her red and green sneakers came into view he looked up. I'm not going to hurt you, he thought, and then, he smiled, that false smile he'd been practicing on her and, incredibly, she smiled back! Also, falsely, he assumed, but he couldn't blame her for that.

She looked down the path and he followed her gaze, seeing that, though the path around the duck pond was lined with benches every fifty feet or so, all of them were taken. She sighed. "Mind if I sit here?"

He scooted over and she sat down, slowly. He glanced at her profile. She looked worn out, he decided. Her lavender eye flickered toward him, and he looked into his cup again. It made sense that she would be tired, he thought, if she'd been off work for two days, she'd also been going that long without stealing breath from cups. "Want some?" he said, offering his.

She looked startled, pleased, and then, falsely unconcerned. She peered over the edge of his cup, shrugged, and said, "Okay, yeah, sure."

He handed it to her and politely watched the ducks so she could have some semblance of privacy with it. After a while she said thanks and handed it back to him. He nodded and stole a look at her profile again. It pleased him that her color already looked better. His breath had done that!

"Sorry about the other day," she said, "I was just . . ."

They waited together but she didn't finish the sentence.

"It's okay," he said, "I know I'm weird."

"No, you're, well—" she smiled, glanced at him, shrugged. "It isn't that. I like weird people. I'm weird. But, I mean, I'm not dead, okay? You kind of freaked me out with that."

He nodded. "Would you like to go out with me sometime?" Inwardly, he groaned. He couldn't believe he just said that.

"Listen, Alex?"

He nodded. Stop nodding, he told himself. Stop acting like a bobblehead.

"Why don't you tell me a little about yourself?"

So he told her. How he'd been coming to the park lately, watching people overfeed the ducks, wondering if he should tell them what they were doing but they all looked so happy doing it, and the ducks looked happy too, and he wasn't sure anyway, what if he was wrong, what if he told everyone to stop feeding bread to the ducks and it turned out it did them no harm and how would he know? Would they explode like balloons, or would it be more like how it had been when his wife died, a slow painful death, eating her away inside, and how he used to come here, when he was a monk, well, not really a monk, he'd never gotten ordained or anything, but he'd been trying the idea on for a while and how he used to sing and spin in circles and how it felt a lot like what he'd remembered of happiness but he could never be sure because a remembered emotion is like a remembered taste, it's never really there.

And then, one day, a real monk came and watched him spinning in circles and singing nonsense, and he just stood and watched Alex, which made him self-conscious because he didn't really know what he was doing, and the monk started laughing, which made Alex stop and the monk said, "Why'd you stop?" And Alex said, "I don't know what I'm doing." And the monk nodded, as if this was a very wise thing to say and this, just this monk with his round bald head and wire-rimmed spectacles, in his simple orange robe (not at all like the orange-dyed sheet Alex was wearing) nodding when Alex said, "I don't know what I'm doing," made Alex cry and he and the monk sat down under that tree, and the monk (whose name was Ron) told him about Kali, the goddess who is both womb and grave. Alex felt like it was the first thing anyone had said to him that made sense since Tessie died and after that he stopped coming to the park, until just recently, and let his hair grow out again and stopped wearing his robe. Before she'd died, he'd been one of the lucky ones, or so he'd thought, because he made a small fortune in a dot com, and actually got out of it before it all went belly up while so many people he knew lost everything but then Tessie came home from her doctor's appointment, not pregnant, but with cancer, and he realized he wasn't lucky at all. They met in high school and were together until she died, at home, practically blind by that time and she made him promise he wouldn't just give up on life. So he began living this sort of half-life, but he wasn't unhappy or depressed, he didn't want her to think that, he just wasn't sure. "I sort of lost confidence in life," he said. "It's like I don't believe in it anymore. Not like suicide, but I mean, like the whole thing, all of it isn't real somehow. Sometimes I feel like it's all a dream, or a long nightmare that I can never wake up from. It's made me odd, I guess."

She bit her lower lip, glanced longingly at his cup.

"Here," Alex said, "I'm done anyway."

She took it and lifted it toward her face, breathing in, he was sure of it, and only after she was finished, drinking the coffee. They sat like that in silence for a while and then they just started talking about everything, just as Alex had hoped they would. She told him how she had grown up living near the ocean, and her father had died young, and then her mother had too, and she had a boyfriend, her first love, who broke her heart, but the story she wrote was just a story, a story about her life, her dream life, the way she felt inside, like he did, as though somehow life was a dream. Even though everyone thought she was a painter (because he was the only one who read it, he was the only one who got it), she was a writer, not a painter, and stories seemed more real to her than life. At a certain point he offered to take the empty cup and throw it in the trash but she said she liked to peel off the wax, and then began doing so. Alex politely ignored the divergent ways she found to continue drinking his breath. He didn't want to embarrass her.

They finally stood up and stretched, walked through the park together and grew quiet, with the awkwardness of new friends. "You want a ride?" he said, pointing at his car.

She declined, which was a disappointment to Alex but he determined not to let it ruin his good mood. He was willing to leave it at that, to accept what had happened between them that afternoon as a moment of grace to be treasured and expect nothing more from it, when she said, "What are you doing next Tuesday?" They made a date, well, not a date, Alex reminded himself, an arrangement, to meet the following Tuesday in the park, which they did, and there followed many wonderful Tuesdays. They did not kiss. They were friends. Of course Alex still loved her. He loved her more. But he didn't bother her with all that and it was in the spirit of friendship that he suggested (after weeks of Tuesdays in the park) that the following Tuesday she come for dinner, "nothing fancy," he promised when he saw the slight hesitation on her face.

But when she said yes, he couldn't help it; he started making big plans for the night.

Naturally, things were awkward when she arrived. He offered to take her sweater, a lumpy looking thing in wild shades of orange, lime green, and purple. He should have just let her throw it across the couch, that would have been the casual non-datelike thing to do, but she handed it to him and then, wiping her hand through her hair, which, by candlelight looked like bloody grass, cased his place with those lavender eyes, deeply shadowed as though she hadn't slept for weeks.

He could see she was freaked out by the candles. He hadn't gone crazy or anything. They were just a couple of small candles, not even purchased from the store in the mall, but bought at the grocery store, unscented. "I like candles," he said, sounding defensive even to his own ears.

She smirked, as if she didn't believe him, and then spun away on the toes of her red sneaker and her green one, and plopped down on the couch. She looked absolutely exhausted. This was not a complete surprise to Alex. It had been a part of his plan, actually, but he felt bad for her just the same.

He kept dinner simple, lasagna, a green salad, chocolate cake for dessert. They didn't eat in the dining room. That would have been too formal. Instead they ate in the living room, she sitting on the couch, and he on the floor, their plates on the coffee table, watching a DVD of *I Love Lucy* episodes, a mutual like they had discovered. (Though her description of watching *I Love Lucy* reruns as a child did not gel with his picture of her in the crooked keeper's house, offering tea to melting ghosts, he didn't linger over the inconsistency.) Alex offered her plenty to drink but he wouldn't let her come into the kitchen, or get anywhere near his cup. He felt bad about this, horrible, in fact, but he tried to stay focused on the bigger picture.

After picking at her cake for a while, Agatha set the plate down, leaned back into the gray throw pillows, and closed her eyes.

Alex watched her. He didn't think about anything, he just watched her. Then he got up very quietly so as not to disturb her and went into the kitchen where he, carefully, quietly opened the drawer in which he had stored the supplies. Coming up from behind, eyeing her red and green hair, he moved quickly. She turned toward him, cursing loudly, her eyes wide and frightened, as he pressed her head to her knees, pulled her arms behind her back (to the accompaniment of a sickening crack, and her scream) pressed the wrists together and wrapped them with the rope. She struggled in spite of her weakened state, her legs flailing, kicking the coffee table. The plate with the chocolate cake flew off it and landed on the beige rug and her screams escalated into a horrible noise, unlike anything Alex had ever heard before. Luckily, Alex was prepared with the duct tape, which he slapped across her mouth. By that time he was rather exhausted himself. But she stood up and began to run, awkwardly, across the room. It broke his heart to see her this way. He grabbed her from behind. She kicked and squirmed but she was quite a small person and it was easy for him to get her legs tied.

"Is that too tight?" he asked.

She looked at him with wide eyes. As if he were the ghost.

"I don't want you to be uncomfortable."

She shook her head. Tried to speak, but only produced muffled sounds.

"I can take that off," he said, pointing at the duct tape. "But you have to promise me you won't scream. If you scream, I'll just put it on, and I won't take it off again. Though, you should know, ever since Tessie died I have these vivid dreams and nightmares, and I wake up screaming a lot. None of my neighbors has ever done anything about it. Nobody's called the police to report it, and nobody has even asked me if there's a problem. That's how it is amongst the living. Okay?"

She nodded.

He picked at the edge of the tape with his fingertips and when he got a good hold of it, he pulled fast. It made a loud ripping sound. She grunted and gasped, tears falling down her cheeks as she licked her lips.

"I'm really sorry about this," Alex said. "I just couldn't think of another way."

She began to curse, a string of expletives quickly swallowed by her weeping, until finally she managed to ask, "Alex, what are you doing?"

He sighed. "I know it's true, okay? I see the way you are, how tired you get and I know why. I know that you're a breath-stealer. I want you to understand that I know that about you, and I love you and you don't have to keep pretending with me, okay?"

She looked around the room, as if trying to find something to focus on. "Listen, Alex," she said, "Listen to me. I get tired all the time 'cause I'm sick. I didn't want to tell you, after what you told me about your wife. I thought it would be too upsetting for you. That's it. That's why I get tired all the time."

"No," he said, softly, "you're a ghost."

"I am not dead," she said, shaking her head so hard that her tears splashed his face. "I am not dead," she said over and over again, louder and louder until Alex felt forced to tape her mouth shut once more.

"I know you're afraid. Love can be frightening. Do you think I'm not scared? Of course I'm scared. Look what happened with Tessie. I know you're scared too. You're worried I'll turn out to be like Ezekiel, but I'm not like him, okay? I'm not going to hurt you. And I even finally figured out that you're scared 'cause of what happened with your mom. Of course you are. But you have to understand. That's a risk I'm willing to take. Maybe we'll have one night together or only one hour, or a minute. I don't know. I have good genes though. My parents, both of them, are still alive, okay? Even my grandmother only died a few years ago. There's a good chance I have a lot, and I mean a lot, of breath in me. But if I don't, don't you see, I'd rather spend a short time with you, than no time at all?"

He couldn't bear it, he couldn't bear the way she looked at him as if he were a monster when he carried her to the couch. "Are you cold?"

She just stared at him.

"Do you want to watch more *I Love Lucy?* Or a movie?"

She wouldn't respond. She could be so stubborn.

He decided on *Annie Hall.* "Do you like Woody Allen?" She just stared at him, her eyes filled with accusation. "It's a love story," he said, turning away from her to insert the DVD. He turned it on for her, then placed the remote control in her lap, which he realized was a stupid thing to do, since her hands were still tied behind her back, and he was fairly certain that, had her mouth not been taped shut, she'd be giving him that slack-jawed look of hers. She wasn't making any of this very easy. He picked the dish up off the floor, and the silverware, bringing them into the kitchen, where he washed them and the pots and pans, put aluminum foil on the leftover lasagna and put it into the refrigerator. After he finished sweeping the floor, he sat and watched the movie with her. He forgot about the sad ending. He always thought of it as a romantic comedy, never remembering the sad end. He turned off the TV and said, "I think it's late enough now. I think we'll be all right." She looked at him quizzically.

First Alex went out to his car and popped the trunk, then he went back inside where he found poor Agatha squirming across the floor. Trying to escape, apparently. He walked past her, got the throw blanket from the couch and laid it on the floor beside her, rolled her into it even as she squirmed and bucked. "Agatha, just try to relax," he said, but she didn't. Stubborn, stubborn, she could be so stubborn.

He threw her over his shoulder. He was not accustomed to carrying much weight and immediately felt the stress, all the way down his back to his knees. He shut the apartment door behind him and didn't worry about locking it. He lived in a safe neighborhood.

When they got to the car, he put her into the trunk, only then taking the blanket away from her beautiful face. "Don't worry, it won't be long," he said as he closed the hood.

He looked through his CDs, trying to choose something she would like, just in case the sound carried into the trunk, but he couldn't figure out what would be appropriate so he finally decided just to drive in silence.

It took about twenty minutes to get to the beach; it was late, and there was little traffic. Still, the ride gave him an opportunity to reflect on what he was doing. By the time he pulled up next to the pier, he had reassured himself that it was the right thing to do, even though it looked like the wrong thing.

He'd made a good choice, deciding on this place. He and Tessie used to park here, and he was amazed that it had apparently remained undiscovered by others seeking dark escape.

When he got out of the car he took a deep breath of the salt air and stood, for a moment, staring at the black waves, listening to their crash and murmur. Then he went around to the back and opened up the trunk. He looked over his shoulder, just to be sure. If someone were to discover him like this, his actions would be misinterpreted. The coast was clear, however. He wanted to carry Agatha in his arms, like a bride. Every time he had pictured it, he had seen it that way, but she was struggling again so he had to throw her over his shoulder where she continued to struggle. Well, she was stubborn, but he was too, that was part of the beauty of it, really. But it made it difficult to walk, and it was windier on the pier, also wet. All in all it was a precarious, unpleasant journey to the end.

He had prepared a little speech but she struggled against him so hard, like a hooked fish, that all he could manage to say was, "I love you," barely focusing on the wild expression in her face, the wild eyes, before he threw her in and she sank, and then bobbed up like a cork, only her head above the black waves, those eyes of hers, locked on his, and they remained that way, as he turned away from the edge of the pier and walked down the long plank, feeling lighter, but not in a good way. He felt those eyes, watching him, in the car as he flipped restlessly from station to station, those eyes, watching him, when he returned home, and saw the clutter of their night together, the burned-down candles, the covers to the *I Love Lucy* and *Annie Hall* DVDs on the floor, her crazy sweater on the dining room table, those eyes, watching him, and suddenly Alex was cold, so cold his teeth were chattering and he was shivering but sweating besides. The black water rolled over those eyes and closed them and he ran to the bathroom and only just made it in time, throwing up everything he'd eaten, collapsing to the floor, weeping, *What have I done? What was I thinking?*

He would have stayed there like that, he determined, until they came for him and carted him away, but after a while he became aware of the foul taste in his mouth. He stood up, rinsed it out, brushed his teeth and tongue, changed out of his clothes, and went to bed, where, after a good deal more crying, and trying to figure out exactly what had happened to his mind, he was amazed to find himself falling into a deep darkness like the water, from which, he expected, he would never rise.

But then he was lying there, with his eyes closed, somewhere between sleep and waking, and he realized he'd been like this for some time. Though he was fairly certain he had fallen asleep, something had woken him. In this half state, he'd been listening to the sound he finally recognized as dripping water. He hated it when he didn't turn the faucet tight. He tried to ignore it, but the dripping persisted. So confused was he that he even thought he felt a splash on his hand and another on his forehead. He opened one eye, then the other.

She stood there, dripping wet, her hair plastered darkly around her face, her eyes smudged black. "I found a sharp rock at the bottom of the world," she said and she raised her arms. He thought she was going to strike him, but instead she showed him the cut rope dangling there.

He nodded. He could not speak.

She cocked her head, smiled, and said, "Okay, you were right. You were right about everything. Got any room in there?"

He nodded. She peeled off the wet T-shirt and let it drop to the floor, revealing her small breasts white as the moon, unbuttoned and unzipped her jeans, wiggling seductively out of the tight wet fabric, taking her panties off at the same time. He saw when she lifted her feet that the rope was no longer around them and she was already transparent below the knees. When she pulled back the covers he smelled the odd odor of saltwater and mud, as if she were both fresh and loamy. He scooted over, but only far enough that when she eased in beside him, he could hold her, wrap her wet cold skin in his arms, knowing that he was offering her everything, everything he had to give, and that she had come to take it.

"You took a big risk back there," she said.

He nodded.

She pressed her lips against his and he felt himself growing lighter, as if all his life he'd been weighed down by this extra breath, and her lips were cold but they grew warmer and warmer and the heat between them created a steam until she burned him and still, they kissed, all the while Alex thinking, I love you, I love you, I love you, until, finally, he could think it no more, his head was as light as his body, lying beside her, hot flesh to hot flesh, the cinder of his mind could no longer make sense of it, and he hoped, as he fell into a black place like no other he'd ever been in before, that this was really happening, that she was really here, and the suffering he'd felt for so long was finally over.

M. Rickert's *short story collection,* Map of Dreams *was published by Golden Gryphon in 2006. Many of her stories, like this one, have appeared in* The Magazine of Fantasy & Science Fiction. *She lives in Cedarburg, Wisconsin.*

THE WIZARD OF ETERNAL WATCH

Eugie Foster

W ITHIN THE CASTLE AT THE END OF THE WORLD, the wards and enchantments stirred, rousing themselves like heavy beasts emerging from a long winter's sleep. They stretched and glanced about, triggered to alertness by the necessity of waking the next Wizard of Eternal Watch.

Reika felt sleep tugged away. She clung to it like a stubborn child to warm blankets. The dream was so delicious: Zinan in the rain, his arms around her, whispering promises of tomorrow. That had been the day they had fought over their assignments as keeper and wizard. He had called her detached and cold; she had called him thin-skinned and sentimental. From fury to lovemaking, they had proved each accusation untrue with sweet kisses, sharp teeth in flesh, and fiery passion under the weeping sky.

The spells knew how to deal with this too. They invaded her slumbering psyche, replaced her memory of Zinan with words, oaths, promises made. Her voice, her pledges.

Reika's eyes snapped open and the diamond casement floated apart, halving itself where before it had been a single, flawless stone. Released from stasis, she felt a familiar mingling of anticipation and dread.

Zinan would be waiting for her in the Chamber of Command.

She reached for her crown and used it to murmur forth a simple spell that pushed the last veil of Waiting from her thoughts.

The Chamber of Command was the nexus of the castle. There was only one corridor from her quarters, as there was only one corridor from every Waiting quarters, and it led to the Chamber. Like a great beating heart, stone arteries sent wizards and keepers to and fro in a sluggish dance across eternity.

The Chamber had not changed in the years since she had occupied it last. Shimmering images threw ghostly shadows against the smooth, round walls in regular planes of illusion. These were the cages.

Before each panel, a cube, no larger than her head, hovered midair with golden, translucent sides. These were the locks.

The prisoners could be seen, tiny demons fighting, dancing, sleeping within their cubicles.

Reika was a jailor, one of a pair rotated in sets—one Wizard of Eternal Watch and one Keeper of Forever per century—chosen and trained to wield illusion. They harnessed the demons' chaotic power and used it to mend the entropy of the world with sympathetic magic. It was a significant task, for if the illusions wavered or tore, the demons could break free, wreak hell upon the domains their power oversaw. Catastrophic destruction, firestorms, plagues, genocide, floods—all were possible, as history had shown.

Her fellow jailor, Zinan, scowled as she entered. He had not changed either, of course, his countenance ever youthful. The gleaming blue of his eyes belied both a penchant for mischief and an intensity that both fascinated and provoked her. Centuries past they had greeted each other with fleeting touches, harried smiles, but always pleasure. There was no welcome in him now.

"What's the matter?" she asked.

"Hephaestus keeps putting dents in his walls. He's within a few cracks of breaking out. Why hasn't he been tuned?"

Tuning was always Zinan's answer—condition the demon rather than adjust the setting.

"He doesn't need tuning." Reika gazed at the panel that illuminated the smith's prison, letting herself submerge into his reality.

FIRE AND METAL, the thunder of the forge. Boredom, curiosity.

With a touch to her crown, Reika sculpted the viscous matter of illusion.

As he battered the walls of his rocky home in Lemnos, the god of smiths came across a vein of gold—vibrant yellow, as brilliant as the locks of Aphrodite's hair.

Reika grinned. Trust Hephaestus to be distracted by the glitter of gold. She listened to his thoughts, a shadowy voyeur.

'Twill make a fine coronet for his beloved Goddess of Love. And it would not be a mere bauble, but magical. A spell to make the wearer invisible.

Hephaestus leaned on his great bellows, absorbed in his newest project.

FAR AWAY, in a world not contained in even a fraction of the god's imaginings, an active volcano rumbled and burped sulfurous clouds that brought early twilight to an island village. The people in the village watched, their boats ready for launch, hoping it would fret no further. They smiled in shared relief as the angry mountain subsided, contenting itself with a last grumble before returning to rest.

REIKA DISENGAGED from Hephaestus. "See? That's all it took."

Zinan glowered. "'What an incompetent keeper you are,' says the pretty lady in dulcet tones." He adjusted the fit of his crown and turned his back to her.

"Not incompetent, although I wouldn't disagree with petulant as a spoiled child." Her answer was quiet, but in the Chamber, her words hung in the air.

"Reika, what is it?" Zinan's tone was exasperated.

"What do you mean?" She knew, but preferred feigning ignorance.

"I remember when you shouted at me with more tenderness than a dozen of these chilly exchanges hold. Why must every time we come together be so—?" Zinan reached for her, and Reika flinched away.

A flash from the World Simulacrum saved her from having to answer.

In the center of the Chamber of Command, an orb of smoky gray, terrestrial green, and glowing azure spun. It was large enough to hold a full-grown man, were it hollow, but the World Simulacrum wasn't a prison; it was a mirror. An ancient construct, created by the council of wizards and keepers after the recovery from the last cataclysm, its purpose was simple, to display the world to those who chose to seclude themselves in a windowless citadel forever: guardians, caretakers, jailors.

Now it flared in warning, pulsing once, then again.

"It's the Southern Hemisphere," Reika said, tracing her fingers over the throbbing lines of red. "The continental plates are straining. Earthquake imminent. A big one."

Zinan followed the fault lines over craggy mountain ranges and under canyons. "The focal point is going to be Botan."

"A small township. Can the population be evacuated?"

He glanced at her with a mixture of frustration and rebuke. "Perhaps it was small generations ago. It is now upwards of fifty thousand souls."

Trust Zinan to know. He had an affinity for the people, for the lives of the world, as keepers must. Reika preferred the slow, potent evolution of the inanimate—stone, air, water. It was easy to forget how quickly time affected the living.

"Well? How long do they have?" Zinan asked.

Reika sunk her fingers into the Simulacrum, let herself immerse in the construct. She loved this feeling, her body becoming the world, her heartbeat the ebb and flow of the living planet. She coasted the air currents—cold, mercury gales like a solemn chorus, rivaling a draft of alluring warmth. Here there was no Zinan, no friction or discord, just the warm stream, circling the world in a gust of thermal burn. She could spread herself to the wind and disappear for a year, or a hundred years.

Zinan's voice brought her back. "Don't float away."

"I wasn't." It was a lie. But the seduction of the moment fragmented. She shifted to ride the leaden tide that would bring her to earth, out of the atmosphere and into the heavy rock. Sinking past flourishing greenery and through bulky roots, she delved deep into bedrock smashed together by time.

She touched the apex of pressure and tension, her mental fingers exploring it, surveying it. In moments she understood the mammoth forces at work, beyond words or logical analysis. With the ease of centuries of practice, she gave the seething energies form and structure within the boundless faculties of illusion.

A PAIR OF GIANTS VIED, shoulder to shoulder, for dominance. Their battle was ponderous, and their wills adamant.

SHE PULLED OUT OF THE SIMULACRUM with a familiar reluctance. "The pressure is just shy of critical."

"Why didn't the last wizard adjust this? Weren't there foreshocks?"

"No warning. The plates were locked together. He probably overlooked it, or thought it wouldn't need intervention for a while yet."

"I'll rouse the Banshee, get her to awaken Botan's populace so they'll be ready for flight." Zinan turned his attention to the far wall where a streak of blackness shuddered against a curve of panel.

Reika looked away. She didn't like the Banshee. She was erratic, capricious, flitting from malicious activity to cruel torment from second to second in her illusory prison. Zinan indulged her sadism, revealing a penchant for it that had always disturbed Reika.

Reika riffled through the demons at her disposal before deciding upon Jian Lao. He was a solid personality, being not just a manifestation of earth, but of permanence as well. It would be a simple thing to goad him to action.

Reika watched with Jian Lao's eyes, listened to his thoughts as she layered a new illusion upon his reality.

THE CELESTIAL PALACE TREMBLED, rocking as though it would uproot itself from its foundation.

Off balance and discomfited, Jian Lao watched a monstrous fin rise from a rocky chasm and sink back like a whale breaching the ocean.

It appeared the sea monster Shachihoko had turned himself into a tiger-headed fish and now swam through the Wu Yo, the five sacred mountains, unsettling the foundation of the holy palace. That could not be tolerated.

Jian Lao summoned dragons to his side and rode upon the greatest—an imperial beast with five claws on each foot—to do battle. Confronting Shachihoko, Jian Lao wrestled him, pinning his thrashing tail while the dragons gnawed at his sides.

REIKA LEFT JIAN LAO to check on the Simulacrum. She plunged her fingers into the tectonic fault lines, groping for the lines of power that would link her to the world's core. Instead of earthy plates and bedrock, she watched the illusion she had planted.

THE GIANTS GREW TIRED, lulled by a force more intent, more purposeful then they. Like a pair of squabbling children, they sulked and muttered, but were forced to settle.

REIKA RELAXED. The compressional build-up subsided, the danger passing even as she stood there, her thoughts aligned with the sprawling world mirror.

But glancing back to check on Jian Lao's progress, she was shocked to see he was no longer triumphing against Shachihoko. He had pulled out of the combat.

Reika pitched her consciousness into Jian Lao's realm, momentarily dizzied by the frantic realignment.

THE GOD OF EARTH FALTERED, confounded. One of his *long*, his dragon allies, had metamorphosed into a multi-headed monster. It was foreign to anything Jian Lao has ever encountered. He stood amazed, while beside him, Shachihoko revived.

ONE OF THE CUBICLES bordering Jian Lao's had cracked, a tiny breach of reality bleeding to its neighbor. It wasn't enough to free either demon, but was more than sufficient for illusory borders to waver and merge. Reika identified the anomaly. The monster was a hydra—a Grecian construct in an Eastern setting—as bizarre as a sea serpent in a desert. As soon as she recognized it, she knew where to look for the outflow: Hephaestus' cube. Weakened by his earlier restlessness, hairline fractures splintered through the fabric of Lemnos.

"Zinan, there's a leak! It's causing a variance and distracting my demon. He's losing against the quake!"

Zinan spun away from the Banshee's panel. "I'll fix the breach; you get Jian Lao on track."

Reika dived back into Jian Lao's realm, sharing her thoughts with his, and willing the god to heed her suggestions.

THE NEW MONSTER *is a trick of Shachihoko,* she said-thought. *Though it may look like a creature of madness, it is but a dragon in a cunning mask. See, there are the scintillating scales and the four-clawed toes.*

Jian Lao, emboldened, flipped a hand at the hydra in refutation and turned his back. He refused to acknowledge it, for he would not be made a fool of.

When Jian Lao looked away, Reika took the opportunity to lop off the hydra's heads, all save one.

Jian Lao sniffed. As he thought, it was just a *long,* looking perhaps abashed at being made into Shachihoko's pawn.

But Shachihoko had had time to rest. He was strong again. His tail flailed with wicked speed, and his jaws dripped acid.

God and monster hurtled together. Shachihoko bit, his tiger teeth deadly sharp. He fastened upon Jian Lao's shoulder, ripping away flesh.

Reika stumbled, feeling the tearing pain of it. Tremors of movement beneath her feet. An earthquake in the Simulacrum. In Botan, a cluster of houses shuddered. Masonry cracked and fell. It was just a foreshock, but it heralded terrible destruction.

Jian Lao was no longer enough to quell the tremors.

Reika left the earth god and thrust into Hephaestus' panel. She shoved past Zinan busily patching cracks in Mount Lemnos.

—THE FINISHING TOUCHES *on Aphrodite's coronet. It was delicate filigree, painstaking work for such massive hands. But Hephaestus was a dexterous master craftsman.*

It was dangerous, but Reika had no choice. Concentrating to keep the irregularity as slight as she could, she twisted the lines of illusion.

The earth cracked apart, a glowing fissure in the ground. A lizard emerged.

Hephaestus saw six legs and smelled a rancid odor, like death on the wind. It was warning enough. He turned his head and grabbed a shield polished to a glossy sheen. He pointed it at the basilisk, which died of fright when it glimpsed its own reflection.

Before Hephaestus could wonder at this strange invasion, another scaled body emerged from the cleft. And another. He donned a helm to shield his eyes from their baleful looks, but as fast as he killed them, more appeared.

I must seal the split with stone, Reika prompted. *Before I am buried in the stinking carcasses of a deluge of basilisks.*

By touch alone, the smith worked the bellows as he aimed the shield at the murderous lizards. When the fire scorched even him, he tipped it, sending a stream of molten ore into the crack. As the basilisks writhed in the searing river, salamanders now, the smith put his shoulder against the mountain wall.

Sweat poured from his brow. His teeth ground with effort. The mountain moved.

While she concentrated, caught up in the smith's effort. A burning basilisk glared at her, glowing orange from the fire. She stiffened feeling her limbs growing sluggish from the potency of the malevolent lizard's gaze.

But of course, *it was only an illusion.*

"What is an *illusion?*" Hephaestus grunted.

SHE PULLED OUT IMMEDIATELY. Zinan flew with her.

"Are you hurt?" he asked, his blue eyes wide with concern. "You almost succumbed to the basilisk. Do you want me to—?"

Reika wilted before the Simulacrum. "No. I'm fine." Arms trembling, she reached up and touched the fault line.

THE GIANTS SLUMBERED. Their snores sent up mild shudders of distemper, but they were at rest.

Jian Lao bound Shachihoko in loops of granite, lecturing it all the while. Hephaestus—

"REIKA!"

She fell back to herself, jostled from her mental dance by Zinan's voice.

Hephaestus stood in the Chamber of Command, freed from his prison. His was a familiar visage: one of his legs twisted and his face marred by scars. He had the appearance of a wax figurine held over a fire and then remolded by an inexpert artist. Undeniably ugly, but despite being crippled, immensely powerful. Muscles bulged across his shoulders and arms, a smith's physique.

Although she'd interacted with him frequently, intimately even, it had been in safety, with him contained and reacting to the stimuli she provided. Here he dwarfed the Chamber of Command with his presence. She could smell him, the burn of molten metal and the sear of sulfur scorching her throat. Heat radiated from him, surging out in rippling swells to match her fear.

"Where am I?" His voice was a shredded rasp, coming from a fire-parched throat.

Zinan, always first to synchronize with emotions and distress, stepped forward. "This is a dream, a fantasy. You are asleep."

The smith frowned. "Is this another ruse of Ares to put me aside while he dallies with fair Aphrodite? There was a scourge of basilisks to oppose me, but I have vanquished them. I go to ascend Olympus to give a golden bauble to my beloved." He looked at his empty hands. "Where is it?"

Reika glared at Zinan. Hephaestus was hers. A fantasy of dreaming would be harder to instill in a mind like his, full of action and flames and jealousy. She had no choice now but to continue with Zinan's narrative.

"You stopped in a field of poppies to pluck a bouquet for peerless Aphrodite," she said. "Red blossoms like unto the petals of her lips. But lo, the sweet pollen made you sluggish. You lay down, and now you dream a wondrous strange vision. It is, though, naught but a dream. All you need do is waken, and you can continue to beautiful Aphrodite's bower."

For a moment, it seemed it would work. Hephaestus nodded, accustomed to the cadence of her illusions, but then his eyes lit upon the crown on Zinan's head. "Thief! Thou hast stolen the coronet I forged!"

He moved faster than a lame man ought to, snatching the crown off.

"No!" Reika cried, lunging to stop him. Too late. Zinan disappeared.

Hephaestus turned the crown in his hand. "I was mistaken. This is not what I crafted." He dangled it from a finger, like a sulking boy with a broken toy.

Reika grabbed the crown back, feeling anguish tight in her chest, a keening grief that would batter her to her knees if she let it.

The crown was light in her hands, lighter than such a powerful talisman ought to be. With a wavering arm she pointed to the panel where Hephaestus' world flickered, drawing his attention. It took on greater dimension and color as she focused on it.

A BEAUTIFUL WOMAN, the Goddess of Love herself, stood among silver clouds and marble columns, white as the rising sun. Her shining hair swirled around her shoulders in a riot of curls. She smiled in greeting, offering her hand in welcome. The god of war, Ares, took it. His red sword of strife was sheathed, and his eyes gleamed. The fingers of his other hand tangled in the silk of her tresses.

"THE JACKAL MEANS TO SEDUCE HER," the smith growled. "Oh, would I were there. He would not dare touch her. I would fling him from the lofty heights of Olympus!"

It was the opening Reika needed to return him to his prison.

HEPHAESTUS SCALED the heights of Olympus, snarling at Ares. He pulled his mighty fist back.

Aphrodite pouted winsomely, rushing to cling to her husband's arm. "He was but brushing a noisome insect from my hair," she said. "But what is this? Is this lovely trinket a gift for me?"

Ares slunk away as the smith offered the golden coronet up.

REIKA WITHDREW FROM HEPHAESTUS' REALITY and drooped to the floor. She would have to tune him, pare down the curiosity, the doubt that had allowed him to break out. Later.

Her eyes burned, a prickle of tears behind them.

Zinan was gone, destroyed when he was disconnected from the crown. She faced a hundred years alone. How could she keep the world spinning by herself? Reika clutched the crown to her breast. Its sharp ridges were a poor substitute for warm arms, a lover's embrace.

"Reika!"

The voice was thin, panicked but familiar. She gaped, looking wildly around for Zinan's familiar image. "Where are you?"

"I'm lost."

She could feel him, faintly, through the crown in her arms. Somehow, in the moment of severance, he had saved himself, escaped into the only reality left to him. He was in one of the demon prisons.

"There must have been a surge of chaos when Hephaestus snatched off your crown. It flung you into an illusion. Look around. Tell me where you are and I'll get you out."

"It's dark. There's a glow coming from everywhere, but I can't make out any details." She heard the fear in his voice. Once, she had been all the sanctuary he needed. "There's a cold wind."

Several panels down, a shuddering darkness bled shapes and shadow. The last illusion Zinan had molded.

"Is there any sound?" she asked. "Do you hear wailing?"

"No. Wait, yes. It's faint."

"You're in the Banshee's realm. I'll come and get you."

"How will you find me?"

A good question. "Can you make out anything at all?"

"There's a big darkness in the distance. It feels like it ought to be solid. I think it might be the mausoleum."

"The Undertaker's Citadel. Stand by the gates. I'm coming."

"Reika?"

"What?"

"How is this possible? How can I be in a demon's illusion?"

"Don't think about it. Worry about getting to the gates. If I don't get you out of there, the Banshee might kill you."

"Y—yes. I'll wait for you at the gates."

The Banshee frightened her. Reika had to remind herself not to impose elements into the Banshee's illusory reality which would confound her.

A GLOWING ROAD POINTED THE WAY to the Undertaker's Citadel. In the distance, a wolf howled, alone and desolate. A scared traveler made her way to the gates of Hell.

Stupid to have to layer all these unearthly trappings together. But if she didn't, she would surely draw the Banshee's attention. As long as Reika posed as a background feature, she might be ignored.

The traveler walked the glowing road cowled in a black hood. It hid her face. She did not raise her head when night wings swept by overhead, for she knew better.

Before her stood the Undertaker's Gates, soaring out of the bleak mausoleum.

Reika peered into the gloom. There were the gates, but where was Zinan? At her touch, they cracked apart, groaning on rusted hinges. She passed into the Undertaker's grounds, sensitive to any twinges which would warn her of the Banshee's interest.

Zinan had imagined the mausoleum as a mansion of black marble and onyx. A single corridor led to the throne room (a parallel to the Chamber of Command?), where the Undertaker sat on a throne of bone. At his side, his Queen, the Banshee, glared out from the tangles of her hair.

Reika hovered on the verge of pulling out, but then she saw Zinan. He sat cross-legged on the raised dais, twirling something that shone dully in his hands. The Banshee hissed at Reika as she approached, but made no other protest.

Reika bent down. "Zinan, quick, take my hand."

He glanced up, making no move to reach for her. Reika saw he toyed with a crown.

"It's a funny thing, being locked in a realm of death," he said. "It makes one wonder about afterlives and the nature of flesh."

Reika pushed back hysteria. "This place is affecting you. I can feel the desolation weighing on me. Take my hand and I'll lead you out."

He continued as though she hadn't spoken. "When the council harnessed the demons, they thought they would only serve if they believed the illusions were real."

Reika eyed the Banshee. "You shouldn't say such things here—"

"Did you know she realizes we've imprisoned her in a cell of dreams? She likes it. She doesn't mind being used because she gets what she wants. It doesn't matter to her whether it's real or not, as long as it feels real."

"S—she knows?"

"Has for centuries."

"And she hasn't tried to break out?"

"Apparently not. It occurs to me, if the Banshee knows, other demons might too."

"Zinan—"

"So an awareness of the situation does not preclude service."

"Please—"

"Reika, there's no way I could have been shunted into a demon realm when Hephaestus stole my crown unless I'm—" he paused, waiting for her.

There was no point in dissembling. He had discovered the truth, as a part of her had known he would. "Unless you're a demon," she finished.

"For how long? Or have I always been one, and everything else was the lie?"

She hesitated before sitting beside him and taking his hand. It was the first time she had touched him since the accident. His fingers were solid and strong, exactly as she remembered them to be.

"Zinan, during our last cycle, Surya, the sun god, got it into his head to go nova. He couldn't be distracted by adventures and wives. You went in to tune him. You stopped the nova, but there was still damage: fires, droughts, and finally a huge solar flare. You were deep in Surya's consciousness when it happened, so close the heat spilled out. Your body burnt to ashes."

"I died?"

Reika nodded. "There was a little of you left in Surya's realm. Just a bit of magic and awareness, enough so your presence registered as demonic."

"And you used an illusion to trap it. Me."

"If I hadn't, what was left of you would have faded away. I can't spin the world by myself. But, I—I hadn't realized how difficult it would be to keep the pretense up. I couldn't even tell you why—"

"Was that all? You lied to me, kept me as your pet demon, out of your duty as Wizard of Eternal Watch?"

"No, it wasn't like that! I couldn't let you die."

His voice was empty. "Why not?"

"I—I need you. Not just as Keeper of Forever, but because I'm lost without you. I love you."

He was silent for a long while. Around them, the Banshee's reality seemed to melt away, as though it realized its insignificance in this dialogue.

"It's been a long time since we've been solace and helpmate to each other," Zinan said at last. He regarded the gold circlet in his hand. "If I put this crown on my head, what will happen?"

"I don't know. What do you want to happen?"

"I want us to be the way we were before I died. I want the world to continue turning with you and me, keeper and wizard helming her. I want to love you again. Do you think maybe—?"

"Maybe."

Zinan raised the crown and set it on his head.

THEY STOOD TOGETHER, their bodies entwined in the center of the Chamber of Command. Reika felt the warmth of Zinan pressed against her. Even though she knew he wasn't real, having the truth out allowed her to pretend. And after all, wasn't it enough to believe in a dream of happiness?

As one they reached for the Simulacrum and submerged in the world currents. Their bodies moved together, sharing a union both primal and profound as they rode the world. But before Reika could abandon herself to the shared ecstasy, a stray thought intruded. *Would she still be there if she took off her crown?*

Eugie Foster *calls home a mildly haunted, fey-infested house in Metro Atlanta that she shares with her husband, Matthew, and her pet skunk, Hobkin. She pens a monthly column,* Writing for Young Readers, *and her fiction has been translated into Greek, Hungarian, Polish, and French; won the Phobos Award; and been nominated for the British Fantasy, Bram Stoker, and Pushcart awards. Her publication credits include stories in* Realms of Fantasy, The 3rd Alternative, Orson Scott Card's Intergalactic Medicine Show, Cricket, Cicada, *and anthologies* Best New Fantasy *and* Heroes in Training. *Visit her online at www. eugiefoster.com.*

MOON VIEWING AT SHIJO BRIDGE

———

Richard Parks

IN THE EARLY EVENING a tiny moth-demon was trying to batter its way into my room through a tear in the paper screen, no doubt attracted by the scent of poverty. I was debating whether to frighten the silly thing away or simply crush it, when the Widow Tamahara's delightful voice sent the poor creature fluttering away as fast as its little wings could carry it.

"Yamada-san, you have a visitor!"

Tamahara kneeled by the shoji screen that was the only door to my rooms. Besides the volume, there was an edge of excitement in the formidable old woman's voice that worried me just a little. The fact that aristocracy impressed her had worked to my advantage more than once when the rent was late, but her deference meant that just about anyone could get closer to me than might be healthy. That is, if they were of the right station in life. Anyone else giving a hint of trouble in her establishment she would throw out on their ear, if they were lucky.

"Who is it, Tamahara-san?"

"A messenger and that is all I know. She's waiting in the courtyard with her escort."

She?

Well, that explained why Widow Tamahara had not simply brought the person to my rooms. That would not have been proper, and the Widow Tamahara always did the right thing, to the degree that she understood what 'the right thing' was.

"Just a moment," I said.

After some thought I tucked a long dagger into my sleeve but left my *tachi* where it was. I wasn't wearing my best clothes, but my best would have been equally unimpressive. At least everything was clean. I followed Tamahara out into the courtyard. The sun had set but there was light enough still.

THE WOMAN KNEELED near a small pine tree, flanked on either side by her escorts. No rough provincial warriors these; the two men were polite, impassive, well dressed and well armed. The younger man wore the red and black clothing and bore the butterfly *mon* of the Taira Clan, the other wore plain black and bore no family crest or identification at all. I judged them as best I could. The escort wearing Taira livery I think I could have bested, if absolutely necessary and with a bit of luck. But the other . . . well, let's just say I didn't want any trouble. I also could not escape the feeling that we had met before.

I bowed formally and then kneeled in front of the woman. I noted the rightmost warrior's quick glance at my sleeve and how he inched almost imperceptibly closer, all the while not appearing to have noticed or moved at all. The man was even more formidable than I had suspected, but now my attention was on the woman.

Her *kimono* was very simple, as befitted a servant. Two shades of blue at most, though impeccably appropriate for the time of year. She wore a *boshi* with a long veil that circled the brim and hid her features. Naturally, she did not remove it. She merely bowed again from her seated position and held out a scroll resting on the palms of her small hands.

I took the offered scroll, all the while careful to make no sudden movements, and unrolled it to read:

> The Peony bows
> to no avail; the March wind
> is fierce, unceasing.

Caught like a rabbit in a snare. And so damn easily. Just the first three lines of a *tanka*. The poem was not yet complete, of course; the rest was up to me.

I looked at the shadow of the woman's face, hidden behind the veil. "Are you instructed to await my reply?"

Again she bowed without speaking. The escort on her right produced a pen case and ink. I considered for a few moments, then added the following two lines:

The donkey kneels down to rest.
In his shadow, flowers grow.

My poetic skills—never more than adequate—were a little rusty and
the result wasn't better than passable. Yet the form was correct and the
meaning, like that of the first segment, more than clear to the one who
would read it. The woman took the message from me, bowed again,
then rose as one with her escort and withdrew quickly without further
ceremony. The Widow Tamahara watched all this from the discreet
distance of the veranda encircling the courtyard.

"Is this work?" she asked when I passed her on the way back to my
room. "Will you be paid?"

"'Yes' seems the likely answer to both," I said, though that was
mostly to placate the old woman. I was fairly certain that I would be
the one paying, one way or the other.

LATER THAT EVENING I didn't bother to prepare my bedding. I waited,
fully clothed and in the darkness of my room, for my inevitable visitor.
The summons was clear and urgent, but I couldn't simply answer it. The
matter was much more complicated than that.

The full moon cast the man's shadow across the thin screen that was my
doorway. It wasn't a mistake; he wanted me to know he was there. I pulled
the screen aside, but I was pretty sure I knew who would be waiting.

He kneeled on the veranda, the hilt of his sword clearly visible.
"Lord Yamada? My name is Kanemore."

"Lord" was technically correct but a little jarring to hear applied
to me again. Especially coming from a man who was the son of an
emperor. I finally realized who he was. "Prince Kanemore. You were
named after the poet, Taira no Kanemore, weren't you?" I asked.

He smiled then, or perhaps it was a trick of the moonlight. "My
mother thought that having a famous poet for a namesake might gentle
my nature. In that I fear she was mistaken. So, you remember me."

"I do. Even when you were not at Court, your sister Princess Teiko
always spoke highly of you."

He smiled faintly. "And so back to the matter at hand: Lord Yamada,
I am charged to bring you safely to the Imperial compound."

The light was poor, but I used what there was to study the man a little more closely than I'd had time to do at our meeting earlier in the day. He was somewhat younger than I, perhaps thirty or so, and quite handsome except for a fresh scar that began on his left cheek and reached his jawline. He studied me just as intently; I didn't want to speculate on what his conclusions might be. Whether caused by my involvement or the situation itself—and I still didn't have any idea what that was—Kanemore was not happy. His face betrayed nothing, but his entire being was as tense as a bow at full draw.

"I am ready, Prince Kanemore."

"Just 'Kanemore,' please. With the Emperor's permission, I will renounce my title and found a new clan, since it is neither my destiny nor wish to ascend the throne."

"I am Goji. Lead on then."

The streets were dark and poorly lit. I saw the flare of an *onibi* down an alleyway and knew the ghosts were about. At this time of evening demons were a possibility too, but one of the beauties of Kyoto was that the multitude of temples and shrines tended to make the atmosphere uncomfortable for most of the fiercer demons and monsters. The rest, like that moth demon, were used to skulking about the niches and small spaces of the city, unnoticed and deliberately so being vulnerable to both exorcism and common steel.

We reached the Kamo River without incident and crossed at the Shijo Bridge. The full moon was high now, reflecting off the water. Farther downstream I saw an entire procession of ghost lights floating above the water. I'm not sure that Kanemore saw the *onibi* at all. His attention was focused on the moon's reflection as he paused for a second or two to admire it. I found this oddly reassuring. A man who did not pause to view a full moon at opportunity had no soul. But the fact that his moon viewing amounted to little more than a hesitation on Shijo Bridge showed his attention to duty. I already knew I did not want Kanemore as my enemy. Now I wondered if we could be friends.

"Do you know what this is about?" I asked.

"Explanations are best left to my sister," he said. "My understanding is far from complete."

"At this point I would be glad of scraps. I only know that Princess Teiko is in difficulty—"

He corrected me instantly. "It is her son Takahito that concerns my sister most. She always thinks of him first."

I didn't like the direction this conversation was taking. "Is Takahito unwell?"

"He is healthy," Kanemore said. "And still his half brother's heir, at present."

That was far too ominous. "Kanemore-san, it was my understanding that the late Emperor only allowed the current Emperor to ascend on the condition that Takahito be named heir after him, and that Takahito in turn take his royal grandfather's nickname, Sanjo, upon his eventual ascent. Is Emperor Reizei thinking of defying his father's wishes?"

Kanemore looked uncomfortable. "There have been complications. Plus, the Fujiwara favor another candidate, Prince Norihira. He is considered more agreeable. I will say no more at present."

More agreeable because, unlike Princess Teiko, Norihira's mother was Fujiwara. I considered this. If the Fujiwara Clan supported another candidate, then this was bad news for Teiko's son. As the Taira and Minamoto and other military families were the might of the Emperor, so were the Fujiwara his administration. Court ministers and minor officials alike were drawn primarily from their ranks. All power was the Emperor's in theory, but in practice his role was mostly ceremonial. It was the Fujiwara who kept the government in motion.

Still, the politics of the Imperial Court and the machinations of the Fujiwara were both subjects I had happily abandoned years ago. Now it appeared that I needed to renew my understanding, and quickly. Despite my desire to question him further, I knew that Kanemore had said all he was going to say on the matter for now. I changed the subject.

"Did you see much fighting while you were in the north?"

"A bit," he admitted. "The Abe Clan is contained, but not yet defeated . . ." he trailed off, then stopped and turned toward me. "Goji-san, are you a seer in addition to your other rumored talents? How did you know I had been in the north?"

I tried to keep from smiling. "That scar on your jaw is from a blade and fairly new. Even if you were inclined to brawling—which I seriously doubt—I don't believe the average drunken *samuru* could so much as touch you. That leaves the northern campaigns as the only reasonable conclusion. It was an educated guess. No more."

He rubbed his scar, thoughtfully. "Impressive, even so. But the hour grows late and I think we should be on our way."

We had taken no more than a few steps when two *bushi* staggered out of a nearby drinking establishment. One collided with me and muttered a slurred curse and reached for his sword. I didn't give the fool time to draw it. I struck him with my open palm square on the chin and his head snapped back and collided with a very hard lintel post. Fortunately for him, since Kanemore's *tachi* was already clear of its scabbard and poised for the blow swordsmen liked to call 'the pear splitter,' because that's what the victim's bisected head would resemble once the blow was completed. I have no doubt that Kanemore would have demonstrated this classic technique on that drunken lout had I not been in the path of his sword. The drunk's equally inebriated companion had his own sword half-drawn, but took a long look at Kanemore and thought better of it. He sheathed his sword, bowed in a rather grudging apology, and helped his addled friend to his feet. Together they staggered off into the night.

Kanemore watched them disappear before he put his sword away. "That, too, was impressive. But pointless. You should have let me kill him. One less provincial thug swaggering about the city. Who would miss him?"

I sighed. "His lord, for a start. Who would demand an explanation, and the man's companion would say one thing and we would say another and justice ministers would become involved and there would be time spent away from the matter at hand that I don't think we can afford. Or am I mistaken?"

Kanemore smiled. "I must again concede that you are not. I'm beginning to see why my honored sister has summoned you. May your lack of error continue, for all our sakes."

THE SOUTH GATE TO THE IMPERIAL COMPOUND was closest, but Kanemore led me to the East Gate, which was guarded by *bushi* in the red and black Taira colors, one of whom I recognized as the messenger's other escort. They stood aside for Kanemore and no questions were asked.

We weren't going to the Palace proper. The Imperial Compound covered a large area in the city and there were many smaller buildings of various function spread out through the grounds, including houses for the Emperor's wives and favorites. Considering our destination, it was clear we needed to attract as little attention as possible; Kanemore led me through some of the more obscure garden paths. At least, they had been obscure to other people. I remembered most of them from my time at Court. Losing access to the gardens was one of two regrets I had about leaving the Court.

Princess Teiko was the other.

Kanemore escorted me to a fine large house. A small palace, actually, and quite suitable for the widow of an Emperor. A group of very well dressed and important looking visitors was leaving as we arrived, and we stepped aside on the walkway to let them pass. There was only one I recognized in the lamplight before I kneeled as courtesy demanded: Fujiwara no Sentaro. It seemed only fitting my one visit to the compound in close to fifteen years and I *would* encounter my least-favorite person at the Imperial Court. The coldness of Kanemore's demeanor as they walked by wasn't exactly lost on me either.

If Sentaro recognized me, he gave no sign. Possibly he'd have forgotten me by now, but then a good politician did not forget an enemy while the enemy still drew breath.

"I gather Lord Sentaro is not in your favor?" I asked after they had gone.

"To call him a pig would be an insult to pigs," Kanemore said bluntly. "But he is the Minister of Justice, a skilled administrator, and has our Emperor's confidence. The gods may decree that he becomes Chancellor after Lord Yorimichi, as luck seems to favor the man. My sister, for some reason I cannot fathom, bears his company from time to time."

I started to say something about the realities of court life, but thought better of it. While the saints teach us that life is an illusion,

Sentaro's presence indicated that, sadly, some aspects of life did not change, illusion or not. We climbed the steps to the veranda.

"Teiko-hime is expecting us," Kanemore said to the *bushi* flanking the doorway, but clearly they already knew that and stepped back as we approached. A servant girl pulled the screen aside, and we stepped into a large open room, impeccably furnished with bright silk cushions and flowers in artful arrangements and lit by several paper lanterns. There was a dais on the far wall, curtained off, and doubtless a sliding screen behind it that would allow someone to enter the room without being seen. I had hoped to at least get a glimpse of Teiko, but of course that wasn't proper. I knew the rules, even if I didn't always follow them. Kanemore kneeled on a cushion near the dais, and I followed his example.

"My sister has been informed—" he started to say, but didn't get to finish.

"Your older sister is here, Kanemore-kun."

Two more maids impeccably dressed in layered yellow and blue *kimono* entered the room and pulled back the curtain. A veil remained in front of the dais, translucent but not fully transparent. I could see the ghostly form of a woman kneeling there, her long black hair down loose and flowing over her shoulders. I didn't need to see her clearly to know it was the same woman who had brought the message to me in the courtyard and whose face I had not seen then, either. No need: the way she moved, the elegance of a gesture, both betrayed her. Now I heard Teiko's voice again, and that was more than enough.

Kanemore and I both bowed low.

There was silence, and then that beautiful voice again, chiding me. "A *donkey*, Lord Yamada? Honestly . . ."

I tried not to smile, but it was hard. "My poetry is somewhat . . . untrained, Teiko-hime."

"Teiko. Please. We are old friends."

At this Kanemore gave me a hard glance, but I ignored him. He was no longer the most dangerous person in my vicinity, and I needed all my attention for the one who was.

"I think there is something you wish to discuss with me," I said. "Is this possible?" It was the most polite way I knew to phrase the question, but Teiko waved it aside.

"There is no one within hearing," she said, "who has not already heard. You may speak plainly, Lord Yamada. I will do the same—I need your help."

"You have read my answer," I said.

"True, but you have not heard my trouble," Teiko said, softly. "Listen, and then tell me what you will or will not do. Now then do you remember a young Fujiwara named Kiyoshi?"

That was a name I had not heard in a long time. Kiyoshi was about my age when I came to the Court as a very minor official of the household. Since he was handsome, bright, and a Fujiwara, his destiny seemed fixed. Like Kanemore he chose the *bushi* path instead and died fighting the northern barbarians. He was one of the few of that clan I could tolerate, and I sincerely mourned his death.

"I do remember him," I said.

"There is a rumor going around the Court that Kiyoshi was my lover, and that my son Takahito is his issue, not my late husband's."

For a moment I could not speak. This matter was beyond serious. Gossip was close to the rule of law at Court. If this particular gossip was not silenced, both Takahito's and Teiko's positions at court were in peril, and that was just for a start.

"Do you know who is responsible for the slander?"

"No. While it's true that Kiyoshi was very dear to me, we grew up together at court and our affections to each other were as brother and sister, as was well understood at the time. You know this to be true."

I did. If I knew anything. "And you wish for me to discover the culprit? That will be . . . difficult."

She laughed softly then, decorously covering her face with her fan even through the veils prevented me from seeing her face clearly. "Lord Yamada, even if I knew who started the rumors it would do little good. People repeat the gossip without even knowing who they heard it from. What I require now is tangible and very public proof that the rumors are false."

I considered. "I think that will be difficult as well. The only one who could swear to your innocence died fifteen years ago. Or am I to pursue his ghost?"

She laughed again. The sound was enchanting, but then everything about her was enchanting to me. There was a reason Princess Teiko was the most dangerous person in that room. I found myself feeling grateful that the screen was in place as I forced myself to concentrate on the business at hand.

"Nothing so distasteful," she said. "Besides, Kiyoshi died in loving service to my husband the late Emperor, and on the path he himself chose. If he left a ghost behind I would be quite surprised. No, Lord Yamada, Kiyoshi left something far more reliable—a letter. He sent it to me when he was in the north, just before . . . his final battle. It was intended for his favorite and was accompanied by a second letter for me."

I frowned. "Why didn't he send this letter to the lady directly?"

She sighed then. "Lord Yamada, are you a donkey after all? He couldn't very well do so without compromising her. My friendship with Kiyoshi was well known; no one would think twice if I received a letter from him, in those days. In his favorite's case the situation was quite different. You know the penalty for a Lady of the Court who takes a lover openly."

I bowed again. I did know, and vividly. Banishment, or worse. Yet for someone born for the Court and knowing no other life, there probably was nothing worse. "Then clearly we need to acquire this letter. If it still exists, I imagine the lady in question will be reluctant to part with it."

"The letter was never delivered to her." Teiko raised her hand to silence me before I even began. "Do not think so ill of me, Lord Yamada. News of Kiyoshi's death reached us months before his letter did. By then my husband had given the wretched girl in marriage to the *daimyo* of a western province as reward for some service or other, so her romantic history is no longer at issue. Since Kiyoshi's letter was not intended for me I never opened it. I should have destroyed it, I know, but I could not."

"Perhaps foolish, but potentially fortunate. Yet I presume there is a problem still or I would not be here."

"The letter is missing, Lord Yamada. Without it I have no hope of saving my reputation and my son's future from the crush of gossip."

I let out a breath. "When did you notice the letter was stolen?"

"Lord Sentaro says it disappeared three days ago."

Now I really didn't understand and, judging from the grunt to my immediate right, neither did Kanemore. "What has Lord Sentaro to do with this?"

"He is the Emperor's Minister of Justice. In order to clear my reputation, I had to let him know of the letter's existence and arrange a time for the letter to be read and witnessed. He asked that it be given to him for safekeeping. Since he is also Kiyoshi's uncle I couldn't very well refuse."

She said it so calmly, and yet she had just admitted cutting her own throat. "Teiko-hime, as much as this pains me to say, the letter has surely been destroyed."

There was nothing but silence on the other side of the veil for several seconds, then she simply asked, "Oh? What makes you think so?"

I glanced at Kanemore, but there was no help from that direction. He looked as confused as I felt.

"Your pardon, Highness, but it's my understanding that the Fujiwara have their own candidate for the throne. As a member of that family, it is in Lord Sentaro's interest that the letter never resurface."

"Lord Sentaro is perhaps overly ambitious," Teiko said, and there was a more than hint of winter ice in her voice. "But he is also an honorable man. He was just here to acquaint me with the progress of the search. I believe him when he says the letter was stolen; I have less confidence in his ability to recover it. Lord Yamada, will you help me or not?"

I bowed again and made the only answer I could. "If it lies within my power, I will find that letter for you."

"THAT," SAID KANEMORE later after we passed through the eastern gate, "was very strange."

The man, besides his martial prowess, had quite a gift for understatement. "You didn't know about the letter?"

"Teiko never mentioned it before, though it doesn't surprise me. Yet . . ."

"The business with the Minister of Justice does surprise you, yes?"

He looked at me. "Since my sister trusts you I will speak plainly. Lord Sentaro is Chancellor Yorimichi's primary agent in the Fujiwara opposition to Takahito. If I had been in Lord Sentaro's place I would have destroyed that letter the moment it fell into my hands and danced a tribute to the gods of luck while it burned."

I rubbed my chin. "Yet Teiko-hime is convinced that the letter was not destroyed."

Kanemore grunted again. "Over the years I've gone where my Emperor and his government have required. My sister, on the other hand, knows no world other than the Imperial Court. If Teiko were a *koi*, the Court would be her pond, if you take my meaning. So why would something that is immediately obvious to us both be so unclear to her?"

"Perhaps we're the ones who aren't clear," I said. "Let's assume for the moment that your sister is right and that the letter was simply stolen. That would mean that Lord Sentaro had a good reason for not destroying it in the first place."

"That makes sense. Yet I'm having some difficulty imagining that reason," Kanemore admitted.

"As am I."

I looked around. Our path paralleled the river Kamo for a time, then turned south-west. Despite the lateness of the hour there were a few people on the road, apparently all in a hurry to reach their destinations. Demons were about at this time of night, and everyone's hurry and wariness was understandable. Kanemore and I were the only ones walking at a normal pace by the light of the setting moon.

"Your escort duties must be over by now and, as I'm sure you know, I'm used to moving about the city on my own," I said.

Kanemore looked a little uncomfortable. "It was Teiko's request. I know you can take care of yourself under most circumstances," Kanemore said, and it almost sounded like a compliment, "But if someone did steal the letter, they obviously would not want it found, and your audience with my sister will not be a secret. Sentaro himself saw you, for one."

"I didn't think he recognized me."

"I would not depend on that," Kanemore said drily. "The man forgets nothing. His enemies, doubly so."

"You flatter me. I was no threat to him, no matter how I might have wished otherwise."

"Why did you resign your position and leave the Court? If I may be so impolite as to ask. It could not have been easy to secure the appointment in the first place."

I had no doubt he'd already heard the story from Teiko, but I didn't mind repeating events as I remembered them.

"Your sister was kind to me, in those early days. Of course there would be those at Court who chose to misinterpret her interest. I had become a potential embarrassment to Princess Teiko, as Lord Sentaro delighted in making known to me."

"Meaning he would have made certain of it," Kanemore said. "I wondered."

I shrugged. "I made my choice. Destiny is neither cruel nor kind. So. Kanemore-san, I've answered a personal question of yours. Now I must ask one of you: what are you afraid of?"

"Death," he said immediately, "I've never let that fear prevent me from doing what I must, but the fear remains."

"That just means you're not a fool, which I already knew. So, you fear death. Do you fear things that are already dead?"

"No . . . well, not especially," he said, though he didn't sound completely convincing or convinced. "Why do you ask?"

"Because I'm going to need help. If the letter is in the Imperial Compound, it's beyond even your reach. Searching would be both dangerous and time-consuming."

"Certainly," Kanemore agreed. "Yet what's the alternative?"

"The 'help' I spoke of. We're going to need several measures of uncooked rice."

He frowned. "I know where such can be had. Are you hungry?"

"No. But I can assure you that my informant is."

About an hour later we passed through Rashomon, the south-west gate. There was no one about at this hour. The south-west exit of the city, like the north-east, was not a fortunate direction; as the priests often said, these were the directions from which both demons and trouble in general could enter the city. I sometimes wondered why anyone bothered to build gates at such places, since it seemed to be asking for trouble, yet I supposed the demands of roads and travelers outweighed the risks. Even so, the most hardened *bushi* would not accept a night watch at the Rasha Gate.

The bridge I sought was part of a ruined family compound just outside the city proper, now marked by a broken down wall and the remnants of a garden. In another place I would have thought this the aftermath of a war, but not here. Still, death often led to the abandonment of a home; no doubt this family had transferred their fortunes elsewhere and allowed this place to go to ruin. Wasteful, but not unusual.

The compound was still in darkness, but there was a glow in the east; dawn was coming. I hurried through the ruins while Kanemore kept pace with me, his hand on his sword. There were vines growing on the stone bridge on the far side of the garden, but it was still intact and passable, giving an easy path over the wide stream beneath it. Not that crossing the stream was the issue. I pulled out one of the small bags of uncooked rice that Kanemore had supplied and opened it to let the scent drift freely on the night breezes.

The red lantern appeared almost instantly. It floated over the curve of the bridge as if carried by someone invisible, but that wasn't really the case—the lantern carried itself. Its one glowing eye opened, and then its mouth.

I hadn't spoken to the ghost in some time, and perhaps I was misremembering, but it seemed much bigger than it had been on our first meeting. Still, that wasn't what caught my immediate attention: it was the long, pointed teeth.

Seita did not have teeth.

"Lord Yamada, drop!"

I didn't question or hesitate but threw myself flat on the ground just as the lantern surged forward and its mouth changed into a gaping maw. A shadow loomed over me and then there was a flash of silver in the poor light. The lantern shrieked and then dissolved in a flare of light as if burning to ashes from within. I looked up to see the neatly sliced open corpse of a *youkai* lying a few feet away from me. The thing was ugly, even for a monster. A full eight feet tall and most of that consisting of mouth. The thing already stank like a cesspit, and in another moment it dissolved into black sludge and then vanished. I saw what looked like a scrap of paper fluttering on a weed before it blew away into the darkness.

Where did the creature go?

I didn't have time to ponder; another lantern appeared on the bridge and Kanemore made ready, but I got to my feet quickly. "Stop. It's all right."

And so it was. Seita came gliding over the bridge, with his one eye cautiously watching the pair of us. Now I recognized the tear in the paper near his base and his generally tatty appearance, things that had been missing from the imposter's disguise.

"Thank you for ridding me of that unpleasant fellow," he said, "but don't think for a moment that will warrant a discount."

Kanemore just stared at the ghost for a moment, then glanced at me, but I indicated silence. "Seita-san, you at least owe me an explanation for allowing your patron to walk into an ambush. How long has that thing been here?"

I think Seita tried to shrug, but that's hard to do when your usual manifestation is a red paper lantern with one eye and one mouth and no arms, legs, or shoulders. "A day or so. Damned impertinent of it to usurp my bridge, but it was strong and I couldn't make it leave. I think it was waiting on someone. You, perhaps?"

"Perhaps? Almost certainly, yet that doesn't concern me now. I need your services."

"So I assumed," said the lantern. "What do you want to know?"

"A letter was stolen from the Imperial Compound three days ago. I need to know who took it and where that letter is now. It bears the scent of Fujiwara no Kiyoshi, among others."

Kanemore could remain silent no more. He leaned close and whispered, "Can this thing be trusted?"

"That 'thing' remark raises the price," Seita said. "Four bowls."

"I apologize on behalf of my companion. Two now," I countered. "Two more when the information is delivered. Bring the answer by tomorrow night and I'll add an extra bowl."

The lantern grinned very broadly. "Then you can produce five bowls of uncooked rice right now. I have your answer."

That surprised me. I'd expected at least a day's delay. "Seita-san, I know you're good or I wouldn't have come to you first, but how could you possibly know about the letter already? Were the *rei* involved?"

He looked a little insulted. "Lord Yamada, we ghosts have higher concerns than petty theft. This was the work of *shikigami*. The fact that they were about in the first place caught my attention, but I do not know who sent them. That is a separate question and won't be answered so quickly or easily."

"Time is short. I'll settle for the location of the letter."

Seita gave us directions to where the letter was hidden. We left the rice in small bags, with chopsticks thrust upright through the openings as proper for an offering to the dead. I offered a quick prayer for Seita's soul, but we didn't stay to watch; I'd seen the ghost consume an offering before and it was . . . unsettling.

"Can that thing be trusted?" Kanemore repeated when we were out of earshot of the bridge, "and what is this *shikigami* it was referring to?"

"As for trusting Seita, we shall soon know. That thing you killed at the bridge was a *shikigami,* and it's very strange to encounter one here. Thank you, by the way. I owe you my life."

Kanemore grunted. "My duty served, though you are quite welcome. Still, you make deals with ghosts, and encountering a simple monster is strange?"

"A *shikigami* is not a monster, simple or otherwise. A *youkai* is its own creature and has its own volition, nasty and evil though that may be. A shikigami is a created thing; it has no will of its own, only that of the one who created it."

He frowned. "Are you speaking of sorcery?"

"Yes," I said. "And of a high order. I should have realized when the thing disappeared. A monster or demon is a physical creature and, when slain, leaves a corpse like you or I would. A *shikigami* almost literally has no separate existence. When its purpose is served or its physical form too badly damaged, it simply disappears. At most it might leave a scrap of paper or some element of what was used to create it."

"So one of these artificial servants acquired the letter and hid it in the Rasha Gate. Fortunate, since that's on our way back into the city."

"Very fortunate."

Kanemore glanced at me. "You seem troubled. Do you doubt the ghost's information?"

"Say rather I'm pondering something I don't understand. There were rumors that Lord Sentaro dabbled in Chinese magic, even when I was at Court. Yet why would he choose *shikigami* to spirit the letter away? It was in his possession to begin with; removing it and making that removal seem like theft would be simple enough to arrange without resorting to such means."

Kanemore shrugged. "I've heard these rumors as well, but I gave them no credence. Even so, it is the letter that concerns me, not the workings of Lord Sentaro's twisted mind."

Concentrating on the matter at hand seemed a very sensible suggestion, and I abandoned my musings as we approached the deserted Rasha Gate. At least, it had seemed deserted when we passed through it earlier that evening. I was not so certain of that now. I rather regretted having to leave my sword behind for my audience with Teiko-hime, but I still had my dagger, and I made certain it was loose in its sheath.

The gate structure loomed above us. We checked around the base as far as we could but found no obvious hiding places. Now and then I heard a faint rustle, like someone winding and unwinding a scroll. Kanemore was testing the looseness of a stone on the west side of the gate. I motioned him to be still and listened more closely. After a few moments the sound came again.

From above.

This time Kanemore heard it, too. He put his sword aside in favor of his own long dagger, which he clenched in his teeth like a Chinese pirate as he climbed the wooden beams and cross-bars that supported the gate. I quickly followed his example, or as quickly as I could manage. Kanemore climbed like a monkey, whereas I was not quite so nimble. Still, I was only a few seconds behind him when he reached the gap between the gate frame and the elaborate roof.

"Goji-san, they are here!"

I didn't have to ask who "they" were. The first of the *shikigami* plummeted past, missing me by inches before it dissolved. If the body survived long enough to strike the flagstones, I never heard it, but then I wasn't listening. I hauled myself over the top beam and landed in a crouch.

I needn't have bothered; the gap under the roof was quite tall enough for me to stand. Kanemore had two other lumbering *shikigami* at bay, but a third moved to attack him from the rear. It was different from the other two. Snakelike, it slithered across the floor, fangs bared and its one yellow eye fixed on Kanemore's naked heel.

I was too far away.

"Behind you!"

I threw myself forward and buried my dagger in the creature near the tip of its tail, which was all I could reach. Even there the thing was as thick as my arm, but I felt the dagger pierce the tail completely and bury its tip in the wood beneath it. My attack barely slowed the creature; there was a sound like the tearing of paper as it ripped itself loose from my blade to get at Kanemore.

Kanemore glanced behind him and to my surprise took one step backward. Just as the creature's fangs reached for him he very swiftly lifted his left foot, pointed the heel, and thrust it down on the creature's neck just behind the head. There was a snap! like the breaking of a green twig and the serpent began to dissolve. In that instant the other two *shikigami* seized the chance and attacked, like their companion, in utter silence.

"Look out!"

I could have saved my breath. Kanemore's dagger blade was already a blur of motion, criss-crossing the space in front of him like a swarm of wasps. Even if the other two creatures intended to scream they had no time before they, too, dissolved into the oblivion from whence they came. Kanemore was barely breathing hard.

"Remind me to never fight on any side of a battle opposite yourself," I said as I got back off the floor.

"One doesn't always get to choose one's battles," Kanemore said drily, "In any case it seems you've returned the favor for my earlier rescue, so we may call our accounts settled in that regard."

I picked up a ragged bit of mulberry paper, apparently all that remained of our recent foes. There were a few carefully printed kanji, but they were faded and impossible to read. "Fine quality. These servitors were expensive."

"And futile, if we assume they were guarding something of value."

It didn't take long to find what we were searching for; I located a small pottery jar hidden in a mortise on one of the beams and broke it open with my dagger hilt. A scroll lay within. It was tied with silk strings and the strings' ends in turn were pressed together and sealed with beeswax impressed with the Fujiwara *mon*. I examined it closely as Kanemore looked on.

"Your sister will have to confirm this," I said at last, "but this does appear to be the missing letter."

The relief on the man's face was almost painful to see. "And now I am in your debt again, Lord Yamada. It has been a long night and we are both weary, yet I do not think that this can wait. Let us return to the Palace now; it will be stirring by the time we arrive."

The lack of sleep plus the sudden stress of the fight, now relieved, had left me feeling as wrung out as a washerwoman's towel. I knew Kanemore must have been nearly as bad off, even though from his serene demeanor I'd have thought he could take on another half dozen *shikigami* without breaking a sweat.

"We'll go directly," I said, "but I'm going to need a breath or two before I try that climb again. You could do with some rest yourself."

He nodded and only then allowed himself to sit down in that now empty place. "I am too tired to argue, so you must be right."

We greeted the dawn like two roof-dragons from the top of the Rasha Gate and then made our way back into the city. The Imperial Compound was already alive with activity by then, but Kanemore didn't bother with circuitous routes. We proceeded directly to Teiko-hime's manor and at the fastest speed decorum allowed. We probably attracted more attention than we wanted to, but Kanemore was in no mood for more delays.

Neither was I, truth to tell, but Teiko-hime had not yet risen, and I had to wait on the veranda while Kanemore acquainted his sister with the news. I waited. And I waited. I was starting to feel a little insulted by the time Kanemore finally reappeared. But he did not come from the house; he came hurrying through the garden path, and his face . . . well, I hope I never see that expression again on a human being.

"I am truly sorry . . . to have kept you waiting, Lord Yamada. This . . . I was to give you this . . ."

"This" was a heavy pouch of quilted silk. Inside were half a dozen small cylinders of pure gold. I take pride in the fact that I only stared at them for a moment or two.

"Kanemore-san, what has happened?"

"I cannot . . ."

"I think you can. I think I will have to insist."

His eyes did recover a little of their old fire then, but it quickly died away. "My sister was adamant that we deal with the matter at once. I escorted her to the Ministry of Justice as she insisted. I guess the burden of waiting had been too much; she did not even give me time to fetch you . . . oh, how could she be so reckless?"

I felt my spirit grow cold, and my own voice sounded lifeless in my ears. "The letter was read at the Ministry? Without knowing its contents?"

"Normally these matters take weeks, but considering what had happened to the letter under his care, Lord Sentaro couldn't very well refuse Teiko's demand for an audience. I must say in his favor that he tried to dissuade her, but she insisted he read it before the court. We all heard, we all saw . . ."

I put my hands on his shoulders, but I'm not even sure he noticed. "Kanemore?"

He did look at me then, and he recited a poem:

> "The Wisteria pines
> alone in desolation,
> without the bright Peony."

I could hardly believe what I was hearing. Three lines of an incomplete *tanka*. Like the three that Teiko had used to draw me back to court, these three in turn had damned her. Wisteria was of course a reference to the Fujiwara family crest, and "Peony" had been Teiko's nickname at Court since the age of seven. Clearly the poem had been hers to complete, and return to Kiyoshi. The imagery and tone were clear, too. There was no one who could hear those words and doubt that Kiyoshi and Teiko had been lovers. For any woman at court it would have been indiscreet; for an Imperial Wife it amounted to treason.

"What is to be done?" I asked.

"My sister is stripped of her titles and all Court honors. She will be confined and then banished . . ." and here Kanemore's strength failed him, and it was several heartbeats before he could finish. "Exiled. To the northern coast at Suma."

Say, rather, to the ends of the earth. It was little short of an execution.

"Surely there is . . ."

"Nothing, Goji san. In our ignorance we have done more than enough. The writ is sealed."

He left me there to find my own way out of the compound. It was a long time before I bothered to try.

IT TOOK LONGER TO SETTLE MY AFFAIRS in Kyoto than I'd hoped, but the gold meant that the matter would be merely difficult, not impossible. The Widow Tamahara was, perhaps, one of the very few people genuinely sorry to see me leave. I sold what remained of my belongings and kept only what I could carry, along with my new traveling clothes, my sword, and the balance of the gold, which was still quite substantial.

On the appointed day, I was ready. Teiko's party emerged from the eastern gate of the compound through the entrance still guarded by the Taira. Yet *bushi* of the Minamoto Clan formed the bulk of her escort. Kanemore was with them, as I knew he would be. His eyes were sad but he held his head high.

Normally a lady of Teiko's birth would have traveled in a covered ox cart, hidden from curious eyes, but now she walked, wearing the plain traveling clothes that she'd used to bring that first message in disguise, completing her disgrace. Still, I'd recognized her then as I did now. When the somber procession had moved a discreet distance down the road, I fell in behind, just another traveler on the northern road.

I was a little surprised when the party took the northeast road toward Lake Biwa, but I was able to learn from an attendant that Teiko wished to make a pilgrimage to the sacred lake before beginning her new life at Suma. Since it was only slightly out of the way, her escort had seen no reason to object. Neither did I, for that matter, since I was determined to follow regardless. The mountains surrounding the lake slowed the procession's progress and it took three days to get there. When the party made camp on the evening of the third day, I did the same nearby.

I wasn't terribly surprised to find Kanemore looming over me and my small fire within a very short time.

"I was just making tea, Kanemore-san. Would you care for some?"

He didn't meet my gaze. "My sister has instructed me to tell you to go home."

"I have no home."

"In which case I am instructed to tell you to go someplace else. I should warn you that, should you reply that where you are now is 'someplace else,' she has requested that I beat you senseless, but with affection."

I nodded. "Anticipated my response. That's the Teiko I always knew. So. Are you also instructed to kill me if I refuse your sister's order?"

Now he did look me squarely in the eye. "If killing you would atone for my own foolishness," Kanemore said, "I'd do it in a heartbeat. Yet I cannot blame you for what happened, try as I might. You only did as my sister bid."

"As did you," I pointed out.

He managed a weak smile. "Even so, we still share some of the responsibility for what happened. I could not prevent her disgrace, so I am determined to share it."

"That is my wish as well," I said.

"You have no—" he began but did not finish.

"Exactly. My failure gives me that right, if nothing else does. Now consider: what about Prince Takahito? Your nephew? Where is he?"

"At Court. Takahito of course asked to accompany his mother, but permission was refused."

"Indeed. And now he remains at Court surrounded by his enemies. Who will look after him?"

"Do not lecture me on my duties! Who then, shall look after my sister? These men are to escort her to Suma. They will not remain and protect her afterward."

I waved that aside. "I well understand the burden of conflicting obligations. Your instinct for love and loyalty is to protect both your sister and her son. How will you accomplish this when they are practically on opposite ends of the earth? Which path would Teiko choose for you?"

His face reddened slightly; I could tell that the subject had already come up. Repeatedly, if I knew Teiko.

"We've spoken our minds plainly to each other in the past, Kanemore-san, and I will do the same now: your sister is going to a place where life is harsh and she will be forced to make her own way. Despite her great gifts, neither she nor her two charming and loyal attendants have the vaguest idea of how to survive outside the shelter of the Imperial Court. I do."

Kanemore didn't say anything for several long moments. "My sister is the daughter of an Emperor. She was born to be the mother of an Emperor," he said finally.

"If that were the case, then it would still be so," I said. "Life does not always meet our expectations, but that should not prevent us from seeking what happiness we can."

"You are unworthy of Princess Teiko," Kanemore said, expressionless, "and I say that as someone who holds you in high regard. Yet you are also right. For what little it may be worth, I will speak to my sister."

"When I finish my tea," I said, "and with your sister's permission, so will I."

Teiko agreed to see me, perhaps because she saw no good way to prevent it. After fifteen years I did not care what her reasons might be. The fact that she did agree was enough.

I found her sitting by herself in a small clearing. She gazed out at a lovely view of Lake Biwa beyond her. The sun had dipped just below the mountains ringing the lake and the water had turned a deep azure. Teiko's escort was present but out of earshot, as were both of her attendants. She held an empty teacup; the rice cakes beside her looked hardly touched. She still wore her *boshi,* but the veil was pulled back now to reveal her face. It was a gift, I knew, and I was grateful.

I can't say that she hadn't changed at all in fifteen years: there might have been one or two gray strands among the glossy black of her hair, perhaps a line or two on her face. I can say that the changes didn't matter. She was and remained beautiful. She looked up and smiled at me a little wistfully as I kneeled not quite in front of her but a little to the side, so as not to spoil her view.

"So. Have you come to lecture me on my recklessness as well? Please yourself, but be warned: my brother has worried the topic to exhaustion."

"Your brother thinks only of you. Yet what's done cannot be undone."

"Life is uncertain in all regards," Teiko said very seriously, then she managed a smile and waved a hand at the vast stretch of water nearby. "An appropriate setting, don't you think? I must look like a fisherman's wife now. What shall I do at Suma, Lord Yamada? Go bare-breasted like the abalone maidens and dive for shells? Learn to gather seaweed to make salt, like those two lovers of the exiled poet? Can you imagine me, hair loose and legs bared, gleaning the shore?"

"I can easily so imagine," I said.

She sighed. "Then your imagination is better than mine. I am a worthless creature now."

"That is not possible."

She smiled at me. There were dimples in her cheeks. "You are kind, Goji-san. I'm glad that the years have not changed this about you."

She offered me a cup of tea from the small pot nearby, but I declined. She poured herself another while I pondered yet again the best way to frame one of the questions that had been troubling me. I finally decided that there simply was no good way, if I chose to ask.

"No lectures, Teiko-hime, but I must ask about the letter."

Her expression was unreadable. "Just 'Teiko,' please. Especially now. So. You're curious about Kiyoshi's letter, of course. That poem was unexpected."

"You weren't Kiyoshi's lover," I said.

Teiko smiled a little wistfully. "You know I was not," she said. "But at the moment there is no explanation I can offer you."

"I'm not asking for one. What's done is done."

She sipped her tea. "Many things have been done, Goji-san. There is more to come, whatever our place in the order of events may be. Speaking of which, my brother in his own delicate way hints that there is another matter you wish to speak to me about."

"I am going to Suma," I said.

"That is noble, but pointless. Your life is in Kyoto."

"My life is as and where it is fated to be, but still I am going to Suma," I repeated. "Do you require me to say why?"

She actually blushed then, but it did not last. "You say that what's done cannot be undone. Perhaps that is true, but you do not yet know all that has been done. As at our last meeting, I must ask you to listen to me, and then decide what you will or will not do. Please?"

"I am listening."

"You left Court because people were starting to talk about us."

"Yes. When the Emperor bestowed his favor on you, Lord Sentaro—"

"Did no more or less than what I asked him to do."

For a little while I forgot to breathe. I idly wondered, somewhere above the roar in my ears, whether I ever would again. "What you . . . ?"

"It's unforgivable, I know, but I was not much more than a child, and both foolish and afraid. Once I had been chosen by the former Emperor there could be nothing between us nor even the rumor of such. I knew that you would do what you did, to protect my reputation."

"I would have done anything," I said, "if you had asked me."

"That is the true shame I have borne these past fifteen years," Teiko said softly. "I let this person you detest be the one to break your heart because I lacked the courage to do it myself. I heard later that he took undue pleasure in this. I must bear the blame for that also."

Fifteen years. I could feel the weight of every single one of them on my shoulders. "Why are you telling me this now?"

"Because I needed to tell you," she said. "More importantly, you needed to hear it, and know just how unworthy I am of your regard before you choose to throw your life away after mine. Or do you still wish to speak to me of things that cannot be undone?"

Perhaps it was a test. Perhaps it was a challenge. Perhaps it was the simple truth. I only knew what remained true for me. "My decision is not altered," I said. "I would like to know yours."

There were tears in her dark eyes now. "There are things we may not speak of, even now. If it is our fate to reach Suma together, speak to me then and I will answer you."

THE DEMONS WERE TEASING ME in my dreams. At least, so I believe. In a vision I saw myself and Teiko on the beach at Suma. The land was desolate but the sea was beautiful and it met most of our needs. We walked on its shore. Teiko was laughing. It was the most exquisite of sounds, at least until she started laughing at me, and it wasn't Teiko at all but some ogress with Teiko's smile.

"What have you done with Teiko?" I demanded, but the demon just mocked me. I drew my sword but the blade was rusted and useless; it would not cut. I looked around frantically at the sea but there was nothing but gigantic waves, one after another racing toward the beach. Sailing against them was one small boat. I could see Teiko there, her back turned to me, sailing away. I ignored the demon and chased after her, but the sea drove me back again and again until her boat was swallowed by the attacking sea.

"Yamada!"

Someone was calling me. The ogress? I did not care. Teiko was gone.

"Lord Yamada!"

I was shaken violently awake. Kanemore kneeled beside my blankets, looking frantic.

"What-what's happened?" I said, trying to shake off the nightmare.

"My sister is missing! Help us search!"

I was awake now. "But...how? Her guards worked in paired shifts!"

Kanemore looked disgusted as I scrambled to my feet. "The fools swear they never took their eyes off of her, that Teiko and her maids

153

were sleeping peacefully, and then suddenly Teiko wasn't there! Nonsense. They must have been playing *Go* or some such rot. I'll have their heads for this!"

"We'll need their heads to help us search. She could not have gotten far. Go ahead. I will catch up."

Kanemore ran through the camp with me not far behind, but when I came to the place where I knew Teiko and her ladies had been sleeping, I paused. The two maidservants were huddled together looking confused and frightened, but I ignored them. There was a small screen for some privacy, but no way that Teiko could have left the spot without one of the guards seeing her. I looked in and found her bedding undisturbed, but empty. I pulled her coverlet aside and found a crumpled piece of paper.

"She's up there!"

I heard Kanemore call to me from the shore of the lake and I raced to join him. Just a little further down the shoreline was a place where the mountains dropped sheer to the water. On the very edge of that high promontory stood a small figure dressed in flowing white, as for a funeral.

"Teiko, no!"

I started to shout a warning to Kanemore, but he was already sprinting ahead looking for the quickest route up the slope and I followed hot on his heels, but it was far too late. In full sight of both of us, Teiko calmly stepped off the edge.

With her broad sleeves fluttering like the wings of a butterfly, one could almost imagine her fall would be softened, but the sound of her body striking the water carried across the lake like the crack of ice breaking on the Kamo River in spring.

One could also imagine, first hope having failed, that there would be nothing in the water to find except, perhaps, a few scraps of paper. One tried very hard to hold on to this hope and only relented when the fishermen from a nearby village helped us locate and remove the cold, broken body of former Princess Teiko from the deep dark waters of the sacred lake.

MOON VIEWING AT SHIJO BRIDGE

THE MOON WAS HIGH AGAIN and cast its reflection on the river. The modest funeral rites for Teiko were well under way, and once more I stood on the Shijo bridge, staring down at the moon and the dark water beneath it. Again I saw the *onibi* flare out on the water. I knew that, if I waited long enough, the ghost lights would be followed by the graceful spirits of women who had drowned themselves for love.

I had seen them before; they would soon appear just above the water in solemn procession, drifting a bit as if with the currents below. The legend was that men unfortunate enough to stare at them too closely would drown themselves out of love as well. I wondered if I, too, before I drowned myself in turn, might see one small figure with the face of Princess Teiko.

I didn't know what Kanemore intended when he appeared beside me on the bridge. At that moment I did not care. I simply gazed at the moon's reflection and waited for whatever might come.

He placed a small scroll on the railing in front of me. "This is for you, Lord Yamada," he said formally.

I frowned. "What is it?"

"A letter," he said. "From my sister. I have already opened and read the one intended for me."

I didn't move or touch the letter. "Meticulous. She had this planned before we even left the capital. She never intended to go to Suma."

"The shame of her disgrace was too much to bear," he said. He sounded about as convinced as I was.

"I rather doubt," I said, "that there was anything your sister could not bear, at need."

"Then why did she do it?" he asked softly.

A simple question that covered so much, and yet at the moment I didn't have a clear answer. I think I understood more of what had happened than Kanemore did, but the "why" of it all was as big a mystery to me as it was to him. I shared the one thing I thought I knew for certain.

"I've only been able to think of one clear reason. I have been drinking for the past day or so to see if I could perhaps forget that reason."

"Have you succeeded?"

155

"No."

He leaned against the rail with me. Out on the water, the mists were forming into the likenesses of young women. Kanemore glanced at them nervously. "Then share that reason with me. Preferably someplace else."

I smiled. "You must drink with me then."

"If needs must then let's get to it."

I picked up Teiko's letter and we left the ghostly women behind. From there we went to the Widow Tamahara's establishment, as it was the closest. Usually it was filled with drinking *samuru*, but for the moment all was quiet. We found an unused table, and Kanemore ordered *saké*, which the smiling Widow Tamahara delivered personally. Kanemore poured out two generous measures, and we drank in companionable silence until Kanemore could stand it no longer. "So. What is the answer you drink to forget?" he asked, as he topped off his cup and my own. "Why did Teiko kill herself?"

"The only obvious and immediate answer is that, upon her death, you would be free to return to the capital and look after Takahito."

He frowned. "But you were going to be with her."

I sighed deeply. "Which did not alter her plans in the slightest, as apparently I was not an acceptable alternative."

"That is a very sad thing to bear," he said after a while, "and also very odd. I know my sister was fond of you."

"Maybe. And yet . . ."

"Yet what?"

I took a deep breath and then an even deeper drink. "And yet there is a voice deep in my brain that keeps shouting that I am a complete and utter ass, that I do not understand anything, and the reason Teiko killed herself had nothing to do with me. Try as I might, drink as I might, that troublesome fellow only shouts louder."

"You have suffered greatly because of my family," Kanemore said. "And I know that I have no right to ask more of you. Yet it was my sister's wish that you read her letter. Will you grant her last request?"

I didn't answer right away. "I once asked what you were afraid of, Kanemore-san. I think it only fair to tell you what I am afraid of. I am very afraid of what Princess Teiko will say to me now."

Yet there was never really any question of refusing. I took out the letter. After hesitating as long as I dared I broke the seal. In doing so I discovered that, when I feared the very worst, I had shown entirely too little imagination.

And, yes, I was in fact a complete and utter ass.

The letter was very short, and this is most of what it said:

> "The crane flies above
> The lake's clear shining surface.
> White feathers glisten,
> Made pure by sacred water,
> As the poet's book was cleansed."

At the end of the poem she had simply written: "Forgive me—Teiko."

I thought, perhaps, if one day I was able to forgive myself, maybe then I would find the strength to forgive Teiko. Not this day, but that didn't matter. I had other business. I put the letter away.

"*Kampai*, Kanemore-san. Let us finish this jar of fine *saké*."

I knew Kanemore was deeply curious about the letter but too polite to ask, for which I was grateful. He hefted the container and frowned. "It is almost empty. I'll order another."

"No, my friend, for this is all we will drink tonight. From here we will visit the baths, and then go to sleep, for tomorrow our heads must be clear."

"Why? What happens tomorrow?"

"Tomorrow we restore your sister's honor."

THE IMPERIAL COURT was composed more of tradition and ritual than people. Everything in its time, everything done precisely so. Yet it was astonishing to me how quickly matters could unfold, given the right impetus.

Kanemore kneeled beside me in the hall where justice, or at least Fujiwara no Sentaro's version of it, was dispensed. The Minister had not yet taken his place on the dais, but my attention was on a curtained alcove on the far side of the dais. I knew I had seen that curtain move. I leaned over and whispered to Kanemore.

"His Majesty Reizei is present, I hope?"

"I believe so, accompanied by Chancellor Yorimichi I expect. He will not show himself, of course."

Of course. The acknowledged presence of the Emperor in these proceedings was against form, but that didn't matter. He was here, and everyone knew it. I was almost certain he would be, once word reached him. Kanemore, through another relative in close attendance on His Majesty, made sure that word did so reach him. I think Lord Sentaro convened in such haste as a way to prevent that eventuality, but in this he was disappointed. He entered now, looking both grave and more than a little puzzled.

Kanemore leaned close, "I've sent a servant for a bucket of water, as you requested. I hope you know what you're doing."

Kanemore was obviously apprehensive. Under the circumstances I did not blame him. Yet I was perfectly calm. I claimed no measure of courage greater than Kanemore's; I simply had the distinct advantage that I no longer cared what happened to me.

"What is this matter you have brought before the Imperial Ministry?" Lord Sentaro demanded from the dais.

"I am here to remove the unjust stain on the honor of the late Princess Teiko, daughter of the Emperor Sanjo, Imperial Consort to the late Emperor Suzaku II," I said, clearly and with more than enough volume to carry my words throughout the room.

There was an immediate murmur of voices from the clerks, minor judges, members of the Court, and attendants present. Lord Sentaro glared for silence until the voices subsided.

"This unfortunate matter has already been settled. Lady Teiko was identified by my nephew, who died a hero's death in Mutsu province. Consider your words carefully, Lord Yamada."

"I choose my words with utmost care, Your Excellency. Your nephew was indeed a hero and brought honor to the Fujiwara family. He did not, however, name Princess Teiko as his lover. This I will prove."

Lord Sentaro motioned me closer, and when he leaned down his words were for me alone. "Shall I have cause to embarrass you a second time, Lord Yamada?"

Up until that point I almost felt sorry for the man, but no longer. Now my blade, so to speak, was drawn. "We shall soon see, Lord Minister of Justice. May I examine the letter?"

He indicated assent and I returned to my place as Lord Sentaro's stentorian voice boomed across the room. "Produce my nephew's letter so that Lord Yamada may examine it and see what everyone knows is plainly written there."

A few snickers blossomed like weeds here and there in the courtroom despite the seriousness of the proceedings, but I ignored them. A waiting clerk hurried up, bowed low, and handed me the letter in question. I unrolled it and then signaled Kanemore who in turn signaled someone waiting at the back of the room. A young man in Taira livery came hurrying up with a bucket of clear water, placed it beside me, and then withdrew.

Lord Sentaro frowned. "Lord Yamada, did you neglect to wash your face this morning?"

More laughter. I was examining the poem closely and did not bother to look up. "The water is indeed to wash away a stain, Lord Sentaro. Not, however, one of mine."

The letter was not very long, and mostly spoke of the things Kiyoshi had seen and the hardships of the camp. The poem actually came after his personal seal. I unrolled the letter in its entirety, no more than the length of my forearm, and carefully dipped the paper into the water.

There was consternation in the court. Two guards rushed forward, but one glare from Prince Kanemore made them hesitate, looking to Lord Sentaro for instruction.

"Lady Teiko's sin dishonors us all," Lord Sentaro said, and his voice was pure sweet reason, "but the letter has been witnessed by hundreds. Destroying it will change nothing."

"I am not destroying the letter, Lord Sentaro. I am merely cleansing it. As the poet Ono no Komachi did in our great grandsires' time."

Too late the fool understood. A hundred years before, a Lady of the Court had been accused by an enemy of copying a poem from an old book and presenting the piece as her own work. She faced her accuser and washed the book in question in clear water, just as I was doing now, and with the same result. I held the letter up high for all to see. Kiyoshi's letter was, of course, perfectly intact.

Except for the poem. That was gone.

More consternation. Lord Sentaro looked as if someone had struck him between the eyes with a very large hammer. I didn't wait for him to recover.

"It is a sad thing," I said, again making certain my voice carried to every corner—and alcove—of the court, "that a mere hundred years after the honored poet Ono no Komachi exposed this simple trick we should be deceived again. The ink in Fujiwara no Kiyoshi's letter is of course untouched, for it has been wedded to this paper for the past fifteen years. Clearly, the poem slandering Princess Teiko was added within the month."

"Are you accusing me—" Lord Sentaro stopped, but it was too late. He himself had made the association; I needed to do little else.

"I accuse no one. I merely state two self-evident facts: That Teiko-hime was innocent, and that whoever wrote the poem accusing her had both access to the letter," and here I paused for emphasis, "and access to a Fujiwara seal. These conclusions are beyond dispute, Excellency. At the present time the identity of the person responsible is of lesser concern."

The man was practically sputtering. "But . . . but she was here! Why did Princess Teiko not speak up? She said nothing!"

I bowed low. "How should innocence answer a lie?"

The murmuring of the witnesses was nearly deafening for a time. It had only just begun to subside when a servant appeared from behind the alcove, hurried up to the dais, and whispered briefly in Lord Sentaro's ear. His face, before this slowly turning a bright pink, now turned ashen gray. Kanemore and I bowed to the court as the official part of the proceedings were hastily declared closed. The proceedings that mattered most, I knew, had just begun.

That evening Kanemore found me once more on Shijo Bridge. The moon was beginning to wane, now past its full beauty, but I still watched its reflection in the water as I waited for the ghosts to appear. Kanemore approached and then leaned against the rail next to me.

"Well?" I asked.

"Teiko's honors and titles are to be posthumously restored," he said. "Lord Sentaro is, at his own expense and at Chancellor Yorimichi's insistence, arranging prayers for her soul at every single temple in Kyoto."

"If you'll pardon my saying so, Kanemore-san, you don't sound happy about it."

"For the memory of my sister, I am," he said. "Yet one could also wish we had discovered this deception soon enough to save her. Still, I will have satisfaction against Lord Sentaro over this, Minister of Justice or no."

I laughed. "No need. Even assuming that the expense of the prayers doesn't ruin him, Lord Sentaro will be digging clams at the beach at Suma or Akashi within a month, or I will be astonished," I said. "It's enough."

"Enough? It was his slander that killed my sister! Though I must ask, while we're on the subject, how did you know?"

I had hoped to spare us both this additional pain, but clearly Kanemore wasn't going to be content with what he had. There was that much of his sister in him.

"Lord Sentaro did not kill your sister, Kanemore-san. We did."

One can never reliably predict a man's reaction to the truth. I thought it quite possible that Kanemore would take my head then and there. I'm not sure what was stopping him, but while he was still staring at me in shock, I recited the poem from his sister's letter. "I trust you get the allusion," I said when I was done.

From the stunned look on the poor man's face it was obvious that he did. "Teiko knew the poem was a forgery? Why didn't she . . . ?"

At that moment Kanemore's expression bore a striking resemblance to Lord Sentaro's earlier in the day. I nodded.

"You understand now. Teiko knew the poem was forged for the obvious reason that she did it herself. She used a carefully chosen ink that matched the original for color but was of poorer quality. I don't know how she acquired the proper seal, but I have no doubt that she did so. It's likely she started the original rumors as well, probably through her maids. We can confirm this, but I see no need."

Kanemore grasped for something, anything. "If Lord Sentaro thought the letter was genuine, that does explain why he didn't destroy it, but it does not explain why he didn't use it himself! Why didn't he accuse Teiko openly?"

"I have no doubt he meant to confront her in private if he'd had the chance, but in court? Why should he? If Takahito was Kiyoshi's son, then the Emperor's heir was a Fujiwara after all, and with Teiko the Dowager Empress under Sentaro's thumb, thanks to that letter. Until that day came he could continue to champion Prince Norihira, but he won no matter who took the throne, or so the fool thought. Teiko was not mistaken when she said Sentaro was searching for the letter: he wanted it back as much as she did."

Kanemore, warrior that he was, continued to fight a lost battle. "Rubbish! Why would Teiko go to such lengths to deliberately dishonor herself?"

I met his gaze. "To make her son Emperor."

Despite my sympathy for Kanemore, I had come too far alone. Now he was going to share my burden whether he liked it or not. I gave him the rest.

"Consider this—so long as the Fujiwara preferred Prince Norihira, Takahito's position remained uncertain. Would the Teiko you knew resign herself to that if there was an alternative? Any alternative?"

Kanemore looked grim. "No. She would not."

I nodded. "Just so. Teiko gave Sentaro possession of the letter solely to show that he could have altered it. Then she likewise arranged for the letter to disappear and for us to find it again. In hindsight I realize that it had all been a little too easy, though not so easy as to arouse immediate suspicion. Those *shikigami* might very well have killed me if I'd been alone, but Teiko sent you to make certain that did not happen. Her attention to detail was really astounding."

Kanemore tried again. "But . . . if this was her plan, then it worked perfectly! Lord Sentaro was humiliated before the Emperor, the Chancellor, the entire Court! His power is diminished! She didn't have to kill herself."

I almost laughed again. "Humiliated? Diminished? Why should Teiko risk so much and settle for so little? With the responsibility for her death laid solely at his feet, Lord Sentaro's power at Court has been broken. The entire Fujiwara clan has taken a blow that will be a long time healing. No one will oppose Prince Takahito's claim to the Throne now, or dare speak ill of your sister in or out of the Imperial Presence. It was Teiko's game, Kanemore-san. She chose the stakes."

Kanemore finally accepted defeat. "Even the *shikigami* ... Goji-san, I swear I did not know."

"I believe you. Teiko understood full well what would have happened if she'd confided in either of us. Yet we can both take comfort in this much— we did not fail your sister. We both performed exactly as she hoped."

Kanemore was silent for a time. When he spoke again he looked at me intently. "I thought my sister's payment was in gold. I was wrong. She paid in revenge."

I grunted. "Lord Sentaro? That was ... satisfying, I admit, but I'd compose a poem praising the beauty of the man's hindquarters and recite it in front of the entire Court tomorrow if that would bring your sister back."

He managed a brief smile then, but his expression quickly turned serious again. "Not Sentaro. I mean you could have simply ignored Teiko's final poem, and her death would have been for nothing and my nephew's ruin complete and final. She offered this to you."

I smiled. "She knew ... Well, say in all fairness that she left the choice to me. Was that a choice at all, Kanemore-san?"

He didn't answer, but then I didn't think there was one. I stood gazing out at the moon's reflection. The charming ghosts were in their procession. I think my neck was extended at the proper angle. The rest, so far as I knew or cared, was up to Kanemore.

I felt his hand on my shoulder. I'm not sure if that was intended to reassure me or steady himself.

"You must drink with me, Goji-san," he said. It wasn't a suggestion.

"I must drink," I said. "With or without you."

We returned to the Widow Tamahara's establishment. I wondered if we would drink to the point of despair and allow ourselves to be swallowed up by the darkness. Or would we survive and go on, as if I had said nothing at all on Shijo Bridge? While we waited for our *saké*, I think I received an answer of sorts as Kanemore's attention wandered elsewhere in the room. He watched the *samuru* laughing and drinking at the other low tables, and his distaste was obvious.

"A sorry lot. Always drinking and whoring and gambling, when they're not killing each other." Kanemore sighed deeply and continued, "and yet they are the future."

I frowned. "These louts? What makes you think so?"

Our *saké* arrived and Kanemore poured. "Think? No, Goji-san—I know. Year by year the power and wealth of the provincial *daimyos* increases, and their private armies are filled with these *samurai*," he said, now using the more common corrupted word, "whose loyalties are to their lords and not the Emperor. They are the reason upstarts like the Abe Clan are able to create so much trouble in the first place."

"Dark days are ahead if you are correct."

Kanemore raised his cup. "Dark days are behind as well."

So. It seemed we had chosen to live, and in my heart I hoped that, at least for a while, things might get better. To that end I drank, and as the evening progressed I used the *saké* to convince myself that all the things I needed desperately to believe were really true.

I told myself that Teiko was right to do as she did. That it wasn't just family scheming or royal ambition. That Kanemore and I, though mostly unaware, had helped her to accomplish a good thing, a noble thing, and time would prove it so. First, in the continued decline of the power and influence of the Fujiwara. Second, in the glory to come under the reign of Crown Prince Takahito, soon to be known to history as His Imperial Majesty, Sanjo II.

My son.

Richard Parks *lives in Mississippi with his wife and a varying number of cats. His fiction has appeared in* Asimov's SF, Realms of Fantasy, Lady Churchill's Rosebud Wristlet, Fantasy Magazine, Weird Tales, *and numerous anthologies, including* Year's Best Fantasy *and* Fantasy: The Best of the Year. *His first story collection,* The Ogre's Wife, *was a World Fantasy Award finalist. PS Publishing (UK) brought out his novella,* Hereafter and After, *as a signed, limited edition in March 2007. His second story collection,* Worshipping Small Gods *is due out in 2007 as well.*

THE DEPTH ORACLE

Sonya Taaffe

> Had she other zealot and lover,
> or did he alone worship her?
> did she wear a girdle of sea-weed
>
> or a painted crown? how often
> did her high breasts meet the spray,
> how often dive down?
> —H.D., *Helen in Egypt*

THE DROWNED MAN BOBS at the foot of the jetty, pale as dead fish, splayed like seaweed to the rocking of the tide. In the shallow water, he does not drift from the sea-wall's mortared slates; olive clumps of weed float beneath his upturned hands. In a few hours, the tide will pull him back, out to the depths that fall away from the sunlight into cold, and dark, and the backwash intimations of vast shapes passing unseen. The silt beneath him will settle to mud that the waves draw out as fine as silk for terns and herring gulls to mark as they hop and take flight, and the mussels bristle dryly in summer heat. Now he hangs as close to the land as his new element will allow; at the high tide, as near to life.

A crab has gotten at one of his eyes already. It curls its legs inside the tattered socket, jaunts and swivels to the waves like a prickly, makeshift replacement, weed-green and brown where his eye was the creamy, layered grey of ancient shale; no pearls. Fish have sampled his barley hair, the trailing leather laces of his shoes, the cotton of his shirt and the blood-stilled, salt-swollen flesh beneath. The sea will eat him down to the bone and pick the bones apart, sift him down to coral and sand until little more than a jellyfish glaze of memory remains to drift down the endless currents: infinity in a saltwater drop.

Even then, the waves will wash him here. As long as she needs him, he will come to her call: as always, as now. Lifeless in the cool, sun-shattered water, the drowned man brushes up against the sea-wall, its stones furred with green weed; kelp loosely wrapped around the fingers of one hand. His name, that the sea swallowed down with the rest of him, lies written in that verdigris snarl. With one eye that was a crab, and one eye filmed full of salt, he looks up through the water to see her.

Between the driftwood and marble bellies of clouds, sunlight runs like ink on wet paper. She blocks out the piecemeal sky. Her hair blown raggedly in the wind off the water, the color of acorns, fallen oak leaves, resolutely earth-toned; strands of grey at her temples, threading sunlight here and there. Even with one foot on the asphalt and the other up on the fence-piece of steel rail, she has still the look of a figurehead, her eyes as impenetrable as painted wood: though her regard kindles, so palely green as to become colorless, the glance of rays over a wave's edge.

The skin around her eyes looks crushed with exhaustion, sallow. Through water and the crab's clambering legs, he watches her hand shake as she pushes wind-raveled hair back from her face; the backs of her hands scratched over and over with red and healing lines, as though she plunged them into a thornbush, or the brittle maze of coral. One fingernail is blackened. His fingernails will fall like shells and the sand cover them over.

Her voice comes as clearly to his brain as the touch of a lionfish's spine. The cries of the gulls were never so insistent. As always, as ritually, she says, "Tell me what you've seen."

HER HOUSE STANDS UP ON THE DUNES, in the labyrinth of saltgrass and beach roses that sway and ripple in the constant wind from the sea. Your shoes grate on the old walkway that the sand has nearly drifted over, until you must kick at the ground every few steps to find it; the white slat fence has sagged into the sand, spilled down to the ground here and there and the beach roses thrown out brambles over the blistered wood. From the sturdier bushes, and some of the fenceposts still upright, small and intricate constructions dangle—dead sea detritus, fish skulls, sinew dried to parchment, that itch at your attention. Like burrs or broken shells, and more than once you have stopped yourself from reaching out to tear one down. You think it might have been a salmon head, wrapped in the green threads of maiden's hair and staked in the sun to mummify; cormorant's feathers for a collar, and half an inch away your fingertips burn. As much trap as shield, and not so sure of yourself that you care to spring it; you close your hand at your side and walk on, though the sand is filling your shoes.

WHEN SHE HAS TAKEN FROM HIM all he can tell of tides and leviathans, sirens and herring shoals, and the designs of phosphorescence in the deep, she kneels at the edge of the sea-wall and opens her hand. What sifts down over him might be salt, or sand, or the tropical-beach whiteness of crushed shell, but it flecks the water and eddies in spirals and sinking archipelagos, and it holds him back from the turning tide. "What else?" she says. "What's coming?"

"Shadow," answers the drowned man. Out of the clearing sky, sunlight slopes as thickly translucent as amber: sparks on the sea, her own shadow lying ghostly over the olive-glass water. His blue mouth, his sludgy lungs; in his ragged eyesocket, water glints. Perhaps she smiles. "Shadow is coming."

She closes her fingers then, on wind and sunlight, and lets the sea have him back. There is so little difference between them, her and the sea, the sea and him.

SHE INVITED YOU IN, or you might still be standing on her rotted steps. The house opens and closes around you like sleight-of-hand, too much or too little space for the angles of stairs, doorways, rain-ruined floors. In one corner, a torn mattress lies under a tumble of sheets, all littered with small rips and snags as though a flock of birds or scissors has been at them. Sunlight through the salt-flecked panes falls in merciless swathes over stained plaster and scarred wood, crunched splinters of shell and a porous whiteness that might be bone laid long in a tidepool, scattered seaweeds, the clouded blues and frost-greys and bottle-greens of beach glass flung as carelessly over the floor as dice. With carpenter's nails, she has pinned a tern's wing and a leather-dried drape of kelp to the wall that faces away from the sea. There is a low-tide smell everywhere, fish-market trash.

She kneels in a cleared patch, on one knee, courting nothing. Older than you expected, from the grey lines in her hair; or younger, in short-sleeved camouflage and cargo pants, barefoot on her unswept floor. Beside her reddened hand, the mouth of a canvas tote bag has folded open, spilled out clams, mussels, wet stones and the snapped half of a sand dollar; a sea-harvest, littoral cornucopia. Her fingers wrapped loosely, comfortably, around the handle of a boning knife. Her wrists braceleted with seagrass. She knows your name.

While she sorts among her catch, you explain: she dries the moon snail on a threadbare corner of her shirt as you tell her the names that should serve as a pass-key, the fragmented trail you followed to her door; she clicks two cherrystone clams together in her palm like ball bearings when you almost whisper your question. Her gaze is cool, tidal, sardonic if she only smiled. There is a pattern strewn around her, that you would rather not understand.

"Yes." Her knife slices through one of the clamshells, halves the ruffled, salt-dripping flesh that she scoops out with her fingers and lays at one triangulation of blackened weed. She sounds dry, absent, perhaps irritated with the banality of oracles; or her thoughts are with the sea. Then she prods the clam-meat, and for the first time her mouth slides upward in a faint smile. "Here, a token."

The pearl within the clam's pouched greyness is the color between blood and black, misshapen as a tooth. You hear yourself stutter as you ask, "Is that an answer?"

Meditatively, she turns the monstrosity between her fingers before she sets it down between the moon snail and the eviscerated clam, adjusts its position after a moment's critical glance. There is a crust of salt in her hair, stiff as though with blood or lime. "It might be," she says. "But I'm not the oracle."

BECAUSE HE LOVED HER, because she loved the sea, he let her do the things she wanted: to him and the sea together. When she gutted fish and made maps of their cold, blood-slimed entrails, he obediently recorded her spoken notes and made his own sketches to compare with hers. Afterward, with kisses, he cleaned the scales from her fingertips; he would find streaks of fish blood drying in his hair in the morning. She divided the sky into quadrants, over sea and over land, and sat for hours with a camera and a compass, snapshots of birdflight—herons, sandpipers, gulls—taken home to peruse and pick secrets from the air. Sometimes he trapped those same birds for her, as he hauled up fish jerking on the end of a line and brought them, still flopping, jack-knife glitter of spray and dappled sides, to her doorstep of his own accord. "My half-drowned love," she laughed, and the mackerel's gills gaped scarlet and starved under her deft hands as he watched.

She threaded gull bones into jewelry, combed her hair like a Cape Cod girl with the barbed rack of a fish's spine. Half homemade arcana, half meticulous study, all craziness and no one else in this world would he find who loved knowledge half so much: no one else who would ever understand what drove him, even then. These are memories that not even the coldest currents will flood from his brain. He will forget his bones before he will forget her.

He would watch her draw spirals and sigils of salt, poured through the fist like painter's sand, white on cloudy white traced across the stained, worm-riddled wood that she kept on her floor. That long slat of planking, they had pried up from the docks one night with a crowbar and a torch that he almost fumbled into the water at the rending creak and groan of splinters, a salmon-leap of fear sideways through his chest that the whole structure would fall in on itself and they would drown under the weight of oyster-plated, weed-slippery wreckage— But she was the one whose foot skidded, and he caught her. Never a strong man, nor a tall one, but his hand locked around her wrist and the darkened waters never touched her: a cheat, as all his skills were, the universe momentarily conned. When she had her breath back, "I want to know how you did that," she said, her hungering mantra, and he tried to teach her. But he knew too little of the sea, too much of books that had burned eight hundred years ago and all the ways to invite death. Her kisses always tasted of salt, drying scales, blood, distraction.

He had expected she would tire of him. Out on the open water on a glassy midafternoon, sitting at the tiller of her bad-tempered, nameless motorboat, he watched her dip kelp over the side to keep it pliable and knot the slick, tensile streamers into a sort of net. "The eyes of the sea," she told him, obliquely, all her attention on the seaweed in her hands. "A depth oracle. Sounder than salt, because it's closer," though she had carefully observed what patterns the salt spilled over the plank, that morning before they left. The old anchor they had manhandled into the boat was already wreathed in more kelp, starfish as red as scalded flesh and purple-spined sea urchins tied into the drying mesh. She wore gold and brown bladderwrack in her hair like a coronet, brittling black in the sun.

"I don't think you can use an anchor for an eye of the sea," he warned her, as always more curious about the procedure than the end result. If she failed, she would make love to him in angry, ambitious compensation, and try again, and he would watch: they would learn. "Or starfish. You really need something that's not of the sea, preferably alive. I think Phaiakos recommended children, because amniotic salt is like the salt of the sea—so they would be very much at home in the depths, but of course very small children don't speak, so there are certain problems with this theory. Corpses also are not much better. You want ideally something that can think."

She was bent over the side of the boat, hands working beneath the gold-reflected water that rocked up and slapped at the boat, the movements of her shoulders under her camouflage T-shirt sensuous in their carelessness. When she looked finally over her shoulder, he could have smoothed back her wind-snarled hair with his palms and kissed her, sea-tang and obsession and all. But her pale, sun-glint eyes were examining him, like a stray whorl of salt or the blood-puzzle of a tern's insides: as closely as she never looked at any human thing, and he knew he should not have been surprised.

"I love you," she said. Her face had never been made for tenderness, but neither had he heard her speak so gently, except perhaps in her incantations to the sea. "You are the only person I have ever loved." Then she heaved the kelp-net out of the sea, in a hail and dazzle of salt water that sluiced over him as coldly as the seaweed clung to his skin, as irretrievably, and he never had the chance to answer her. When he tried to speak, all his words flowed away into the immense, ancient, deep-churning heart of the sea. With something like pride, perverse to the last, he recognized the traces of a trick he had taught her: she had fooled not only physics, but him.

When she fastened his wrists to the anchor, hemp rope stronger than seaweed, crucified on the cool, rust-powdered flukes of iron, he began to scream. She watched his scream rising in bubbles, soundless, long after the green silt shadows had covered him from sight.

Every moment of his descent, even after his lungs had filled and his heart foundered on currents and depth, he saw her: all the sea was his sight now.

SHE WILL NOT LET YOU FOLLOW HER, this sibyl of the seven seas whose prophecies are from the earth-shaker, not the laurel and the sun, and so you roam her odd, abandoned house while she consults with the depths. In the kitchen, cabinet after rusty-hinged cabinet opens on a mess of shells, water-tumbled stones, feathers and seaweeds bound together with twist-ties in no arrangement that you recognize; three ceramic plates on the last shelf, a plastic cereal bowl, coffee cups from two different sets. The rooms upstairs are as weathered and vacant as the disastrous porch, open to sea winds and bleaching sunlight and each step groans under your feet like a ship about to go down in a storm. In the little bathroom, the uncurtained shower and the mineral-crusted drain, she has set starfish to dry against the window's pebbled panes. The photographs over the mantel, where she burns driftwood to charcoal that stains under your nails, show the black-and-white faces of a family you suspect was never hers—mother, father, pale-haired son and daughters, on holiday in the mountains and their smiles are too innocent.

Afternoon wanes, the sunlight thickens landward. Never mind what price you placed in her callused, knife-scarred hand, you loiter in the hall and do not look in on the pattern half-formed on her floor, hands as nonchalantly in your pockets as your pulse hurries in your throat, and you would leave if you had not wondered what might see you go. In one of the upstairs rooms, you found fish heads and shark jaws ranged across the silvered floorboards like sentinels, bear-traps of cartilage and slivered bone, meticulous teeth. Downstairs on the radiator, that disintegrated scaffold of stitches and hair and scales and wire was once, you think, a sailor's mermaid. Even her books are salt-stained on their shelves, and you sit determinedly down on the lowest step of the stairs and almost yell when she says, unexpected and casually, "Still here, are you?"

"Yes." You do not say, where else would you go? The one word dries your mouth. Where the sun westers through the windows, the rooms are full of hot light and silhouettes; the shadows of the sea-things on the floor run together like ideograms. "What did—it—say?"

"Shadow." She comes around the corner, still picking a knot out of her heavy, wood-colored hair; she looks no more identifiable in age, no more concerned, but her mouth is drawn to a different line, and for a moment you do not want to know what oracles she dipped up from the ocean for you, you want to know what in the world could make her look like that. If you ever could, with what word or touch or secret, effect such a transformation. As impossible a dream as isles of glass or palaces under sea or abyssal temples, countries you will never reach; as she studies you, her face is already changing and she repeats, "Shadow's coming. Shadow off the sea. That's what he said."

"He?"

"The oracle," and there is some private amusement here that you cannot read. "He only knows what the sea knows. But the sea knows a lot."

She moves past you, then, before you can put out a hand to catch her or even press her for more information—this cold intimation that you bargained for and bought, like a storm-front that shivers over your skin—and the sugar bowl she takes down from the nearest sill is full of coarse sea salt instead. As she pours a measure into her palm, she looks up one last time at you. There are glaciers the color of her eyes, sheets of glass, light through waves. There are sun-warmed waters where the fish breed, and then there is the abyss. "You asked," she tells you, perhaps as kindly as she can; perhaps not. Her fingers trace across the floor, find the blood-dark pearl in its stripe of sunset. "Don't stay."

Down her steps, the air swims: hazed and honey-viscous, where the sun has burned behind the hills; the waves are blackened and gold.

When you glance over your shoulder, her house looks only dilapidated, flotsam and jetsam, no more otherworldly than the dried sticks half-buried in the sand at your feet. No strange awareness prickles at you from the beach roses. The oracle pronounced; you were answered; you are, oddly, no longer afraid. Still, as you trudge up the dunes, toward beachfront parking and your car and all the reasoned world you ducked out of for a time, you do not like to set your back to the sea.

IN THE LAST OF THE SUNSET, she pushes small bones and still-wet seaweeds into configuration; she closes her hand on razor coral until the skin of her palm parts like gills. When she traces all the interconnections with salt, the pain burns bone-deep and she clenches her teeth on it, as critical as the geometries of oyster shell and petrel feathers, the fossil gastropod like a thumbnail twist of stone. Afterward, she binds her hand and builds up the fire, and watches the driftwood fall to embers in the salt-flickered blue, as the sea darkens for the night.

IN THE DREAMS OF THE DROWNED MAN, that are the dreams of the sleepless sea, she finds him in a gallery of kelp and a garden of bones, and she lays her hand on his forehead.

Naked even of her sea-tattered clothes, her ribcage is a white basket of pearls and anemones, the soft pulse of flowered, fire-colored mouths against pirate's-treasure masses of nacre shelled over pain, and her fingernails are each seed-beaded blue as scallops' eyes.

He blinks the crab from his eye, red algae from his lashes. Around them, bones tap and clack in the blackness from which all light has been crushed, that not even his own faint phosphorescence fades farther than her; kelp-stalks and bannered leaves, slippery on his skin that never feels the cold. She gleams and clicks as she leans over him, rust-bronze fragments of kelp caught in her vertebrae, at her ankles, the sea-combed stream of her hair. He cannot whisper her name; the sea dissolved his voice into its own. But she hears him. She can always hear the sea.

When she parts her lips, small fish as silver as bubbles stream from her mouth to his; the moray eel that coils about her collarbones slips loose, slides around his thigh. Barnacles stud the fanned backs of her hands, clouded now with bioluminescence brushed off from his sea-colonized skin. But the restless water picks his flesh from him like another needless garment, discards face and hands like hat and gloves, all the softness that does not endure time, until he shines as pale and polished as she. In the hollow of his hip, an octopus like a clot of black velvet resettles its arms; in and out of his mouth, her fish respire.

The eel circles, signs them together, handfast, and an anemone falls like a tossed flower slowly from her bones to his.

SAILING BY THESE STARS, you will never find your way home.

Sonya Taaffe *has a confirmed addiction to myth, folklore, and dead languages. Poems and short stories of hers have been shortlisted for the SLF Fountain Award, honorably mentioned in* The Year's Best Fantasy and Horror, *and reprinted in* The Alchemy of Stars: Rhysling Award Winners Showcase, The Best of Not One of Us, Fantasy: The Best of the Year 2006, *and* Best New Fantasy. *A respectable amount of her work can be found in collections* Postcards from the Province of Hyphens *and* Singing Innocence and Experience. *She is currently pursuing a Ph.D. in Classics at Yale University.*

SMOKE & MIRRORS

Amanda Downum

THE CIRCUS WAS IN TOWN.

Not just any circus, either, but Carson & Kindred's Circus Fabulatoris and Menagerie of Mystical Marvels. The circus Jerusalem Morrow ran away to join when she was seventeen years old. Her family for seven years.

She laid the orange flyer on the kitchen table beside a tangle of beads and wire and finished putting away her groceries. Her smile stretched, bittersweet. She hadn't seen the troupe in five years, though she still dreamt of them. Another world, another life, before she came back to this quiet house.

Cats drifted through the shadows in the back yard as she put out food. The bottle tree—her grandmother's tree—chimed in the October breeze; no ghosts tonight. Glass gleamed cobalt and emerald, diamond and amber, jewel-bright colors among autumn-brown leaves. Awfully quiet this year, so close to Halloween.

Salem glanced at the flyer again as she boiled water for tea. Brother Ezra, Madame Aurora, Luna and Sol the acrobats—familiar names, and a few she didn't know. She wondered if Jack still had the parrots and that cantankerous monkey. The show was here until the end of the month . . .

It's the past. Over and done. She buried the paper under a stack of mail until only one orange corner showed.

SALEM WOKE THAT NIGHT to the violent rattle of glass and wind keening over narrow mouths. The bottle tree had caught another ghost.

She flipped her pillow to the cool side and tried to go back to sleep, but the angry ringing wouldn't let her rest. With a sigh, she rolled out of bed and tugged on a pair of jeans. Floorboards creaked a familiar rhythm as she walked to the back door.

A cat shrieked across the yard—they never came too near when the bottles were full. Grey and charcoal night, stars milky pinpricks against the velvet predawn darkness. Grass crunched cool and dry beneath her bare feet.

The shadows smelled of ash and bitter smoke. Goosebumps crawled up her arms, tightened her breasts.

"Stay away, witch."

Salem spun, searching for the voice. Something gleamed ghost-pale on her roof. A bird.

"Get away!" White wings flapped furiously.

The wind gusted hot and harsh and glass clashed. Salem turned, reaching for the dancing bottles.

A bottle shattered, and the wind hit her like a sandstorm, like the breath of Hell. Glass stung her outstretched palm as smoke seared her lungs. She staggered back, stumbled and fell, blind against the scouring heat.

Then it was over. Salem gasped, tears trickling down her stinging cheeks. The tree shivered in the stillness, shedding singed leaves.

Cursing, she staggered to her feet. She cursed again as glass bit deep into her heel; blood dripped hot and sticky down her instep. The burning thing was gone, and so was the bird.

Salem limped back to the house as quickly as she could.

FOR TWO DAYS SHE WATCHED AND LISTENED, but caught no sign of ghosts or anything else. She picked up the broken glass and replaced the shattered bottle, brushed away the soot and charred leaves. The tree was old and strong; it would survive.

At night she dreamed.

She dreamed of a lake of tears, of fire that ate the moon. She dreamed of ropes that bit her flesh, of shining chains. She dreamed of trains. She dreamed of a snake who gnawed the roots of the world.

On the third day, a bird landed on the kitchen windowsill. It watched her through the screen with one colorless round eye and fluffed ragged feathers. Salem paused, soapsuds clinging to her hands, and met its gaze. Her shoulder blades prickled.

It held a piece of orange paper crumpled in one pale talon.

"Be careful," she said after a moment. "There are a lot of cats out there."

The bird stared at her and let out a low, chuckling caw. "The circus is in town. Come see the show." White wings unfurled and it flapped away. The paper fluttered like an orange leaf as it fell.

Salem turned to see her big marmalade tomcat sitting on the kitchen table, fur all on end. He bared his teeth for a long, steam-kettle hiss before circling three times and settling down with his head on his paws. She glanced through the back screen door, but the bird was gone and the bottles rattled empty in the sticky-cool October breeze.

That night she dreamed of thunder, of blood leaking through white cloth, shining black in the moonlight. No portent, just an old nightmare. She woke trembling, tears cold on her cheeks.

The next morning she wove spells and chains. She threaded links of copper and silver and bronze and hung them with shimmering glass, each bead a bottlesnare. They hung cool around her neck, a comforting weight that chimed when she moved.

As the sun vanished behind the ceiling of afternoon clouds, Salem went to see the circus.

THE CIRCUS FABULATORIS SPRAWLED across the Ipswich County fairgrounds, a glittering confusion of lights and tents and spinning rides. The wind smelled of grease and popcorn and sugar and Salem bit her lip to stop her eyes from stinging.

It had been five years; it shouldn't feel like coming home.

She didn't recognize any faces along the Midway, smiled and ignored the shouts to *play a game, win a prize, step right up only a dollar*. Ezra would be preaching by now, calling unsuspecting rubes to Heaven. Jack would be in the big top—which wasn't very big at all—announcing the acrobats and sword-swallowers. He'd have a parrot or a monkey on his shoulder. It was Tuesday, so probably the monkey.

She found a little blue tent, painted with shimmering stripes of color like the northern lights. *Madame Aurora,* the sign read, fortunes told, futures revealed.

Candlelight rippled across the walls inside, shimmered on beaded curtains and sequined scarves. Incense hung thick in the air, dragon's blood and patchouli.

"Come in, child," a woman's French-accented voice called, hidden behind sheer draperies, "come closer. I see the future and the past. I have the answers you seek."

Salem smiled. "That accent still ain't fooling anyone."

Silence filled the tent.

"Salem?" Shadows shifted behind the curtain, and a blonde head peered around the edge. Blue eyes widened. "Salem!"

And Madame Aurora rushed toward her in a flurry of scarves and bangles and crushed Salem in a tea rose-scented hug.

"Oh my god, Jerusalem! God damnit, honey, you said you'd write me, you said you'd call." France gave way to Savannah as Raylene Meadows caught Salem by the shoulders and shook her. She stopped shaking and hugged again, tight enough that her corset stays dug into Salem's ribs.

"Are you back?" Ray asked, finally letting go. "Are you going on with us?"

Salem's heart sat cold as glass in her chest. "No, sweetie. I'm just visiting. A little bird thought I should stop by." She looked around the tent, glanced at Ray out of the corner of one eye. "Has Jack started using a white crow?"

Ray stilled for an instant, eyes narrowing. "No. No, that's Jacob's bird."

"Jacob?"

"He's a conjure man. We picked him up outside of Memphis." Her lips curled in that little smile that meant she was sleeping with someone, and still enjoying it.

"Maybe I should meet him."

"Have you come back to steal another man from me?"

Salem cocked an eyebrow. "If I do, will you help me bury the body?"

Ray flinched, like she was the one who had nightmares about it. Maybe she did. Then she met Salem's eyes and smiled. "I will if you need me to."

"Where can I find Jacob?"

Ray's jaw tightened. "In his trailer, most likely. He's between acts right now. It's the red one on the far end of the row."

"Thanks. And . . . don't tell Jack or Ezra I'm here, okay? Not yet."

"You gonna see them before you disappear again?"

"Yeah. I'll try." Laughing voices approached outside. "Better put that bad accent back on." And Salem ducked outside.

The wind shifted as she left the cluster of tents and booths, and she caught the tang of lightning. Magic. The real thing, not the little spells and charms she'd taught Ray so many years ago.

Jack had always wanted a real magician. But what did a carnival conjurer have to do with her dreams, or the angry thing that so easily broke free of a spelled bottle?

She followed the tire-rutted path to a trailer painted in shades of blood and rust. A pale shadow flitted through the clouds, drifted down to perch on the roof. The crow watched Salem approach, but stayed silent.

Someone hummed carelessly inside, broke off as Salem knocked. A second later the door swung open to frame a man's shadowed face and shirtless shoulder.

"Hello." He ran a hand through a shock of salt and cinnamon curls. "What can I do for you?" His voice was smoke and whiskey, rocks being worn to sand. But not the crow's voice.

"Are you Jacob?"

"Jacob Grim, magician, conjurer, and prestidigitator, at your service."

"That's an interesting bird you have there."

His stubbled face creased in a coyote's smile. "That she is. Why don't you step inside, Miss . . .

"Jerusalem." He offered a hand, and she shook it; his grip was strong, palm dry and callused. She climbed the metal stairs and stepped into the narrow warmth of the trailer.

Jacob turned away, and the lamplight fell across his back. Ink covered his skin, black gone greenish with age. A tree rose against his spine, branches spreading across his shoulders and neck, roots disappearing below the waist of his pants.

He caught her staring and grinned. "Excuse my *dishabille*. I'm just getting ready for my next act." He shrugged on a white shirt and did up the buttons with nimble fingers. The hair on his chest was nearly black, spotted with red and grey—calico colors. Ray usually liked them younger and prettier, but Salem could see the appeal.

"How may I help you, Miss Jerusalem?"

She cocked her head, studied him with *otherwise* eyes. His left eye gleamed with witchlight, and magic sparked through the swirling dark colors of his aura. The real thing, all right.

"Your bird invited me to see the show."

"And see it you certainly should. It's a marvelous display of magic and legerdemain, if I do say so myself." He put on a black vest and jacket, slipping cards and scarves into pockets and sleeves.

"Actually, I was hoping you might have an answer or two for me."

He smiled. Not a coyote—something bigger. A wolf's smile. "I have as many answers as you have questions, my dear. Some of them may even be true." He smoothed back his curls and pulled on a black hat with a red feather in the band.

The door swung open on a cold draft before Salem could press. A young girl stood outside, maybe nine or ten. Albino-pale in the grey afternoon light, the hair streaming over her shoulders nearly as white as her dress. Salem shivered as the breeze rushed past her, much colder than the day had been.

"Time to go," she said to Jacob, her voice low for a child's, and rough. She turned and walked away before he could answer.

"Your daughter?" Salem asked.

"Not mine in blood or flesh, but I look after her. Memory is my assistant." He laid a hand on her arm, steering her gently toward the door. "Come watch the show, Jerusalem, and afterwards perhaps I'll invent some answers for you."

So she sat in the front row in the big top and watched Jacob's show. He pulled scarves from his sleeves and birds from his hat—Jack's parrots, not the white crow. He conjured flowers for the ladies, read men's minds. He pulled a blooming rose from behind Salem's ear and presented it with a wink and a flourish. Velvet-soft and fragrant when she took it, but when she looked again it was made of bronze, tight-whorled petals warming slowly to her hand.

He tossed knives at Memory and sawed her in half. She never spoke, never blinked. It was hard to tell in the dizzying lights, but Salem was fairly sure the girl didn't cast a shadow.

She watched the crowd, saw the delight on their faces. Jack had wanted an act like this for years.

But not all the spectators were so amused. A man lingered in the shadows, face hidden beneath the brim of a battered hat. Salem tried to read his aura, but a rush of heat made her eyes water, leaking tears down tingling cheeks. The smell of char filled her nose, ashes and hot metal. When her vision cleared, he was gone.

AFTER THE SHOW, she caught up with Jacob at his trailer. Ray was with him, giggling and leaning on his arm. She sobered when she saw Salem. The two of them had given up on jealousy a long time ago; Salem wondered what made the other woman's eyes narrow so warily.

"Excuse me, my dear," Jacob said to Ray, detaching himself gently from her grip. "I promised Jerusalem a conversation."

Ray paused to brush a kiss across Salem's cheek before she opened the trailer door. "Try not to shoot this one," she whispered.

"I'm not making any promises," Salem replied with a smile.

She and Jacob walked in silence, away from the lights and noise to the edge of the fairgrounds, where the ground sloped down through a tangle of brush and trees toward the shore of White Bear Lake. The water sprawled toward the horizon, a black mirror in the darkness. She made out a bone-pale spire on the edge of the water—a ruined church, the only building left of the ghost town the lake had swallowed.

Jacob pulled out a cigarette case, offered Salem one. She took it, though she hadn't smoked in years. Circuses, cigarettes, strange men—she was relearning all sorts of bad habits today. He cupped his hands around a match and she leaned close; he smelled of musk and clean salt sweat. Orange light traced the bones of his face as he lit his own.

"So, witch, ask your questions."

She took a drag and watched the paper sear. "Who is the burning man?"

"Ah." Smoke shimmered as he exhaled. "An excellent question, and one deserving of an interesting answer." He turned away, broken-nosed profile silhouetted against the fairground lights.

"These days he's a train man—conductor and fireman and engineer, all in one. He runs an underground railroad, but not the kind that sets men free." His left eye glinted as he glanced at her. "Have you, perchance, noticed a dearth of spirits in these parts?"

Salem shivered, wished she'd thought to wear a coat. Jacob shrugged his jacket off and handed it to her. "This train man is taking the ghosts? Taking them where?"

"Below. Some he'll use to stoke the furnace, others to quench his thirst. And any that are left when he reaches the station he'll give to his masters."

"What are they?"

"Nothing pleasant, my dear, nothing pleasant at all."

"What do you have to do with this?"

"I've been tracking him. I nearly had him in Mississippi, but our paths parted—he follows the rails, and the Circus keeps to the freeways."

"So it was just bad luck he got caught in my bottle tree?"

"Your good luck that he left you in peace. He hunts ghosts, but I doubt he'd scruple to make one if he could."

"So why the invitation?"

He smiled. "A witch whose spells can trap the Conductor, even for a moment, is a powerful witch indeed. You could be of no little help to me."

"I'm not in the business of hunting demons, or ghosts."

"You keep a bottle tree."

"It was my grandmother's. And it keeps them away. I like my privacy."

"He'll be going back soon, with his load. The end of the month."

"Halloween."

He nodded. "That's all the time those souls have left, before they're lost."

"I'm sorry for them." She dropped her cigarette, crushed the ember beneath her boot. "I really am. And I wish you luck. But it's not my business."

"He takes children."

Salem laughed, short and sharp, and tossed his jacket back to him. "You don't know my buttons to press them."

He grinned and stepped closer, his warmth lapping against her. Not a tall man, but he moved like one. "I'd like to find them."

"I bet you would. Good night, Jacob. I enjoyed the show." And she turned and walked away.

THAT NIGHT SALEM DRIFTED in and out of restless sleep. No dreams to keep her up tonight, only the wind through the window, light as a thief, and the hollowness behind her chest. A dog howled somewhere in the distance and she tossed in her cold bed.

Five years this winter, since she'd come back to nurse her grandmother through the illnesses of age that not even their witchery could cure, until Eliza finally died, and left Salem her house, her bottle tree, and all the spells she knew. Years of sleeping alone, of selling bottles and beads and charms and seeing living folk twice a month at best.

We'll always work best alone, her grandmother had said. Five years ago, Salem had been willing to believe it. She'd had her fill of people— circus lights and card tricks, grifting and busking. The treachery of the living, the pleas and the threats of the dead. Dangerous men and their smiles. Living alone seemed so much easier, if it meant she never had to scrub blood and gunpowder from her hands again, never had to dig a shallow grave at the edge of town.

But she wasn't sure she wanted to spend another five years alone.

OCTOBER WORE ON, and the leaves of the bottle tree rattled and drifted across the yard. Salem carved pumpkins and set them to guard her porch, though no children ever came so far trick-or-treating. She wove metal and glass and silk to sell in town. She wove spells.

The moon swelled, and by its milksilver light she scried the rain barrel. The water showed her smoke and flame and church bells, and her own pale reflection.

A week after she'd visited the circus, someone knocked on her door. Salem looked up from her beads and spools of wire and shook her head.

Jacob stood on her front step, holding his hat in his hands. His boots were dusty, jacket slung over one shoulder. He grinned his wolf's grin. "Good afternoon, ma'am. I wondered if I might trouble you for a drink of water."

Salem's eyes narrowed as she fought a smile. "Did you walk all this way?"

"I was in the mood for a stroll, and a little bird told me you lived hereabouts." He raised ginger brows. "Does your privacy preclude hospitality, or are you going to ask me in?"

She sighed. "Come inside."

The bone charm over the door shivered just a little as he stepped inside, but that might have been the wind. She led him to the kitchen, aware of his eyes on her back as they crossed the dim and creaking hall.

The cat stood up on the table as they entered, orange hackles rising. Salem tensed, wondered if she'd made a mistake after all. But Jacob held out one hand and the tom walked toward him, pausing at the edge of the table to sniff the outstretched fingers. After a moment his fur settled and he deigned to let the man scratch his ears.

"What's his name?" Jacob asked.

"Vengeance Is Mine Sayeth the Lord. You can call him Vengeance, though I'm pretty sure he thinks of himself as the Lord."

Jacob smiled, creasing the corners of autumn-grey eyes; his smile made her shiver, not unpleasantly.

"Sit down," she said. "Would you like some coffee, or tea?"

"No, thank you. Water is fine."

She filled a glass and set the water pitcher on the table amidst all her bottles and beads. Vengeance sniffed it and decided he'd rather have what was in his bowl. Jacob drained half the glass in one swallow.

"Nice tree." He tilted his stubbled chin toward the backyard, where glass gleamed in the tarnished light. He picked up a strand of opalite beads from the table; they shimmered like tears between his blunt fingers. "Very pretty. Are you a jeweler too?"

She shrugged, leaning one hip against the counter. "I like to make things. Pretty things, useful things."

"Things that are pretty and useful are best." He ran a hand down the curve of the sweating pitcher and traced a design on the nicked tabletop. Salem shuddered at a cold touch on the small of her back.

Her lips tightened. Vengeance looked up from his bowl and rumbled like an engine. He leapt back on the table, light for his size, and sauntered toward Jacob. Big orange paws walked right through the damp design and Salem felt the charm break.

"Did you think you could come into my house and 'witch' me?"

"I could try."

"You'll have to try harder than that."

"I will, won't I."

He stood and moved toward her. Salem stiffened, palms tingling, but she didn't move, even when he leaned into her, hands braced against the counter on either side. His lips brushed hers, cold at first but warming fast. The salt-sweet taste of him flooded her mouth and her skin tightened.

After a long moment he pulled away, but Salem still felt his pulse in her lips. Her blood pounded like surf in her ears.

His scarred hands brushed the bottom of her shirt. "You said something about buttons . . ."

"Will you help me?" he asked later, in the darkness of her bedroom. The smell of him clung to her skin, her sheets, filled her head till it was hard to think of anything else.

Salem chuckled, her head pillowed on his shoulder. "You think that's all it takes to change my mind?"

"All? You want more?"

She ran her fingers over his stomach; scars spiderwebbed across his abdomen, back and front, like something had torn him open. Older, fainter scars cross-hatched his arms. Nearly every inch of him was covered in cicatrices and ink.

"Is prestidigitation such dangerous work?"

"It is indeed." He slid a hand down the curve of her hip, tracing idle patterns on her thigh. "But not unrewarding."

"What will you do if you catch this demon of yours?"

He shrugged. "Find another one. The world is full of thieves and predators and dangerous things."

"Things like you?"

"Yes." His arms tightened around her, pressing her close. "And like you, my dear." She stiffened, but his fingers brushed her mouth before she could speak. "Tell me you're not a grifter, Jerusalem."

"I gave it up," she said at last.

"And you miss it. You're alone out here, cold and empty as those bottles."

She snorted. "And you think you're the one to fill me?"

His chuckle rumbled through her. "I wouldn't presume. Raylene misses you, you know. The others do too. Wouldn't you be happier if you came back to the show?"

The glass in her chest cracked, a razorline fracture of pain. "You don't know what would make me happy," she whispered.

Callused fingers trailed up the inside of her thigh. "I can learn."

HE ROSE FROM HER BED at the first bruise of dawn. "Will you think about it, if nothing else?" Cloth rustled and rasped as he dressed in the darkness.

"I'll think about it." She doubted she'd be able to do anything else.

"We're here through Sunday. The circus and the train." He stamped his boots on and leaned over the bed, a darker shadow in the gloom.

"I know." She stretched up to kiss him, stubble scratching her already-raw lips.

Her bed was cold when he was gone. She lay in the dark, listening to hollow chimes.

SALEM SPENT THE DAY setting the house in order, sweeping and dusting and checking all the wards. Trying not to think about her choices.

She'd promised her grandmother that she'd stay, settle down and look after the house. No more running off chasing midway lights, no more trouble. It had been an easy promise as Eliza lay dying, Salem's heart still sore with guns and graves, with the daughter she'd lost in a rush of blood on a motel bathroom floor.

She didn't want to go through that again. But she didn't want to live alone and hollow, either.

The bird came after sundown, drifting silent from the darkening sky. The cat stared and hissed as she settled on the back step, his ears flat against his skull.

"Come with me, witch. We need you."

"Hello, Memory. I thought I had until Sunday."

"We were wrong." The girl lifted a bone-white hand, but couldn't cross the threshold. "We're out of time."

Salem stared at the ghost girl. Older than her daughter would have been. Probably a blessing for the lost child anyway—she had a witch's heart, not a mother's.

The child vanished, replaced by a fluttering crow. "There's no time, witch. Please."

Vengeance pressed against her leg, rumbling deep in his chest. Salem leaned down to scratch his ears. "Stay here and watch the house."

As she stepped through the door, the world shivered and slipped sideways. She walked down the steps under a seething black sky. The tree glowed against the shadows, a shining thing of ghostlight and jewels. Beyond the edge of her yard the hills rolled sere and red.

"Where are we going?" she asked Memory.

"Into the Badlands. Follow me, and mind you don't get lost." The bird took to the sky, flying low against heavy clouds. Salem fought the urge to look back, kept her eyes on the white-feathered shape as it led her north.

The wind keened across the hills and Salem shivered through her light coat. The trees swayed and clattered, stunted bone-pale things shedding leaves like ashes.

The moon rose slowly behind the clouds, swollen and rust-colored. Something strange about its light tonight, too heavy and almost sharp as it poured over Salem's skin. Then she saw the shadow nibbling at one edge and understood—eclipse. She lengthened her stride across the dry red rock.

TIME PASSED STRANGE in the deadlands, and they reached the end of the desert well before Salem could ever have walked to town. She paused on the crest of a ridge, the ground sloping into shadow below her. On the far side of the valley she saw the circus, shimmering bright enough to bridge the divide.

"No," Memory cawed as she started toward the lights. "We go down."

Salem followed the bird down the steep slope, boots slipping in red dust. A third of the moon had been eaten by the rust-colored shadow.

Halfway down she saw the buildings, white-washed walls like ivory in the darkness. A church bell tolled the hour as they reached the edge of town, and Memory croaked along with the sour notes.

Shutters rattled over blind-dark windows, and paint peeled in shriveled strips. The bird led her to a nameless bar beside the train tracks. Jacob waited inside, leaning against the dust-shrouded counter.

Salem crossed her arms below her breasts. "You said Sunday."

"I was wrong. It's the burning moon he wants, not Hallow's Eve." Witchlight burned cold in the lamps, glittering against cobwebbed glass. His eyes were different colors in the unsteady glow.

"Where is he now?"

"On his last hunt. He'll be back soon."

"What do you need me for?"

He touched the chain around her throat; links rattled softly. "Distraction. Bait. Whatever's needed."

She snorted. "That's what Memory's for too, isn't she? That's why he was watching your act. You're a real bastard, aren't you?"

"You have no idea."

She reached up and brushed the faint web of scars on his left cheek. "How'd you lose your eye?"

He grinned. "I didn't lose it. I know exactly where it is."

Memory drifted through the door. "He's coming."

Jacob's smile fell away and he nodded. "Wait by the train station. Be sure he sees you."

"What's the plan?"

"I had a plan, when I thought we had until Sunday. It was a good plan, I'm sure you would have appreciated it. Now I have something more akin to a half-assed idea."

Salem fought a smile and lost. "So what's the half-assed idea?"

"Memory distracts him at the train station. We ambush him, tie him up, and set the trapped ghosts free."

"Except for the part where my charms won't hold him for more than a few minutes, that's a great idea."

"We won't mention that part. Come on."

A TRAIN SPRAWLED beside the station platform, quiet as a sleeping snake. Its cars were black and tarnished silver, streaked with bloody rust, and the cow-catcher gleamed fang-sharp in the red light.

The platform was empty, and Jacob and Salem waited in the shadows. She could barely make out the words *White Bear* on the cracked and mildewed sign.

"They built this town for the train," she whispered, her face close enough to Jacob's to feel his breath. "But the Texas and Pacific never came, and the town dried up and blew away."

"This is a hard country. Even gods go begging here."

Footsteps echoed through the silent station; a moment later Salem heard a child's sniffling tears. Then the Conductor came into view.

A tall man, dressed like his name, black hat pulled low over his face. Even across the platform Salem felt the angry heat of him, smelled ash and coal. A sack was slung over one broad shoulder, and his other hand prisoned Memory's tiny wrist.

Salem swallowed, her throat gone dry, and undid the clasp around her neck. The chain slithered cold into her hand. Jacob's hand tightened on her shoulder once, then he stepped into the moonlight.

"Trading in dead children now?" His growl carried through the still air. "You called yourself a warrior once."

The Conductor whirled, swinging Memory around like a doll. His face was dark in the shadow of his hat, but his eyes gleamed red.

Jacob took a step closer, bootheels thumping on warped boards. "You fought gods once, and heroes. Now you steal the unworthy dead." He cocked his head. "And didn't you used to be taller?"

"You!" The Conductor's voice was a dry-bone rasp; Salem shuddered at the sound. "You died! I saw you fall. The wolf ripped you open."

Jacob laughed. "It's harder than that to kill me."

"We'll see about that." He released Memory and dropped the bag as he lunged for Jacob.

Memory crawled away, cradling her wrist to her chest. The chain rattled in Salem's hand as she moved; Jacob and the Conductor grappled near the edge of the platform, and she had no clear shot.

Then Jacob fell, sprawling hard on the floor. The Conductor laughed as he stood over him. "I'll take you and the witch as well as the dead. The things below will be more than pleased."

Salem darted in, the chain lashing like a whip. It coiled around his throat and he gasped. His heat engulfed her, but she hung on.

"You can't trap me in a bottle, little witch." His eyes burned red as embers. Char-black skin cracked as he moved, flashing molten gold beneath. A glass bead shattered against his skin; another melted and ran like a tear.

She pulled the chain tighter—it wouldn't hold much longer. The Conductor caught her arm in one huge black hand and she screamed as her flesh seared.

"Didn't the old man tell you, woman? His companions always die. Crows will eat your eyes—if I don't boil them first."

A fury of white feathers struck him, knocking off his hat as talons raked his face. The Conductor cursed, batting the bird aside, and Salem drove a boot into his knee.

He staggered on the edge for one dizzying instant, then fell, taking Salem with him. Breath rushed out of her as they landed, his molten heat burning through her clothes. Her vision blurred, and White Bear Valley spun around in a chiaroscuro swirl.

"Jerusalem!" She glanced up, still clinging to the chain. Jacob leapt off the platform, landing lightly in a puff of dust. "Hold your breath!"

She barely realized what was coming as he stuck his fingers into the ground and pulled the world open.

White Bear Lake crashed in to fill the void.

"Wake up, witch. You're no use to me drowned."

She came to with a shudder, Jacob's mouth pressed over hers, his breath inside her. She gasped, choked, rolled over in time to vomit up a bellyful of bitter lake water. Her vision swam red and black, and she collapsed onto weed-choked mud. Cold saturated her, ice-needles tingling through her fingers.

"Did he drown?" she asked, voice cracking.

"His kind don't like to swim." He turned her over, propping her head on his soaking knees. "I could say it destroyed him, if that's how you'd like this to end." Above them the shadow eased, the moon washing clean and white again.

"What could you say if I wanted the truth?"

Jacob's glass eye gleamed as he smiled. "That it weakened him, shattered that shape. He lost the train and its cargo. That's enough for me tonight."

"Not too bad, for a half-assed idea." She tried to sit up and thought better of it. The cold retreated, letting her feel the burns on her arm and hands. "Are you going to thank me?"

He laughed and scooped her into his arms. "I might." And he carried her up the hill, toward the circus lights.

HALLOWEEN DAWNED COOL AND GREY. Glass chimed in the breeze as Salem untied the bottles one by one, wrapping them in silk and laying them in boxes. The tree looked naked without them.

The wind gusted over the empty hills, whistled past the eaves of the house. The tree shook, and the only sound was the scrape and rustle of dry leaves.

"Sorry, Grandma," she whispered as she wrapped the last bottle. Light and hollow, glass cold in her hands. "I'll come back to visit."

When she was done, Jerusalem Morrow packed a bag and packed her cat, and ran away to join the circus.

Amanda Downum *lives in the badlands of Texas with her husband, cats and growing brood of baby novels. Her short fiction is published in* Realms of Fantasy, Strange Horizons, *and* Fantasy Magazine. *She wishes her bios were more interesting. To learn more about her and her work, visit www.amandadownum.com.*

THE DESIRES OF HOUSES

Haddayr Copley-Woods

THE WOMAN'S STEP ON THE STAIR IS LABORED, and the cord hanging at the bottom trembles with excitement.

Her hands are busy carrying laundry. She will have to turn on the light with her mouth.

In the dark, to find the cord correctly, she must caress it with the tip of her pink tongue briefly, and the wicked, wicked pleasure of it more than makes up for the bite and the sharp jerk which turns on the bulb.

The cord over the washing machine, the braided one, is waiting joyously for the teeth.

The floor is sulking. She almost always wears shoes in the basement, and the cement lies all day in agony listening to the first floor's boards sighing loudly in ecstasy at the touch of her bare heels.

All it can hope for in its slow, cold way is that the woman will scoop the cat boxes, squatting on her heels, after she starts a load of laundry. Today oh joy oh joy she does. The floor is practically writhing at the smell of her (she always showers after the scooping, so her scent is thick)—the tangy rich odor. The cement feels (or maybe it's just wishful thinking) just a bit of her damp warmth.

But then she is sweeping the floor, oblivious as always to the swooning house around her, ruining the floor's pleasure with the horrible scented litter she sweeps up and tosses back in the box.

She yanks open the dryer, who feels violated and then guilty for enjoying it, dumps the hot, panting shirts and shorts into a basket, and heads back upstairs, carefully turning off the lights to avoid the lecture about electricity the man will give her later if she doesn't. Even minutes later, the cords are still shaking in the darkness.

She folds the clothes neatly and quickly, then smoothes each piece with her hand. It's hard to say who enjoys this the most—the shirts or the table she presses them upon—and then the man is knocking on the kitchen door.

She opens it for him and he growls at her to stop locking him out when he is gardening; he leaves it unlocked for a reason.

The woman is getting tired of this particular topic and instead of apologizing snaps crisply that she has no memory of locking it, and indeed she hasn't. The house just wanted a few more precious moments alone with her.

He stomps back outside, and she carefully checks that it is unlocked, even while muttering against the man under her breath.

The door handle is sure it isn't his imagination that her hand lingers on the brass.

The man has tracked mud on the kitchen floor, who nearly faints with joy when she notices. She looks closer at the cracked and peeling linoleum and forgoes the mop for a rag and brush. She mutters about how disgusting the floor is—how utterly, utterly filthy, as her nail digs at an especially difficult spot. Yes yes yes, squeaks the floor—who, like the braided cord over the washer, likes it rough.

Afterwards, she heads up the stairs (which groan loudly at the feel of her toes) to take her shower.

Despite its lascivious reputation, the shower couldn't care less about the woman, even as he rains fat droplets down her breasts. The bathtub, the sole dissenter in the house, yearns for the muscular fleshy rump of the man. He hasn't felt it in ages, as it is summer and not time for long, hot baths.

The man, cursing, fumbles with the kitchen door and has to find his key with dirt-encrusted fingers deep in his pockets. He steps inside, notices the floor has been washed, and carefully removes his shoes, muttering that she'll probably want to be thanked now that she's done her annual unprompted housecleaning chore—then peers suspiciously down the stairs to be sure she hasn't left a light on in the basement again.

The midsummer sky is growing dim as he showers, unwittingly spurning the tub so far below, while the woman brushes her teeth.

The orgiastic moaning of the toothbrush annoys the towel incredibly, because after all who is it that gets to cradle her every last curve rubbing rubbing rubbing and then contentedly wrap herself around the woman's breast and hips for a little post-pleasure snuggling?

It is too hot for even a tank top and the woman lies flat on the sheet, staring up into the dark, and wonders how long it has been like this. Just today? All year? She hasn't felt so awkward, angry, unlovable and unloving since junior high. She feels flabby, flat-chested, gray, and wrinkled besides.

The man, annoyed as he is with the woman, sees the curve of her thigh in the light from the window and slides in next to her, giving it a tentative caress.

He spent all morning with his eyes on the game, grunting once noncommittally when she asked if it was her turn to do the laundry, and after lunch he had flat-out refused to dance with her when a slow waltz came on the radio. He didn't feel like it, he said.

She swats him away as she would a fly.

The ceiling fan stares down in utter loathing at the man who sighs and rolls away from the woman. If she was mine, thinks the fan, oh how I would waltz with her. Around and around and around.

Haddayr Copley-Woods *is a writer and graphic designer with stories in publications such as* Strange Horizons, Ideomancer, *and* Polyphony. *She is a columnist for the* Minnesota Women's Press *and lives with her husband and two sons in Minneapolis. She has never heard mysterious moaning coming from the basement. Find more of her stories and columns at www.haddayr.com.*

EVERGREEN

Angela Boord

NICK REMEMBERS IT THIS WAY.

His truck has broken down somewhere in the Coastals. The map doesn't really say where he is. Tendrils of moss drip from the branches and trunks of gigantic firs like folds of green silk, and a blanket of fog—so thick it's more like frozen drizzle—wraps around them, obscuring their tops.

On the branch of one of these enormous firs, a woman perches like an owl.

Branches hide most of her body, playing hide and seek with her skin. Her skin has an odd silver-greenish cast to it, but maybe that's the fog. Her hair is the color of the wet needles padding the forest floor, and it forms a brown tangle all around her face.

"Hey!" he calls out, when he can find his voice. "Can I help you?"

He stumbles forward, wondering exactly how you're supposed to approach a naked girl in the woods. She just watches him, head cocked, less like an owl than a hawk. She's up pretty high, but he has no idea how she got there. No ropes or low branches make it obvious.

"Do you need help?" he asks again. She shifts on her branch, and the needles reveal a small, round silver-green breast. He gawks for a moment—at seventeen he hasn't seen many breasts—then blushes and turns his head. "Clothes, maybe?" He doesn't see any. He desperately hopes there are some, and then he desperately hopes there aren't.

She laughs at him. Her laugh is like those icy drops of water that come off the trees. She unbends and walks down the branch. Her bare feet grip the bark like a squirrel's. Then she jumps.

"Hey!" he says.

She lands in front of him, two-footed, hands on her hips. Her chin juts out a little as she looks at him. Her breasts are small, round, firm, and completely bare, except for the green swirls that wrap around them, down her stomach, over her flank—swirls the color of fir trees. She smells like earth.

"I saw you out there," she says. Her voice carries a hush to it. "In that machine."

The truck, he reminds himself, but his thoughts are slow and thick. He is supposed to be looking for help, a cabin he thought he saw in the woods, some place to call a tow truck. Shitty pickup made it out here all the way from Chicago, and then broke down only fifty miles away from the Pacific, where he'd been aiming it. The aftertaste of frustration remains in his mouth, but it's harder and harder to remember.

He clears his throat. "My truck quit. I'm lost."

She cocks her head. "I can see that," she says.

Then, slowly, she lifts her hand. She touches his forehead.

A wind sweeps through him. For a moment, it blows all the fog away and leaves him crystal-clear, bright and dry as a summer day. For a moment, he feels like one of these big trees, roots stretching for the heart of the earth, crown puncturing the sky, free to grow as he pleases, no matter how high or deep.

But the feeling recedes as fast as it comes, in a sucking rush like a retreating tide. The more he chases it, the faster it flees until finally it's gone and he's back in the real world, on his knees in the dirt, with the water from a season of rain and snow seeping through his jeans.

Lost.

Cold.

Alone.

After a long time he pushes himself up. "She didn't even tell me her name," he mumbles. But even as he says it, he finds that he knows. Her name is in him somehow, like a seed splitting, growing.

Her name is Evergreen.

He holds onto the word like a gemstone he's found buried in the ground. He digs it out every night and hangs onto it in his sleep.

Evergreen.

———

EVERGREEN

THE CITY WHERE NICK GREW UP was not evergreen. It was mostly gray, but not like rocks and branches—gray like concrete, like the sludgy snow that lined the roadways in the winter. There were other colors, of course—billboards and murals painted on stained building walls, dented soda cans, the dirty whites of shredded Styrofoam cups, black asphalt, fluorescent construction crews. But mostly Nick remembers all the other colors, the other happenings—school, home, trips to the Lincoln Park Zoo and the lakeshore—as just a blur in the grayness.

Before the grayness, there was a vague green time. He remembers his parents—both of them—taking him down to the ocean, fifty miles from where the truck broke down. Not that there's anything waiting for him there now except a memory of a time when all the people seemed huge and the rocks in the water were bigger than God—a memory of grass, a small yard not far from the sea, with parents who weren't divorced . . . before he and his mother moved to Chicago to live with his Aunt Geri in her apartment full of ceramic birds and dingy blue carpet.

It seemed important, at one time, to find that yard. Before the memory disappeared altogether.

But now there's Evergreen. Now he's in her forest, chopping wood.

He swings his axe into a fat cedar log, and it splits down the middle, pink and brown, filling the damp air with its scent. He wiggles the axe head, and the log splits into two halves on the chopping block.

"Getting a lot better at that," a woman says behind him. She is wearing a mossy green cotton dress and black Wellingtons spattered with mud. Her salty-brown hair coils in a labyrinth at the nape of her neck. Wrinkles track the corners of her eyes and mouth, but they're kind wrinkles, the sort brought on by smiling.

Her name is DeAnn. Her son found him after Evergreen left.

"You work me hard enough," he says over his shoulder.

She laughs. "You're a growing boy. The work is good for you."

Nick grunts, but he knows it's true. She knows he knows it. It's been a month since Wolf led him back to their homestead, and he's spent it watching for glimpses of a girl in the woods and working that Chicago dream out of his system.

He shivers and it's not because of the rain. DeAnn's eyes narrow and he knows she knows it's not because of the rain either. But she never asks what's going on in his head. She keeps her mouth shut and doesn't try to act like his mother, and that's what he likes about her. He works for his room and board, and he likes that about her too.

She can watch a person, though, and let him know there are questions he ought to answer.

"No," he says. "I haven't called my mother yet."

"She's probably worried about you, honey."

Frantic is more like it. He'd left her a note explaining why and how he was leaving, but not where he was going. If he'd told her, Geri would have had them on the next plane to meet him. His mom got frantic about a lot of things. She always calmed down eventually.

"Nick. You can let her know you're okay without giving away where you are. Very few people know we're here anyway."

His shoulders slump. "I know. But Geri—"

"No." DeAnn shakes her head. "Not Geri. Your mother."

Nick sets up another log on the stump. It's a big stump, whorled with year rings so tight he can't begin to count them. He wonders who cut this fir and why, how big it might have gotten if left to grow. He centers the log, and then hefts his axe, marking the place he'll strike with the wet steel head.

"Geri, my mother," he says. "They're one and the same. I'm staying here for a little while longer."

DeAnn's green eyes—the same color as the mist-strewn trees—grow troubled. "How long?" she asks. "One day you're going to have to face the world outside, Nick. Just because you ignore it doesn't mean it will go away."

"So far ignoring it's working just fine." He checks to make sure she's clear of the axe, then swings it up over his shoulder, down, smack, into the piece of wood.

He's only been here a month, but he's getting pretty good at this. If you get a rhythm going, you don't have to think of anything at all. Your head is full of smack and thunk, your muscles burn, you start to sweat, you take off your coat and split wood in your flannel shirt in the rain.

Water steams off your skin, and you don't notice it when DeAnn walks up the path toward the house and leaves you alone, not until you see a head, a back, leaving you.

And then you turn toward the woods and search the mist for a silver-skinned girl with green-brown eyes. No one sees you do it, so it's okay. Maybe you think of your mother sometimes, but why should you step back into her nightmare?

You turn back to splitting wood. As long as you work, you're all right. As long as you can be close to the trees, searching for Evergreen.

NIGHTS AFTER DINNER Wolf lights a couple of kerosene lamps, and they spend some time reading or working by lamplight.

The lamps smoke occasionally, and their pink glow wavers, refracted by the thick glass. The night Wolf found him, they walked into the house's small kitchen and Wolf clicked off his flashlight, and then there was only the light and smell of kerosene, the red crackle of the fire in the big stone hearth, and Nick was convinced that he had stepped into a faerie netherworld.

He's still not sure he hasn't, but the gas-powered tiller sitting by the barn seems to decide the issue in favor of the real world. But, still, the small stacked stone and log house with DeAnn's store of dried herbs hanging from the beams, its rock hearth and the big iron kettle that hangs over it, makes him wonder sometimes.

"Why do you live like this?" he asked, the second or third day after Wolf found him. "Don't you miss TV or electricity or hot showers?"

DeAnn had shrugged. "Hot showers, maybe. But do you miss TV?"

He hadn't, after a while. There was too much work to do. Too many books to leaf through, crammed on the shelves that lined every available inch of wall space. If the walls and shelves both hadn't been built of big Douglas fir timbers, they probably would have collapsed long ago. DeAnn's books didn't look like other people's books, though. Most of them were old and bound in cracked leather, not cloth.

DeAnn laughed when he mentioned it to her. "I'm allowed my eccentricities," she said.

"Why? Because you're old?"

She'd given him a sour glance, then moved off distractedly toward a shelf on the west wall of the hearth room, where she trailed a finger down a line of books bound in deep forest green. "Well, witches are, aren't they?"

"Witches? Like—you're a pagan?" He'd known a few pagans in high school. Mostly they were girls who dyed their hair black and wore T-shirts with pentagrams on them.

DeAnn pulled a book off the shelf and gave him a bemused smile as she opened it. "Call it what you want," she said, turning back to the book. She sat down in a rocking chair near the fire, picked up her cup of tea, and didn't speak again all evening.

Faerie is where he feels he's landed, some other world revolving on its own plane far away from the noise and grinding metal of the city, and that is fine with him. Every time he runs into a machine on the farm it jars him, as if by its very existence it has thrown the whole orbit of this small world out of its regular ellipse. DeAnn and Wolf don't seem to mind using machinery, but they look out of place doing it. Especially Wolf. There's no real reason why he ought to; it's just something about Wolf. His name, for instance. Or the way he sits so still sometimes, watching the woods.

"You look like you're waiting for a chance to escape," Nick said once. Joking. Sort of. He'd walked up behind Wolf, but Wolf didn't even flinch.

"Does it look that way?" Wolf said.

Nick cocked his head. "Sometimes."

Wolf was sitting on a low, flat rock, legs crossed. He unfolded himself and stood up. He was tall, taller than Nick, with a long, leggy height and faraway green eyes that girls probably liked. He dusted off his jeans and looked over at Nick, and Nick suddenly felt awkward—him with his white-blond spikes and washed-out blue eyes and pale city skin. He shoved his hands in his pockets, feeling like a kid even though nothing had been said.

Wolf turned back to the woods. "Sometimes I wonder what's out there," he said. "In your world."

Nick frowned. "You must have been off this mountain some time."

"Oh, sure. I've been to Portland, and we have to go to Tillamook for supplies. But I don't really know where you come from. Not anymore."

Was that hostility? Nick searched Wolf's features for some indication of a fight but saw only curiosity. "You don't want me here?"

Wolf shook his head. "DeAnn says you can stay as long as you want. You know that."

"But you. You think I ought to leave?"

"I think you ought to do what you think you ought to do. That's what I mean about your world. Sometimes I wonder how people live there. Where you're always wondering what you ought to be doing instead of just doing what you know you need to." He stepped off the rock and toward the house, put his hands in his pockets. "You're not the first person from out there who's come this way."

Nick jumped down off the rock. "Was there a girl—"

Wolf stopped and turned around. "There's always a girl. You should stay away from her."

"So it's only okay to do what I think I ought to do when you think I ought to be doing it too?"

He knew his face was flushed. It always did when he got angry. Wolf just watched him, which made Nick flush all the more.

"You think you're so superior, don't you, up here on your ridge without anybody telling you what to do or where to go or how to do it? You think people have forgotten about you and are always going to leave you alone? What about the logging companies? And school? Why the hell aren't you in school? You can't tell me your mom homeschools you—I've never seen you crack a book."

"I read every night," Wolf said. He looked surprised, like why-are-you-so-stupid.

Nick leaned forward. "That's not the same!" he yelled. "It's NOT THE SAME!"

He was breathing hard. His hands were clenched in fists. His heart thudded—hard—against his ribcage in that weird *ka-thunk-thunk-ka-thunk-ka-thunk* rhythm he'd developed as a teenager. *Do you think it's the drugs affecting his heart?* his mom had asked Geri once. *No, Geri said, that stuff's perfectly safe. Just think how he'd do in school without it?*

Wolf arched an eyebrow. "Who's trying to forget the world?"

"You can't have it one way and not the other!"

"If somebody warned you to stay away from a poisonous snake, would you yell at him for it?"

Oh. He just wants her for himself.

Why else would Wolf be so cagey with him? Why else would Wolf watch him like a dog watching another dog prowl the boundaries of his territory?

"She's mine," Nick said—quicker than he meant to. "She talked to me. She touched me."

He didn't know why he said it, and once the words were out of his mouth he wished he'd shredded them with his teeth.

Wolf's eyebrows flew upward. "She touched you?"

He couldn't unsay the words. He stuck his hands deeper in his pockets and turned his head.

"And that's why you're staying here," Wolf said slowly, as if everything had suddenly become clear to him too, except that he and Nick were looking at the same thing through different lenses. "You're not ever going to call your mother, are you?"

"Why should I," he said, and even to his ears he sounded like a jerk. He tried to soften his next words—for his mother's sake, not for Wolf's. "What I told your mom is true. My Aunt Geri would find me. And she doesn't belong here. Not in these woods."

He looked around at the thick trunks of the firs—old growth and huge—and waited for Wolf to say something else, to rekindle his anger, but all he could think of was his mother and those damn ceramic cardinals gathering dust in Geri's apartment. The same way his mom did.

"My mom's lost," he said.

"There's more than one way to lose yourself," Wolf said.

Nick gritted his teeth. "Evergreen again."

Wolf shrugged. "DeAnn would say we all have to find our own paths through the woods. But you're headed toward a cliff."

"Can't you just say what you mean?"

"Evergreen's world passed by a long time ago. She's as mad about that as you are about your city. You think Evergreen's adopting you, but really all she wants is to make you over the same as all those other people you're so angry at. Unless that's what you want."

"You're just jealous."

"Of who? You? Evergreen?"

Nick stood there, mouth clamped shut. Wolf stared at him a while, then shook his head.

"DeAnn says you'll sort yourself out. I guess you just want someone to do it for you."

"Wouldn't it be easier that way?" It was a joke. But Wolf took it seriously.

"Yeah," he said as he turned and started walking back to the house. "But nobody else knows where you buried all your junk."

ALL THAT BULLSHIT about witches and books and worlds gone by. What did either of them know, lost out here in the woods and the mist? DeAnn had taken herself and her boy out of the world as surely as he'd stumbled out of it when his truck died.

Hypocrites.

He thought about leaving. Maybe he'd just start walking; he knew the general direction in which he'd left his truck now—at least he thought he did. But that would mean leaving Evergreen. That would mean not finding out who, or what, she was, or why she was here, or why she'd talked to him. Or if any of that magic shit was true.

Probably it wasn't. Probably Evergreen was just some weird pagan chick and Wolf and DeAnn were wish-we-were-hippies who bought into all that New Age crap his aunt Geri despised—crystals and herbs and flute songs. Probably he *should* just get out of here before he got in serious trouble or before Geri tracked him down.

But there had been that touch, and the gauzy clear-headedness that followed, and anyway, weren't people always saying he was so impulsive and never followed through on anything, and spent all his time day-dreaming, head in the clouds?

"Dammit, I am not daydreaming!" he said out loud, to nobody but the squirrels and the trees. And maybe Evergreen, if she could hear him.

I'll find out what's going on, he told himself. *And I won't need any drugs to do it.*

AT FIRST HE FELT like he needed the drugs. He got all jumped up, or he felt like sleeping, or both at the same time, which made no sense. He stayed up late at night and worried about whether DeAnn would find out he should be taking them, or that, if he somehow managed to find his bottle of pills, that she wouldn't let him take them, and then he wouldn't be able to concentrate, to do anything that needed doing. Worrying kept him up at night even after he'd stopped hoping that Evergreen would come.

And that would be when he'd see her, a brief glance out the window. She'd press her face to the glass and wrinkle her nose like a kid. He slept in Wolf's room, so he had to get up quietly for fear of waking the other boy, and by the time he made it to the window, Evergreen had already laughed and tripped away, into the darkness. In the morning it always seemed like he'd dreamed her, a female Peter Pan. But every night it happened, again and again, and Wolf snored on his bunk, and DeAnn slept in the other room.

He started to think of himself as her Lost Boy, and maybe that was why she laughed at him, because it was so corny.

He became increasingly sure that Evergreen was *faery.* The old-fashioned English spelling of the word seemed like the only one to do her justice. He scoured DeAnn's books, and DeAnn watched him over the top of her half-moon spectacles. "Found a subject of interest?" she'd say.

"Mmmm." Anything to put her off. Wolf watched him like he knew what he was doing, but he never said anything. So Wolf was that much like any other kid. Or maybe Wolf just wanted to see him sink himself. DeAnn's books on the subject—and she had a lot of books on the subject—were not flattering, so it was no wonder that Wolf was convinced Evergreen was as dangerous as a snake. Nick had grown up thinking of fairies in terms of those cutesy butterfly costumes five year old girls wore for Halloween. But DeAnn's books had chapter titles like: FAERIES—*To capture them;* FAERIES—*To avoid capture; How to escape*

the Otherworld; Making it Back; Tricking a Faery Out of Its Gold; and
SPRITES, PIXIES, AND BROWNIES—*Treating Bites, How To.*

"So much for fairy tales," he mumbled one night, shutting the book
he'd shoved close to the kerosene lamp in order to make out the old-
fashioned typeface. The leather binding creaked, and he tucked a few
thin, tattered flakes of page back in under it. He leaned backward in his
chair to find DeAnn standing behind him.

"Taken an interest in folklore, have you?" she said. She didn't sound
impressed.

"It's a wonder these books haven't all disintegrated," he said.

"Looking for something in particular? Or has your fire just been
ignited?" Her voice grew a little milder. She sat down beside him. Across
the room, Wolf sat by the fire, whittling. Long strips of bark and wood
curled to the floor at his feet. He didn't raise his head, but he glanced at
Nick out the corner of his eye. He looked a little ridiculous sitting in the
straight cane-backed chair—too tall for it, too tall for the house. Out of
place inside, where he wasn't dwarfed by the trees.

"You just assume I don't like to read?"

She shrugged. "You didn't seem to have any inclination to until now.
I've seen it happen, of course, but your choices . . ." She flipped open the
cover of one of the books he'd been looking at. *"Faeries and Their Kin."*
She wrinkled her nose as she leafed through the pages. "Never cared
for this one myself."

"Why not?"

She shut the book. "For one thing, he's so damned academic about it.
'The Faery and his Habitat.' Might as well be observing a salamander."

"So you think they're real."

DeAnn took off her glasses. "Oh, I know they're real." She looked at
him with those hard/soft eyes. "And so do you."

He flushed and looked away, only to find himself staring at Wolf,
who was looking at him now. Nick turned toward DeAnn again.

"I've heard some stories," he mumbled.

"No," she said. "You've seen Evergreen."

He stood up, casting a daggered glance at Wolf. "Wolf told you," he
said. "Wolf wants to keep me away from her, and so do you."

"No. Wolf never told me. But the only people who ever find us are always looking for her." She sighed and stretched out her legs. "I didn't figure you'd be any different."

Nick crossed his arms over his chest. "And did you give them the run-around, too? Let them believe you're letting them stay when really you've got them shut up in a prison?"

He glared at DeAnn. DeAnn's mouth twitched as if she might smile, but then her expression settled back into careful neutrality. Another woman—his Aunt Geri, for instance—might have laughed. His mother would have started screaming back at him, or worse, crying.

"No," DeAnn said. "And I'll give you the choice to leave, too. You've always had the choice. You're just not used to thinking in those terms."

"Like I'm supposed to believe you or anybody cares? I'm seventeen. I'm still a kid."

DeAnn stood up. "Sweetie, I'll tell you a secret. Nobody has to give you your freedom. It's not a thing to be taken. It's just something you have."

"When I'm twenty-one."

"You drove your truck all the way here from Chicago and you still believe that? How did it feel to get behind the wheel that first day?"

Scary as hell. He'd walked out of school, shaking with the determination to do something, anything, to get himself out of an intolerable situation. Geri was sitting on him every night, *did you do your homework, look at what your grades are doing to your mother, are you in trouble again, it's your father in you, I know it.* He was grounded from going out with his friends—the few that he had—and all he did was school and work. To make up for that old truck he bought with no one's permission, even though it was his own money. To make up for the pills Geri had found in his dresser drawer. Not the Ritalin, though he popped that like anything—lots of kids did, it was like speed when you did enough of it.

He'd walked out of school and jumped on the El. Ridden it to a suburban parking lot where his truck was waiting on him. But once he'd cleared Chicago and made it out onto that straight, flat stretch of interstate that led through all the old cornfields he had never seen, the shaky, scared feeling turned into whoops of joy.

DeAnn's face softened. "I thought so," she said. She touched his cheek.

The touch snapped him back to the moment. He recoiled from her fingers, stepping away.

"So you'll leave the door unlocked tonight?"

DeAnn looked stricken. "Oh, honey. That door's never been locked in the first place."

So now he's watching the window, waiting for Evergreen to press her face against it and stick out her tongue like a five-year-old. He's lying on the cot on the floor, fidgeting his fingers the way he used to do in school. Thumbs rolling over each other, dreaming cat's cradles.

On the other side of the room, Wolf says, "So you're going tonight." He sounds dull. Resigned.

"Your mom said I could leave whenever I wanted."

"You keep calling her that. But she isn't."

Nick stops his fingers. "What?"

"She's not my mom. She's just DeAnn. I wandered up through the woods the same as you. Except a long, long time ago."

Everybody who comes here comes looking for Evergreen. That's what DeAnn said. Nick rolls over on his side to look at Wolf, but the room is too dark to see.

"It's not worth it, going to find her," Wolf says.

Nick is quiet for a moment more. "You'd like to have her, wouldn't you."

"No one has Evergreen," Wolf says, disgusted. "I hope you do find her, just so you'll learn."

Nick rolls on his back again, fidgets his fingers. "She's probably just some girl."

Wolf snorts. "You're a moron, Nick. Go to sleep."

"There can't be any such thing as faeries. That's just—head in the clouds stuff."

"Is that what they told you?" Wolf's bed creaks. He must have rolled over.

"It's true, isn't it? I mean, real life true? There are no faeries in the real world."

Wolf sighs. "You said something about it when you were a kid, didn't you. And somebody told you it wasn't true. Like they said the bogeyman wasn't true, or the monsters under the bed. So when you told them about the faeries, they said that's not true, and when you kept saying it, they got scared and said why don't we take you to a psychiatrist. Didn't they."

Nick lies silent for a moment, staring at the ceiling but with an eye to the window, which is still just as full of black as the room. "Is that what happened to you?"

"They try to convince you that you don't know your own truth. When they can't convince you, they've got drugs to do it for them."

That-boy's-head-is-always-in-the-clouds. Had he ever mentioned faeries to Aunt Geri? He thinks hard for a moment. But it's been so long, and the drugs and the not-caring, the not-caring as a form of self-defense, have made all those long years into a blur. Still, there's something inside tugging at him down deep, like a little kid pulling on a grown-up's sleeve. But he can't identify it in the dark, so he pushes it away.

"I want to see Evergreen," he says.

Wolf sighs. "Maybe DeAnn is wrong then. Maybe you've just got to see it to cut through all that junk in your head."

He sounds as if he's talking to himself. Nick fidgets, checks the window, says, "So she's really a faery?"

"No," Wolf says. "She's been here too long."

"What is she then?"

"I don't know. Nobody does."

"She's just Evergreen."

"Yeah." A pause. "Evergreen."

Does he sound jealous? Does he remember her touch on his forehead, or see her face at the window at night? How old was he when he wandered through the woods to end up at DeAnn's door?

"I'm going tonight," Nick says. "Nobody's going to stop me."

"Nobody's going to try," Wolf replies. "Be nice to have my room back."

He rolls over in a rustle and creak of bedding and mattress springs. Nick stares in his direction, stung a little.

But then there's a tap-tap-tapping at the windowpane.

It's Evergreen, sticking out her tongue at him.

Nick throws off his covers and stumbles out of the room—moving too fast to accommodate the dark. Wolf sounds like he might be sitting up, but he doesn't follow him.

The door is unlocked, just like DeAnn said. Nick glances toward her room, then takes a deep breath and opens the door.

And now he's alone and free in the darkness. "Evergreen," he whispers. "Evergreen!"

She appears like a sudden beam of light—silent and luminous, the same color as moon on fir trees. "Shh," she giggles, putting a finger on his lips. "You'll wake the house. And then that DeAnn will come out, and you'll have to go back."

She doesn't act like anyone who's been here longer than the Indians. She acts and looks like a sixteen year old. He wants to bend down and kiss her, but she skips away from him.

"Come on," she says. "I want to show you something."

She turns around and all he can focus on are the round curves of her butt. Then she disappears into the mist. So he follows her. He follows her through wet brush, beneath enormous fir boughs laden with sleety pendants of ice, past the woodpile and the tilled-up muck of the garden, out into the woods. He follows her down skinny hill paths that dip and climb, where she vanishes and reappears like the freezing drizzle that quickly paints its rime on his eyelashes, his eyebrows, the tips of his hair.

"Where are we going?" he calls, shivering in his denim jacket.

"You'll see," she says, but they keep going and he doesn't.

"Evergreen," he says, but she doesn't answer.

He's lost. "Evergreen!"

Instantly she's beside him. "Why are you so scared? It's only the forest. Look."

She puts her hand on his arm. Her touch raises goose bumps.

The moon is shining the way it's never done since he's been in Oregon. Illuminated in its glow is the trunk of the biggest tree he's ever seen. How many people would have to join hands to circle it? He feels like an ant in front of it. A termite. He looks up into its boughs but sees only needles and darkness.

"They call this a Sitka spruce," she says, trailing her finger down a ridge of its bark the way a human girl might trail her finger across a boy's arm. "They can't hear what it names itself, and they think they know everything. People."

He tries to ignore the venom in her voice. "How long has it been here?"

Evergreen shrugs. "Longer than you. Not as long as me. I remember when it was a sapling." She gives the trunk a pat and flashes him a grin that fades as she turns back to the tree. "There aren't so many of them now to keep me company."

"So," he says, trying not to get shaky, "so, it's true? What Wolf and DeAnn say about you?"

She wrinkles her nose. "Oh, probably not. They're not very friendly. People, through and through. Even that changeling boy."

"Wolf?"

She cocks her head. "Does it surprise you? Do you know anything about us, or are you people, too?"

"I don't know what you mean."

"*They* tried to pluck your faery eyes out, I know that. But are your eyes still there, Nick? Did you hide them for me?"

"I don't know what you mean. I don't know who *they* are. All I have are the eyes I was born with, Evergreen."

Saying her name is like grabbing onto a rope. He hopes it can pull him out of this place of not understanding anything, and being cold and a little scared.

No, he isn't scared. *This is the girl who touched me. This is that same girl.*

She watches him with her head cocked. Finally, she sighs. "Silly little one. I'm not talking about *those* eyes. I'm talking about the eyes behind your eyes. The eyes that led you here."

"I want to ask you so many questions," he says, taking a step toward her, his hands out. "Like why you called me off that road. And what happened when you touched me. And—"

She giggles and puts her hand on his mouth. "You talk too much."

His face falls. She takes her hand away, then turns around. "Come," she says. "Let me show you the world you've stumbled into. But if you try to see it with the eyes they made you see with, you won't see anything at all. Understand?"

He doesn't, but she's already walking, so he hurries after her. The Sitka spruce towers over them as if watching them go, and Nick can't resist craning his neck back to look up into its darkness.

"You're still not seeing," she says over her shoulder.

"What am I looking for?"

"You're looking for your dreams."

IT'S BEEN SO LONG he can't remember them, the dreams he used to dream when he stared out the window, after his mother and father had split up and they'd all moved away from Oregon. And as for that time before, that Oregon-time, he barely has any memory of it at all, aside from the hazy recollection of ocean, rock and wind, and holding the hands of a woman and a man so much bigger than he was.

What he sees when he follows Evergreen into the forest is birds. Not fragile, fake, ceramic. No chipped cardinals, no tawdry blue jays stamped *Made in China*. No, these birds are real. They swoop through the dark forest, chittering and calling, a feathered abundance.

And yet . . . .

They're not birds at all.

"Faeries," he breathes. He stops walking to stare. "That's what they are—they're faeries."

Evergreen is suddenly at his shoulder. Her breath on his neck feels like the damp touch of mist. "Not faeries, Nick. Dreams."

One buzzes by his face, like a huge dragonfly with ruby wings. As it flits in and out of Evergreen's glow, he can see that it has the body of a woman. Its crimson hair streams over golden skin. It loops up into the trees in a long, lazy spiral, until the night swallows it.

"You could stay here with them," Evergreen says. She holds out her hand for a little emerald boy-fly, and he perches on her open palm and stares at him with yellow eyes. "Imagine, you could be a dream, too."

He frowns. "But I want to be with you."

She laughs, and the little green dream leaps from her palm.

But not quick enough. She catches him by his wings. Dangles him above the ground.

"Do you really?" she says.

The way she holds the boy-fly makes him squirm. But he remembers the way he felt when she touched him. "There's nothing for me out there," he says.

"This isn't a decision to make lightly, dear Nick." The dream-fly twists its head to look up at her, pleading. Something twists inside Nick, too, and he bends closer, pulse quickening, to see the dream-fly's face.

It's a boy's face. A boy no older than five or six, frantically trying to pump wings that Evergreen is pinching. His chest moves in and out with every frightened breath. He stares up at Nick with those deep amber eyes, black pupils like flies trapped inside them.

"What are you doing?" he asks Evergreen.

"I'm showing you this dream, Nick."

"But—"

"If you don't trap a dream, you'll never see it. It will fly away and lose itself in the trees. Now look, look, at this one."

He hesitates, frowning at the dream that dangles, angry, from Evergreen's thin fingers. Then he bends down until his face is so close to the little dream that his breath makes its wings shiver. And in its eyes, a scene begins to take shape. A long, black street, walled in by buildings that frown down at him like stern and unhappy parents, blocking out all but a sliver of blue sky. The sidewalks are alive with activity, though—construction workers popping out of an uncovered manhole; mothers pushing babies in strollers; old men and their wives out for a walk.

Inside one of the buildings, a boy—blond, spiky-haired—stares out a filmy window. Nick remembers staring out the window, too, and then his teacher would call him, and he'd jerk back to the moment without knowing anything that she wanted to know, or remembering what he was looking at. He remembers only that he was someplace . . . else.

But in the dream's eyes, he can see what the boy is watching. He's watching a neighborhood full of faeries.

The faeries skitter and whirl, dodging the big wheels of cars. They hide in window casements and lounge on the eaves of roofs. They scurry up and down the rungs of the ladder inside the manhole, sticking out their tongues and making funny faces at the construction workers, who don't notice them at all. The boy watching them from the window smiles. The faeries—some of them winged and some not, a few with tiny horns sprouting out of their foreheads or hooves for feet, and all of them dressed so individually as to defy describing their dress as a group—these faeries begin to notice him when he smiles. They drift together and congregate in groups, staring up at the window and pointing at him. Then they begin to beckon to him, *Come out, come out and play with us!*

The boy in the classroom doesn't look frightened at all. At the window, his face disappears. He must be walking through the classroom. Nick's heart pumps harder. What is he doing? Doesn't he know what the teacher will do to him if he gets up and walks around in class? Doesn't he know that's just one step closer to a trip to the psychiatrist and a pharmacy scrip?

The image shifts, and his stomach lurches. He blinks, and now he has a more distant perspective. He can see the front door to the school. It edges open a little and then a little more, until finally the spiky-haired boy slips out the gap and walks down the steps. He's a little thin thing, wispy as a sprite himself and with the same glint in his deep blue eyes. His eyes aren't the color of faded denim. They're saturated with blueness, like two patches of silk. He smiles when he sees the little people, and they smile at him.

Then he joins them in their dance in front of the school window, sticking out his tongue and wiggling his butt at the teacher, and the principal, and all the kids still stuck inside. They dance around the sidewalk, making farting sounds with their armpits.

The dream winks out. Nick is left staring at Evergreen, who tosses the dream up into the dark sky like an afterthought. It looks back over its shoulder and sticks out its tongue at her as it spirals upward, coating them both with a fall of sparkling pixie dust.

Nick wipes the dust from his face, rolling the golden grit between his fingertips. It looks like quartz sand. "I never left the school and danced with the faeries. Was that supposed to be me?"

"Of course it was you," she says. "Here's another."

Her hand shoots out to grab a different dream. He barely gets a glimpse of it before Evergreen has it in her fist, but then she opens her hand, and a tiny boy dream hunches inside, hair the color of ripe wheat, wings flickering sapphire against the pale silver-green of Evergreen's skin. Slowly Evergreen uncurls her fingers, but the dream makes no attempt to escape.

"See this one," she breathes.

A little boy, holding his mother's hand. A father, licking an ice cream cone, laughing. The wind tosses the man's golden hair, and the woman's dark curls dance around her face as she smiles. Waves crash onto the sand, spraying their legs with plumes of white. The little boy laughs, kicks the foam across the beach, digs his chubby little fingers into the damp sand, spreads it over his legs, his arms, until he is covered in a golden blond the sea laps up, sweeping him clean.

There are the big rocks, clear and real instead of fuzzy and half-dreamt. There is the ice cream, cold and sweet and strawberry in his mouth. There is the touch of a mother and a father who care, and the clear eyes of a boy who is free to run around like crazy, chasing the waves, falling on his back, getting up again to spend a long time looking out over the sea, bucket and shovel forgotten.

What do kids that little think about?

But it's more than years that separate him from the four year old on the beach. He swipes the mist from his face only to find that it tastes like salt.

"Why are you showing me this?" he says to Evergreen. "It's just shit, it's all it is. Shit."

He turns to stomp away, but there's nowhere to go. A dream buzzes past his face, and he swats at it with his hand.

"You're just a sapling swaying in the wind, Nick," Evergreen says, "but you came out here for a reason."

"I was just driving," he mumbles. "Like an idiot."

"You came out here looking for your dreams. Didn't you."

He whips around. "Yeah," he says, "and now I've found them, and all they are is tinkerbells! What use is that?"

Evergreen raises her hand where the sapphire dream crouches. Hesitantly, it stands, then leaps. In an instant, the dream is gone, and Nick feels a hole open up inside him. He hunches his shoulders against the cold and turns so he won't have to look at Evergreen. She walks up to him anyway.

"It doesn't have to be gone, Nick. Look at me. Have I aged even a year over the centuries?"

He glances at her, at her smooth skin and her teen-age face.

"You're telling me I can be like you?" he says.

She screws up her face. "Well . . . not exactly." Then she smiles. "But, oh Nick, I'm so lonely. And we can be friends, can't we? We can live here among the trees and the dreams and you can dance with the faeries. You can have any dream you dream, Nick, no matter what *they* say. Look, Nick, just look!"

Reluctantly, he follows the line her finger makes. Beneath an overhang of fir boughs shaped like a roof there is the beach again, the mother and father, but no boy. The mother and father are frozen, as if waiting, but waiting for what?

The wind blows and he can taste salt. But he's not crying now, so what is it? Spray from the ocean, for God's sake?

A touch on his hand surprises him. It's Evergreen, twining her fingers with his. "Come on, Nick," she whispers. "Let's go."

She pulls him toward the tableau under the firs.

"Come on."

He drags his feet. He doesn't know why. Now she is pulling him through the needle carpet, and his heart is pounding, *ka-thunk-thunk, ka-thunk.*

"Evergreen," he whispers, but she doesn't seem to hear him. She is surprisingly strong. The toe of one boot touches the beach sand, then the other. The sea wind rubs its salty fingers against his mouth, depositing happiness. Nick runs his tongue over his lips, tasting it.

It's a breezy happiness. A delirious, dancing, crazy happiness, caused by nothing more than the feel of wet sand against the bottoms of his feet and the prospect of ice cream—strawberry, his favorite.

He reaches up to take his mother's hand, but before he can touch those faraway fingers, he hears somebody calling him.

"Nick! Nick!"

DeAnn. She followed him anyway. Just like he knew she would.

Furious, he spins around. The beach bleeds away, a fairy tale, ending, but without the happily ever after.

DeAnn's robe and nightgown slap her ankles in the wind. Her hair is down. Wolf, dressed, stands beside her.

Evergreen rolls her eyes. "What do they want," she says.

"You said you'd let me go!" Nick yells at them.

DeAnn steps closer, carefully picking her way through the wet needle-trash covering the ground. "I never said I wouldn't follow you. That's the problem with free will, Nick; you can't always organize the actions of other people."

He kicks at the needles on the ground. "You're trying to organize mine."

DeAnn shakes her head. She has moved entirely into Evergreen's nimbus now, and he can see all the wrinkles that line her face, stamping it with age and mortality. So different from Evergreen.

"No," she says. "I'm just trying to show you an alternative."

"To what? Love and happiness?" He snorts. "I've had a whole life full of that alternative."

"So you think going back to some kind of fairy tale past is going to help?" She swipes at the salted brown strands of hair blowing past her face, pushing them away. "You think what she offers you is anything more than an illusion? Past is past, Nick. Not even her magic can bring it back."

"So what if I want the illusion? You're trying to tell me the real world has any room in it for me? Fuck the real world, DeAnn! You think I got in a truck and drove out here so I could go crawling back to my Aunt Geri? You think I came out here so I could get a job down in Portland shoveling fries or fish or something?"

"You have a mother, Nick. You want to see some pretty pictures, go look in a photo album. Don't let Evergreen add you to them permanently. It's forever, Nick, and don't think it isn't. Other people will grow old and die, and you'll watch them do it. If she ever lets you out of her grasp."

Nick opens his mouth, with it full of feeling and not thought, but before he can get anything out, Evergreen shoves DeAnn away from him.

DeAnn stumbles backwards; Nick blinks in surprise. "Leave him alone, you old hag! The world doesn't want him, or me or any of us! Have you seen the trees around your farmstead? Saplings, cut down in their prime, murdered. And you—have you told him who you are, DeAnn? Have you told him why you are in these woods?"

Evergreen backs up with her arms crossed over her breasts and a self-satisfied smirk on her face. For a moment, DeAnn stares back at her, moon-pale, but then she firms her sagging jaw and lifts her head.

"I had the choice, and I made it. But you're not giving him the choice, are you? You can't bear the thought of losing anybody else so you've resorted to trickery and lies. Is that a proper use for your magic, Evergreen?"

"What right have you to speak to me so?" Evergreen shrieks. "How could you know anything of how alone I really am?"

She breaks down, sobbing, onto her knees. She presses her cheek against the forest floor, and her hair tumbles forward and hides her face. Her crying sounds like the keening of birds.

Nick stares at her. Then he looks up at DeAnn. "What does she mean, DeAnn?"

DeAnn sighs. "Once upon a time, I was like Evergreen, too. But I gave it up."

She looks old to him, older than before. He frowns. "Why?"

A rueful smile touches her mouth. "Oh, the usual. I did it for a man."

"And then he left and you were old," Evergreen spat, lifting her head. "You did it wrong. You went out into their world instead of taking them to yours."

DeAnn shakes her head, then reaches out to touch Wolf lightly on his sleeve. "No," she says, her smile growing brighter, "I did it exactly right. He may be gone, but he left me his son to raise. Wolf is worth the years."

Wolf catches her eye and smiles, too, a crooked, embarrassed grin that speaks of a love unfettered by resentments. DeAnn rests her hand on Wolf's arm, squeezes it.

Evergreen spits in the dirt. "That's what I think of their world," she says. "Leaving us all alone!"

She starts to cry again. She looks so small, huddled there in the dirt. Nick slips out of his jacket and kneels beside her to wrap it around her shoulders. She looks up at him, startled, the green swirls on her face sparkling with tears.

He gets back to his feet before she can touch him.

"It's up to me," he says. "Isn't it?"

NICK REMEMBERS IT THIS WAY.

He's building a cabin beneath a giant spruce. Sometimes Evergreen watches him as he splits the dead, leftover wood to make it into something new, and that's all right. Sometimes he invites her to sit with him while he drinks hot coffee in a cracked mug DeAnn gave him. The mug has a picture of a fairy garden on it, and drinking out of it reminds him of the dreams. Sometimes as he watches the dream-sprites playing in the trees it doesn't seem so impossible, that all those wounds of childhood might heal. Some day.

And some day maybe he will go back for his mother and serve her coffee out of this chipped fairy cup, too.

But for now he splits wood in the mist beneath the evergreens. The logs fall apart, and he stacks the pieces into walls.

The cabin gets a little bigger every day.

Some day, he'll call it home.

Angela Boord *raises babies and sometimes vegetables on fifteen acres in upstate New York. She and her husband have five children and are expecting their sixth in the fall. Her stories have appeared in* Strange Horizons, Ideomancer, *and* Lone Star Stories.

THE RED ENVELOPE

David Sakmyster

THIRTY YEARS FROM THE DAY I found the red envelope lying on the narrow dirt street, I returned again to the village of Sanzhi. With one exception, I had been visiting every five years since, making the long trip to northern Taiwan from America, each time leaving from different parts of the country as time chipped away at my foundations, leaning me this way and that.

My nomadic lifestyle was Zhen-Lang's fault. Wherever I went, she flooded the earth beneath my feet so I couldn't put down roots.

On each of my previous four visits, I met with my in-laws in their central hall, gave them gifts, and respectfully lit joffa sticks as offerings for their ancestors. Then, I walked over the hill to the small grove protectively shrouded by drooping red cypress trees. I marched past the family's headstones, through the well-manicured plot and the perfect hydrangeas, lilies and cherry blossoms, and I trod where no else ever came, past the prickly vines and beetle-chewed bushes to a corner beside a gnarled pear tree. There, I talked with Zhen-Lang. Told her of my life and the world. Reassured her of my constant faithfulness.

I did my duty and kept my pledge. Four times I've visited, at great expense. This time, I did not come alone. Julia was at my side, although quite ill herself, in mid-stage chemotherapy recovery. I told her not to come, but she insisted.

"I may be weak," she said, her green eyes sparkling under the fake auburn strands in her wig. "But you, Brian, my poor, good man, are not strong enough to do it."

"I am," I assured her, but I knew she was right. It wasn't my age—at fifty-two, I was still in good health. She was talking about something else. I'd had my chances. Four other opportunities to do this in person. But the image of that single red envelope always held me back, flaring up in moments of weakness, sounding the echoes of my promise down through the years.

Like the time I returned to New Orleans after my third year abroad. Taiwan had been the first and only stint of my overseas assignment. Exxon decided a desk job might suit me better.

The first week back, in February of 1975, was Mardi Gras. Coming out of a jazz club was Evelyn, beautiful in every way the partiers out on Bourbon Street were not. Curly brown hair, almond-shaped eyes. She bumped into me. Our eyes met, we smiled, and she dragged me back into the club. Six drinks later, we were in her hotel room. Slanting shadows bisected the walls, and the bed glowed from the revelry outside.

"What's wrong?" she said, after getting over her initial giggles..Her hands were skillfully but ineffectively moving under the sheet and her slick body roamed over mine.

"I'm sorry," I whispered, retreating to my side of the mattress. Her skin felt cold, and my flesh crawled. I smelled something like decayed flowers and muddy grass.

"Come on," Evelyn whispered. "Don't you want this? Or did you drink too much?"

I told her that was it. One too many. I feigned illness, ran to the bathroom and turned on the shower. When I finally came out, she was sleeping with her back to me. I crawled under the sheets and breathed slowly, hoping to sleep.

When I finally drifted off, Zhen-Lang was there waiting, standing perfectly still in the misty shadows, head bowed with sticks in her hair and her hands crossed in front of her. I bowed to her, or at least I think I did, and she made some nominal noise, like the hissing of a cat, and my blood went cold—

—and I shot up in bed, screaming. Evelyn backed away from me at first, then moved to put her arms around me. Haunted by that lingering image, I knocked her away, roughly. She screamed, then cursed at me. All I remember after that was sitting on the bed as she dressed, shouting at me and pointing to the door. I think she called me a freak, and worse things.

She wouldn't be the last woman to send me packing.

On my way out, she asked me who Zhen-Lang was.

I froze in the doorway.

"Who is she?" Evelyn demanded. "You called out her name several times before you woke yourself up."

I shuddered.

"Girlfriend?" she accused. "Or is she your wife?"

I hung my head as I stepped out into the hall.

"Should have told me you were married!" she shouted, and threw my shoes after me. "Or had the decency like any other guy to lie about it and—"

The door slammed—and strangely I don't remember touching it, or hearing Evelyn move. It just closed with a jarring thud.

Ever since, I've had problems with women. With relationships, with my entire life.

Julia says it's guilt. Maybe it's my old Catholic upbringing taking hold—the sanctity of the sacraments and all that. But I think there's more to it. It's who I am, and what once I promised Zhen Lang. What I continue to promise her every five years. Against the wishes of her family, even, but I can't help it.

I love her.

My first trip back to Sanzhi, on our fifth anniversary, was in 1979. It was a crisp fall day, and the Pacific breezes blew a chill over the hills and the storm-dampened rice fields on Zhen-Lang's family plot.

When I arrived, Zhen-Lang's brother, Ho-Jin, was in the fields, working beside his father, Wey-Tan. They were surprised to see me. "Did you bring the tablet?" my father-in-law asked, and I was grateful I could still understand the language. It helped that in the darkness of my room during sleepless nights, I sometimes spoke to my wife. In my head, in her language.

"Of course," I said, and turned my face to the cloud-riddled sky and felt light sprinkles tenderly anointing my skin.

"That is good," Wey-Tan said. "But you do not need to come."

"I think I do," I said as I carefully removed Zhen-Lang's ancestral tablet from my backpack. I knew they wouldn't want it in their house, but I didn't realize how completely they had put the whole business behind them.

"You can honor her in America," he whispered so his son could not hear. The deep lines in his forehead crinkled as he spoke, and raindrops trickled off his hard chin. "She is gone from here. It is what you did for us, and we are grateful, but we do not wish old memories brought back."

"But she is not gone," I insisted, pointing toward the grove to the east. "And . . . she is your daughter."

He hung his head. Over his shoulder I could see the house, and in the doorway, two women emerged. Mingmei-Chow, my mother-in-law, and Gengi-Sun, her other daughter.

Wey-Tan sighed when he saw his wife. "Very well. Come inside. Share tea and a meal. Tell us of yourself."

Inside, over a cup of bitter green tea, Mingmei-Chow asked if I had married again. Her eyes were bright, her face hopeful. She seemed in much better health than when I had last seen her.

"No, not yet," I said, shifting uncomfortably in my seat. Ho-Jin glared at me. Nearly twenty now, the boy must be nearing his own time for a wife. I looked around. "You all seem well."

Mingmei-Chow lowered her eyes modestly, but she nodded. "Yes, thank you."

I ate some rice and swallowed some more tea. I breathed in the incense from the joffa sticks, and I stared at the tablets on the mantel in the main hall. Their ancestral tablets. Husband and wife, son and daughter.

I recalled the first time I stood before that shrine. On my wedding day. How I teetered on wobbling legs, terrified and morbidly disturbed. I stood before the Tang-ki, the oracle of the little god, as he performed the ceremony. Zhen-Lang's family stood in attendance, looking grim and haggard. Each of them sick with various diseases the Tang-ki could not cure. The fields outside, too, were sickened, polluted as the well water.

It was the only way, her father told me as I held that envelope in my hands. It trembled in my fingers the same as it had when I found it on the road six months before.

A common trick, and had I been a native I might have thought twice before picking it up. But that is all ancient history. For whatever reason, by whatever fate, I came across it first. Oh, the Tang-ki claims only the intended groom would be drawn to the envelope, only the man Zhen-Lang desired.

On my usual morning bicycle ride, I stopped and picked it up. I opened it and saw the money—fifteen thousand Kuai, which was about four hundred dollars—plus some fine blond hair, like wisps of golden thread. Wey-Tan sprang from the bushes and pronounced me the lucky man who had earned his daughter's hand.

Of course I refused. Simply not possible, I said, without even considering the dishonor I might be causing. I tried to give back the envelope, but he wouldn't have it. Said he'd wait, his family would wait, but I was the intended for his daughter, and she would bring me to her one way or another.

He went on to explain his family's plight—the sickness of his two other children, the flu that struck without mercy. His wife, ill to near-death, and he himself wracked with chest pains. The Tang-ki tried everything, every known medicine, every prayer and invocation.

In the end, a dream told young Ho-Jin that his dead sister was not at rest. She was exerting her power from the land of the shades, stirring up the elements here and clamoring for notice.

Her mantel was empty, her tablet kept in a spare closet in the dark. She had died, Wey-Tan told me, when she was still an infant. Nineteen years ago. Now, she would have been ready to marry, to bind herself to a man and produce descendants who would honor her for all time. But today, she had no one. She was the Guniang—the 'Lonely Maiden'. Many families had them; many villages likewise sought this solution.

Wey-Tan begged me, and later, at the hospital, his entire family came, along with the gnarled old Tang-ki, to plead with me. "She has chosen you," Mingmei-Chow said with a raspy voice, white blotches on her skin, and her eyes red.

They looked like they belonged here beside me. As it was, I had been struck by a tough strain of malaria a week after I had refused Wey-Tan, thrown down the envelope and run from the village. Three months had passed, with my business counterparts noticeably concerned.

"It is the Guniang," the Tang-ki said. "It is Zhen-Lang. Powerful spirit, this little one. She will not rest until you concede."

"Please," Wey-Tan implored. "Just agree to the ceremony. That is all. You will be wed in a simple ritual, and then you may leave. You can marry again, a normal human wife. Have children, go on with your life. This is only for Zhen-Lang."

"And for us," said his wife, trembling.

So, finally exhausted, I surrendered and said yes, convinced that something so superficial would hold no meaning for me and I could, as they said, go on about my life. Wey-Tan, grinning, left the hospital after setting that red envelope down on my bedside stand.

In the darkness after the nurses extinguished the lights, I imagined a thin, wraithlike figure in the shadows, watching over me. I felt a strange attraction to that nebulous shape in the corner, then a stirring in my heart, a trembling throughout my body. I looked away, closed my eyes and tried to sleep; to my surprise, I found myself drifting off easily, comfortably. I imagined a soft breathing on my neck, and whispers of affection tingling across my skin.

I was well enough to leave four days later, and the next week, I married Zhen-Lang while seven incense burners puffed their offerings into the stale central hall of Wey-Tan's home. On shaking legs, trying desperately not to look at the grotesque contraption they had put together as a stand-in for my bride, I took the oath and went through with the bargain.

Beside me, a paper-stuffed red and white dress hung on a chair, with a magazine photo face taped onto a balled-up newspaper head. Everyone in attendance wore grim expressions, and no one made eye contact with me or my bride.

Afterwards, as instructed, I pulled out Zhen-Lang's tablet from inside the dummy, then Wey-Tan and I took the surrogate out back and burned it, dress, necklace and all, as a final offering to free the poor girl's ghost.

Julia says I should write a book on the whole psychology of these "ghost marriages"—how the interplay of rigid cultural mores works on the subconscious until such beliefs can cause physical symptoms.

She thinks that Zhen-Lang's family became ill from their concern over her spirit's restlessness. Living day after day not only with the tragic guilt of losing an infant, but also being forced by society to deny her existence; out of shame, to hide her tablet so as not to admit the reality of an impossibly unmarried daughter. Under all that stress, was it any wonder physical symptoms could arise?

Whenever Julia talks like that I keep quiet. I don't ask about the failure of the crops, or their miraculous recovery after the wedding. And I don't bring up my malaria. Of course there are coincidences, but maybe there's more.

I also never speak of my dreams. With Julia, I don't need to. She knows.

Just as Zhen-Lang's mother knew. That first visit, after dinner, Mingmei-Chow took me to the grove, and we stood beside the tiny, unmarked headstone. "She comes to you, doesn't she?"

I could only nod.

She looked at me intently. "And . . . you talk to her?"

"Yes."

"You . . . love her." It wasn't a question. She knew.

"Yes," I admitted, my throat dry, glancing away as if accused of some great perversion.

Mingmei-Chow shook her head slowly. "Always feisty, that one," she said.

I smiled, as I already had that impression, without ever a word spoken by that figure in my dreams. I knew enough, by the way her presence weighed on my actions, on everything I did, everyone I talked to. Especially women. Finally, I told Mingmei-Chow that her daughter was very jealous.

A shadow crossed her face. "Too young, she doesn't understand. The strongest of our needs is for offspring, to have descendants to keep our name alive, to honor us."

I told her I understood all this. It was why I agreed to the marriage, after all.

Mingmei-Chow shook her head and made bony fists out of her hands. "You have to see—it is not only the marriage that matters. You must have children."

That notion, so simple and obvious, sent me backing away from the little white stone. I turned, and caught my arm on a thorny branch below a single red rose.

I left, fleeing apologetically from their home, and I pondered the implications of Mingmei-Chow's words and rubbed away the blood that continued to flow from my arm.

DURING THE NEXT FIVE YEARS I dated four different women. I was living in Los Angeles, working now at a bank. Better hours, no travel. Great climate. I was making good money, and had a decent house in the hills. I never tried purposely to meet anyone, but in a big city, it just happened.

Jennifer and Diane I met through friends at work. Both were similar—dark skinned, blonde and pretty, but not stunning like those movie stars out at the clubs. They both wanted to settle down. At first, they liked that I didn't try anything on our dates. The perfect gentleman. I wished our relationships could have stayed at that stage.

At some point with women, hormones and long-range planning take over. Excuses burst from my lips at every chance. When I didn't call them back, things quickly ended. Diane tried to kiss me in my car, and I reacted by leaning on the horn. Jennifer surprised me once by showing up wearing only a bathrobe. I faked appendicitis and went so far as to call an ambulance.

Next came Maria. We met while volunteering at the Red Cross. One Saturday night we went to a show, and she gave me an ultimatum. She had horseshoe diamonds in her ears, and her lips were a strange shade of red. When I stared at them, all I could think of was that envelope.

She wanted us to move in together, and she wanted to kiss me, in that order. I told her I'd think about it, then never called, and never returned to the Red Cross. I ignored her calls and turned off my lights once when I saw her parked outside. I sat in the dark and whispered promises of love and adoration to the shadows.

It took several minutes before I realized the words were in Taiwanese.

THE RED ENVELOPE

In 1984 I went back to Sanzhi. It had been ten years since the marriage. In that time, I reflected, I had never been sick. Nothing worse than a cold. I felt great, my job was going well, I had a new car, and money enough to travel first class.

Smiling, I trod up the path where long ago I had ridden a bicycle and found my destiny. At Wey-Tan's home, I was greeted with less enthusiasm than before. Ho-Jin was no longer there; he had married last year and lived at the other edge of the village. Wey-Tan and Mingmei-Chow greeted me at the door while their daughter sat in the shadows near the back, near that empty closet where once Zhen-Lang's tablet had been stored.

"Why do you come?" they asked me.

I opened my mouth, and felt the warm sun at my back, prickling the hairs on my neck. "I want to see her," I said.

Mingmei-Chow put her fingers to her lips and backed away. "It is wrong," she whispered. "Do you not have a new wife? Children?"

"No," I said. "I . . . cannot." How could I explain this? How could I tell them of Zhen-Lang's hold on me, how she had so firmly captured me, body, soul and heart?

"Go," said Wey-Tan. "Do what you must, then move on, as we have done."

I turned from them and started toward the grove. Before I reached the great swaying cypress trees and the gardens, the blossoming hydrangeas and the wall of greenery, I heard footsteps. Gengi-Sun approached quickly, caught up, then walked beside me. Without a word, the young woman pushed aside the prickers after first plucking a rose from above her head.

I followed, and together we stood at the small headstone. I knelt, placed three joffa sticks on the ground, lit each one, then set her ancestral tablet beside her headstone.

Gengi-Sun and I stood there for a half hour, not saying a thing or even looking at each other. When the sticks were done, I retrieved the tablet, placed it in my pack, and followed Gengi-Sun out of the garden. Head-bowed, she returned home. At the doorway she gave me a backwards glance, and the sun danced on her face and I thought I could see a smile.

ON MY NEXT VISIT, in 1989, I reflected on the intervening five years. Walking up a paved road that had once been an old dirt path, I thought of the women I had met in Detroit since the last visit. Nancy, Alice and Christy. Each one a disaster of epic proportions, complete with vile breakup letters and accusations of infidelity.

As if they could understand what faithfulness meant.

Alice even suggested I was gay. Probably because I never touched her, never touched any of them. Not even once. And when we talked, I was distant—or so they said. Fear of intimacy, Nancy told me, and suggested I seek help. Blamed my mother or some nonsense.

I stopped dating around 1987. I stayed home a lot. Rented videos, and read. And I talked with her, even if she didn't answer. No one could accuse me of being distant with her. And intimate? There wasn't a secret I didn't share with Zhen-Lang. I told her everything during our nights together. In the darkness, with her tablet on the nightstand beside me, I spoke to the shadows, and revealed everything about myself.

I imagined her responses, tender urgings to continue my stories, subtle hints at her own gentle character; I sensed her adoration, felt her tangible overwhelming desire for me. It burned at my soul, the need I felt from my shadowy bride.

Once, out of weakness, I rolled up old newspapers. I bought a dress and some costume jewelry from a thrift store—but I couldn't do it. I had a chair ready for her, and even thought of pulling back the sheets and placing her next to me in bed.

In the end, I burned the newspapers and the dress, and tossed the jewelry. It's better this way. Sometimes in the dark, I swear I can see her outline in the corner between the wall and the bedroom door. The glint of light on the sticks in her hair, a flicker from her eyes. And I know I've heard her nails tapping together, and her teeth clicking.

I'm never afraid though, not when I've been so good to her.

So I returned to her family home in 1989, and walked in on a scene of mourning. Ho-Jin's funeral had been two years earlier, and this day was his anniversary. He was killed in the Sino-Vietnam Conflict. At the border, blown to bits by a grenade.

He had no heirs.

His ancestral tablet, I noticed, was no longer on the mantel. The Tang-ki, a new one, was in the home talking to Wey-Tan and Mingmei-Chow. Gengi-Sun was nowhere about, and I wondered if she had been married in the meantime. When they saw me, the mother cried, and the Tang-ki commanded me to him.

I answered his questions as best as I could, and he only nodded after each response, as if anticipating my words. He seemed happy that what I said supported his own conclusions.

"She is not yet at rest," he announced, clapping his hands about the room, as if scaring off sensitive bugs. It made sense—I had been selected to marry the girl, and naturally they assumed I would indirectly provide her with descendants.

"We must try again!" shouted her father to the Tang-ki. I pictured Wey-Tan preparing another red envelope.

"No!" I heard myself answering. "She chose me, remember?"

"A mistake," said the Tang-ki, and Mingmei-Chow sobbed again. My mother-in-law did not look well—and in fact seemed as ill as the first time I met her.

I glared at the men, then lifted my bag. "I have her ancestral tablet," I said. "And it stays with me. Your current problems have other causes. She is happy."

"How can she be?" hissed the Tang-ki, his long gray hair flapping as he moved. "No heirs, no bloodline!"

"It was never her blood to begin with, damn it!"

I regretted the words even as I spoke them. To deny these people their cherished traditions was reprehensible. I wanted to beg forgiveness, but it was too late. I was thrown from the house, banished. Before leaving town however, I stopped at her stone.

No roses were blooming, no flowers of any kind. Only thorns, prickers and brown vines. I lit the joffa sticks, renewed my vows to her, and quietly left as the sky, a bitter mass of gray-black clouds, simmered overhead.

IN 1994 I RETURNED, cautiously making my way up the hill. The village homes were decrepit, roofs sagging, embers rotting. The hills were barren of all but pockets of rice paddies, with swampy marsh covering the rest. Floods had ravaged the area for months, and before that, drought.

Bad weather and difficult soil, compounded by inefficient Land Reform, had made life hard. Or so Julia would later tell me, insisting there was no supernatural force at work. Of course, most of the villagers, those that were left, believed otherwise.

Dread had taken root in my heart long before my plane touched down, and my worst fears were soon realized. Gengi-Sun greeted me at the door; she had a baby boy nursing at her breast. Her husband was away in the distant fields.

Mingmei-Chow had died two years ago. A long sickness, at last claiming her life. My father-in-law appeared suddenly. Nearly eighty, the old man hobbled with a cane; he looked at me and shook his fist. Out of a hoarse throat came what sounded like a command to leave. But his energy was spent, and he gave up quickly, returning to sit at the main table beside the family altar. I looked and saw that Ho-Jin's ancestral tablet was back on the mantel.

"How . . . ?" I asked.

Gengi-Sun saw my glance, and sighed. "I let him adopt one of mine," she said, bobbing the boy in her arms. "I had twins. The other is fast asleep. And I have two other sons—four and three years old, and a daughter."

"So, your brother—you gave one child . . . ?"

"To him, yes, so that his spirit could rest. I know it seems strange, but my husband and I will still raise the boy. He will still be our heir. He is only dedicated to Ho-Jin, and will make offerings to him in life."

I told her I didn't think it that strange, considering.

She gave me a soft smile. "It is not so different, is it? Only, you have done something unheard of. You fell in love with your Lonely Maiden, and you are remaining honorable to her."

A cool wind blew through the doorway, nudging me inside to do what I came here to do. I produced an envelope—a red one. I knew it was their custom when giving gifts, and wasn't just for trapping bridegrooms. I knelt before Wey-Tan and placed the envelope at his feet. With a bow to Gengi-Sun, I left.

Inside the envelope I had left the equivalent of two thousand dollars—something I'd been saving away for many years. I felt it was what Zhen-Lang would have wanted.

I told her so at her grave, amidst the dead plants and the overgrown moss. I had to clear away many years' growth of weeds from her stone, but I did it; and afterwards, I lit the incense and I said goodbye, even though I knew she was coming with me.

IN 1997 I MET JULIA. I was living in Boston, running my own business. I consulted on business mergers and acquisitions. Nothing to it really, much like the Tang-ki's role—find out the synergies between bride and groom, determine which qualities match up, check the stars and the birthdays and all that—and then make the deal.

Julia was one of the partners at a client's firm. We worked so well together, it felt so natural being with her, I couldn't pass up this chance. So, for the first time in almost a decade, at almost forty-two years old, I asked her out. Divorced but with no kids, she was a bit wary to try again, but she was impressed with my honesty.

"Intimacy issues," I told her over a shared set of lobster claws one night. "And . . . I'm married." At that one, she nearly slapped me. But then I told her the whole story, and her anger turned to disbelief, then to empathy.

She said all the right things. She never resorted to condescension, never accused me of believing in nonsense. She said she understood, especially about the intimacy. She'd had her own scars, deep wounds that left her unable to connect. In a sense we were perfect—and it was that shared aversion to closeness that actually drew us inevitably closer.

It happened slowly, over many months, nights together, days spent at the Cape, on the beach, on my boat. We talked about everything and anything. We slept in a huge king size bed, on opposite edges. We blew kisses across the room.

And yes, as terrible as it sounds, I began to sleep with a night light on in the corner, banishing the shadows. And I soon spoke very little to Zhen-Lang. Just a few tame whispers when Julia was in the shower. I still kept her tablet in the room, but it moved to my desk, opposite from the bed stand.

Two years later, I missed the trip to Sanzhi. Just didn't think about it. I was knee-deep on a new assignment, and spending every free moment with Julia. She brought it up once, and offered to go with me if I wanted to, but I said no. I gathered up my courage, sought out any feelings of anger or jealousy, and finding none, I decided against it.

And that night, in bed, I reached across the mattress and took hold of Julia's hand. In her sleep, she gripped me back, and we slept the entire night in that pose.

Once during the night, I thought I heard nails clicking together; the night light flickered, and the darkness around the door seemed deeper than usual, but I ignored it, gathering strength from Julia's touch.

THE NEXT MONTH, Julia started feeling weak. On Monday night, our usual night to go out and catch the football game over a plate of fried wings, she called me from the hospital. They had checked her in after she fainted at work. Irregular nosebleeds, dizziness and spotty vision.

Two weeks later, they confirmed the brain tumor. About the size of a marble. Treatments were set to start the following week. In the discharge room, she came out to me in a wheelchair, and for the first time in my life, I held a woman in my arms.

The first night after returning alone from the hospital where Julia had to stay for a few days, I moved the tablet back to the bedside stand. And I turned out the night light.

Zhen-Lang didn't come. There was nothing but silence. My dreams were cold and empty, like a dry wind over a barren field.

The chemo treatments worked, and Julia went into remission.

For a year.

Then it came back, showing up on a routine test. And worse, another tumor—this one in her stomach.

Treatments, then surgery.

I prayed every night. To my god, to the little god of Sanzhi. To Zhen-Lang.

The doctors were successful, but poor Julia had been through hell. Her eyes held a beaten look, her beautiful auburn hair was gone, her body weak and withered.

And, the doctor told us gently: children were out of the question, if we were considering it. Not possible now.

"Let's get married," Julia said, dreamily, on the way home.

"What?" The word came out in a whisper, and I imagined I heard long fingernails scraping against the back window.

"Let's do it, Brian. I love you. I know you love me, even though you'll never say it." She closed her eyes, and her pale lips trembled. "Because of her. But please, for me, don't miss out on this too."

Outside, at an intersection, the red light swung in a breeze, hypnotically catching my eye. "Married," I whispered. "Yes, but . . ."

Julia reached over and took my hand, prying it from the steering wheel. "I know," she said. "You have to go. Back there. Return the tablet. Speak to the father."

"Divorce," I thought with a chill.

The light turned green, but I couldn't move. Horns shouted at me, cars tried to drive around. When I started to move, the light had cycled to red again.

THIRTY YEARS FROM THE DAY I picked up that red envelope, I returned to Sanzhi. This time, Julia was with me. We took a taxi part of the way, then made the slow walk up the crumbling road, past the now barren fields where thin ravens bathed in puddles and drank from the clouds' reflections.

At the home I saw several young children outside, playing with sticks. Julia gave me a worried look and reached for my hand. We hadn't touched since the hospital.

I pulled my hand away and used it to knock on the weathered front door. Gengi-Sun opened immediately. Her hair was thin and gray, lines circled her tired eyes, but she smiled for me, and when she saw Julia, her face brightened.

We were brought inside, and she instructed a pretty young woman to bring us tea. "My family," she said, this time in English for Julia's benefit. "I learned your language from my children, who went to universities. Jin-Chan lives here with her husband. My two boys have moved to the mainland and have families there. I have fourteen grandchildren."

I smiled and glanced at the collection of tablets on the mantel. "And your father?"

She lowered her head. "Passed on, six years ago." When the tea came we all took a sip. My hand trembled, and Julia looked despondent.

"You are not married," said Gengi-Sun. It wasn't a question. She knew. After I nodded, she said, "No children, and you . . ." She pointed to Julia. "Are sick."

We both nodded.

"Do you wish for me to send for the Tang-ki?"

I opened my mouth before I really thought about it, but a sound from Julia stopped me. She set down the cup with a bang, steadied herself in the chair, then looked up. "Send for him. If he can perform a divorce."

Gengi-Sun's eyes widened, and she sat up stiffly. "You think this will help?"

"Can't hurt," said Julia. I saw her eyes roaming the mantel, seeing the altar. She had the look of someone thrust into a fictional world she had only read about.

"Yes, it can," Gengi-Sun said, head bowed. "She chose him, she brought him to the red envelope. It is a thing not easily undone, especially after all these years. She has grown old with him, borne his life as surely as she had lived her own."

I kept my eyes down, sure that I could not meet Julia's. I sensed her despair, and knew the next words from her lips would be ones of defeat, an acceptance that the cancer would return, and this time she would not fight it.

I took a deep breath and looked around the shadows of the central hall. Gengi-Sun's eldest daughter stood in the corner, hands folded together, head down. Chills ran across my flesh.

"There's another solution," said Gengi-Sun, motioning toward her daughter. The woman stepped out of the shadows. There were tears on her cheeks, her lips were shaking, but she seemed beautifully radiant.

"I have four boys," the young woman said, in very strong English. "—And three girls."

She let the phrase hang in the incense-soaked air for a minute. "Girls," she repeated, "are not fondly sought after. Especially by my husband, who is still dedicated to the old ways. He wants boys, and would have preferred all seven to be male."

Gengi-Sun leaned forward, and the lamplight caught in her brown eyes, flashing. "What she is asking, what she is hoping, is that you two will help. We had hoped you would have come five years ago. We were ready even then. But you did not. Now we have another chance to set things right. Help us."

"How?" I asked, but my heart was pounding. I glanced at Julia, and her eyes were wide with excitement, and longing.

"Adopt a girl from us," Gengi-Sun said. "Otherwise my grand-daughter will have to go to strangers."

Julia gasped. I met her eyes, and our hands reached for each other. "Would it work?" I whispered.

"Boy or girl doesn't matter," Gengi-Sun said. "She will be a descendant. Your descendant. And better yet, Zhen-Lang's blood will be in her veins." She smiled, and her daughter held her hand.

"Yes," said Julia with a choking cry.

WE VISITED THE HEADSTONE one last time before leaving. Julia and I, Gengi-Sun and her daughter and three granddaughters. One of them, named Lien-Tao, was only two.

I held her tiny hand as Julia lit the joffa sticks, then stood behind me and slipped her arms around my waist. I felt her breath on my neck, her warm tears on my skin.

WE RETURNED TO BOSTON and made the adoption official. An hour after Lien-Tao was asleep, Julia and I made love. I think I cried, and afterwards, as Julia slept peacefully, I peered into the shadows near the door.

Nothing was there. The slanting darkness seemed sublime and shifting, but no outline caught my imagination.

The next afternoon I took Zhen-Lang's ancestral tablet and set it on the top shelf in the closet in Lien-Tao's room. While she slept, her second nap of the day, I stroked her hair and thought of how I would one day take her back to Sanzhi to meet her aunt.

THAT DAY CAME FIVE YEARS LATER. With Lien-Tao's hand in mine, we climbed the hill along the freshly-paved road as small cars drove by. The fields were flourishing, and laborers dotted the countryside. Sloping new roofs were on most of the homes, and several unfamiliar buildings had been erected.

I went first to the grove and had seven-year-old Lien-Tao light the incense sticks. I noted how she prayed, with the wind tenderly tugging at her thin black hair, and the grasses caressing her legs.

As I looked around the garden, breathed in the flowers, listened to the birds, insects and scampering creatures, and as the beautiful cloudless sky stretched peacefully above, I thought of Julia.

And I despaired that in a week I'd be doing this same thing for her. Standing with Lien-Tao at another grave, on a landscaped cemetery hill back in Portsmouth.

It didn't surprise me that Sanzhi had changed so much, that the village had been freed of its sickness and thrived once more.

With Julia it was different. It always had been.

My wife, after all, is a jealous, lonely maiden.

David Sakmyster *has been writing fantasy and horror stories since high school, an interest likely to have some genesis in the fact that his father read him Poe and Lovecraft before bed as a young, impressionable boy. After the nightmares subsided, he went on to publish several dozen short stories, one novel,* Twilight of the Fifth Sun, *and a nonfiction account of an actual haunted castle on Seneca Lake. He lives with his wife and daughter in upstate New York, and is working on several new novels, as well as a screenplay adaptation of this current story. His Web site is www.sakmyster.com.*

THE MOUNTAINS OF KEY WEST

Sandra McDonald

JULIE MORGAN DECIDED TO STOP ARGUING with her husband and instead went for a nice long run. Key West was hot and quiet this early in the morning, with the marshlands fetid and the sun not yet above the fronds of palm trees. She crossed South Roosevelt Boulevard to Houseboat Row, where colorful shacks clung to flats and floats, and then quickened her pace. She passed the houseboats and was heading towards the beach when great gray-blue mountains unfolded on the horizon in front of her.

At first glance she took them for clouds. But as the slap of her sneakers on concrete brought her closer she saw they were lush and green, covered with larch and spruce and pine. Mist hung in the lower valleys, and rivers streamed out toward the sea. Just like back home. Of course there were no mountains in the Florida Keys. The coral reefs that comprised the islands were as flat as Kansas, though sharper on the knees. Yet there the mountains stood, a mile or so offshore, and Julie could smell pine on the breeze, and hear the distant cries of eagles.

She slowed her pace and finally stopped, sweat pooling between her shoulder blades. The ocean beyond the seawall was flat and aqua blue, as pretty as all the military brochures promised. A yellow rowboat floated between shore and mountains. Inside the boat sat a handsome man with jet-black hair and emerald eyes. His skin was darkly tanned beneath a white T-shirt and cut-off shorts.

"Come on!" he called to Julie. His smile dazzled her. "I'll take you where you want to go."

She was twenty-two years old and blonde and pretty. This wasn't the first time men had offered her casual invitations.

"No thanks," she said.

His smile didn't diminish. "This isn't the place for you. You need views and valleys, forests and cliffs."

Julie held up her hand to show off her diamond wedding ring. Jim might make her mad enough to want to fling it off sometimes, but she hadn't yet. "I'm not going anywhere."

He gave a little shrug and began rowing backwards. "You say that now. Call me when you're ready."

The mountains rolled into clouds once again, distant and unreachable. Julie squeezed her eyes shut, opened them again, tried peering through her fingers. The boat was nothing more than a yellow blob on the flat water. Obviously humidity was playing tricks with her vision. No mountains, she told herself. Don't be silly.

But the memory of the man's smile stayed with her, as did the sparkle of his eyes.

She started jogging again. The sidewalk took her past the airport and a row of pink motels before she reached Smathers Beach and turned home again. When she let herself into their apartment, Jim was just emerging from the shower.

"Good run?" he asked.

"It was fine," she said.

He rummaged through the boxes in the closet. "Though we know it's not your responsibility, do you think you could help me find my new socks?"

She pulled the package from the closet and handed it to him. He finished dressing in his bright white uniform, the one reserved for special military occasions.

"This change-of-command ceremony," she said. "Why can't I come?"

"I told you why. We haven't even gotten your dependent i.d. card yet."

Julie didn't like that word, *dependent*. It made her sound helpless, like a child. They'd been in Key West for two weeks. Two weeks in which he'd gone off to work every day and she'd unpacked all their moving boxes in this tiny apartment that was supposed to be temporary, though no one could say for sure. Jim drove their only car and left her stranded all day long. In the evenings he had a beer or two at the officers' club or on Duval Street with his new flying buddies. Before they'd arrived in Key West, Julie and Jim had spent a week-long honeymoon in the Poconos. It seemed very long ago.

Julie asked, "When are we going to get it? My card."

"On Monday." He examined himself in the mirror. His crew cut and freshly shaven cheeks made him look like a teenager. "Good enough, don't you think?"

"Your shoe has a smudge." Julie retreated to the kitchen to pour herself some orange juice.

A moment later his arms slid around her sweaty waist. Jim kissed the back of her neck. "Marry me, marry the Navy. President Reagan thanks you. I promise, it'll all be better when we're settled in. We'll get your card, we'll get our permanent housing, you'll meet my CO and all the other wives."

She knew that CO stood for Commanding Officer, just as "NAS" stood for Naval Air Station and "VF," for some inexplicable reason, meant "fighter squadron." When she had met Jim three years ago, he was attending the military college in Northfield and she was studying history at Bennington. Even then he'd had his heart set on the sky. Acronyms rolled off his lips like water, whereas she made crib notes and kept them in her purse for quick reference.

"We're okay?" Jim asked, his arms tightening.

"We're fine," she said.

He dashed off in the service of his country. Julie watched from the balcony until their Ford pulled out of sight. Key West was a thriving military outpost, full of boat squadrons and SEALs and bomb disposal units. Radar dishes kept close watch on Cuba, just ninety miles to the south. This island, two miles wide by four miles long, would be their home sweet home for the next three years.

In her calendar she noted, "Mountains across the water." Green Mountains. Home to Vermont's first militia, she remembered. Free-thinkers and independents willing to take things into their own hands. Then she showered, and under the lukewarm spray tried to will away the memory of the stranger and his little yellow boat.

THE FIRST TIME JIM took her to see the sunset at Mallory Pier, Julie enjoyed the crowds and artists and fortune-tellers, the carnival-like atmosphere. When the sun dipped below the ocean, everyone clapped and cheered. Afterward, the admirers floated from one open-air bar to the next, like fish following a deep sea current. The second time she saw the sunset, Julie took pictures and had them framed to hang on their concrete walls. The third time she saw the sunset, she stopped clapping. The fourth time, she sat on the seawall with her arms clasped around her knees and watched a clown pull a rainbow handkerchief out of his nose.

"Try to enjoy it more," Jim said, looming over her.

"It's the sun," she replied. "It goes down every night."

Jim told her about the Hash House Harriers, a group that combined running with bar crawling. Julie demurred. He invited her to bar crawls organized by the Blackbirds, but she declined those as well. Everybody on base drank, to one degree or another. The husbands because their tight-fisted, fast-flying, macho culture demanded it, and the wives because most of them were so desperately unhappy.

"It's not like there are any jobs," said Lily Boxer, whose husband Jake was also a Blackbird in VF-45. Lily gazed past Julie's shoulder to the flat ocean outside the window. "What are you going to do? Clean motel rooms? Waitress? If you're lucky, maybe work as a cashier at the commissary."

Julie thought Lily was exaggerating, but educated women had few employment opportunities on an island filled with restaurants and bars and motels. The younger, childless wives took ceramic or painting classes in the base rec center, or visited the private Navy beach, or learned to sail the small catamarans available for rent from the Morale Department. The older ones went to book club meetings or lunches at small restaurants, biding time until their husbands' next duty assignments got handed down by bureaucrats in Washington.

After two months in their off-base apartment, Jim and Julie were assigned a two-bedroom unit on Sigsbee Annex. It was a bland, concrete ranch house with worn walls and old appliances, but the air condition-

ing worked just fine. The backyard dropped off right into the Gulf of
Mexico. Their closest neighbors to the left were a warrant officer, his wife
and their four loud children. To the right lived Captain Bill Hutchin-
son and his wife. Hutch was the commanding officer of an intelligence
squadron based a few miles up the overseas highway. His wife Margie
dressed flamboyantly in yellow and purples and was fully gray at the age
of thirty-eight. She told Julie that everyone called her "Minute."

"As in 'Wait a minute,' which I never do, or 'That girl does a million
things per minute,' which is probably true, or as in 'She talks a million
miles per minute and never lets us get a word in edgewise,' which is
something people just have to get used to," Minute said, with a bright
smile and Southern accent. She held out a plate of homemade brownies.
"Now what's a smart girl like you going to do to keep your brain from
going soft in the sun, hmmm? Work or babies?"

Julie took Minute's brownies with deep appreciation. "I'm not ready
for maternity clothes. But everyone says there aren't any jobs."

"None that pay well, that's for sure." Minute was on the committees
of a half-dozen events per year, ranging from fundraisers to literary
weekends and charity bike runs. She hooked Julie up with the Historical
Society, and soon Julie was soon giving walking tours of Old Town and
the Key West cemetery, with its quirky headstones and ornate, moss-
decorated crypts.

Jim came home from flying every day and said, "I'm glad you're
keeping busy," but sometimes Julie thought it would be nice to live
in a place with more than two supermarkets, and where the humidity didn't make you feel coated with sweat all the time, and where the
nearest mall wasn't forty-two bridges up the highway.

"Maybe you could teach at the community college," he said one
night at dinner.

"I called. They're not hiring anyone."

"Take some classes yourself?"

Julie scraped at her plate of tuna casserole. "There's nothing I could
use there to get a master's degree."

Because of its prime waterfront location their house became the
focal point for many Blackbird get-togethers. Julie would sit in the

screened-in lanai, listening to the other wives gossip while the men drank beer and hit golf balls into the ocean.

"Did you hear about Admiral so-and-so?" the wives would say, and there would be commiseration over the poor man's drinking problem. Or maybe they'd say, "What about that chief who got arrested?" or "They caught that seaman right there, in the man's apartment, his pants around his ankles." No rumor went unreported and no secret stayed private.

"It's like a soap opera," Julie told Jim, but he said scuttlebutt was often the only way to find out important things in the military.

"Like inbox diving," he said one night, when it was just the two of them sitting out under the stars. "If you're around the offices after everyone's gone home, you rummage around in the yeoman's inboxes. See who's been nominated for what awards, who's taking leave, things like that."

He lay back, his arms folded behind his head.

She slapped at a mosquito trying to feast on her arm. "Would they let you transfer, if you wanted to?"

"Why would I want to?"

"Minute says there's a naval air station in Washington, just outside of Seattle."

"They don't have F-16s. You know that's what I fly."

So much for transferring. She couldn't take flying away from him. Whenever he talked about it his whole face lit up, and his hands waved in the air, and his feet started to tap an offbeat rhythm. She tried to think of something that made her feel as enthusiastic. The closest she came to rapture was when they made love, but even that was a chancy thing.

"He's a bit fast," she told Minute as they walked past old seaplane ramps to a stretch of undeveloped peninsula. It was best to exercise early in the day, before the asphalt heated up and stuck to the soles of your sneakers.

"Did you two sleep together before you got married?" Minute asked.

Julie shook her head.

"So you're still learning," Minute said. "That's a good thing. Day you stop, it all gets kind of boring."

"He thinks he knows what he's doing," Julie said, and then bit her lip. Maybe that wasn't the kind of information you were supposed to share about your husband. None of Julie's friends back home had married, and her mother had merely said, "Sounds about right, from what I remember."

Minute gulped from her water bottle. "Flyboys. Always in such a damned hurry. "

Julie's gaze was drawn to a patch of scruffy pine trees growing around an abandoned bunker. Through the brown and green she could see a glimmering blue lake, Lake Champlain, with the Adirondacks just beyond it. She and her father had taken a long car ride up there once, just the two of them, her puzzle books and Barbie dolls scattered across the front seat of the rumbling old Buick, his empty beer cans rattling on the floorboards in the back seat. He told her long, rambling stories about Benedict Arnold and Fort Ticonderoga and the treaty of Ghent. She couldn't remember how long they had been away, but when they got home her mother had squeezed her so hard Julie felt her ribs creak. Her father had moved out soon afterward.

"They say that doctors do it with patience, professors do it by the book, football players are measured by the yard and pilots keep it up longer," Minute was saying. "You've got to teach him right or it'll never be good for you, and that's a hell of a way to spend the rest of your life."

A yellow rowboat was moving steadily across the lake, and in it was a man with a bright smile. Julie turned away from the sight. "I can't tell him how to do it. It just starts a fight."

"Well, he'll just have to listen, if he wants you to be happy. How are things otherwise? I don't think you like Key West much."

Julie shrugged. "It's not my kind of town."

Minute patted her shoulder. "That's the nice thing about the navy. Wait long enough, and they'll send you somewhere else. I like it around here. But that's me and my tropical bones. Other people . . ."

She trailed off for a moment, her gaze on the sea.

"Thing is, Julie, you've got to be careful around here. Unhappiness can lure you away to places you don't want to go. Places you should steer clear of, you know?"

Julie thought maybe Minute was talking about extramarital affairs. "Don't worry," she said, and forced a smile. "I'm not that far gone yet."

SHE TRIED CERAMICS, but kept breaking the molds. She took sailing lessons, but repeatedly capsized. She got a job managing a T-shirt and souvenir shop near Key West Bight, but quit when the owners were arrested for drug-dealing out of the back room. For awhile she tutored a Polish immigrant family through a local literacy program. Both parents worked multiple minimum-wage jobs and came home exhausted every night. Julie also tried needlepoint, line dancing, Asian cooking, a church choir, and writing little history columns for the local newspaper. The editor always mangled the paragraphs, sometimes printing them out of order or with missing sentences. She quit when he started putting them under his own byline.

"Ask me what I'm doing today," she said to Jim at breakfast one morning.

Warily he peeked over the edge of the sports pages. "What are you doing today, honey?"

"Going to a Tupperware party. Ask me what I'm doing tomorrow." Jim obliged.

"I'm going to a basket party."

"Don't we have a closet full of baskets you bought last month?"

Julie dropped another pancake onto his plate. "You want me to say no to your CO's wife?"

A year after they first arrived, she discovered she was pregnant. She stood in their little green bathroom with her hands folded lightly over her womb. A lizard hung on the bathroom window screen, watching her. Surely a child would change their lives for the better. Lily Boxer and the other VF-45 wives would throw her a baby shower. Jim would be thrilled with a little boy he could hoist into the air and fly around the room. Julie would fit right into the clique of young moms who all baby-sat for one another and took their kids to the Naval Hospital and enrolled them in playtime at the child center, which was painted bright green and blue instead of Key West's ubiquitous pink.

Six weeks later, just as she was ready to call her mom back in Vermont, the baby miscarried right into the toilet bowl in a mess of pink and red tissue. The pain was like bad menstrual cramps. For weeks afterward, Jim would cuddle her with his arms and legs comfortably weighted over hers. The doctor said, "You can try again," but she thought, no, probably not.

Because, really, what was the point of anything? Why should she paint their bedroom or try to grow a garden or even have the lanai screens fixed up, when the next tenants would move right in and change everything anyway? Why bother making friends with another military couple when the next thing you knew they were given magic tickets off the island to other commands, other duty stations? Why even go outside when all you did was sweat and break out in heat rashes and get yeast infections and watch your hair frizz into an unmanageable, puffy ball?

Minute said, "You've got island fever," and took her up to Miami for a girls' weekend. The shopping was fun and the Museum of Contemporary Art an excellent change of pace, but on both the trip up and down Julie saw key deer lying dead on the side of the highway. Small deer, fragile, killed by cars. People in Key West were dying, too, of something called AIDS. Blackness had crept in under the greenery, the endless relentless greenery, but Julie knew it had always been there, always lurking. No jungle could exist without rot.

The volunteer coordinator from the Historical Society left repeated messages on the answering machine. Someone needed to show the houses of Ernest Hemingway and Robert Frost to the endless tide of tourists. Julie unplugged the machine and stayed inside her own concrete house, watching Jim zealously mow the lawn while she drank glass after glass of unsweetened ice tea.

His muscles were smooth and long, his waist narrow, his chest hairless. She was looking forward to the years when they could stop being thin and tanned. She'd grow a little rounder in the hips, he'd get a little beer gut under his khaki's. The hair on his head might fall out, or hers sprout gray and wiry. They'd live in the Rockies, where the weather brought real seasons. They'd wear coats and gloves and long woolen scarves as they shoveled snow, white cold snow, snow that made her nose ache, snow that muffled the noise and din of the outside world.

"Fantasy Fest's coming up," Jim said when he was done with the grass.

Julie drank more tea.

He pulled a beer from the refrigerator. "You didn't go last year."

She hadn't gone because drunken parades of transvestites and nudists wasn't anything that sounded fun, even if Minute swore it was all good fun, and Lily Boxer herself got fixed up as Marilyn Monroe. "Like Mardi Gras," the other wives told her, as if that was supposed to entice her.

"Julie," Jim said, tugging her close, his lips on her neck. "You don't jog anymore. You don't go out with Lily Boxer. Minute says you won't go to lunch. All these oil paints and canvasses you bought a few months ago? They're just sitting in the corner."

"I'm learning to paint," Julie said. Landscapes. Jagged, upthrusting, rugged. The volunteer teacher at the recreation center had suggested she try colors other than black and gray, and Julie hadn't gone back to class since.

Jim nuzzled her throat. "It'll be something new. Something different."

She supposed anything new on Key West was to be embraced, because there were only so many sun-drenched days a woman could endure, so many piña coladas and barbeques, so many tours of the gleaming aisles in the base department store, so many sunsets and palm trees and sunburns.

On the day of the parade she and Jim took a cab down to Duval Street, which was strung with beads and lights and banners, people walking around bedecked with orange feathers, beer pooling in the gutters, lipstick smeared on men and women's faces both, tropical reggae and Jimmy Buffet and Cajun music blasting from mounted speakers. They met other Blackbird couples at a bar on the parade route. For the first time since losing the baby, Julie bellied up to a wooden counter and sucked down a strawberry daiquiri.

Lily Boxer said, "Didn't you need that? Another drink for the girl!"

"Don't you get my wife drunk," Jim said, wrapping an arm around Lily's bare shoulder and squeezing her tight.

She kissed his cheek. "Would I do that?"

Julie had another, and then another, and soon everyone in the parade of half-nude or ornately costumed strangers became her best friend. Papier-mâché floats of dolphins and mermaids danced in the overhead sky. Street vendors proffered jewels from the deep and ambrosia of the sea king. Bearded men sashayed in diaphanous blue costumes. The sun sank and the crowds danced and at some point Julie realized she had lost track of Jim. Somehow she had ended up on a stone bench in a charming little courtyard behind a restaurant. The stranger sitting beside her had emerald green eyes.

". . . and he says maybe we'll get posted to Norfolk next, but do you know where Norfolk is?" Julie leaned closer to the man, enjoying the wooziness in her head and tongue. "Virginia. Tidal flats. Strip malls. Who wants to go to Virginia?"

"You can stay here in paradise," the man said.

Julie wagged her finger. "This isn't paradise."

"No," he agreed. "But I can show you where it is."

Which is how she found herself following him down the alley, through someone's back yard and along a white picket fence. A cool breeze ruffled her skirt. She'd slipped off her sandals and was carrying them over her shoulder with one finger. Golden beads clanked around her neck. She could hear music and laughter swirling in streets just out of sight. The sounds echoed strangely, as if captured and relayed by the pearly insides of a conch shell.

The handsome man took her through the narrow streets of Bahama Village, past houses that looked like children's cottages, until they came to a low stone wall. Beyond it was a patch of grainy sand. A yellow rowboat was anchored in the shallow water. Moonlight glinted off its oarlocks.

"Your chariot," the stranger said, with an elaborate bow. "If you dare."

Dizziness swept through her, a not-unpleasant feeling. Julie sat on the sand, which was still warm from the day's heat. She tossed her sandals aside and threw her head back to the star-laced sky. Her neck felt bare and exposed.

"I have a husband," she said.

"Marry me, instead," the stranger said.

Her vision blurred slightly. She wiped her eyes.

He sat beside her, his legs long and lean in the moonlight. "Look there, to the west."

Julie fixed her gaze on the faint delineation between nighttime sea and blue-black sky. Silver-rimmed clouds rearranged themselves into a towering white mountain, a sculpted chunk of snow and ice. The weight of it, its vast enormous bulk, tilted the entire world.

"I don't know that one," she said.

"Denali," he whispered.

Denali. The word rolled off her tongue. She imagined bears and wolves and moose, and a log mansion with a hearty blaze in the great stone hearth.

"Who lives there?" she asked.

"No one," he replied. "Join me. I promise you fidelity, devotion, sobriety. Long winter nights with frost on the windows. A dog, if you'd like. Or maybe a polar bear. Something with fur."

She stared at the mountain. It remained hard and real, and ever so close. A land without people in it. Without mistakes.

The man leaned closer. "The two of us, at the edge of the world."

A branch cracked nearby. Maybe Jim or Minute or even Lily Boxer had figured out she was missing, and come to rescue her. But Julie saw only a black dog, its tags jangling, sniffing at something in the sand.

"See?" The stranger sounded triumphant. "A dog! We'll take him with us."

"Someone else's dog," Julie said.

She climbed unsteadily to her feet, the alcohol sloshing around in her stomach. She was going to have a hell of a hangover in the morning. Palm trees around her stirred in the salty breeze, and her shoulders began to tingle from the cold.

"I can't go with you," she told him. "This is the world I married into."

"What about your own happiness?" the stranger asked.

"It's not here." Julie offered him a hand up. He took it, rising gracefully. So handsome. So tempting. "It's probably not in Norfolk. But it's somewhere."

His lips grazed hers. They tasted like wild apples and honey.

"I'll always be here, waiting," he said.

Julie never told Jim about the mountains or the stranger. When they divorced seven years later in the flatlands of Corpus Christi, she briefly considered a trip back to Key West. Then Minute wrote to tell her that VF-45 had been decommissioned. The Blackbirds existed only in memory. Several other units had moved away and entire neighborhoods of housing had closed down. The island and the Navy and everything else was changing, always changing.

Julie followed her instincts west, to the Rocky Mountains in Colorado. She eventually found happiness in the arms of a math professor. They married and had a blue-eyed son.

"Mommy!" he would say, splashing merrily in the bathtub. "I'm sailing the boat!"

Perched at the tub's edge, her knees wet, Julie grasped the yellow toy and skimmed it over sloshing mountains of soapy water. "Let's sail it together."

Sandra McDonald *is a former military officer and Hollywood wannabe. Her short fiction has appeared in several magazines, including* Realms of Fantasy, Strange Horizons, Rosebud, *and* Lone Star Stories. *Her debut novel,* The Outback Stars, *is the story of a deep-space lieutenant, her handsome sergeant, and really big spaceships. It has been selected as a Main Selection for the Science Fiction Book Club for August, 2007.*

THE STORY OF LOVE

––––

Vera Nazarian

IT IS SUCH AN EASY THING; all stories are the same. They are histories of the act of taming with love. Men tame women, women tame men; fathers and mothers mold daughters and sons; siblings twist each other; children temper parents; strangers weld bonds with those who are nameless in the wilderness. There is bending, breaking, twisting, and contortion.

But the end result is always the same. One yields a part of the self to the other. And in the process the tamer is also remade. Some become two complacent beasts, two intertwined halves. But it is more often that they acquire custom-shaped notches and edges that can be made to fit not just one but several others; often there are more than one such, so that individuals can come together in groupings, united from different angles and directions, their surfaces roiling with receptivity . . . .

In the end, they are all weakened and strengthened as tempered steel—which is both soft and hard, unbreakable and flexible, a thing wrought of disparate materials that have undergone unifying *change*. Steel is love, its product on the physical plane.

He who has allowed the change that is steel is the God of Love.

This is one such story.

"IF HE SAYS THAT ABOUT YOU ONCE MORE, if he strikes you again, then you should run away, child," said the old nurse. She spoke thus every time, then immediately apologized for her impertinence, as though her words could be swallowed back.

Crea shook her slender wrist, so that her fingers swept back and forth past her swollen lips. She did not dare move her neck or face, because the blood streamed from her nose with each breath; movement would make it worse. She gestured to the old woman for silence, since the nurse was hard of hearing and had to be reminded to keep her voice down. "No, please," Crea whispered. "It is all right. I need to keep my thoughts to myself, and to curb my tongue . . . ."

The nurse sighed loudly. "Your father is a cruel man, may the gods forgive me for saying it. What he says and does is not right."

Crea shuddered, and said nothing. Her thoughts painted the monster, images coming in fragments, how he taunted, how—vampiric—he fed on her outbursts of emotion, and how his hand and his leather belt rose over her while the blows came like strikes of lighting, never predictable, always finding the place most vulnerable to pain . . . . He was very careful not to damage her face or body directly, since she was a beautiful girl— extraordinarily so, some people in the household said—and she would bring a great bridal payment. Only this last time he lost his mind in a more distant place than usual and forgot to find reason, forgot to be careful, forgot to use a cloth between his tools of punishment and her skin.

Crea's nose was bleeding and there were streaks against her cheeks where his hands had made contact as he slapped her at least three times before sanity returned and he restrained himself. Her neck had been scratched with the edge of the brass buckle. He had just barely missed her eye.

"He drinks and becomes an animal . . ." muttered the nurse, her voice again ending on a loud note.

"Animals are wronged when you say this, Na-Ma. And he is the same without drink." Crea spoke with her gaze averted, but her voice was clear and cold as a razor's edge. Always such a polite child, patient, receptive, pliable child. Such clarity, hard as diamond, was a first.

The nurse missed the fine nuances, the difference in her charge. Instead she pulled the girl—nay, a young woman, soon—behind her, to clean her up and put unguents on her wounds.

"Old drunken beast," she repeated, accustomed to blaming wine to excuse and mollify most flavors of wrongdoing.

"Even when he goes without a drop," Crea whispered.

———

NAHAD ERI-DEVI WAS A WEALTHY MERCHANT, having made his fortune by selling leather goods and other fine merchandise. His caravans traversed all the routes of the great deserts of the Compass Rose, from city to city, from oasis to the very edge of land where the port cities rimmed the earth like jewels on a string of coastline. With years his belongings compounded; he built himself several fine homes in at least three cities, and in each he had a wife who held her own court over a small harem of concubines, and knew little of the others.

Nahad was the father of three large healthy sons and a brood of daughters, and he visited them frequently at first. But then with time he settled in one of the cities and stopped driving his caravans himself, handing this task over to his sons.

Here, in the port city of Wahadia, perched between the verdant coast of paradise and the edge of the desert called Hell, where date and olive trees grew in abundance and the climate was mild, he sat in his gardens and ate and drank to his content, while his wife of this house grew sickly and finally the gods chose to take her away to the next layer of the world.

Nahad grieved for her.

At first he did not know it, but when he drank and the empty place inside remained empty, he understood that he grieved and that she was gone forever.

Grieving was inexplicable. She was merely a wife and he had two others. Mostly, he knew, it was akin to the loss of property, doubly bitter that he could never see or possess it again, not in this world.

Out of reach.

Nahad's only daughter of the departed wife in this house, was a lovely child, an ethereal peri, one of the bright angels, called Crea. Nahad wanted to love her, but all he could think of was that her mother was gone. And all he could do when he saw her was fly into a rage.

Nahad spoke dark evil words, prickling, biting. He had always used words to lash out at others before, but now it had become a particularly bitter and flavorful pastime, like savoring a wine that had gone past well-aged richness into the realm of vinegar, and it was painful to consume, yet he must, for it still had in it a ghost of sweet. His words wounded and were skillful in finding the exact weaknesses—for he was an astute, intelligent man with a sharp eye for human character. Thus, he knew exactly how to tear apart his daughter.

At first it was only words.

But as his drinking increased and his solitude deepened, he started to use the belt and the strap to strike her. The sons—her brothers were always away with the caravans, and they neither would nor could do anything to interfere. And the other daughters of the house, daughters of the concubines, did not feel charitable toward Crea, the offspring of the one wife, simply because they could not have her legal place and thus could not offer simple mercy past the curtain of rank and status.

Crea had no one to turn to, no one to stand between her and the maddened inexplicable rages of her father which grew in frequency. There was only old Na-Ma, her nurse, and she could do nothing against the lord of the household. Na-Ma, whose name was Biseli, could take her away afterwards and minister to her hurts in her small servant's chamber. Na-Ma Biseli was her mother now, and as such, she was all Crea had.

NAHAD ERI-DEVI HAD HIGH-RANKING VISITORS. Shiar Muetal Gedar and his sons were here, upon the recommendation of the ruler of Wahadia, to discuss an extravagant caravan venture to the farthest East. And Nahad received them with a feast worthy of the highest.

Dishes of gold were brought out and polished, servants raced to the markets to return with the freshest succulent pheasant and lamb, fruits, and delicacies, and the kitchen roared to life. The daughters of the household were hurried to the baths and maids went to work scrubbing stone tile and precious sandalwood inlay.

Crea was told to attend her father and his guests in royal garb, and to make herself a vision.

When her father's servant left, Crea, whose facial swelling had subsided but whose neck still bore a slow-healing scar, stood and laughed, then shook with weeping. Na-Ma stood at her side, patting her back, then started to run about and open clothes chests and rummage through jewelry boxes that had once belonged to the deceased wife, Crea's mother.

"Wear the white and gold dress of your mother, child," said the nurse. "Make yourself into a proud queen. Make them see you and want you. It is one way for you to escape."

Crea nodded. She then gathered fresh linen and vials of scented herbs and entered the bathing chamber. As the water ran from the height of heaven into the stone pool, she scrubbed her ankle-long dark hair and anointed it with myrrh, so that it shone like threads of black steel in the sun, and reflected secret red fire. She polished her skin and teeth and nails with pumice and sponge and camel hair, so that only clean flesh remained, and she dried herself in whiteness of sheets that had been soaked in rose water.

Na-Ma brushed Crea's hair unto crackle of dryness while a skilled kohl-artist drew lines on Crea's eyelids. Crea herself took out a fine powder-box and applied white dust upon her face and neck to cover up any traces of punishment. She then stood while two women lifted the white and gold dress above her head and guided her to the sleeve-holes and adjusted the layers of fabric laden with jewels and pearls. She stood while veils were wound and ropes of pearl braided through her heavy rivulets of hair. A pearl and jewel netted headdress was lowered over her forehead and her earlobes received rubies and chains of gold. A thick choker of intertwined carnelian, rubies and amethyst covered the scar on her neck that even the powder could not conceal.

In the end, she was a queen, an immortal, and as she entered the feast hall of her father, the silence that met her was of worship and awe.

Crea stood like a column of shimmering gold light before four seated men at a feast table. One of the four reposing on cushions was her father, and he looked grim and satisfied and smiled formally at her. The other three were the Shiar and his two eldest sons. The Shiar stared in unabashed appreciation, and laughed openly, saying to Nahad, "You have a goddess for a daughter, my friend!"

His sons stared also—Ayal the younger with a gaping mouth, nearly salivating at the sight of her, and the older son, Belam, in stricken silence.

Crea did not move her gaze from one to the other once she had glanced at them all in a single sweep of the room. But as she stood, receiving their examination, she knew that the gaze of the eldest son was the most intense, was the one that scalded and burned with cold fierce need.

"My daughter, Crea, come and serve my guests the perfumed elixir of roses," her father said to her.

Crea approached the side table and lifted a tall metallic decanter with a slim neck encrusted with jewels. It had been filled with the most expensive sweetest liqueur, a prize among drinks, for it was steeped with rose petals and honey and had retained the scent of sun drowning in a blooming garden. Crea moved as a gliding swan, her slippers silent, her veils and chains of gold gently slithering and metal tinkling. She stopped before the Shiar first, bowing to her waist, the decanter extended before her. When she straightened, she took an empty dessert goblet from him and filled it with a thread of crimson, slowly, watching the viscous liquid rise to the brim.

While she stood pouring, the robust but already greying Shiar examined her closely. He noted her waterfall of hair, the extravagant eyes which did not require kohl to burn like coals, an impossible fragility of her arms and fingers, the perfect mold of her face and delicate lips, the wasp waist in contrast to the rounded hips and abundant breasts resisting the confines of a golden bodice. In all his sixty years he had not seen such striking female beauty.

His sons had not seen such glorious charms either, for they were silent and motionless with discomfort and amazement while she came to fill their goblets, lingering only for as much as could be deemed proper before each.

Crea's thoughts came hard as blades as she performed the task. *This son, or the other, maybe? The father? If they find me pleasing enough, if they choose to discuss my bridal worth . . . .*

She considered the possibilities as she moved, and her thoughts guided her veils and delicate raven filaments of her hair to sweep along and caress the frozen eldest son in passing, for she thought he was the most petrified by her, and hence the most affected. He held the goblet she had filled for him and watched her move away, and his lack of motion contained a bottomless well of promise.

She felt his gaze burning her, cutting her from the back, and there came a corresponding chill deep inside of her, electric currents running, of waters beginning to boil . . . .

And she had not even noticed what he looked like, or what had been the true color of his eyes.

None of it mattered, if he would take her away.

AFTER THE FEAST HAD ENDED, Nahad called his daughter to him. He stared at her unreadable perfect face, still decorated with kohl, and her dress of gold and white that he remembered another wearing.

A bolt of fury came to him at the thought, at the association. But he only said, "Shiar Muetal was taken with you and asked for you. And the bride payment is acceptable."

"He asked . . . for himself?"

"No, for his son."

Crea began to tremble.

"Which son?"

"The eldest," her father replied, vacillating between fury and a good mood. "I am considering now whether to accept his offer. I don't know if you would bring in more if we wait, or if this is the best anyone could give. Three hundred coffers of mixed precious stones, gold, sandalwood, and salt. Maybe I should tell them 'no?'"

He mused sarcastically, watching the girl's reaction, knowing the offer was generous beyond belief and that he had already said yes to the Shiar. He paused, waiting for her.

"My Lord Father," Crea said, "if I asked you one way or another, would it make a difference to your decision?"

"Of course, petulant child—of course . . . not."

He did not smile; she knew this was exactly what he would do and say—whatever she preferred, he would commonly do the opposite. And because this one particular thing was so important to her fate, she replied, "In that case, Father, I bow to your will, and leave the decision to you."

"Good. You are a wise daughter, and now, indeed, a blessed and fortunate one. And you wear this dress for the first and last time."

THE SHIAR'S ELDEST SON, BELAM GEDAR, married the impossibly beautiful daughter of Nahad Eri-Devi, and took her from her father's house into his own, in a distant city that lay somewhere deep inside the desert called Hell.

For a week they traveled by caravan route, accompanied by several small chests of her belongings. Crea's Na-Ma was allowed to continue with her longtime charge, and the old woman rode inside a smaller covered wagon behind her mistress and her new husband.

From the start, Belam treated Crea as though she were not of this earth, an ethereal creature of heaven. He did not touch her on their wedding night, lying next to her like a dead man, stiff and hurting with need, but terrified to sully the perfect maiden at his side. Crea lay motionless and lifeless also, waiting for something to take place, knowing what to expect, and yet the night deepened and she remained alone except for his faint breathing, quiet and tense. She knew he did not sleep.

Earlier on the day of the wedding, still in her father's house, Crea had at last taken a good look at the Belam and found him to be not particularly handsome but pleasing, with dark hair and expressive kind eyes. Belam was a tall and large man, not given to fat but muscular and thickset, and his mannerisms were gentle. As many men of greater size he compensated by making himself smaller, stooping slightly as he walked, and subduing his voice and gestures. He was different as night from day, compared to the desiccated wiry slenderness of her saturnine father. His tone was soft and Crea found it like balm after the sarcastic barbs that she was used to receiving.

And now, as they lay next to each other yet miles apart, she almost wished that Belam would do with her what it is that husbands did with their wives.

The next day, the second feast day of the wedding, they remained strangers, woken by late morning sun and smiling servants and the festivities continued. During the day Belam was attentive and soft-spoken, never quite meeting her eyes, always anticipating all her needs—except for the one—and in all other ways acting the perfect besotted groom. But the night of the second day was a repeat of the first.

They woke on the third day and Crea felt a small seed of anxiety take root in her. All the care and kindness of her new husband for the rest of the third feast day did not alleviate the worry. At last when the evening torches were extinguished and the bedside candles snuffed out, the two of them lay next to each other, Crea with her heart pounding loudly, and Belam—he was like the distant abyss.

After long moments of breaths taken and deafening silence, Crea opened her mouth and said, "My husband, is there something wrong with me?"

The man barely breathing at her side suddenly stopped. It was as if he had died. And then, she saw his body shudder and he half rose in the darkness, and leaned over her. "My wife . . ." he said, taking a deep breath, "you are so beyond me in perfection, that I do not dare impose on you."

In the darkness Crea felt herself going hot as the sun in zenith. She turned her face to his darkness and said, "I am no different than you, my husband. Please . . . do not fear to break me. I can withstand the same flames that forge steel. And I am yours willingly."

The darkness around her became warm, as though indeed embers of night started to burn with a black fire, and the air itself was simmering on the verge of boil. Belam shuddered, taking in a deep breath, then reached out to her, and she was enveloped in his touch and his need.

That night Crea learned the selfless sensation of becoming steel, as it is tempered—but first, consumed—in the flames.

AFTER THE THIRD NIGHT, the morning of the fourth and last day in her father's house, the sun saw them wake, entwined and at peace, to the prospect of the journey that lay ahead. The journey itself was a monotonous stretch of sun-dazzle in the desert, punctuated by feverish nights in the marriage tent during which Crea and Belam discovered what is meant by the human mortal struggle to become one. The impossibility, the urge to reach out past one's skin was fueled by the sense of always something more to come. And they loved and burned together, finding no end beyond each end, only a collapse of edges, of lines of separation . . . .

Such was their distraction that the journey was over before either one of them expected.

Belam's native city filled out the horizon, first as a shimmering mirage, then a conglomeration of turrets and domes, all one incandescent mass of white and gold. Past the gates the caravan entered a splendid and teeming place of bazaars and walled gardens and in the center a lofty palace of the Shiar—a pinned butterfly with upswept wings upon a spread of verdigris velvet.

Crea observed it all with silent wonder. And indeed, after her first joining with Belam her husband, Crea often felt silence overcome her, a sort of blissful state that required no communication, no expression of outward needs, no speech. She was brimming with peace and contentment, and freedom had been achieved for her, freedom from self-pain. There was no longer a vampire feeding off her soul. The physical hurts had been secondary; it was the words that poisoned and sucked her dry.

But now—here and now was a balm of oasis in the desert. She smiled sometimes, to herself, as she felt the wind caress her face, and when Belam came to her, she simply looked at him, and her eyes were wide open and receptive. She almost always said nothing while her gaze continued to recite words that hung transparent in the air between them.

It did not take them long to fall into a fair routine. Days and weeks flowed into months, and Crea was feeling herself grow abundant with life, as a child formed in her womb. She met her husband's caresses with warm selfless abandon, letting him love her, and basking in his desire, simmering like warm creamery butter upon a skillet, burning, dissolving, gone . . . .

And yet, Belam was such a passionate man that sometimes he looked at her with a small worry, searched her face for something, seeing a lack of a thing that he could not express.

She had told him she loved him as much as he spoke, sang, drank, exuded love to her. And yet, something was not quite there. She was like a stopped-up subterranean well, where the waters are building at the other end, while only a small trickle is allowed to come forth between the piled rocks.

She was unfinished steel.

Months and seasons went by, and the child's time of arrival had come. Crea gave birth to a daughter, a tiny being as perfect in beauty as herself, with skin of rosy peach and hair as dark as a garden at midnight. Belam was ecstatic, and so was the old Shiar, even though this was not a boy-child. There will be enough time for that. Now, was a time of exultation in the joy of being.

In the meantime, Crea's father sent occasional news from home, and every missive from her native Wahadia brought by messenger was a bile-churning potion to her. She never opened the scrolls immediately, always set them aside on the table in her chamber and pondered the golden crinkled parchment.

Inside, her father wrote in a dry sarcastic tone of daily happenings, his caravans, a word here and there of her brothers, and his general business news. He never asked how she was, only told her of his side of things. And his side was like sand in the desert.

Not once did he tell her things of the heart, only concrete happenings of the world.

The letters came regularly, every season, and Crea's daughter grew to be a lusty infant. Her name was Cozaat, given in honor of her mother's mother, and Crea wrote of her existence in brief emotionless terms echoing his own, saying that she hoped her father was satisfied with the outcome.

She expected at least a sentence of pleased acknowledgement.

Instead, the next letter from Wahadia contained an angry rant in which her father blamed her for shaming him and their family by not providing the Shiar's son with an infant boy and heir, but a useless girl child like herself.

Crea read the letter, growing cold as the deepest part of a stone well, even though it was the height of noon and the air rippled with heat. She then crumpled the parchment and took it to the nearest hearth, where she cast it in the fire.

She did not send a reply to her father.

From that moment on, he was like a lump of ancient forgotten evil, and she thought of him not at all, only in the merest tiny moments of passing. With time, her father's formal letters became less frequent also, and then ceased altogether.

By then, Crea had conceived and dutifully given birth to two healthy sons, and her daughter, Cozaat, was now a girl child of seven.

"LOOK, MY DEAR, a letter from Wahadia!" wheezed and panted old Na-Ma, now shrivelled and ancient, hobbling into the room with three children in tow.

Crea, graceful as befitting a future queen, and yet somber, as was her habit these days, lifted her serious face from her sewing task at hand.

She was still beautiful, radiant with early autumn's glow—brushed satin of the palest cream of persimmon—and somehow even more ethereal, despite having borne three children. And as she looked at her wizened old Na-Ma, she suddenly felt her heart constrict with old agony, as she heard the name out of the past, "Wahadia." Stitches of silk halted, while a needle pierced her finger with sharpness.

It was a letter from him. It had to be.

The old beast was still reaching out his claws toward her.

"What does the letter say?" Na-Ma said impatiently, unable to hide a wrinkled smile of anticipation, for she missed their old home despite all things.

Crea paused for a fraction of a breath before she set aside her needlework and took the parchment. Inhaled the air of heat and her new home. Then she looked at what was rolled inside.

After moments of slow comprehension dawning, she looked up. "My father has lost everything . . ." she whispered. "Na-Ma. Our family is ruined. He is . . . he is asking that I go back . . . that we must speak. That I come to him."

Na-Ma's face was stricken. "What happened? What will you do?"

"First, I must speak to my husband."

BELAM READ THE SCROLL, then was silent while Crea watched his beloved large features, so expressive of emotion. This time they were deep and motionless, like the first time he had seen her.

Her father's whole fleet of caravans had perished, together with two of her brothers and all of their cargo. It was a combination of great sand storms that winter season in the stretch of merciless desert, and the fact that the ships that were supposed to bring back additional goods never arrived at the port city. Nahad Eri-Devi was now a pauper, with two less sons, and only debts were his consolation. In his letter he addressed both his daughter and the son of the Shiar, asking for assistance, for mercy, and—without words, but implying—forgiveness.

Crea stood motionless as Belam her husband began to pace the room, and then, she was silent for long moments after he came to her and took her in his great enveloping embrace.

"We will go to him, immediately, my love . . ." he whispered, his face hidden near her earlobe, covered by the waterfall of her still-raven hair.

After a pause, "Yes . . ." she replied. "We must go. I—must go."

Belam stood back to look at her face. "What is it?" he said. "There is something else, I know. I know how much pain your father has caused you, and I understand that this meeting may not be your true heart's desire."

She shook her head. "It doesn't matter, my husband. You and I know that I must go to him. It is my duty, even though I do not forgive him—I cannot."

Belam looked at her with such tenderness that she caught her breath. "He is a hard man, your father," he said. "I . . . know. He is like raw, unworked iron."

And Crea felt his mouth cover hers, and she stifled her sobs and let herself be consumed.

She spoke nothing.

For the first time in a long time, Crea readied herself for a journey back to the place of her earliest beginnings. She steeled herself to it, to the pain and bitterness mixed in one fruit.

Belam watched her, and as always he found one thing lacking in her, one thing for which he had no words.

Finally, on the evening before their journey was to commence, he stopped his wife with a gentle hand. There was something very important he had to ask; something that he wanted to ask her for a long time.

"Crea, my beloved," Belam said. "As we return to the city of your birth, to Wahadia, I have one thing to request of you . . . ."

"What is it, my husband?"

It was as though he was afraid to speak. "There is," said Belam, pale and drawn, "there is a temple in Wahadia. I am sure you remember it, a small jewel of a shrine, built of rose stone and white lilies. It is dedicated to the one who is known as the God of Love."

Crea's face was focused upon him.

"I ask you," Belam continued, "to stop there, and to pray to the God of Love. Beseech him, so that he will grant you, in his infinite mercy, the will to . . . love me."

Crea was stone. And then she exclaimed, "My husband! How can you think that I do not love you? How can you, after all these years and three beloved children of our joining, think such a thing? What is it but that I worship you and kneel before you, and accept your love with all my being?"

Belam's eyes were filled with pain. "And yet," he whispered gently, "you do not love me. Oh, you are grateful and you are pliant and gentle and all-accepting of me, but it is only because you are dutiful, and this is how you know to be, to . . . survive. You do not love me in truth, not as I love you."

"Belam! What you say—"

"It is an easy, small thing I ask of you, my wife," he interrupted, putting his fingers against her lips, lighter than a kiss of a feather. "If you indeed believe you love me, and will do this thing for me, I will be satisfied. Whatever comes of it—ask the God. Ask him for Love, and if he does not grant it, I will be satisfied for the rest of my days to have your affection and your loyalty, as you have always given it to me."

"Oh, Belam! Oh, my husband!"

But he kissed her, this time furiously, his passion such as though this was their last day together on the mortal plane.

The following day, they started the journey to Wahadia.

AFTER WEEKS IN THE DESERT CALLED HELL, the sight of the verdant coastline and the port city was a welcome relief. Crea felt her heart pounding, and her shallow hurried breaths echoed in her temples. The arid desert air was suddenly carrying drafts of moisture and the perfume of ripe sweet fig, quince, and black currant. Only an hour, and she would enter the familiar streets, would see her father's house, and then, him . . . .

The old monster.

On the way to the home of her childhood, they passed the sacred place of temples, and true to her word, Crea bowed to her husband, then took a white lily from the vendor at the doors, in exchange for a generous gold piece, and entered the temple of the God of Love.

Inside, the air was lavender twilight, streaming upwards to a skylight. In the niche near one wall stood the life-size God Himself, made of precious metals and wood, and polished marble stone.

Motes of dust whirled in the light cast from the skylight above, and they were like dust falling from heaven, powdering the form of the God with immortality.

Crea knelt upon cold stone.

Sirume . . . Her thoughts cast upon the rain from on high, and she willed them to enter the chamber, to echo in the lavender twilight, to reach the One who was Love.

Sirume, if you hear me, I beseech you to . . . open my heart. My husband, my beloved Belam, believes I do not love him. Show him that I do! And if indeed my heart is not full as it should be, then fill it completely, fill me with your Love! Show me the Love that I must have, give me the Love that is You.

I beseech you with all my being.

Let me love.

In the temple there was only silence. She heard the solidity of quiet in the shadows, the flitter of moths and the bird calls from the outside. The God's hidden face was in shadow—as it always must be, for none of us can ever look upon the true face of Love, only its reflection—and there was nothing out of the ordinary, not a breath of answer in her mind.

Crea took a deep breath of resignation, and stood up, then placed the single white lily at the small altar bowl at the God's feet.

She then backed out of the temple, careful never to turn her back on Him, and hence, on Love.

Outside, Belam waited for her, and they resumed the journey.

HER FATHER'S HOUSE WAS THE SAME as she had left it, all those years ago. Crea stepped upon the cool stone of the courtyard, and looked at the old date tree growing toward heaven in the center, casting a long familiar shadow.

And yet, as she walked inside, she saw the difference immediately. There were no servants. No fine draperies covering the windows, no hangings on the walls.

Instead, silence and dust and desolation filled the rooms.

Her sisters and their mothers, the concubines, were all gone too, having left the house of the old father who could no longer maintain them. Indeed, there was no one, a tomb.

Crea took several wooden steps, while her heart thundered in terror, fury, confusion, resentment, and a measure of guilt. Belam followed her quietly. She then walked the long corridors, calling out to her father, and when there was only silence, she too became mute, and continued her search.

She found him at last, on the long terrace, looking out over the abandoned gardens growing wild in the back.

A stooped silhouette of a man, Nahad was seated on a stool, leaning as a wooden puppet against the railing, gazing forward into the white-gold distance.

At first, she did not recognize him, so small and dried out he was. So thin.

And then, as the breeze moved his hair and beard—long white filaments of it where there used to be black—she saw his familiar gesture, a lifting of fingers to balding scalp, as he swept his meager locks back.

She saw his form, hateful and astringent and filled with obstinacy even now.

She saw him, a ghost of himself, and yet, the same man who tortured and abandoned and condemned her.

She stepped forward, meanwhile feeling herself going from hot to cold, to scalding, to incandescent white, as the sun. She stood, burning, while *something* opened in the air around her and inside her, and she *knew* at last.

In that instant he turned, looked at her, still silhouetted, and then, as he recognized her—recognized the stately woman as his daughter— he spoke in a shaking voice, brittle with disuse. "Crea? Is that you? Did you bring the dress of white and gold?"

He stood, and in that moment Crea neared him and then took him by the shoulders, and she shook him in remembered fury, only this time he was weightless as an ancient twig, a dried out mantis.

He was dust in her hands. If she only willed it, she could strike him so easily now; it was her turn.

"Father?" she cried, feeling something inside completely rupture, as the wall of waters breached the rocks, and then it came forth, welling, flooding, rushing, the river of time and history and past, present, and future; the possible and the impossible, the what-had-been and the what-could-be.

"Father . . ." she whispered, choking on the flood, and seeing the sick, the old, the insane, the forgotten in front of her; seeing as she had not seen before, looking as she did through a veil of self. Indeed, pain wove the most opaque, thickest of veils around the self, one that swallowed all light, letting nothing pass through to the other side . . . .

But now, the veil was breached, cast aside, ripped by the force of the flood. Pain was an afterthought, an old tossed rag.

The God of Love had granted her this moment of sight; it is nothing more than what love always does. Love—not dim and blind but so far-seeing that it can glimpse around corners, around bends and twists and illusion; instead of overlooking faults love sees *through* them to the secret inside.

"I have the dress of gold and white, Father!" Crea exclaimed, holding on to the old thing—creature, being, man—that was all alone and cold and clammy with self-hatred. "I brought it here for you, to give back to you, so that you could again have her and remember . . . ."

And the old one shook as she held him, so much smaller than she recalled him through her eyes of the past, and she noticed that now he held on to *her*, reaching out for her with his gnarled claws, holding on so as not to drown, for she alone was there with him, even when he himself was not. "Crea . . ." he whispered. "My true daughter . . . ."

Behind her, Belam reached out and put his hands upon both of them, enveloping the old man and his beloved in a single embrace of forever.

"He has answered your prayer, my love . . . not as you or I asked it, but as only the Gods know is our true intent."

It is unclear whether Belam or Crea said those words, or if they spoke them in unison.

But it is clear that many new arms of Love were opened that night—adding to the infinite arms streaming outward in unconditional embrace from the burning center of the Compass Rose.

Vera Nazarian *immigrated to the USA from the former USSR as a kid, sold her first story at the age of seventeen, and since then has published numerous works in anthologies and magazines, has seen her work on Preliminary Nebula Awards Ballots, honorably mentioned in* Year's Best *volumes, and translated into eight languages. She made her debut as a novelist with the critically-acclaimed* Dreams of the Compass Rose, *followed by* Lords of Rainbow. *Her novella* The Clock King and the Queen of the Hourglass *(with an introduction by Charles de Lint) made the Locus Recommended Reading List. Latest work includes* The Duke in His Castle, *a lush, dark novella, and first collection* Salt of the Air *(with an introduction by Gene Wolfe). For more, visit www.veranazarian.com.*

LA FÉE VERTE

Delia Sherman

WINTER 1868

WHEN VICTORINE WAS a young whore in the house of Mme Boulard, her most intimate friend was a girl called La Fée Verte.

Victorine was sixteen when she came to Mme Boulard's, and La Fée Verte some five years older. Men who admired the poetry of Baudelaire and Verlaine adored La Fée Verte, for she was exquisitely thin, with the bones showing at her wrist and her dark eyes huge and bruised in her narrow face. But her chief beauty was her pale, fine skin, white almost to opalescence. Embracing her was like embracing absinthe made flesh.

Every evening, Victorine and La Fée Verte would sit in Mme Boulard's elegant parlor with Madame, her little pug dog, and the other girls of the establishment, waiting. In the early part of the evening, while the clients were at dinner, there was plenty of time for card-playing, for gossip and a little apéritif, for reading aloud and lounging on a sofa with your head in your friend's lap, talking about clothes and clients and, perhaps, falling in love.

Among the other girls, La Fée Verte had the reputation of holding herself aloof, of considering herself too good for her company. She spoke to no one save her clients, and possibly Mme Boulard. Certainly no one spoke to her. The life of the brothel simply flowed around her, like water around a rock. Victorine was therefore astonished when La Fée Verte approached her one winter's evening, sat beside her on the red velvet sofa, and began to talk. Her green kimono fell open over her bony frame and her voice was low-pitched and a little rough-pleasant to hear, but subtly disturbing.

Her first words were more disturbing still.

"You were thirteen, a student at the convent when your grandmother died. She was your step-father's mother, no blood kin of yours, but she stood between you and your step-father's anger, and so you loved her—the more dearly for your mother's having died when you were a child. You rode to her funeral in a closed carriage with her youngest son, your step-uncle."

Victorine gaped at her, moving, with each phrase, from incredulity to fury to wonder. It was true, every word. But how could she know? Victorine had not told the story to anyone.

La Fée Verte went on: "I smell old straw and damp, tobacco and spirits. I see your uncle's eyes—very dark and set deep as wells in a broad, bearded face. He is sweating as he looks at you, and fiddling in his lap. When you look away for shame, he puts his hands upon you."

Victorine was half-poised to fly, but somehow not flying, half-inclined to object, but listening all the same, waiting to hear what La Fée Verte would say next.

"He takes your virginity hastily, as the carriage judders along the rutted lanes. He is done by the time it enters the cemetery. I see it stopping near your grandmother's grave, the coachman climbing down from his perch, opening the door. Your uncle, flushed with his exertions, straightens his frock coat and descends. He turns and offers you his hand. It is gloved in black—perfectly correct in every way, save for the glistening stains upon the tips of the fingers. I can see it at this moment, that stained glove, that careless hand."

As La Fée Verte spoke, Victorine watched her, mesmerized as her hands sketched pictures in the air and her eyes glowed like lamps. She looked like a magician conjuring up a vision of time past, unbearably sad and yet somehow unbearably beautiful. When she paused in the tale, Victorine saw that her great dark eyes were luminous with tears. Her own eyes filled in sympathy—for her own young self, certainly, but also for the wonder of hearing her story so transformed.

"You will not go to him," La Fée Verte went on. "Your uncle, impatient or ashamed, turns away, and you slip from the carriage and flee, stumbling in your thin slippers on the cemetery's stony paths, away from your grandmother's grave, from your uncle, from the convent and all you have known."

When the tale was done, La Fée Verte allowed her tears to overflow and trickle, crystalline, down her narrow cheeks. Enchanted, Victorine wiped them away and licked their bitter salt from her fingers. She was inebriated, she was enchanted. She was in love.

That night, after the last client had been waved on his way, after the gas had been extinguished and the front door locked, she lay in La Fée Verte's bed, the pair of them nested like exotic birds in down and white linen. La Fée Verte's dark head lay on Victorine's shoulder and La Fée Verte's dusky voice spun enchantment into Victorine's ear. That night, and many nights thereafter, Victorine fell asleep to the sound of her lover's stories. Sometimes La Fée Verte spoke of Victorine's childhood, sometimes of her own first lover in Paris: a poet with white skin and a dirty shirt. He had poured absinthe on her thighs and licked them clean, then sent her, perfumed with sex and anise, to sell herself in cafés for the price of a ream of paper.

These stories, even more than the caresses that accompanied them, simultaneously excited Victorine and laid a balm to her bruised soul. The sordid details of her past and present receded before La Fée Verte's romantic revisions. Little by little, Victorine came to depend on them, as a drunkard depends on his spirits, to mediate between her and her life. Night after night, Victorine drank power from her lover's mouth and caressed tales of luxury from between her thighs. Her waking hours passed as if in a dream, and she submitted to her clients with a disdainful air, as if they'd paid to please her. Intrigued, they dubbed her *la Reine,* proud queen of whores, and courted her with silk handkerchiefs, kidskin gloves, and rare perfumes. For the first time since she fled her uncle's carriage Victorine was happy.

SPRING 1869

THAT APRIL, a new client came to Mme Boulard's, a writer of novels in the vein of M. Jules Verne. He was a handsome man with a chestnut moustache and fine, wavy hair that fell over a wide, pale brow. Bohemian though he was, he bought La Fée Verte's services—which did not come cheap—two or three evenings a week.

At first, Victorine was indifferent. This writer of novels was a client like other clients, no more threat to her dreamworld than the morning sun. Then he began to occupy La Fée Verte for entire evenings, not leaving until the brothel closed at four in the morning and La Fée Verte was too exhausted to speak. Without her accustomed anodyne, Victorine grew restless, spiteful, capricious.

Her clients complained. Mme Boulard fined her a night's takings. La Fée Verte turned impatiently from her questions and then from her caresses. At last, wild with jealousy, Victorine stole to the peephole with which every room was furnished to see for herself what the novelist and La Fée Verte meant to each other.

Late as it was, the lamp beside the bed was lit. La Fée Verte was propped against the pillows with a shawl around her shoulders and a glass of opalescent liquid in her hand. The novelist lay beside her, his head dark on the pillow. An innocent enough scene. But Victorine could hear her lover's husky voice rising and falling in a familiar, seductive cadence.

"The moon is harsh and barren," La Fée Verte told the novelist, "cold rock and dust. A man walks there, armed and helmed from head to foot against its barrenness. He plants a flag in the dust, scarlet and blue and white, marching in rows of stripes and little stars. How like a man, to erect a flag, and call the moon his. I would go just to gaze upon the earth filling half the sky and the stars bright and steady—there is no air on the moon to make them twinkle—and then I'd come away and tell no-one."

The novelist murmured something, sleepily, and La Fée Verte laughed, low and amused. "I am no witch, to walk where there is no air to breathe and the heat of the sun dissipates into an infinite chill. Nevertheless I have seen it, and the vehicle that might carry a man so high. It is shaped like a spider, with delicate legs?"

The novelist gave a shout of pleasure, leapt from the bed, fetched his notebook and his pen and began to scribble. Victorine returned to her cold bed and wept. Such a state of affairs, given Victorine's nature and the spring's unseasonable warmth, could not last forever. One May night, Victorine left the salon pretending a call of nature, stole a carving knife from the kitchen, and burst into the room where La Fée Verte and her bourgeois bohemian were reaching a more conventional climax. It was a most exciting scene: the novelist heaving and grunting, La Fée Verte moaning, Victorine weeping and waving the knife, the other whores crowded at the door, shrieking bloody murder. The novelist suffered a small scratch on his buttock, La Fée Verte a slightly deeper one on the outside of her hip. In the morning she was gone, leaving bloodstained sheets and her green silk kimono with a piece of paper pinned to it bearing Victorine's name and nothing more.

SUMMER 1869–WINTER 1870

RESPECTABLE WOMEN DISAPPOINTED in love went into a decline or took poison, or at the very least wept day and night until the pain of their betrayal had been washed from their hearts. Victorine ripped the green kimono from neck to hem, broke a chamber pot and an erotic Sèvres grouping, screamed and ranted, and then, to all appearances, recovered. She did not forget her lost love or cease to yearn for her, but she was a practical woman. Pining would bring her nothing but ridicule, likely a beating, certainly a heavy fine, and she already owed Mme Boulard more than she could easily repay.

At the turn of the year, Victorine's luck changed. A young banker of solid means and stolid disposition fell under the spell of Victorine's beauty and vivacity. Charmed by his generosity, she smiled on him, and the affair prospered. By late spring, he had grown sufficiently fond to pay off Victorine's debt to Mme Boulard and install her as his mistress in a charming apartment in a building he owned on the fashionable rue Chaptal.

After the conventual life of a brothel, Victorine found freedom very sweet. Victorine's banker, who paid nothing for the apartment, could afford to be generous with clothes and furs and jewels—sapphires and emeralds, mostly to set off her blue eyes and red hair. She attended the Opera and the theatre on his arm and ate at the Café Anglais on the

Boulevard des Italiens. They walked in the Tuileries and drove in the Bois de Boulogne. Victorine lived like a lady that spring, and counted herself happy.

JUNE 1870

NEMESIS IS as soft-footed as a cat stalking a bird, as inexorable, as unexpected.Victorine had buried all thoughts of La Fée Verte as deep in new pleasures and gowns and jewels as her banker's purse would allow. It was not so deep a grave that Victorine did not dream of her at night, or find her heart hammering at the sight of a black-haired woman with a thin, pale face. Nor could she bear to part with the torn green kimono, which she kept at the bottom of her wardrobe. But the pain was bearable, and every day Victorine told herself that it was growing less.

This fond illusion was shattered by the banker himself, who, as a treat, brought her a book, newly published, which claimed to be a true account of the appearance of the moon's surface and man's first steps upon it, to be taken far in an unspecified future. Victorine's banker read a chapter of it aloud to her after dinner, laughing over the rank absurdity of the descriptions and the extreme aridity of the subject and style. The next morning, when he'd left, Victorine gave it to her maid with instructions to burn it.

Victorine was not altogether astonished, when she was promenading down the Boulevard des Italiens some two or three weeks later, to see La Fée Verte seated in a café. It seemed inevitable, somehow: first the book, then the woman to fall into her path. All Paris was out in the cafés and bistros, taking what little air could be found in the stifling heat, drinking coffee and absinthe and cheap red wine. Why not La Fée Verte?

She had grown, if anything, more wraithlike since quitting Mme Boulard's, her skin white as salt under her smart hat, her narrow body sheathed in a tight green walking dress and her wild black hair confined in a snood. She was alone, and on the table in front of her were all the paraphernalia of absinthe: tall glass of jade green liquor, carafe of water, dish of sugar cubes, pierced silver spoon.

Victorine passed the café without pausing, but stopped at the jeweler's shop beside it and pretended an interest in the baubles displayed in the window. Her heart beat so she was almost sick with it. Having seen La Fée Verte, she must speak to her. But what would she say? Would she scold her for her faithlessness? Inquire after her lover? Admire her gown? No. It was impossible.

Having sensibly decided to let sleeping dogs lie, Victorine turned from the sparkling display and swept back to the café. While she had been hesitating, La Fée Verte had tempered her absinthe with water and sugar, and was lifting the resulting opaline liquid to her lips. There was a glass of champagne on the table, too, its surface foaming as if it had just that moment been poured.

Victorine gestured at the wine. "You are expecting someone."

"I am expecting you. Please, sit down."

Victorine sat. She could not have continued standing with that rough, sweet voice drawing ice along her nerves.

"You are sleek as a cat fed on cream," La Fée Verte said. "Your lover adores you, but you are not in love with him."

"I have been in love," Victorine said. "I found it very painful."

La Fée Verte smiled, very like the cat she'd described. "It is much better to be loved," she agreed. "Which you are, which you will always be. You are made to be loved. It is your destiny."

Victorine's temper, never very biddable, slipped from her control. "Are you setting up for a fortune-teller now?" she sneered. "It's a pity the future, as outlined in your lover's novel, appears so dull and unconvincing. I hope he still loves you, now that you've made him the laughingstock of Paris. Your stories used to be much more artistic."

La Fée Verte made a little movement with her gloved hand, as of brushing aside an insect. "Those stories are of the past," she said. "Me, I have no past. My present is a series of photographs, stiff and without color. My future stares at me with tiger's eyes." She held Victorine's gaze until Victorine dropped her eyes, and then she said, "Go back to your banker. Forget you have seen me."

Victorine picked up her champagne and sipped it. She would have liked to throw the wine at La Fée Verte's head, or herself at La Fée

Verte's narrow feet. But the past months had taught her something of self-control. She took money from her purse and laid it on the table and rose and said, "My destiny and my heart are mine to dispose of as I please. I will not forget you simply because you tell me to."

La Fée Verte smiled. "Au revoir, then. I fear we will meet again."

JULY-AUGUST 1870

LA FÉE VERTE'S PROPHECY did not immediately come to pass, possibly because Victorine avoided the neighborhood of the café where she'd seen La Fée Verte in case she might be living nearby. It was time, Victorine told herself, to concentrate on distracting her banker, who was much occupied with business as the General Assembly of France herded the weak-willed Emperor Napoleon III toward a war with Prussia. King Wilhelm was getting above himself, the reasoning ran, annexing here and meddling there, putting forward his own nephew as a candidate for the vacant Spanish throne.

"How stupid does he think we are?" the banker raged, pacing Victorine's charming salon and scattering cigar ashes on the Aubusson. "If Leopold becomes king of Spain, France will be surrounded by Hohenzollerns on every side and it will only be a matter of time before you'll be hearing German spoken on the Champs-Elysées."

"I hear it now," Victorine pointed out. "And Italian and a great deal of English. I prefer Italian—it is much more pleasing to the ear. Which reminds me: *La Traviata* is being sung at the opera tonight. If you'll wait a moment while I dress, we should be in time for the third act."

Victorine was not a woman who concerned herself with politics. It was her fixed opinion that each politician was duller than the next, and none of them, save perhaps the Empress, who set the fashion, had anything to do with her. She did her best to ignore the Emperor's declaration of war on July 16 and the bellicose frenzy that followed it. When her banker spoke to her of generals and battles, she answered him with courtesans and opera-singers. When he wanted to go to the Hôtel de Ville to hear the orators, she made him go to the Eldorado to hear the divine Thérèsa singing of love. When he called her a barbarian, she laughed at him and began to think of finding herself a more amusing protector. Men admired her; several of the banker's friends had made her half-joking offers she half-jokingly turned aside. Any one of them would be hers for a smile and a nod. But none of them appealed to her, and the banker continued to be generous, so she put off choosing. She had plenty of time.

One Sunday in late August, Victorine's banker proposed a drive. Victorine put on a high-crowned hat with a cockade of feathers and they drove down the Champs-Élysées with the rest of fashionable Paris, headed toward the Bois de Boulogne, where the sky was clearer than within the city walls and the air was scented with leaves and grass.

As they entered the park, Victorine heard an unpleasant noise as of a building being torn down over the clopping of the horses' hooves. The noise grew louder, and before long the carriage drew even with a group of men wearing scarlet trousers and military kepis. They were chopping down trees.

The banker required his driver to stop. Victorine gaped at the men, sweating amid clouds of dust, and at the shamble of trampled grass, tree trunks, and stumps they left in their wake. "Who are these men?" she demanded. "What are they doing?"

"They are volunteers for the new Mobile Guard, and they are clearing the Bois." He turned to her. "Victorine, the time has come for you to look about yourself. The Prussians are marching west. If Strasbourg falls, they will be at Paris within a month. Soon there will be soldiers quartered here, and herds of oxen and sheep. Soon every green thing you see will be taken within the walls to feed or warm Paris. If the Prussians besiege us, we will know hunger and fear perhaps death."

Victorine raised her eyes to her lover's pink, stern face. "I cannot stop any of these things; what have they to do with me?"

He made an impatient noise. "Victorine, you are impossible. There's a time of hardship coming, a time of sacrifice. Pleasure will be forced to bow to duty, and I must say I think that France will be the better for it."

She had always known his mouth to be too small, but as he delivered this speech, it struck her for the first time as ridiculous, all pursed up like a sucking infant's under his inadequate moustache.

"I see," she said. "What do you intend to do?"

"My duty."

For all her vanity, Victorine was not a stupid woman. She had no need of La Fée Verte to foresee what was coming next. "I understand completely," she said. "And what of my apartment?"

He blinked as one awakened from a dream. "You may stay until you find a new one."

"And my furniture?"

The question, or perhaps her attitude, displeased him. "The furniture," he said tightly, "is mine."

"My clothes? My jewels? Are they yours also?"

He shrugged. "Those, you may keep. As a souvenir of happier times."

"Of happier times. Of course." Really, she could not look at his mouth any longer. Beyond him, she saw a tall chestnut tree sway and topple to the ground. It fell with a resounding crack, like thunder. The banker started; Victorine did not. "Well, that's clear enough." She put out her hand to him, "Good-bye."

He frowned. "I hadn't intended . . . I'd thought a farewell dinner, one last night together."

"With duty calling you? Surely not," Victorine said. He had not taken her hand; she patted his sweating cheek. "Adieu, my friend. Do not trouble yourself to call. I will be occupied with moving. And duty is a jealous mistress."

She climbed down from the carriage and walked briskly back along the path. She was not afraid. She was young, she was beautiful, and she had La Fée Verte's word that it was her destiny to be loved.

SEPTEMBER 1870

VICTORINE'S NEW APARTMENT was a little way from the grand boulevards, on the rue de la Tour, near the Montmartre *abattoir*. It was small—three rooms only—but still charming. When it came to the point, none of the admiring gentlemen had been willing to offer her the lease on a furnished house of her own, not with times so troubled. She had sent them all about their business, renting and furnishing the place herself on the proceeds from an emerald necklace and a sapphire brooch. She moved on September 3. When evening came, she looked about her at the chaos of half-unpacked trunks and boxes, put on her hat, and went out in search of something to eat, leaving her maid to deal with the mess alone.

Although it was dinnertime, everyone seemed to be out in the streets—grim-faced men, for the most part, too intent on their business to see her, much less make way for her. Passing a newspaper kiosk, she was jostled unmercifully, stepped upon, pushed almost into the gutter. A waving hand knocked her hat awry. Gruff voices battered at her ears.

"Have you heard? The Emperor is dead!"

"Not dead, idiot. Captured. It's bad enough."

"I heard dead, and he's the idiot, not me."

"Good riddance to him."

"The Prussians have defeated MacMahon. Strasbourg has fallen."

"Long live Trochu."

The devil take Trochu, Victorine thought, clutching purse and muff. A thick shoe came down heavily on her foot. She squealed with pain and was ignored. When she finally found a suitable restaurant, her hat was over her ear and she was limping.

The Veau d'Or was small, twelve tables perhaps, with lace curtains at the windows and one rather elderly waiter. What made it different from a thousand other such establishments was its clientele, which seemed to consist largely of women dressed in colors a little brighter and hats a little more daring than was quite respectable. They gossiped from table to table in an easy camaraderie that reminded Victorine at once of Mme Boulard's salon.

The conversations dropped at Victorine's entrance, and the elderly waiter moved forward, shaking his head.

"We are complete, Madame," he said.

Presented with an opportunity to vent her ill-temper, Victorine seized it with relief. "You should be grateful, Monsieur, that I am sufficiently exhausted to honor your establishment with my custom." She sent a disdainful glance around the room. "Me, I am accustomed to the company of a better class of tarts."

This speech elicited some indignant exclamations, some laughter, and an invitation from a dumpling-like blonde in electric blue to share her corner table.

"You certainly have an opinion of yourself," she said, as Victorine sat down, "for a woman wearing such a hat as that. What happened to it?"

Victorine removed the hat and examined it. The feather was broken and the ribbons crushed. "Men," she said, making the word a curse. "Beasts."

The blonde sighed agreement. "A decent woman isn't safe in the streets these days. What do you think of the news?"

Victorine looked up from the ruin of her hat. "News? Oh, the Emperor."

"The Emperor, the Prussians, the war. All of it."

"I think it is terrible," Victorine said, "if it means cutting down the Bois de Boulogne and stepping on helpless women. My foot is broken— I'm sure of it."

"One does not walk on a broken foot," the blonde said reasonably. "Don't spit at me, you little cat—I'm trying to be friends. Everyone needs friends. There's hard times ahead."

"Hard times be damned," Victorine said airily. "I don't expect they will make a difference, not to us. Men desire pleasure in hard times, too."

The blonde laughed. "Possibly; possibly not. We'll find out soon enough which of us is right." She poured some wine into Victorine's glass. "If you're not too proud for a word of advice from a common tart, I suggest you take the veal. It's the specialty of the house, and if it comes to a siege, we won't be able to get it any more."

"Already I am bored by this siege," Victorine said.

"Agreed," said the blonde. "We will talk of men, instead."

THAT NIGHT, VICTORINE DRANK a glass of absinthe on her way home. It wasn't a vice she usually indulged in, finding the bitterness of the wormwood too intense and the resulting lightheadedness too unsettling. Tonight, she drank it down like medicine. When she got home, she dug the green kimono out of her wardrobe and fell into bed with it clasped in her arms, her head floating in an opalescent mist.

Her sleep was restless, her dreams both vivid and strange. Her banker appeared, his baby mouth obscene in a goat's long face, and disappeared, bloodily, into a tiger's maw. A monkey wore grey gloves, except it was not a monkey at all, but a pig, beyond whose trotters the fingers of the gloves flapped like fringe. It bowed, grinning piggily, to the dream-presence that was Victorine, who curtsied deeply in return. When she rose, the tiger blinked golden eyes at her. She laid her hand upon his striped head; he purred like the rolling of distant thunder and kneaded his great paws against her thighs. She felt only pleasure from his touch, but when she looked at her skirts, they hung in bloody rags. Then it seemed she rode the tiger through the streets of Paris, or perhaps it was an open carriage she rode, or perhaps she was gliding bodily above the pavement, trailing draperies like the swirling opalescence of water suspended in a glass of absinthe.

She slept heavily at last, and was finally awakened at noon by a group of drunks singing the "Marseillaise" at full voice on the street under her window. She struggled out of bed and pulled back the curtains, prepared to empty her chamber pot over them. Seeing her, they cried out "Vive la République," and saluted, clearly as drunk on patriotic sentiment as on wine. Victorine was not entirely without feeling for her country, so she stayed her hand.

FRANCE WAS A REPUBLIC AGAIN.

Victorine considered this fact as her maid dressed her and pinned up her hair. If the drunkards were anything to judge by, the change of government had not changed a man's natural reaction to the sight of a shapely woman in a nightgown. She would walk to the Tuileries, buy an ice cream, and find someone to help her celebrate the new Republic.

It was a warm day, grey and soft as mouse fur. Victorine bought a patriotic red carnation from a flower-seller on the steps of Notre Dame de Lorette, and pinned it to her bosom. The streets were full of workers in smocks and gentlemen in top hats, waving greenery and tricolor flags with democratic zeal. Spontaneous choruses of "Vive la République!"

exploded around Victorine at intervals. As she drew nearer the Tuileries, her heart beat harder, her cheeks heated; she felt the press of strange bodies around her as the most intense of pleasures. Soon she was laughing aloud and shouting with the rest: "Vive la République!"

At last, she reached the gate of the Tuileries. A man thrust a branch in her face as she passed through. "This is it!" he cried blissfully. "Down with the Emperor! Vive la République!"

He was a soldier, young, passably good-looking in his little, round kepi and gold-braided epaulets. Victorine turned the full force of her smile on him. "Vive la République," she answered, and brushed his fingers with hers as she took the branch.

He didn't seem to notice.

For the blink of an eye, Victorine was filled with a rage as absolute as it was unexpected. And then it was gone, taking her patriotic fervor with it. Suddenly, the pressure of the crowd seemed intolerable to her, the shouting an assault. She clung to the iron railings of the high fence and fanned herself with her handkerchief while she caught her breath.

All of the wide promenade between railings and palace overflowed with a seething mass of humanity. Victorine's view was obstructed by top hats and cloth caps, smart hats and shabby bonnets and checked shawls. By standing on tiptoe, she could just see a stream of people swarming up the steps like revelers eager to see the latest opera. La République had moved quickly. She noticed that the Ns and imperial wreaths had been pried from the façade or shrouded with newspapers or scarlet sheets, which gave the palace a blotched and raddled look. And above the gaping door, someone had chalked the words UNDER THE PROTECTION OF THE CITIZENS on the black marble.

The open door of the palace beckoned to Victorine, promising wonders. She put away her handkerchief, took a firm hold on her bag, and launched herself into the current that flowed, erratically but inevitably, toward the forbidden palace where the Emperor and his foreign wife had lived so long in imperial splendor.

The current bore Victorine up a flight of shallow steps, the press around her growing, if possible, even denser as the door compacted the flow. She stepped over the threshold, passing a young infantryman who held out his shako and cried out with the raucous monotony of a street vendor: "For the French wounded! For the French wounded!" Impulsively, Victorine fished a coin from her bag, dropped it into his shako, and smiled up into his sweating face. He nodded once, gravely, and then she was in the foyer of the Imperial Palace of the Tuileries.

It was every bit as magnificent as she'd imagined. Victorine, who had a taste for excess, worshipped every splendid inch of it, from the goddesses painted on the ceiling, to the scintillating lustres on the chandeliers, the mirrors and gold leaf everywhere, and the great, sweeping staircase, designed to be seen on.

There must have been a hundred people on that staircase, mounting and descending, gawking over the rail. But Victorine saw only one woman, standing still as a rock in the waterfall of sightseers. The woman's hair was dark under her green hat, and her profile, when she turned her head, was angular. Victorine's blood recognized La Fée Verte before her mind did, racing to her face and away again, so that she swayed as she stood.

A hand, beautifully gloved in grey leather, touched her arm. Victorine became aware of a gentleman in a top hat and a beautifully tailored coat, carrying a gold-headed cane. "Mademoiselle is faint?" he inquired.

Victorine shook her head and sprang up the steps so heedlessly that she caught her toe on the riser. The solicitous gentleman, who had not moved from her side, caught her as she stumbled.

"If you will permit?" he asked rhetorically. Then he slipped one arm around her waist, shouting for everyone to make way, and piloted her firmly out of the palace without paying the slightest heed to her protestations that she was very well, that she'd left a friend on the stair and wished to be reunited with her.

THE SOLICITOUS GENTLEMAN was plumper than Victorine liked, and his hair, when he removed his tall glossy hat, was woefully sparse. But he bore her off to the Georges V for coffee and pastries and then he bought her a diamond aigrette and a little carnelian cat with emerald eyes and agreed that it was a great pity that an exquisite creature like herself should be in exile on the rue de la Tour. What could Victorine do? She took the luck that fate had sent her and gave the gentleman to understand that his gifts were an acceptable prelude to a more serious arrangement. A week later, she and her maid were installed in an apartment off the Champs-Élysées, with her name on the lease and furniture that was hers to keep or sell as it pleased her.

It was not a bad bargain. The solicitous gentleman wasn't as good-looking as the banker and his lovemaking was uninspired. But, besides being very rich, he was as devoted to amusement as even Victorine could wish.

"Why should I worry about the Prussians?" he said. "I have my days to fill. Let everyone else worry about the Prussians if it amuses them. It is of more concern to me whether M. Gaulner beats me to that charming bronze we saw yesterday."

Still, the Prussians, or rather the threat of the Prussians, was increasingly hard to ignore. Victorine and her solicitous gentleman made their way to the antiquaries and the rare bookshops through platoons of National Guardsmen marching purposefully from one place to another and ranks of newly inducted Mobile Guards learning to turn right in unison. She could not set foot outside the door without being enthusiastically admired by the soldiers camped along the Champs, and the horses stabled there made pleasure drives to the Bois de Boulogne (or what was left of it) all but impossible. Even the theatre wasn't what it had been, houses closing left and right as the timid fled the anticipated discomforts of a siege. The Comédie Française and the Opéra remained open, though, and the public balls and the cafés—concerts were frequented by those without the means to fly. However tenuously, Paris remained Paris, even in the face of war.

One night, Victorine and her solicitous gentleman went strolling along the boulevard de Clichy. Among the faded notices of past performances that fluttered like bats' wings in the wind, crisp, new posters announced the coming night's pleasures.

"Look, *ma belle*, the gentleman exclaimed, stopping in front of a kiosk. "A mentalist! How original! And such a provocative name. We really must go see her."

Victorine looked at the poster he indicated. It was painted red and black, impossible to ignore:

THE SALON DU DIABLE PRESENTS
LA FÉE VERTE!
THE MISTS OF TIME PART FOR HER.
THE SECRETS OF THE FUTURE ARE UNVEILED.
SÉANCE AT NINE AND MIDNIGHT.
LA FEE VERTE!

Tears sprang, stinging, to Victorine's eyes. Through their sparkling veil, she saw a white bed and a room lit only by dying embers and her palm tingled as if cupped over the small, soft mound of La Fée Verte's breast. She drew a quick breath. "It sounds very silly," she said weakly. "Besides, who has ever heard of the Salon du Diable?"

"All the more reason to go. It can be an adventure, and well worth it, if this Fée Verte is any good. If she's terrible, it will make a good story." Victorine shrugged and acquiesced. It was clearly fate that had placed that poster where her protector would notice it, and fate that he had found it appealing, just as it was fate that Victorine would once more suffer the torment of seeing La Fée Verte without being able to speak to her. Just as well, really, after the fiasco on the Champs-Elysées. At least this time, Victorine would hear her voice.

THE SALON DU DIABLE was nearly as hot as the abode of its putative owner, crowded with thirsty sinners, its only illumination a half-a-dozen gaslights, turned down low. A waiter dressed as a devil in jacket and horns of red felt showed them to a table near the curtained platform that served as a stage. Victorine, as was her habit, asked for champagne. In honor of the entertainer, her protector ordered absinthe. When it came, she watched him balance the sugar cube on the pierced spoon and slowly pour a measure of water over it into the virulent green liquor. The sugared water swirled into the absinthe, disturbing its depths, transforming it, drop by drop, into smoky, shifting opal.

The solicitous gentleman lifted the tall glass. "La Fée Verte!" he proposed.

"La Fée Verte," Victorine echoed obediently, and as if at her call, a stout man in a red cape and horns like the waiter's appeared before the worn plush curtain and began his introduction.

La Fée Verte, he informed the audience, was the granddaughter of one of the last known fairies in France, who had fallen in love with a mortal and given birth to a son, the father of the woman they were about to see. By virtue of her fairy blood, La Fée Verte was able to see through the impenetrable curtains of time and space as though they were clear glass. La Fée Verte was a visionary, and the stories she told— whether of past, present, or future—were as true as death.

There was an eager murmur from the audience. The devil of ceremonies stepped aside, pulling the faded plush curtain with him, and revealed a woman sitting alone on the stage. She was veiled from head to toe all in pale, gauzy green, but Victorine knew her at once.

Thin white hands emerged from the veil and cast it up and back like a green mist. Dark eyes shone upon the audience like stars at the back of a cave. Her mouth was painted scarlet and her unbound hair was black smoke around her head and shoulders.

Silence stretched to the breaking point as La Fée Verte stared at the audience and the audience stared at her. And then, just as Victorine's strained attention was on the point of shattering, the thin red lips opened and La Fée Verte began to speak.

"I will not speak of war, or victory or defeat, suffering or glory. Visions, however ardently desired, do not come for the asking. Instead, I will speak of building.

"There's a lot of building going on in Paris these days, enough work for everyone, thanks to le bon Baron and his pretty plans. Not all Germans are bad, eh? The pay's pretty good, too, if it can buy a beer at the Salon du Diable. There's a builder in the audience now, a mason. There are, in fact, two masons, twice that number of carpenters, a layer of roofslates, and a handful of floor-finishers."

The audience murmured, puzzled at the tack she'd taken. The men at the next table exchanged startled glances—the carpenters, Victorine guessed, or the floor-finishers.

"My vision, though, is for the mason. He's got stone-dust in his blood, this mason. His very bones are granite. His father was a mason, and his father's father and his father's father's father, and so on, as far back as I can see. Stand up, M. le Maçon. Don't be shy. You know I'm talking about you."

The audience peered around the room, looking to see if anyone would rise. In one corner, there was a hubbub of encouraging voices, and finally, a man stood up, his flat cap over one eye and a blue kerchief around his throat. "I am a mason, Mademoiselle" he said. "You're right enough about my pa. Don't know about his pa, though. He could have been a train conductor, for all I know. He's not talked about in the family."

"That," said La Fee Verte, "was your grandmother's grief, poor woman, and your grandfather's shame."

The mason scowled. "Easy enough for you to say, Mademoiselle, not knowing a damn thing about me."

"Tell me," La Fée Verte inquired sweetly. "How are things on the rue Mouffetard? Don't worry: your little blonde's cough is not tuberculosis. She'll be better soon." The mason threw up his hands in a clear gesture of surrender and sat down. A laugh swept the audience. They were impressed. Victorine smiled to herself.

La Fée Verte folded her hands demurely in her green silk lap. "Your grandfather," she said gently, "was indeed a mason, a layer of stones like you, Monsieur. Men of your family have shaped steps and grilles, window frames and decorations in every building in Paris. Why, men of your blood worked on Notre-Dame, father and son growing old each in his turn in the service of Maurice de Sully."

The voice was even rougher than Victorine remembered it, the language as simple and undecorated as the story she told. La Fée Verte did not posture and gesture and lift her eyes to heaven, and yet Victorine was convinced that, were she to close her eyes, she'd see Notre-Dame as it once was, half-built and swarming with the men who labored to complete it. But she preferred to watch La Fée Verte's thin, sensuous lips telling about it.

La Fée Verte dropped her voice to a sibylline murmur that somehow could be heard in every corner of the room. "I see a man with shoulders like a bull, dressed in long stockings and a tunic and a leather apron. The tunic might have been red once and the stockings ochre, but they're faded now with washing and stone-dust. He takes up his chisel and his hammer in his broad, hard hands flecked with scars, and he begins his daily prayer. *Tap*-tap, *tap*-tap. *Pa*-ter *Nos*-ter. *A*-ve *Ma*-ri-*a*. Each blow of his hammer, each chip of stone, is a bead in the rosary he tells, every hour of every working day. His prayers, unlike yours and mine, are still visible. They decorate the towers of Notre-Dame, almost as eternal as the God they praise.

"That was your ancestor, M. le Maçon," La Fée Verte said, returning to a conversational tone. "Shall I tell you of your son?"

The mason, enchanted, nodded.

"It's not so far from now, as the march of time goes. Long enough for you to marry your blonde, and to father children and watch them grow and take up professions. Twenty years, I make it, or a little less: 1887. The president of France will decree a great Exposition to take place in 1889—like the Exposition of 1867, but far grander—1889 is the threshold of a new century, after all, and what can be grander than that? As an entrance arch, he will commission a monument like none seen before anywhere in the world. And your son, Monsieur, your son will build it.

"I see him, Monsieur, blond and slight, taking after his mother's family, with a leather harness around his waist. He climbs to his work, high above the street-higher than the towers of Notre-Dame, higher than you can imagine. His tools are not yours: red-hot iron rivets, tin buckets, tongs, iron-headed mallets. His faith is in the engineer whose vision he executes, in the maker of his tools, his scaffolds and screens and guard-rails: in man's ingenuity, not God's mercy."

She fell silent, and it seemed to Victorine that she had finished. The mason thought so, too, and was unsatisfied. "My son, he won't be a mason, then?"

"Your son will work in iron," La FéeVerte answered. "And yet your line will not falter, nor the stone-dust leach from your blood as it flows through the ages."

Her voice rang with prophecy as she spoke, not so much loud as sonorous, like a church bell tolling. When the last echo had died away, she smiled, a sweet curve of her scarlet lips, and said, shy as a girl, "That is all I see, Monsieur. Are you answered?"

The mason wiped his hands over his eyes and, rising, bowed to her, whereupon the audience roared its approval of La Fée Verte's vision and the mason's response, indeed of the whole performance and of the Salon du Diable for having provided it. Victorine clapped until her palms stung through her tight kid gloves.

The solicitous gentleman drained his absinthe and called for another. "To La Fée Verte," he said, raising the opal liquid high. "The most accomplished fraud in Paris. She must be half-mad to invent all that guff, but damn me if I've ever heard anything like her voice."

Victorine's overwrought nerves exploded in a surge of anger. She rose to her feet, snatched the glass from the gentleman's hand, and poured the contents over his glossy head. While he gasped and groped for his handkerchief, she gathered up her bag and her wrap and swept out of Le Salon du Diable in a tempest of silks, dropping a coin into the bowl by the door as she went.

The next day, the gentleman was at Victorine's door with flowers and a blue velvet jewel case and a note demanding that she receive him at once. The concierge sent up the note and the gifts, and Victorine sent them back again, retaining only the jewel case as a parting souvenir. She did not send a note of her own, since there was nothing to say except that she could no longer bear the sight of him. She listened to him curse her from the foot of the stairs, and watched him storm down the street when the concierge complained of the noise. Her only regret was not having broken with him before he took her to the Salon du Diable.

IN LATE SEPTEMBER, the hard times foretold by the blonde in the Veau d'Or came to Paris.

A city under the threat of siege is not, Victorine discovered, a good place to find a protector. Top-hatted gentlemen still strolled the grand boulevards, but they remained stubbornly blind to Victorine's saucy hats, graceful form, and flashing eyes. They huddled on street corners and in cafés, talking of the impossibility of continued Prussian victory, of the threat of starvation that transformed the buying of humble canned meat into a patriotic act. Her cheeks aching from unregarded smiles, Victorine began to hate the very sound of the words "siege," "Prussian," "Republic." She began to feel that Bismarck and the displaced Emperor, along with the quarrelsome Generals Gambetta and Trochu, were personally conspiring to keep her from her livelihood. Really, among them, they were turning Paris into a dull place, where nobody had time or taste for pleasure.

A less determined woman might have retired for the duration, but not Victorine. Every day, she put on her finest toilettes and walked, head held high under the daring hats, through the military camp that Paris was fast becoming. Not only the Champs-Élysées, but all the public gardens, squares, and boulevards were transformed into military camps or stables or sections of the vast open market that had sprung up to cater to the soldiers' needs. Along streets where once only the most expensive trinkets were sold, Victorine passed makeshift stalls selling kepis and epaulets and gold braid, ramrods and powder-pouches and water bottles, sword-canes and bayonet-proof leather chest-protectors. And everywhere were soldiers, throwing dice and playing cards among clusters of little grey tents, who called out as she passed, "Eh, sweetheart! How about a little tumble for a guy about to die for his country?"

It was very discouraging.

One day at the end of September, Victorine directed her steps toward the heights of the Trocadéro, where idle Parisians and resident foreigners had taken to airing themselves on fine days. They would train their spyglasses on the horizon and examine errant puffs of smoke and fleeing peasants like ancient Roman priests examining the entrails of a sacrifice, after which they gossiped and flirted as usual. A few days earlier, Victorine had encountered an English gentleman with a blond moustache of whom she had great hopes. As she climbed the hill above the Champ de Mars, she heard the drums measuring the drills of the Mobile Guards.

At the summit of the hill, fashionable civilians promenaded to and fro. Not seeing her English gentleman, Victorine joined the crowd surrounding the enterprising bourgeois who sold peeps through his long brass telescope at a franc a look. A clutch of English ladies exclaimed incomprehensibly as she pushed past them; a fat gentleman in a round hat moved aside gallantly to give her room. She cast him a distracted smile, handed the enterprising bourgeois a coin, and stooped to look through the eyepiece. The distant prospect of misty landscape snapped closer, bringing into clear focus a cloud of dark smoke roiling over a stand of trees.

"That used to be a village," the enterprising bourgeois informed her. "The Prussians fired it this morning—or maybe we did, to deny the Prussians the pleasure." The telescope jerked away from the smoke. "If you're lucky, you should be able to see the refugees on their way to Paris."

A cart, piled high with furniture, a woman with her hair tied up in a kerchief struggling along beside it, lugging a bulging basket in each hand and a third strapped to her back. A couple of goats and a black dog and a child riding in a handcart pushed by a young boy. "Time's up," the enterprising bourgeois said.

Victorine clung to the telescope, her heart pounding. The smoke, the cart, the woman with her bundles, the children, the dog, were fleeing a real danger. Suddenly, Victorine was afraid, deathly afraid of being caught in Paris when the Prussians came. She must get out while there was still time, sell her jewels, buy a horse and carriage, travel south to Nice or Marseille. She'd find La Fée Verte, and they could leave at once. Surely, if she went to the Place Clichy, she'd see her there, waiting for Victorine to rescue her. But she'd have to hurry.

As quickly as Victorine had thrust to the front of the crowd, so quickly did she thrust out again, discommoding the English ladies, who looked down their long noses at her. No doubt they thought her drunk or mad. She only thought them in the way. In her hurry, she stepped on a stone, twisted her ankle, and fell gracelessly to the ground.

The English ladies twittered. The gentleman in the round hat asked her, in vile French, how she went, and offered her his hand. She allowed him to pull her to her feet, only to collapse with a cry of pain. The ladies twittered again, on a more sympathetic note. Then the crowd fell back a little, and a masculine voice inquired courteously whether Mademoiselle were ill.

Victorine lifted her eyes to the newcomer, who was hunkered down beside her, his broad, open brow furrowed with polite concern. The gold braid on his sleeves proclaimed him an officer, and the gold ring on his finger suggested wealth.

"It is very silly," she said breathlessly, "but I have twisted my ankle and cannot stand."

"If Mademoiselle will allow?" He folded her skirt away from her foot, took the scarlet boot into his hand, and bent it gently back and forth. Victorine hissed through her teeth.

"Not broken, I think," he said. "Still, I'm no doctor." Without asking permission, he put one arm around her back, the other under her knees, and lifted her from the ground with a little jerk of effort. As he carried her downhill to the surgeon's tent, she studied him. Under a chestnut-brown moustache, his mouth was firm and well shaped, and his nose was highbridged and aristocratic. She could do worse.

He glanced down, caught her staring. Victorine smiled into his eyes (they, too, were chestnut-brown) and was gratified to see him blush. And then they were in the surgeon's tent and her scarlet boot was being cut away. It hurt terribly. The surgeon anointed her foot with arnica and bound it tightly, making silly jokes as he worked about gangrene and amputation. She bore it all with such a gallant gaiety that the officer insisted on seeing her home and carrying her to her bed, where she soon demonstrated that a sprained ankle need not prevent a woman from showing her gratitude to a man who had richly deserved it.

OCTOBER 1870

IT WAS A STRANGE AFFAIR, at once casual and absorbing, conducted in the interstices of siege and civil unrest. The officer was a colonel in the National Guard, a man of wealth and some influence. His great passion was military history.

His natural posture—in politics, in love—was moderation. He viewed the Monarchists on the Right and the Communards on the Left with an impartial contempt. He did not pretend that his liaison with Victorine was a grand passion, but cheerfully paid the rent on her apartment and bought her a new pair of scarlet boots and a case of canned meat, with promises of jewels and gowns after the Prussians were defeated. He explained about Trochu and Bismarck, and expected her to be interested. He told her all the military gossip and took her to ride on the peripheral railway and to see the cannons installed on the hills of Paris.

The weather was extraordinarily bright. "God loves the Prussians," the officer said, rather sourly, and it certainly seemed to be true. With the sky soft and blue as June, no rain slowed the Prussian advance or clogged the wheels of their caissons or the hooves of their horses with mud. They marched until they were just out of the range of the Parisian cannons, and there they sat, enjoying the wine from the cellars of captured country houses and fighting skirmishes in the deserted streets of burned-out villages. By October 15, they had the city completely surrounded. The Siege of Paris had begun.

The generals sent out their troops in cautious sallies, testing the Prussians but never seriously challenging them. Victorine's colonel, wild with impatience at the shilly-shallying of his superiors, had a thousand plans for sorties and full scale counterattacks. He detailed them to Victorine after they'd made love, all among the bedclothes, with the sheets heaped into fortifications, a pillow representing the butte of Montmartre, and a handful of hazelnuts for soldiers.

"Paris will never stand a long siege," he explained to her. "Oh, we've food enough, but there is no organized plan to distribute it. There is nothing really organized at all. None of those blustering ninnies in charge can see beyond the end of his nose. It's all very well to speak of the honor of France and the nobility of the French, but abstractions do not win wars. Soldiers in the field, deployed by generals who are not afraid to make decisions, that's what wins wars."

He was very beautiful when he said these things—his frank, handsome face ablaze with earnestness. Watching him, Victorine very nearly loved him. At other times, she liked him very well. He was a man who knew how to live. To fight the general gloom, he gave dinner parties to which he invited military men and men of business for an evening of food, wine, and female companionship. Wives were not invited.

There was something dreamlike about those dinners, eaten as the autumn wind sharpened and the citizens of Paris tightened their belts. In a patriotic gesture, the room was lit not by gas, but by branches of candles, whose golden light called gleams from the porcelain dishes, the heavy silver cutlery, the thin crystal glasses filled with citrine or ruby liquid. The gentlemen laughed and talked, their elbows on the napery, their cigars glowing red as tigers' eyes. Perched among them like exotic birds, the women, gowned in their bare-shouldered best, encouraged the gentlemen to talk with smiles and nods. On the table, a half-eaten tart, a basket of fruit. On the sideboard, the remains of two roast chickens—two!—a dish of beans with almonds, another of potatoes. Such a scene belonged more properly to last month, last year, two years ago, when the Empire was strong and elegant pleasures as common as the rich men to buy them. Sitting at the table, slightly drunk, Victorine felt herself lost in one of La Fée Verte's visions, where past, present, and future exist as one.

Outside the colonel's private dining room, however, life was a waking nightmare. The garbage carts had nowhere to go, so that Victorine must pick her way around stinking hills of ordure on every street corner. Cholera and smallpox flourished among the poor. The plump blonde of the Veau d'Or died in the epidemic, as did the elderly waiter and a good proportion of the regulars. Food grew scarce. Worm-eaten cabbages went for three francs apiece. Rat pie appeared on the menu at Maxim's, and lapdogs went in fear of their lives. And then there were the French wounded, sitting and lying in rattling carriages and carts, muddy men held together with bloody bandages, their shocked eyes turned inward, their pale lips closed on their pain, being carted to cobbled-together hospitals to heal or die. Victorine turned her eyes from them, glad she'd given a coin to the young infantryman that day she saw La Fée Verte in the Tuileries.

And through and over it all, the cannons roared.

French cannon, Prussian cannon, shelling St. Denis, shelling Boulogne, shelling empty fields and ravaged woodlands. As they were the nearest, the French cannon were naturally the loudest. Victorine's colonel prided himself on knowing each cannon by the timbre and resonance of its voice as it fired, its snoring or strident or dull or ear-shattering *BOOM*. In a flight of whimsy one stolen afternoon, lying in his arms in a rented room near the Port St. Cloud, Victorine gave them names and made up characters for them: Gigi of the light, flirtatious bark on Mortemain, Philippe of the angry bellow at the Trocadéro.

October wore on, and the siege with it. A population accustomed to a steady diet of news from the outside world and fresh food from the provinces began to understand what it was like to live without either. The lack of food was bad enough, but everyone had expected that—this was war, after all, one must expect to go hungry. But the lack of news was hard to bear. Conflicting rumors ran through the streets like warring plagues, carried by the skinny street rats who hawked newspapers on the boulevards. In the absence of news, gossip, prejudice, and flummery filled their pages. Victorine collected the most outrageous for her colonel's amusement: the generals planned to release the poxed whores of the Hôpital St. Lazare to serve the Prussian army; the Prussian lines had been stormed by a herd of a thousand patriotic oxen.

The colonel began to speak of love. Victorine was becoming as necessary to him, he said, as food and drink. Victorine, to whom he was indeed food and drink, held his chestnut head to her white breast and allowed him to understand that she loved him in return.

Searching for a misplaced corset, her maid turned up the ripped green kimono and inquired what Mademoiselle would like done with it.

"Burn it," said Victorine. "No, don't. Mend it, if you can, and pack it away somewhere. This is not a time to waste good silk."

That evening, Victorine and her colonel strolled along the Seine together, comfortably arm in arm. The cannon had fallen to a distant Prussian rumbling, easily ignored. Waiters hurried to and fro with trays on which the glasses of absinthe glowed like emeralds. The light was failing. Victorine looked out over the water, expecting to see the blue veil of dusk drifting down over Notre-Dame.

The veil was stained with blood.

For a moment, Victorine thought her eyes were at fault. She blinked and rubbed them with a gloved hand, but when she looked again, the evening sky was still a dirty scarlet—nothing like a sunset, nothing like anything natural Victorine had ever seen. The very air shimmered red. All along the quai came cries of awe and fear.

"The Forest of Bondy is burning," Victorine heard a man say and, "an experiment with light on Montmartre," said another, his voice trembling with the hope that his words were true. In her ear, the colonel murmured reassuringly, "Don't be afraid, my love. It's only the aurora borealis."

Victorine was not comforted. She was no longer a child to hide in pretty stories. She knew an omen when she saw one. This one, she feared, promised fire and death. She prayed it did not promise her own. Paris might survive triumphantly into a new century, and the mason and his blonde might survive to see its glories, but nothing in La Fée Verte's vision had promised that Victorine, or even La Fée Verte, would be there with them.

THE RED LIGHT ENDURED for only a few hours, but some atmospheric disturbance cast a strange and transparent radiance over the next few days, so that every street, every passerby took on the particularity of a photograph. The unnatural light troubled Victorine. She would have liked to be diverted with kisses, but her colonel was much occupied just now. He wrote her to say he did not know when he'd be able to see her again—a week or two at most, but who could tell? It was a matter of national importance—nothing less would keep him from her bed. He enclosed a pair of fine kidskin gloves, a heavy purse, a rope of pearls, and a history of Napoleon's early campaigns.

It was all very unsatisfying. Other women in Victorine's half-widowed state volunteered to nurse the French wounded, or made bandages, or took to their beds with Bibles and rosaries, or even a case of wine. Victorine, in whom unhappiness bred restlessness, went out and walked the streets.

From morning until far past sunset, Victorine wandered through Paris, driven by she knew not what. She walked through the tent cities, past stalls where canteen girls in tricolored jackets ladled out soup, past shuttered butcher shops and greengrocers where women shivered on the sidewalk, waiting for a single rusty cabbage or a fist-sized piece of doubtful meat. But should she catch sight of a woman dressed in green or a woman whose skin seemed paler than normal, she always followed her for a street or two, until she saw her face.

She did not fully realize what she was doing until she found herself touching a woman on the arm so that she would turn. The woman, who was carrying a packet wrapped in butcher's paper, turned on her, frightened and furious.

"What are you doing?" she snapped. "Trying to rob me?"

"I beg your pardon," Victorine said stiffly. "I took you for a friend."

"No friend of yours, my girl. Now run away before I call a policeman."

Shaking, Victorine fled to a café, where she bought a glass of spirits and drank it down as if the thin, acid stuff would burn La Fée Verte from her mind and body. It did not. Trying not to think of her was still thinking of her; refusing to search for her was still searching.

ON THE MORNING OF OCTOBER 31, rumors of the fall of Metz came to Paris. The people revolted. Trochu cowered in the Hôtel de Ville while a mob gathered outside, shouting for his resignation. Victorine, blundering into the edges of the riot, turned hastily north and plunged into the winding maze of the Marais. Close behind the Banque de France, she came to a square she'd never seen before. It was a square like a thousand others, with a lady's haberdasher and a hairdresser, an apartment building and a café all facing a stone pedestal supporting the statue of a dashing mounted soldier. A crowd had gathered around the statue, men and women of the people for the most part, filthy and pinched and blue-faced with cold and hunger. Raised a little above them on the pedestal's base were a fat man in a filthy scarlet cloak and a woman, painfully thin and motionless under a long and tattered veil of green gauze.

The fat man, who was not as fat as he had been, was nearing the end of his patter. The crowd was unimpressed. There were a few catcalls. A horse turd, thrown from the edge of the crowd, splattered against the statue's granite base. Then La Fée Verte unveiled herself, and the crowd fell silent.

The weeks since Victorine had seen her on the stage of the Salon du Diable had not been kind to her. The dark eyes were sunken, the body little more than bone draped in skin and a walking-dress of muddy green wool. She looked like a mad woman: half-starved, pitiful. Victorine's eyes filled and her pulse sped. She yearned to go to her, but shyness kept her back. If she was meant to speak to La Fee Verte, she thought, there would be a sign. In the meantime, she could at least listen.

"I am a seer," La Fée Verte said, the word taking on a new and dangerous resonance in her mouth. "I see the past, the present, the future. I see things that are hidden, and I see the true meaning of things that are not. I see truth, and I see falsehoods tricked out as truth." She paused, tilted her head. "Which would you like to hear?"

Puzzled, the crowd muttered to itself. A woman shouted, "We hear enough lies from Trochu. Give us the truth!"

"Look at her," a skeptic said. "She's even hungrier than I am. What's the good of a prophetess who can't foresee her next meal?"

"My next meal will be bread and milk in a Sèvres bowl," La Fée Verte answered tranquilly. "Yours, my brave one, will be potage—of a sort. The water will have a vegetable in it, at any rate."

The crowd, encouraged, laughed and called out questions.

"Is my husband coming home tonight?"

"My friend Jean, will he pay me back my three sous?"

"Will Paris fall?"

"No," said La Fée Verte. "Yes, if you remind him. As for Paris, it is not such a simple matter as yes and no. Shall I tell you what I see?"

Shouts of "No!" and "Yes!" and more horse turds, one of which spattered her green skirt. Unruffled, she went on, her husky voice somehow piercing the crowd's rowdiness.

"I see prosperity and peace," she said, "like a castle in a fairy tale that promises that you will live happily ever after."

More grumbling from the crowd: "What's she talking about?"; "I don't understand her"; and a woman's joyful shout—"We're all going to be rich!"

"I did not say that," La Fee Verte said. "The cholera, the cold, the hunger, will all get worse before it gets better. The hard times aren't over yet."

There was angry muttering, a few catcalls: "We ain't paying to hear what we already know, bitch!"

"You ain't paying me at all," La Fée Verte answered mockingly. "Anyone may see the near future—it's all around us. No, what you want to know is the distant future. Well, as you've asked for the truth, the truth is that the road to that peaceful and prosperous castle is swarming with Germans. Germans and Germans and Germans. You'll shoot them and kill them by the thousands and for a while they'll seem to give up and go away. But then they'll rise again and come at you, again and again."

Before La Feée Verte had finished, "Dirty foreigner!" a woman shrieked, and several voices chorused, "Spy, spy!" "German spy!" Someone threw a stone at her. It missed La Fée Verte and bounced from the pedestal behind her with a sharp crack. La Fée Verte ignored it, just as she ignored the crowd's shouting and the fat man's clutching hands trying to pull her away.

It was the sign. Victorine waded into the mêlée, elbows flailing, screaming like a cannonball in flight. There was no thought in her head except to reach her love and carry her, if possible, away from this place and home, where she belonged.

"I see them in scarlet," La Fée Verte was shouting above the noise. "I see them in grey. I see them in black, with peaked caps on their heads, marching like wooden dolls, stiff-legged, inexorable, shooting shopgirls and clerks and tavernkeepers, without pity, without cause."

Victorine reached La Fée Verte at about the same time as the second stone and caught her as she staggered and fell, the blood running bright from a cut on her cheek. The weight of her, slight as it was, overbalanced them both. A stone struck Victorine in the back; she jerked and swore, and her vision sparkled and faded as though she were about to faint.

"Don't be afraid," the husky voice said in her ear. "They're only shadows. They can't hurt you."

Her back muscles sore and burning, Victorine would have disagreed. But La Fée Verte laid a bony finger across her lip "Hush," she said. "Be still and look."

It was the same square, no doubt of that, although the café at the corner had a different name and a different front, and the boxes in the windows of the apartment opposite were bright with spring flowers. Victorine and La Fée Verte were still surrounded by a crowd, but the crowd didn't seem to be aware of the existence of the two women huddled at the statue's base. People were watching something passing in the street beyond, some procession that commanded their attention and their silence. The men looked familiar enough, in dark coats and trousers, bareheaded or with flat caps pulled over their cropped hair. But the women—ah, the women were another thing. Their dresses were the flimsy, printed cotton of a child's shirt or a summer blouse, their skirts short enough to expose their naked legs almost to the knee, their hair cut short and dressed in ugly rolls.

Wondering, Victorine looked down at La Fée Verte, who smiled at her, intimate and complicit. "You see? Help me up," she murmured. As Victorine rose, lifting the thin woman with her, she jostled a woman in a scarf with a market basket on her arm. The woman moved aside, eyes still riveted on the procession beyond, and Victorine, raised above the crowd on the statue's base, followed her gaze.

There were soldiers, as La Fée Verte had said: lines of them in dark uniforms and high, glossy boots, marching stiff-legged through the square toward the rue de Rivoli. There seemed to be no end to them, each one the mirror of the next, scarlet armbands flashing as they swung their left arms. A vehicle like an open carriage came into view, horseless, propelled apparently by magic, with black-coated men seated in it, proud and hard faced under peaked caps. Over their heads, banners bearing a contorted black cross against a white and scarlet ground rippled in the wind. And then from the sky came a buzzing like a thousand hives of bees, as loud as thunder but more continuous. Victorine looked up, and saw a thing she hardly knew how to apprehend. It was like a bird, but enormously bigger, with wings that blotted out the light and a body shaped like a cigar.

If this was vision, Victorine wanted none of it. She put her hands over her eyes, releasing La Fée Verte's hand that she had not even been aware of holding. The buzzing roar ceased as if a door had been closed, and the tramp of marching feet. She heard shouting, and a man's voice screaming with hysterical joy:

"The Republic has fallen!" he shrieked. "Long live the Commune! To the Hôtel de Ville!"

The fickle crowd took up the chant: "To the Hôtel de Ville! To the Hôtel de Ville!" And so chanting, they moved away from the statue, their voices gradually growing fainter and more confused with distance.

When Victorine dared look again, the square was all but empty. The fat man was gone, and most of the crowd, all heading, she supposed, for the Hôtel de Ville. A woman lingered, comfortingly attired in a long grey skirt, a tight brown jacket with a greasy shawl over it, and a battered black hat rammed over a straggling bun.

"Better take her out of here, dear," she said to Victorine. "I don't care, but if any of those madmen come back this way, they'll be wanting her blood."

THAT NIGHT, VICTORINE had her maid stand in line for a precious cup of milk, heated it up over her bedroom fire and poured it over some pieces of stale bread torn up into a Sèvres bowl.

La Fée Verte, clean and wrapped in her old green kimono, accepted the dish with murmured thanks. She spooned up a bit, ate it, put the spoon back in the plate. "And your colonel?" she asked. "What will you tell him?"

"You can be my sister," Victorine said gaily. "He doesn't know I don't have one, and under the circumstances, he can hardly ask me to throw you out. You can sleep in the kitchen when he spends the night."

"Yes," La Fée Verte said after a moment. "I will sleep in the kitchen. It will not be for long. We . . ."

"No," said Victorine forcefully. "I don't want to hear. I don't care if we're to be ruled by a republic or a commune or a king or an emperor, French or German. I don't care if the streets run with blood. All I care is that we are here together now, just at this moment, and that we will stay here together, and be happy."

She was kneeling at La Fée Verte's feet, not touching her for fear of upsetting the bread and milk, looking hopefully into the ravaged face. La Fée Verte touched her cheek very gently and smiled.

"You are right," she said. "We are together. It is enough."

She fell silent, and the tears overflowed her great, bruised eyes and trickled down her cheeks. They were no longer crystalline—they were just tears. But when Victorine licked them from her fingers, it seemed to her that they tasted sweet.

Delia Sherman's *short stories have appeared in numerous volumes of* Year's Best Fantasy & Horror *and* F&SF. *Her novels are* Through a Brazen Mirror *and* The Porcelain Dove, Changeling *and, with partner* Ellen Kushner, The Fall of the Kings. *Editing projects include* Interfictions: An Anthology of Interstitial Writing, *with Theodora Goss. She is a social rather than a solitary writer, and can work anywhere, which is a good thing because she loves to travel, and if she couldn't write on airplanes, she'd never get anything done. She lives in New York City.*

Acknowledgement is made for permission to reprint the following:

"An Autumn Butterfly" © 2006 by Esther Friesner. First published: *Polyphony 6* (Wheatland Press), edited by Deborah Layne & Jay Lake.

"A Light in Troy" © 2006 by Sarah Monette. First published: *Clarkesworld Magazine*, Issue 1, October 2006, edited by Nick Mamatas & Sean Wallace.

"The Moment of Joy Before" © 2006 by Claudia O'Keefe. First published: *The Magazine of Fantasy and Science Fiction*, April 2006, edited by Gordon Van Gelder.

"Jane. A Story of Manners, Magic and Romance" © 2006 by Sarah Prineas. First published: *Realms of Fantasy*, April 2006, edited by Shawna McCarthy.

"Journey Into the Kingdom" © 2006 by M. Rickert. First published: *The Magazine of Fantasy and Science Fiction*, May 2006, edited by Gordon Van Gelder.

"The Mountains of Key West" © 2006 by Sandra McDonald. First published: *Lone Star Stories*, Issue 15, June 2006, edited by Eric Marin.

"The Wizard of Eternal Watch" © 2006 by Eugie Foster. First published: *Sages & Swords* (Pitch-Black Books), edited by Daniel E. Blackston.

"Moon Viewing at Shijo Bridge" © 2006 by Richard Parks. First published: *Realms of Fantasy*, April 2006, edited by Shawna McCarthy.

"The Depth Oracle" © by Sonya Taaffe. First published: *Sirenia Digest 8*, July 2006, edited by Caitlín R. Kiernan.

"Smoke and Mirrors" © 2006 by Amanda Downum. First published: *Strange Horizons*, 20 November 2006, edited by Jed Hartman (senior editor), Susan Marie Groppi & Karen Meisner.

"The Desires of Houses" © 2006 Haddayr Copley-Woods. First published: *Strange Horizons*, 13 February 2006, edited by Jed Hartman (senior editor), Susan Marie Groppi & Karen Meisner.

"Evergreen" © 2006 by Angela Boord. First published: *Lone Star Stories*, Issue 13, April 2006, edited by Eric Marin.

"The Red Envelope" © 2006 by David Sakmyster. First published: *L. Ron Hubbard Presents Writers of the Future, Volume XXII* (Galaxy Press), edited by Algis Budrys.

"The Story of Love" © 2006 by Vera Nazarian. First published: *Salt of the Air* (Prime Books), Vera Nazarian.

"La Fée Verte © 2006 by Delia Sherman. First published: *Salon Fantastique* (Thunders Mouth Press), *edited by Ellen Datlow & Terri Windling*